THE MOGUL'S RELUCTANT BRIDE

BILLIONAIRE BRIDES OF GRANITE FALLS

ANA E ROSS

CEDAR TREES PUBLISHERS

THE MOGUL'S RELUCTANT BRIDE

Edited by Crazy Diamond Editing
Cover Design by Najla Qamber Designs

www.anaeross.com

Billionaire Brides of Granite Falls Series

The Doctor's Secret Bride

The Mogul's Reluctant Bride

The Playboy's Fugitive Bride

The Tycoon's Temporary Bride

With These Four Rings: Wedding Bonus

Beyond Granite Falls Series

Loving Yasmine

Desire's Chase

Pleasing Mindy

Billionaire Island Brides Series

Seduced by Passion (2022)

To my fabulous team of Beta Readers: Dinah, Shirlyn, Renita, Monica, Lena, Sharon, Shunta, and Angie.

PROLOGUE

Kaya cupped her little hands over her ears and hummed the tune to her favorite song, "You Are My Sunshine". But as hard as she tried to drown out the noise, she could still hear her mother's angry screams and her father's booming voice coming from inside.

Finally, her father's heavy footsteps thumped across the floor. As he opened the door, she jumped up from the front step of the apartment where they'd made her sit while they yelled at each other.

He smiled at her. He always smiled at her, even when he was mad with everybody else.

"Are we going to the zoo now, Daddy?" She'd waited all week to go to the zoo with him. She'd waited all week to see him.

He crouched down beside her. "No, baby. We're not going to the zoo today."

Tears filled her eyes and her lips trembled. "But you promised. You promised you'd take me to the zoo. Please, Daddy." She placed her hands on his broad shoulders.

"I'm sorry, Kaya, baby. But your—"

"Kay! Kay! Get in here before I whip your behind."

Kaya's heart beat hard and fast inside her chest when her mother appeared at the door with a cigarette between her fingers.

Her father stood up. "Go on," he said. "You heard your momma."

Kaya balled her fists and glared at her mother. "No!" Her long braids slapped across her face as she shook her head in defiance. "I won't go inside. I want to go with my daddy."

"Get out of here!" her mother screamed at her father. "Don't talk to her. Don't you ever talk to her again or I'll have your—"

"Okay, Nadine. I'm going." William Brehna smiled at his little girl again. "Bye Kaya, baby. Daddy loves you."

"Daddy!" Kaya screamed as he walked down the steps.

"You stay away from that man." Her mother grabbed her arm, hauled her inside, and kicked the door shut. "He's a no good—"

"He's good. He's my daddy. He's my daddy." Tears spilled down her cheeks as she glared at the puffy-eyed dragon with a curly stream of smoke oozing out of her mouth.

Nadine Brehna glared at her daughter then marched into the only bedroom in the apartment and slammed the door.

Kaya ran to the window in the living room and watched her father get into his car. But instead of driving off, he just sat there.

It could have been seconds, minutes, hours—a five-year-old had no concept of time, only the reality of abuse and loneliness.

She jumped up with joy when he got out of the car and came back up the walkway. She ran to the door, threw it open, and leaped into his arms. "Oh, Daddy, we're going to the zoo." She didn't really care if they went to the zoo, or the park, or if they only went for a walk around the block. She needed so much to be with her daddy.

He was the only happiness she had.

He pried her arms from around his neck and pressed a cold

metal object into her hand. "This is for you, Kaya." He set her on the step and knelt in front of her, his big white teeth sparkling in the morning sun. "It belonged to your great-great-grandfather."

A big lump settled in Kaya's chest when she saw tears in her father's eyes. She'd never seen her daddy cry before. "You can keep it, Daddy. I don't need it." She wiped at his tears with trembling fingers.

Her father held her hands and dropped wet kisses into her palms. "Don't you ever lose this locket, Kaya. It contains a code to a box in a bank, but don't go to the bank until you're eighteen."

He made her say the name and location of the bank several times until she remembered it.

"And don't let your momma know you have this locket. You hear me, baby girl?"

"Yes, Daddy." Kaya gazed at the object then slid it into the pocket of her shorts.

"Daddy has a fistful of love for you. Always and forever," he said with a tear-soaked smile, pressing his fist to his chest. He pulled her close and hugged her tightly.

She wound her arms around his neck, his black beard grazing her soft cheeks, his spicy odor seeping under her tender skin. She never wanted to let him go.

But he tore away, tears gushing down his dark cheeks. "Goodbye, Kaya. I love you, baby. I'll *always* love you, my little princess."

"Daddy!" Kaya called as he staggered down the walkway. Somehow, in her five-year-old heart, she knew she would never see him again. "Daddy, don't leave me. Please don't leave me here. Daddy! Daddy—"

"Kay! Kay! I told you to come inside!"

Her mother grabbed her by the arm. Kaya fought her with

every bit of strength in her lithe body. But it was no use. Through her tears, amidst her screams, she watched the taillights of her father's car disappear around the corner. When she collapsed on the step, too weak to fight anymore, her mother dragged her inside as if she were a rag doll.

"What did I tell you, Kay?"

"It's Kaya. Kaya! My name is Kaya. It means 'Stay and don't go back.' My daddy told me."

"Well, I don't see that man who gave it to you around here, do I? You want me to tell you where he is, Kay?"

"*You* made my daddy go away. *You* made him leave. I hate you. I hate you! I—"

Her skinny frame rocked from the force of the slap across her face, and a million bright stars shot across her vision, momentarily blinding her.

"You can think about how much you hate me while you're in there." Nadine opened the closet door and threw her daughter atop a heap of smelly coats, old shoes, and dilapidated cardboard boxes filled with junk. "You're not coming out 'til you apologize for your rude mouth."

"I don't care! I don't ever want to come out! I don't ever want to see your ugly face ever again!"

"Suits me fine. You can stay in there for the rest of your miserable life, you ungrateful little brat." Nadine slammed the door.

Kaya pulled the object her father had given her from her pocket, and closing her fingers around it, she stuffed her fist into her mouth as a fresh batch of tears rolled down her cheeks, stinging the tender spot where her mother had slapped her.

"Why, Daddy? Why did you leave me here?"

Kaya wept her little broken heart out, and when she had no more tears, when there was no energy left in her small body, she curled up in the musky darkness and went to sleep.

CHAPTER ONE

Eighteen years later...

"There must be some mistake, Steven." Kaya Brehna's hands tightened around the arm of the chair.

"I really wish there was, Kaya."

"They— they left nothing?"

"Nothing," the man behind the mahogany desk reiterated with a shake of his head.

Kaya pressed an unsteady hand to her chest. Her heart raced with fear, and her mind swam in a pool of confusion and uncertainty. Even though she'd never had a close relationship with Lauren, when Steven had called with the news of her sister and brother-in-law's deaths, and that they had named her guardian of their children, Kaya had dropped everything to be with her nephew and two nieces.

Up until a minute ago, she had every reason to believe that nine-year-old Jason, four-year-old Alyssa, and two-month-old Anastasia were financially secure. She hadn't met the children until yesterday, but the minute she saw them, Kaya knew she could never abandon them. She was all set to put her life on hold to nurse them through this most grievous time of their lives, but how on earth could she do that after what the executor of Michael and Lauren's will just told her?

They died bankrupt.

Nothing made any sense.

Forcing back the hysteria in her throat, Kaya struggled to her feet, and braced her hands against the edge of the desk. "Steven, I've worked in the homes of some of the wealthiest people in Florida. I know money when I see it. That three-story, eight-bedroom mansion my sister lived in is worth millions, yet, you're telling me she died penniless?"

"I'm sorry to give you more bad news, Kaya, but, yes, those are the facts I'm afraid." His tone was apologetic, as if he was the one who had caused her dilemma.

"Well, in light of that, Steven, I can't stay in Granite Falls now. I have no choice but to return to Palm Beach, and take the children with me."

Steven rose and strolled around the desk. "I'm aware that you and your sister weren't very close, Kaya, and that there are events about her life you may not be aware of. But I was Michael and Lauren's friend as well as their attorney, and if there's one thing I do know, it's that they would not want you to take their children to Florida. Granite Falls is their home."

"*Was,* Steven. *Was.*" Kaya threw her hands up in frustration. "Everything is changed now. I was willing to settle down in Granite Falls, put my life on hold for a while, until they got used to me as their caregiver, but that option is off the table. My career in Palm Beach is the only fighting chance I have to provide a decent living for all of us."

"I understand the financial dilemma you're facing, but it wouldn't be wise to uproot the children so soon after the loss of their parents. They have ties in Granite Falls. Ties that shouldn't be severed at this precarious time of their lives."

"And their strongest tie is Bryce Fontaine, I suppose," she said, rather grudgingly. Bryce was the children's godfather, and from what Kaya had learned from friends of the family who were gathered at the house when she arrived yesterday, he was a very present figure in the children's lives.

"Bryce is a big part of their lives," Steven voiced her thoughts out loud. "Despite the fact that you are their aunt and only living relative, they will need him to get them through this tragedy. He has been like a second father to them, ever since they were born, and now that Michael is gone, they will need him more than ever."

Kaya tried to ignore the insinuations in Steven's words. She needed no reminders that the children didn't know her, that they'd never met her until yesterday. If only she'd been more congenial toward her sister, met her halfway. A few weeks ago, Lauren had invited her up to celebrate Michael's fiftieth birthday. She'd agreed to come, and they'd promised to take care of her travel arrangements. But unable to get past her juvenile sibling resentment, she'd reneged at the last minute. If she'd come up like she'd promised, she would have seen her sister and met Michael and the kids, but she hadn't.

"When is Bryce coming back?" she asked Steven. She was still to meet this Bryce, who'd been on a skiing trip in Switzerland the day Michael and Lauren died.

"His jet could be landing anytime soon. You know what that means for Jason." His brows drew together and his blue eyes clouded with unease. "I can't force you to stay in Granite Falls, Kaya. I can only strongly advise that you consider sticking with your initial plans to remain here, at least for now."

Kaya walked over to the window and stared out across the parking lot. She felt as listless as the wind-blown snowflakes tumbling aimlessly to the ground. Steven was right about keeping the children in a familiar environment, around familiar faces. But what was she to do? They were destitute. Returning to Florida was her only option. Even there, with three children to support, she could still end up broke, like Michael and Lauren.

Kaya never anticipated that her life could spiral out of control so quickly and unexpectedly. There was only one other time in her life when she'd been this scared—the day she saw her father for the last time.

She raised a hand to her chest and closed her fingers around the locket that her father had given her when she was five years old—the one with the code to a safety deposit box. Her father had instructed her not to go to the bank until she was eighteen, and now, even after five years, Kaya was still awed at the contents of that safe.

She'd had the jewel appraised, and almost fainted when she learned how much it was worth. Her father had left a letter explaining how he'd come into possession of the gem. He'd written that he wanted her to know that it wasn't stolen. Unsure of what to do with it, Kaya had just left it alone. Had her father given Lauren a similar gem? Had Lauren sold her inheritance to purchase *L'etoile du Nord,* her multimillion-dollar estate? Had she squandered the rest on an extravagant lifestyle that she couldn't maintain?

Kaya sighed as the questions surged through her mind. Steven was right again. There was so much about her sister's life she didn't know. What she did know was that the contents in that safe was all she had of her father's memory, the only tangible bond she had to her ancestry. She couldn't bear the thought of parting with it, even though it would solve her newly acquired financial problems, and set her and the children up for life. But that was asking too much. It wasn't fair that she should have to spend her inheritance on Lauren's children. She had preserved her heirloom, while Lauren had wasted hers on a big...

Kaya turned from the window as the only other solution took

root in her mind. "The estate," she said, walking back over to Steven. "It's worth millions, hopefully more than Michael and Lauren owed their creditors. If I sell the estate, I can—"

"Um, Kaya, you can't sell that estate."

"Why not? Don't tell me there's a lien against it." That faint thread of hysteria was back in her voice. If their father had given Lauren the same kind of gem he had given her, Lauren could have paid cash for the estate. Did she mortgage it off to sustain her luxurious lifestyle?

"No. There's no lien against it," Steven said.

Kaya breathed a sigh of relief. "Well then, why can't I sell it?"

"Because it didn't belong to Michael and Lauren. It doesn't belong to the children."

Kaya's mouth dropped open. "What do you mean it didn't—doesn't belong to them? If it isn't their estate, then whose is it?"

"Mine. *L'etoile du Nord* belongs to me," came a rumbling voice behind her.

Kaya spun around, her heart flying to her throat when her eyes collided with the powerful bronze body of the man standing on a pair of legs that would make a Viking proud.

Bryce Fontaine, New England's business mogul—CEO and president of Fontaine Enterprises—in the flesh.

He was far more handsome than his pictures portrayed, she thought, staring in admiration as he bent his snow-dusted head to get his large frame through the door.

The ample shoulders, stretching beneath a dark-green sweater, the sharp chin, and generous mouth, all spoke of power and resolute strength. The man possessed a captivating presence and an air of authority that made you stop and take note when he entered a room. She was taking note—a lot of notes.

If Kaya had to sum Bryce Fontaine up in one word, it would be *"intimidating"*.

A tingling sensation generated in Kaya's belly and traveled south to her thighs, and then to her knees, making them go weak. She slumped against the edge of the desk and tried to bring her escalated breathing under control.

Steven walked over and met him near the door. Even Steven —who was about six feet, two inches tall—had to roll his head back to face the giant, as they talked in low voices.

Steven had called Bryce the night of the tragedy, but a blizzard in the Alps had delayed his return. He must have flown all night, Kaya thought, taking in his stubbled chin and disheveled appearance that made him seem even more imposing.

When Kaya had enquired about the hunk in her sister's family pictures, Libby—Steven's fiancée, and a close friend of the family—had given her a short version of his accomplishments.

Bryce Fontaine had started out in real estate—buying up a substantial amount of land in Granite Falls and the neighboring towns, then quickly expanded to the rest of the business world. He devoured companies from glass blowing to computer software programing, and as he'd just claimed, he also owned the estate on which her sister lived.

Seemed like the man owned the entire town, she thought, recalling driving by the Youth Performing Arts Center, Granite Falls Towers, and Country Club, to name a few buildings and skyscrapers that bore his name. His signature was everywhere in Granite Falls. He'd even built an airport with a runway long enough to accommodate his private jets and those of his friends, Libby had told her.

As if sensing her scrutiny, he turned his head and pinned her with a calculating stare. Breathless seconds ticked by before he stepped around Steven and headed in her direction. A compelling energy seemed to coil within him at each step he took.

Forcing her legs to support her, Kaya pushed off the desk as he came to a stop and towered over her. His gaze was bold and penetrating. His eyes, enigmatic and unfathomable, were like midnight's deepest black. As she gazed up at him, Kaya had the dizzying sensation of falling into blackness. She'd never felt so susceptible to a man in all her life. He could reach out and take a hold of her, do anything he wanted to her, this very moment, and there was not a damn thing she'd be able to do about it. Vitality zinged through her bloodstream, even as her body began to shiver from an unfamiliar awareness. How could she feel this vivacious and weak at the same time? Kaya wondered, as she once again leaned on the desk for support.

If he could cause her to lose control of her motor skills by just looking at her, then God help her.

"Bryce," Steven said, coming to stand next to the titan, "this is Lauren's sister, Kaya Brehna. Kaya, Bryce Fontaine."

Bryce shook the hand the petite woman with a thick curtain of dark-brown curls tumbling off her small shoulders offered him. Such soft honey-hue skin, he thought as he gazed into her beautiful brown eyes—eyes like little Alyssa's. Where Alyssa's were innocent and mischievous, Kaya's were mesmerizing, large and exotic, with tones of soft amber that seemed to speak to him from within. He could easily lose his way in those spellbinding eyes, he thought.

"It's a pleasure, Miss Brehna," he said, releasing her and ordering his brain to buffer the bolt of electricity charging through him. It had been ages since the touch of a woman caused his heart to pound out an erratic rhythm. He didn't know what to make of it.

"It's nice meeting you, too, Mr. Fontaine," she said in a soft unsteady voice.

Bryce smiled as her dark, long lashes came down to shield her eyes from his.

Steven cleared his throat, reminding Bryce that there was someone else in the room.

"I'll leave you two alone to get acquainted while I make a phone call," Steven said, walking into an adjoining room and closing the door.

"Take your time," Bryce said, his gaze following Kaya's movements as she laced and unlaced her fingers in front of her. He wondered if she was this nervous in the company of all men, or was it just him. He let his ego believe it was just him. He was so used to assertive women who let him know up front exactly what they wanted from him. It was a welcome change to encounter one who was still shy, demure, who made a man feel like a man. Protective. Male —pumped full of adrenaline in anticipation of the chase, he thought as his eyes took in the radiance of her heart-shaped face and her full, pouty, sexy lips. How he would so love to test their subtlety, feel them quiver, then open to accept him.

If he'd passed Kaya on the street, in a restaurant, or pulled up beside her at a traffic light, Bryce knew he would have given her a second look, maybe a third. He most certainly would have asked for her number.

And to think he could have had it months ago when Lauren had been telling him that she wanted him to meet her sister. He'd shut Lauren down because he hadn't wanted to jeopardize their friendship. What if he'd met Kaya and didn't like her? Well, that wasn't an issue anymore. He'd met her and he liked her, too much, he realized at the stirring in his loins. But the outcome would have been the same, because when he'd had his fill of little Kaya, he would have walked away like he always did. His friendship with Lauren had meant too much to him. It still did, even though she was gone. So there was no messing with her little sister. *Stand down, boy.*

"So, here we are," she said, raising her head to offer him a heart-stopping smile.

"Yes, here we are." Dear God, he was dumbstruck. Only once in his life had Bryce ever felt this powerless to a woman.

"Why are you looking at me like that?" she asked, crossing her arms about her.

Bryce shook his head. "I'm sorry," he said to cover his enthrallment. "It's just that you look nothing like Lauren. You're so petite, and Lauren was—well, Lauren." He formed a generous figure in the air with his hands. "I expected some small hint of resemblance, at least."

"Maybe it's because we were half-sisters," she said, a smile lighting the soft features of her face.

"Half-sisters?" He tilted his head to one side. "Lauren told me she had a younger sister, but she never elaborated. I just assumed you had the same parents." He frowned as he studied her. "I didn't think you'd be this young, either." He hadn't thought anything of her at all, since he never expected to ever meet her. She couldn't be much older than twenty-two or three. Lauren had to be at least ten years her senior.

His eyes appraised her petite form, dressed in a cream sweater and a knee-length skirt. Even in her black high-heel boots, the top of her head hardly made it to his chest. She looked very soft, very warm, very female—his ideal type. Lauren knew him well. A fond smile touched his lips at the memories of his friend, his sister, whom he missed so much already.

"Let's just say Eli Brehna would never have been nominated Father of the Year," Kaya said as her fingers closed around a fist-shaped locket resting against her chest. "Neither Lauren nor I ever spoke about it."

He wanted to ask her about the "it" she and Lauren never

spoke about, but knew it was not the right time. He and Lauren had been very close, yet she'd never mentioned "it".

Whatever secret they'd shared, Lauren had taken it to the grave with her. He wondered how much she'd told Kaya about him, about...

"I was also surprised when I saw your pictures, Mr. Fontaine."

"Please, call me Bryce. There's no need for formality between us."

"Okay, then I'm Kaya." Her lips spread on a warm smile. "As I was saying, Michael was a lot older than Lauren, so when she wrote that you were best friends, I assumed you were his age. Besides, there aren't many thirty-something-year-old men out there who've built billion-dollar empires from the ground up."

"When I want something, I just go out and get it."

"I'm just the same way. I believe in fighting for what I want. I let nothing stand between me and my heart's desires."

Bryce smiled. "We have something in common already, I see."

"It would seem as if we do, Bryce." Her brown eyes sparkled, and her lips quivered on an inviting smile, one that lit up her eyes this time and caused the amber hues around her irises to shimmer.

Bryce's heart responded with a leap, ever so slight. He liked the soft sound of his name falling from her exquisite lips. Tightening his jaw, he blanketed the warm feelings it generated in him. No need to travel down troublesome paths. Paths that would lead to nowhere, and that would only leave him in a lingering state of frustration. Kaya was in Granite Falls for one reason only—her sister's funeral. When it was over, she'd be going back to Florida, and he may never see her again. *He hoped.*

He turned and held the back of a chair. "Have a seat, Kaya.

We may as well be comfortable while we discuss the children's welfare."

She nodded and sat down.

Bryce sat down in the chair facing her, his heart heavy at the thought of discussing the gruesome reason he'd left Switzerland, just hours after his jet landed. He hadn't even gotten the chance to attack the slopes, burn off the frustrations that had driven him there in the first place. "Who's taking care of them?" he asked Kaya, deciding it was best to just tackle the issue they'd been avoiding since he walked into the office.

"Libby," she answered.

"Great." He would have gone directly to the house, but when he'd called Steven and learned that Lauren's sister would be in his office, he'd opted to meet her here. They had a lot to discuss and he'd rather not do it with the kids around. "How are they coping?"

"Alyssa's fine, as resilient as a rubber ball," she answered with a gentle softness in her voice. "But Anastasia has been fussy, and Jason, well—"

She started that nervous twisting of her hands again. She couldn't be scared of a little boy. "What about Jason?" Bryce asked, fighting the urge to reach out and cover her hands with his.

"He's in denial. He completely ignores me. Samantha Kelly, the grief counselor from their church, came by last night, but he wouldn't talk to her. He thinks his parents went to Switzerland with you, and that you're bringing them home."

Bryce frowned. "Why does he think that?"

"Well, they died the same day you left for Switzerland, remember?"

"Yes, but—"

"You've taken the family to Europe on your jet several times, so in Jason's mind, his parents merely took another trip with you.

Samantha called it a coping mechanism, and she thinks you're the only one who can get Jason to accept the truth."

Bryce felt pressure building in his chest. Propping his elbows on his knees, he buried his face in his hands, groaning inwardly. If Michael and Lauren's deaths seemed so inconceivable to him, he could only imagine what it was like for Jason losing both his parents so suddenly and tragically.

Many times he'd put smiles on the children's faces when he'd replaced a broken toy. How could he attempt to fix their little broken hearts when he could never bring their parents home?

Fate had dealt them a crushing blow, and he would have to see them through this most frightening period of their lives. He would be there for them—night and day until... Bryce slowly raised his head and stared at Kaya. "When I walked in, you were discussing the option of selling my estate. Why?"

She blushed and glanced away briefly. "I didn't know *L'etoile du Nord* belonged to you. I'm just trying to close out Michael and Lauren's affairs as soon as possible so that the children and I can get on with our lives. As you know, Michael had no relatives and I'm the only family Lauren had."

"And I imagine coming here for the funeral and finally meeting the children will give you some closure and a measure of peace when you return to Florida." He paused as the door to the adjacent office opened and Steven rejoined them. "I can assure you, the children will be well cared for. I love them dearly, and I'll raise them as if they were my own."

"Um, Bryce," Steven interjected. "That wouldn't be necessary."

"On the contrary, Steven, it's absolutely crucial. There's no one else to take care of them."

Steven shot Kaya a furtive glance. "There *is* someone else, Bryce."

"Who?"

"Kaya. Michael and Lauren named her legal guardian. She has full custody of the children, and she's planning to take them to Florida after the funeral."

Kaya watched a kaleidoscope of emotions flitter across Bryce's face. *Shock. Confusion. Hurt. Betrayal.*

He staggered out of his chair and slammed a fist on the desk. "They did *what?*"

Anger.

Kaya jumped and hugged her arms about her middle tightly, her eyes flashing back and forth from Bryce to Steven, then back to Bryce.

"Michael and I were closer than most brothers, for God's sake. I loved Lauren like a sister. I adore those kids. How could they ever doubt that?"

"Bryce, believe me, when they asked me to write the will, I raised those same points on your behalf. But they were quite certain about what they wanted."

"When did they make this ridiculous decision?"

"About a year ago."

Kaya sat up straight. A year ago was when Lauren tracked her down and began sending her pictures of the children. She'd invited her to come up and meet the family. But old fears had kept her away.

Bryce turned his mercurial eyes on her. His big hands were clenched into fists. His broad shoulders heaved from his deep, harsh breathing.

The mixture of hurt and betrayal in his eyes resonated in her own tormented heart. He'd just lost his dearest friends, and now he was about to lose his godchildren whom he obviously adored.

"They didn't even know her." He flung his hands in the air. "They might as well have pulled a stranger off the streets and asked her to raise their kids. That's what you are. A stranger. To all of us!" He took a threatening step toward her.

Kaya felt his despair in the pit of her stomach, but she steeled herself against the looming threat and pushed to her feet. "Bryce, I know how hurt and betrayed you must feel right now. But I'm the only living relative the children have."

"I'm the closest thing to family they have, Kaya. The fact that people share the same blood doesn't make them family. You don't know those kids, and they certainly do not know you."

"They'll come to know me. They'll even love me in time," she said, forcing stability into her voice.

"They love me now," he grounded through clenched teeth. "I've been in their lives from the moment each one of them was born. Where were you?"

In high school. But she was sure that's not what he meant.

"I'm not the kind of godfather who ignores them all year then drop by with expensive gifts on Christmas and birthdays. Which is a lot more than I can say for you, their only living relative, who never even took the time to visit her sister."

That hurt far more than Kaya ever thought it would. But she gathered courage from the knowledge that even though she and Lauren were estranged, her sister still named her legal guardian of her children.

Lauren had her reasons. Kaya didn't know what they were. What she did know was that she would not fail her sister. She had failed her in life by not reaching out to her, meeting her halfway; she would not fail her in death by walking away from her children. She would fulfill her request, no matter the cost.

Kaya glanced at Steven, hoping he would intervene on her behalf. He shrugged and spread his hands, obviously reluctant to take sides in a dispute between an old friend and a new client.

"I hope you haven't told the kids about your absurd plans." Bryce's acerbic tone drew her back to his scowling face.

"Of course not. They have enough to deal with already. I'll tell them when the time is right."

"It'll never be right, Miss Brehna."

So they were back to last names.

He looked her over judiciously. "You're a career woman whose main priority in life, I'm certain, is to climb the corporate ladder of success. It's not easy for a single woman to raise a child alone."

"And how would you know?" Kaya retorted, hands on hips.

"I employ a few of them, Miss Brehna. I overhear their complaints. Can you honestly tell me you're ready to sacrifice all you've worked for to raise three children you don't even know?"

Kaya knew it wouldn't be easy, and that it may even jeopardize her job at Pearson's Interior Decorating. Wayne had already pointed out the demands her new position as head designer would have on her time, not to mention her obligation to the clients she'd left hanging when she got the call from Steven.

And then there was Jack, her fiancé, whom she still hadn't told she'd inherited three little orphans. Jack was adamant about not having children after they were married. She never thought she wanted children, either, until she met these three who had Eli Brehna's blood flowing through their veins. Was she picking up a heavier load than she could hoist over her shoulders, much less carry?

"You have no idea what you're getting yourself into, do you?" Bryce was like a hound dog, sniffing out her fears. "You're already neck-deep in financial problems or you wouldn't have been thinking about selling my estate. You probably can't even afford the funeral."

The funeral. Kaya hadn't even thought of that after Steven dropped the bombshell on her earlier. When she'd thought there was money to pay for the funeral, she'd picked out two elaborate coffins, and hadn't bothered to give a second thought to the expense of keeping them in the funeral home. Well, she'd have to go a cheaper route now, and get Michael and Lauren buried as quickly as possible. Tomorrow.

"This is what we're going to do, Miss Brehna." Bryce glared down at her as if she were one of his insubordinate employees. "I'll pay for Michael and Lauren's funeral, then I'll even pay for a first class ticket back to Florida for you. Better still, I'll have my pilot fly you back in my jet. I'll reimburse all expenses you've incurred so far. Just sign the kids over to me and you can leave Granite Falls as freely and as unencumbered as you came." He pulled a checkbook from his back pocket, and opened it. "Name your price, Miss Brehna."

Kaya seethed at his arrogance, his assumption that he could buy her. In all of her twenty-three years on this planet, she never had this strong a desire to slap someone across the face. Too bad it was beyond her immediate reach.

"Money isn't everything, *Mr. Fontaine*. It can buy a lot of luxuries, I'd grant, but it cannot buy love. I love my nephew and nieces. In time, they'll grow to love me. Love is a price you certainly cannot afford."

His eyes narrowed to dark slits as he tossed the checkbook on the desk. "You obviously have no idea who you're dealing with, Miss Brehna. I promise, I will—"

"Time out," Steven finally interjected, coming to stand between them. "I realize emotions are running high right now. But you both need to stop before you say something you'll regret. Let's get Michael and Lauren buried, then you two can work out the details over the children."

"Actually, there's nothing to work out," Kaya stated in the calmest voice she could muster under the circumstances. "Steven, I would like you to prepare the necessary papers to finalize my custody of the children so I can get out of this town as soon as possible."

She threw her head further back to encounter Bryce's angry glare. Even though he'd managed to push her within a hair's breadth of striking him, she knew what drove him. He was fighting for three little kids who weren't even related to him when her own parents had walked away without a backward glance. For that, she admired him, and for the children's sake she would try to get along with him.

In spite of that, she had to let him know that she didn't scare easily. Her years in foster homes where she had to fight for what was hers, then fight some more to hold on to it, had instilled a warrior's spirit in her. She wasn't backing down. Not for him. Not for anyone.

"Mr. Fontaine, I'm sorry we had to meet under such tragic circumstances. I can see that you care about your godchildren and want what's best for them. But, I'm their family, and good or bad, rich or poor, family is the most important thing to a child. I wouldn't get in the way of your relationship with them. You can visit them whenever you want. But get this, I'm not signing them over to you, or anyone else. Ever."

Bryce could barely contain his fury as he watched her sashay across the floor, pull a leather jacket from the coat rack, and snatch up a handbag from a corner table.

The second Steven closed the door behind her, Bryce exploded. "The nerve of that woman! Who does she think she is?"

"Their aunt and legal guardian." Steven ran his fingers through his hair, a helpless, skeptical twist to his lips.

"You are my friend. You should have told me what Michael and Lauren had done."

"Bryce, you know I couldn't do that. They were my friends

too, but they were also my clients. I owed them certain fiduciary rights. Loyalty and confidentiality—"

"You dare talk to me about loyalty, Steven? Where was their loyalty to me and to their defenseless children?" Bryce shook his fists in the air and began to pace the floor. "She's taking them to Florida. Michael and Lauren would not want their children living anywhere but in Granite Falls. This is their home."

"I pointed that out to Kaya. I don't know if it did any good." Steven sighed. "If I'd seen this coming, I would have instructed them to include some kind of condition on her guardianship. It's beyond my power. Kaya has custody, clear and free."

Bryce came to a halt in front of Steven. "It may be beyond your power, but it isn't beyond mine. I'm not going to stand by and let that woman take those kids from their home, from people they've known all their lives. People they know and trust. People who love them."

"Bryce, I don't want you going off—"

He cut Steven off with a flip of his wrist. "I don't care what I have to do, or whose neck I have to step on to keep those kids in Granite Falls. I will *not* lose them, Steven. I will not lose them!"

CHAPTER TWO

Kaya pulled her rental into the four-car garage at *L'etoile du Nord*. She slammed her palms against the steering wheel, releasing the anger and frustration that had been stewing inside her since she left Steven's office.

She never thought it possible that anyone could awaken that raging little girl she'd buried years ago, but Bryce Fontaine had done it. Kudos to him.

She'd been looking forward to his return, mainly for Jason's sake. Now she wished she'd never laid eyes on the man. He was the most arrogant, overbearing, egotistic male she'd ever met.

Dangerous, too, since he had enough money and power to break her. He could keep her tied up in a custody battle for the next hundred years if he wanted. And from the imminent rage in his black eyes and thunderous voice, Kaya had no doubt that was exactly what he intended to do. He would fight to keep the kids in his life because he loved them.

He shared a mutual love and trust with his godchildren—the kind of love and trust that would take her months, if not years to build. Especially when it came to Jason who'd made it clear that he did not like her.

The courts would look favorably on their emotional ties to Bryce, and take into consideration that Bryce was older, shared a history with each of them, and was far more financially capable of taking care of all of them. She was twenty-three years old, a stranger to them, had no experience with children, had no clue how to be a parent, and would probably be broke in three months.

Yes, it was true that she had a piece of paper that gave her legal rights to them, but Kaya had spent enough time in Florida's child welfare system to know that a notarized piece of paper wasn't enough. She'd witnessed a lot of cases where the courts ruled against legal rights because they didn't think it was in the best interest of the child—her own case was one of those where best interest won out over legal and maternal rights. Kaya knew now exactly how all those parents who'd fought for their children and lost them felt. She knew how Nadine felt when she lost custody of her. The only difference was that Nadine hadn't really fought for her; she'd used her parental rights for her own selfish reasons that had nothing to do with love. The courts had been on little Kaya's side, and had made the right decision in her favor. Would they do the same for Jason, Alyssa, and Anastasia?

If she were honest with herself, Kaya knew she couldn't expect the courts to side with her in this case. She couldn't think of one person who would be on her side. Not one.

Kaya sighed as she exited the car and walked toward the mudroom. The shock of learning about Michael and Lauren's sudden deaths, inheriting the children, then finding out they didn't have a penny to their names—all in two days—was hard enough to fathom. She never thought she'd have to fight for them, too.

The thought of losing her nephew and nieces to Bryce Fontaine left a hollow feeling in the pit of Kaya's stomach, and as she sat on the bench in the mudroom to shed her boots, she squeezed her eyelids together to stop the stinging tears from falling. If she lost them, she had no one to blame but herself. A stupid, childish grudge against her sister could cost her the three most precious things that have ever entered her life. She had to find a way to keep them.

Kaya opened her eyes and stared at the white ceiling. "God, help me. Make a way for me to keep the children, please."

As an adult, Kaya didn't practice any religion, but as a child, she'd lived in a few foster homes where the norm was to attend church on Sundays. She'd sat in the congregation with her foster families and listened, unimpressed, as people shared miracles that God had done in their lives. Before she'd become a ward of the state of Florida, Kaya had spent years praying for her father to come back and take her out of the hellhole he'd left her in. Since God never answered that prayer, she'd stop believing in miracles.

From what she'd learned about Michael and Lauren, it seemed as if they'd been regular church attendees, so perhaps God would grant this wish—not for her, but for Michael and Lauren and their children's sakes.

Feeling a little more balanced in spirit, Kaya got up and opened the door that led into the house. But as she entered the palatial foyer and took in the grandeur of the marble Grecian columns separating several richly furnished areas of the first floor, and the myriad of Palladian windows that afforded breathtaking views of Crystal Lake and the rolling mountains behind it, Bryce's claim rang loud and clear in her ears.

Mine. L'etoile du Nord belongs to me.

This was Bryce Fontaine's house. And she'd bet anything that in that big head of his, he thought that he owned everything in it, including her sister's children. Yet, she thought, biting into her lower lip, nowhere in this house, not even in the third-floor unfinished master suite, was there a sign that Bryce Fontaine lived here.

Why didn't *he* live here? Why were her sister and her family living in his house? And why didn't anybody bother to tell her what was going on?

Lauren never explained anything about her private life in their occasional snail-mail correspondences. She'd merely sent pictures of the family with short notes to explain them, but at the end of each letter, she expressed her wish that the two of them would have a chance to meet again, get to know each other, and talk about their father. It was the last part that always got to Kaya. Back then, she had no desire to talk to Lauren about the father who'd chosen Lauren and her mother over her. Today, she'd give anything to sit down with her sister and learn about the man she'd once loved with all her little heart and soul.

"Auntie Kaya, you're home. You're home."

Kaya looked up at the sound of the cheerful voice and the pitter-pattering of feet on the landing linking the two sprawling staircases to the second floor. She smiled as Alyssa, with Snoopy clutched under one arm, raced down a flight of steps as quickly as her little legs would carry her.

All of Kaya's doubts vanished at the glee on the little girl's face. She couldn't remember anyone ever being this excited to see her, but she could remember being just as excited to see her father when she was a little girl. She dropped her purse on a nearby table and opened her arms as Alyssa ran to her.

"Hey, baby." She hugged the dark-brown, curly-headed child and kissed her relentlessly. How could she have forgotten she had Alyssa on her side? This darling little child had accepted her without question. She was Kaya's glimmer of hope, her assurance that all would work out for the best.

Alyssa was still too young to understand the sudden void in her life, and last night at bedtime when she'd asked where her mommy and daddy were, Kaya had simply told her that they had gone to heaven.

"Did they go for a vacation? Can I go to heaven to see them, Auntie Kaya?" she'd asked.

"One day, honey. One day," Kaya had replied on a sob.

"You didn't kiss Snoopy," Alyssa said, holding up her favorite stuffed animal that was once white and fluffy, but was now a tattered dull grey from four years of heavy loving.

Kaya gave Snoopy a tight-lipped peck on his scruffy black nose. She refused to think of the plethora of germs crawling all over that dog. Snoopy went everywhere with Alyssa, even to the bathroom.

"Did you bring me a present, Auntie Kaya?" Alyssa fiddled with the locket around Kaya's neck.

"Not this time, sweetie." Kaya gazed into her sparkling eyes —Eli Brehna's eyes, eyes that she'd also inherited, eyes that Nadine cursed each time she looked at her daughter.

"Why didn't you bring me a present, Auntie Kaya?"

"Because when Little Brownie Locks was climbing up the snowy mountain," she began while tickling Alyssa's tummy, "she met a big bad bear who scared her so much…" Kaya growled for emphasis. "Little Brownie Locks was so frightened, she forgot all the important things she had to do, and she ran all the way home, screaming, 'Mommy, Mommy, the big bad bear is after me. Mommy, Mommy, help me.'"

As Alyssa screamed in delight, the parallelism of that tale to her encounter with Bryce made Kaya's heart race. She'd been so preoccupied with his threats, she'd forgotten to stop at the quilt shop in town to pick up a new dress for one of Alyssa's many dolls. She'd learned last night that Alyssa was a doll collector, and never said no to a new one, not even duplicates.

"Tickle me some more, Auntie Kaya," Alyssa yelled, wriggling around in her arms.

Kaya obliged and pressed her close as she giggled uncontrollably. Kaya breathed in the sounds of joy. Anything was better than the ominous cloud hanging over the house, waiting to burst and drench their hearts with sorrow. She took a few wavering steps and plopped down on the sofa closest to the deep-ledged fireplace that separated the living and dining areas.

For a few moments, she gazed out at the winter wonderland beyond the tinted glass windows. She was surrounded with a white calmness, so different from the unceasing din of Palm Beach. *Life will be very different for these children in Palm Beach*, she thought, turning her attention to Alyssa who was now fiddling with her locket again. "Where's everybody?" she asked.

"Jason's in his room and Miss Libby is in Stasia's room." Alyssa clapped her hand over her mouth, her eyes opening wide. "Shhhh." She brought her lips close to Kaya's ear. "Miss Libby says be quiet 'cause she's putting Stasia to bed."

Kaya chuckled. "Now you tell me after all that screaming you just did." Thank God the house was huge, and that the nursery was on the second floor on the opposite side of house.

"I thought I heard you."

Kaya smiled at the freckled-face redhead descending the stairs. She'd known Libby for less than twenty-four hours and she already felt as if they were close friends.

Kaya had felt very welcomed since she'd stepped off the plane in Manchester to find a Fontaine Enterprises jet, albeit a small one, waiting to fly her to Granite Falls. She'd arrived at *L'etoile du Nord* to meet Libby and Steven, Ethan Bennett—whom she learned was Jason's best friend—and his mother, Adrianna. She'd also met Pastor Reuben Kelly and his wife Samantha from Granite Falls Community Church. They'd all raced to the house the night Michael and Lauren died, and had stayed with the children until Kaya arrived.

If it was one thing that was made clear to Kaya right away, it was that the children had a strong support system in place. They'd shown up in the time of a crisis, and Kaya was grateful for the time they'd spend with her and the children, but once they felt that she could handle the situation, they'd returned to their families and lives. Pastor Kelly had a church to run and Samantha had other clients to attend to. Adrianna had two more children at home—a toddler and an infant—and Libby had a previously scheduled bridal dress fitting.

If Kaya were to be honest with herself, she'd admit that after everyone went home last night, leaving her all alone with a screaming infant, she'd been tempted to catch the first flight back to Florida this morning. But when Alyssa had crawled into her bed in the early hours of dawn, wrapped her arms about her neck and told her that she loved her, all thoughts of running had been vanquished from Kaya's mind. This situation was different from any she'd ever faced, and she knew she was already messing up, big time, but she wasn't a quitter. She wasn't going to quit these kids just because her circumstance looked impossible to overcome.

"Is she sleeping?" Kaya asked, jutting her chin at the monitor in Libby's hand.

Libby set the monitor on the marble table in front of the sofa and sat down beside Kaya. "I got her to take a couple ounces of formula. That will hold her for a little while. She misses nursing." She rolled her eyes in Alyssa's direction.

Kaya nodded her understanding. Samantha had instructed them not to say anything to Alyssa about her parents' deaths until Bryce was back. Samantha thought he should be the one to tell her since he'd been like a father to her for her entire life. Only now did Kaya understand the gravity of those words. Would Samantha testify on Bryce's behalf in a custody battle?

Kaya swallowed and smiled at the child sitting on her lap. "Alyssa, can you go play with your dolls for a while? I need to talk with Miss Libby."

"I wanna stay with you." Alyssa tightened her hand around Kaya's waist. "I'll be quiet and not interrupt."

"I know you'll be quiet, but I need to talk about some grownup stuff with Miss Libby. It's just for a little while. Okay?"

Alyssa pouted and reluctantly climbed off her lap. "Will you play dolls with me?"

"In a little while."

"Okay, Auntie Kaya. Don't forget, now."

"I wouldn't. I promise."

Alyssa skipped across the floor and descended three short steps that led into a playroom near the kitchen area.

"So, how did your meeting with Steven go?" Libby asked.

"Interesting." Kaya noted the sparkle in Libby's eyes at the mention of her fiancé. Kaya never felt enthusiastic when she spoke about Jack, thought of him, or even when she was with him. He seemed more like an old familiar friend than a fiancé. The sight of him caused her no real delight, just a warm comfortable feeling, like she would get from slipping on a cozy sweater on a chilly evening, and being grateful that it still fit, and could do its job.

But her heart was pounding out of control at the mere thought of Bryce Fontaine. Her fingers still tingled from his touch, and those gnawing pangs in the core of her belly were back at the memory of his dark probing eyes, sexy brown lips, and bronzed giant stature.

The man had set her on fire with just one look.

Kaya let out a harsh breath. "Is he always so damned arrogant?"

"Who, Steven?" A frown wrinkled Libby's forehead.

"No. The *godfather*."

"Oh." Libby split a wry, freckled smile. "You met Bryce."

"Collided with Bryce would be a more accurate account." Kaya had to bite back her impression of the man since Libby worked at Fontaine Enterprises as head of the accounting department. "Why didn't you tell me this house belonged to him?"

Libby shrugged. "I assumed you knew. Didn't you and your sister talk?"

"I wish we did. Then I might understand why Bryce thinks her children belong to him. He went ballistic when he heard I'd inherited them and that I was taking them to Florida with me. For a minute there I thought he was the biological father instead of the godfather."

Libby dropped her gaze and her expression turned somber.

"What is it, Libby? Is there something I should know, besides what I don't already?"

"Bryce loves these kids, Kaya. It would break his heart if you took them away from here."

"So do you and Steven, but I don't see you going into a rage over it."

"It's different for Bryce. Ever since—"

"Ever since what?" Kaya prompted when Libby stopped.

"Bryce experienced a horrific heartbreak a few years ago, Kaya. It changed him in more ways than any of us anticipated, even his parents. He still hasn't recovered from it. Just go easy on him, okay? I know he can be a real pain in the ass sometimes, but his heart is always in the right place."

That was hard for Kaya to believe after the way he'd tried to pay her off. She should have known there was something profound driving that man. He'd been warm and charming when she'd first met him, then in the space of a heartbeat, he'd turned into a raging tyrant. Now Libby was telling her that the omnipotent Bryce Fontaine wasn't that invincible after all. He was human and vulnerable like the rest of them.

"What happened to him, Libby?" The depth of Kaya's

curiosity, the force of her need to know more about the man who rubbed her in all the wrong ways, surprised even her.

"I shouldn't have said anything." Libby shot to her feet and clasped her hands over her mouth as if to keep more gossip from spilling out.

Kaya followed her up. "But you did. And you can't leave me hanging like this. Maybe, if I know what's going on in his head, I could better understand his irrational behavior."

"Would it change your mind about taking the kids to Florida with you?"

"I don't know."

Libby eyed her speculatively. "Just forget I said anything. When and if Bryce wants you to know about his past, he'll tell you. Please, don't tell him that I mentioned it. He trusts very few people in this world, and two of them just died. I don't want to give him a reason not to trust me."

"Okay, I wouldn't. I wouldn't say anything." Accepting that any more discussions about Bryce were over, Kaya walked to the fireplace and stretched her hands toward the leaping flames behind the glass-enclosed hearth. Libby was clearly concerned about ruining her relationship with Bryce. Not only was the man domineering and intimidating, he had his entourage of loyal disciples to protect and defend him.

In spite of the internal havoc he was already causing to her being, and the obstacles he could place in her path to retaining custody of the children, Kaya couldn't help but wonder about the painful experience Bryce had suffered.

Whatever it was, she was certain that he didn't want her pity or her sympathy. He wasn't the kind of man to wear his heart on his sleeve, either. She'd only spent a few minutes in his presence, but she already had him figured out. Bryce Fontaine wasn't the kind of man who would let anyone know he was hurting, emotionally or physically. He was proud.

Sensing someone was watching her, Kaya gazed across the wide open space of the first floor. Sure enough, Jason was standing in an informal dining area off the kitchen, observing her. Even from a distance, she felt the disdain in his silver-grey eyes.

He was the most light-footed child she'd ever known. She could hear Alyssa coming from a mile away, but Jason made his presence known only when he was ready. Several times yesterday, she'd caught him eyeing her like a full-bellied cat would eye a bird with a broken wing—not knowing whether or not to be bothered.

Unlike Alyssa, he'd been wary of her, but politely civil when she first arrived. But last night it all changed when she'd offered to tuck him in. He'd screamed at her, telling her that she was not his mother and to leave him alone. Then he'd slammed his bedroom door in her face.

He'd given her a glimpse of Little Kaya. After her father walked out on her, she'd become filled with rage. Nadine had tried to beat it out of her, to no avail. As Kaya thought about it, she realized that it was only after Nadine abandoned her and she was placed in foster care that her anger began to subdue. She wasn't mad at the world; she was just mad at Nadine. It was Nadine's fault that her father had left. Kaya wished her father had fought for her, like Bryce was prepared to fight for Jason and his sisters. *Oh, to know love like that.*

Jason sauntered up to Libby, ignoring Kaya altogether. "Miss Libby, when are Uncle Bryce and Mommy and Daddy coming home?"

"Soon, Jason." Kaya gave Libby a silencing shake of the head.

"Yeah, soon," Libby backed her up.

She didn't want him to know that Bryce was back, not until she figured out how to deal with the man. As she watched Jason's shoulders droop, Kaya felt like someone was snipping little pieces of her heart out with a pair of giant scissors. His moment of truth was near.

"Can I stay at your place until they come home?"

Libby rested her hands on his shoulders. "I'll tell you what. I have to go into town to run some errands. Would you like to come along for the ride? We can stop at Mountainview Café and have a bowl of Miss Eloise's homemade clam chowder that you love."

"Okay, and maybe if Ethan is there, I can see him?"

"Yeah, maybe." Libby ruffled his curly black hair.

Kaya wished she could have been the one to cause the hint of a smile that flitted across Jason's face. She knew that deep down inside, he was a sweet kid. She wanted so much to put her arms around him, tell him that she loved him.

"Ethan's grandmother owns the café," Libby told Kaya.

Kaya nodded. "I see."

"Run on upstairs and put on some warm clothes." Libby tugged on the sleeve of Jason's T-shirt. "We don't want you getting sick."

He left without giving Kaya a second glance.

"I don't mean to take over," Libby added when they were alone again. "But he's been cooped up in this house for two days, now. It's school winter break, and he would have been out on the ski trails with his father every day if—" She shrugged. "You know."

"I understand." Kaya placed a hand on her shoulder. Nobody seemed to want to utter the words, "dead" or "died". "You know them better than I do. I get it."

"Auntie Kaya, me and my dollies are ready for tea," Alyssa called from the playroom.

"I'll be right there."

Libby cleared her throat. "Um, my sister asked me to pick up my niece, Courtney, from daycare. She's Alyssa's age, and if you don't mind, I'd like to take her with me, too. Anastasia is asleep and I'm sure you could use some rest."

"What do I tell Bryce when he comes knocking?" She could just imagine his ire at not finding *his* children at home.

"Use the time to talk. Get to know him. He's a good man, Kaya. You'll see that once you get past his hard exterior."

Kaya doubted that very much. "I feel awful you're using your week off from work to help me out when you have a summer wedding to plan," she said.

"I'll have plenty of time for wedding plans. The kids are much more important right now." She gave Kaya's arm a comforting squeeze. "Jason will come around. Just give him time."

Time? Time was one luxury Kaya didn't have. Not with Bryce Fontaine breathing down her neck.

As she paced the nursery with a screaming Anastasia in her arms, Kaya wondered why Bryce still hadn't shown up with the sheriff and the town's two cops in tow.

On the other hand, she was grateful he hadn't. With Jason and Alyssa gone, she'd used the alone time to get some important things done—like asking the undertaker to use his least expensive caskets since she now knew that the funeral cost was coming out of her pocket. She would love to give her sister and brother-in-law a more glamorous burial, but she had to watch every penny she spent from now on.

She'd also called Jack at his job, and was holding until he got off the line with a supplier when Anastasia's whimpers came through the monitor. She'd hung up with semi-regret. She wasn't looking forward to having a conversation about her new charges with Jack. He didn't really like kids. Needy and annoying were his constant description of them. *Dah!*

She'd agreed to marry him—not because she also disliked children, but because she wasn't planning on having any. She'd been too afraid that she'd turn out to be as despicable a mother as Nadine. But now that she'd inherited three little ones, Kaya knew she'd do everything in her power to see that they were loved and well taken care of. She could only hope that Jack's attitude towards children would change once he met hers.

"Hush, baby," Kaya whispered as Anastasia hit a higher note, causing a horrendous ringing in her ears. She'd changed her, tried to feed her, unsuccessfully, then sang, terribly off-key, every lullaby she could pull from her childhood memories. But Anastasia refused to be comforted. As a last resort, Kaya had finally called Dr. LaCrosse, the children's pediatrician, only to be told that he was on his honeymoon. The physician who was filling in for him was in surgery and he would call her back when he was out. She was still waiting.

"Please, Stasia. Stop crying," Kaya begged, rocking her gently in the crook of her arm. "I wish I knew what was wrong with you, but I don't. Please—"

"Why is she screaming like that? I heard her all the way from the courtyard."

Kaya tensed at the deep voice rising above the piercing cries. She spun around. Bryce's imposing figure hugged the doorway. He'd shaved, and changed into jeans and a pullover shirt that lay snugly against the hard muscles of his flat stomach, wide powerful chest, and broad shoulders.

She'd told herself that nothing he did or said would shake her confidence. But as she gazed into his censuring eyes, Kaya's heart began to pound with fear of the trouble he could cause her.

He pushed away from the door, picked up a pink blanket from the changing table and draped it over his shoulder. "You told me she's been fussy, not that she's been trying to start an avalanche around us. Give her to me." He towered over Kaya, arms outstretched.

"I can handle it." Kaya tightened her hold and backed up a step. His demand to give Anastasia to him was tantamount to the one he'd made in Steven's office to hand over custody of all the children to him. "I don't need your help," she said tersely.

"Oh, really?" he drawled, his eyes laced with skepticism. A humorous smile played at the corner of his mouth as he took in her petite framed swallowed up in one of Lauren's huge sweaters.

Kaya took another backward step, only to discover he'd cornered her between the crib and a chest of drawers. Realizing he was not going to move, she pressed her bare feet into the lambskin throw rug and held her ground. As unbearable as the screams were, it would be worse if Bryce proved he was more adept than her at handling a fussy baby. It would be one more weapon he could use against her in court.

Kaya's mind fast-forwarded. *"Your Honor, when I walked into the nursery, Miss Brehna was holding the screaming infant, little Anastasia. It was clear that she had no idea what she was doing, and that the child had been crying for quite some time. If I hadn't shown up when I did, I— I—" His voice would crack deliberately. "I tremble to think what could have happened to that baby. We've heard of young inexperienced mothers who have shaken their babies…" A tear would slip from his eye. "I thank God that I got there in time to prevent another tragedy."*

Bastard!

"Kaya, just give her to me. Come on."

Kaya shook her head and rewound to the present. She glared at Bryce and tightened her hold on Anastasia

"This screaming isn't good for her lungs, and quite frankly it's hard on my ears." Bryce reached out again, his dark eyes daring her to disagree with him.

Kaya glanced down at the red-faced, squirming child in her arms, wanting so much to be the one to give her comfort, to get her used to the idea that her auntie Kaya, and no one else, was now her sole provider. Pride tempted her to ignore Bryce, but sensibility pushed her to hand over the baby since all of her novice attempts at calming her had failed. "Okay. Okay. You can have her."

As she placed Anastasia in his arms, Bryce's scent, his nearness, and the brush of his fingertips against her arms sent a host of dizzying sensations rushing through Kaya. Their eyes locked, and somewhere in the blackness of his, Kaya detected a flash of lust. Elemental need. Unadulterated want. She knew that look. She'd encountered it many times from a multitude of men. But she'd never been this terrified of her reaction to it.

It was exciting, suffocating, and weakening, all in one. Yet, she found herself powerless or unwilling to avert her gaze. Another reason she'd agreed to marry Jack was that he never looked at her that way. Perhaps Jack never really looked at her, just through her and around her. He'd never *seen* her. She felt comfortable with him. *Too comfortable.*

Kaya let out the breath she'd been holding when Bryce took a step backward and shifted his gaze to the baby. In that spellbinding moment, Bryce had awakened something deep inside her. *Curiosity?* No. She told herself that it was antipathy. He was on a mission to destroy her. It would be in her best interest not to lose sight of that fact. His penetrating stare was one of intimidation. That was all it was.

She watched as he cradled Anastasia's tiny head in one of his large hands and clasped the other around the scrawny little body. Ignoring the flailing arms and legs, he raised her close to his face and began to sing a song Kaya had never heard before.

Sweet baby child, hush, don't you cry

Momma's gone away for a little while
Soon she'll be home with a bright happy smile
And she'll hug and rock, her sweet baby child
Sweet baby child, hush, don't you cry...

As she listened to the words that would never come to pass, tears pooled in Kaya's eyes. Lauren was gone, not for a while, but forever. She would never kiss, nor hug, nor rock her sweet baby child again.

In the midst of her troubling thoughts, the deep, soothing rhythm of Bryce's voice resonated through Kaya, melting away her fears and frustrations over his meddling.

She felt blessed relief.

The man could sing a fledgling from the safety and comfort of its nest, she thought, watching him pace back and forth with Anastasia in his arms. Luther Vandross had nothing on him. With a voice so beautiful, so touching, he could have been a star.

Anastasia apparently thought so, too, because as Bryce chanted the chorus over and over again, her screams eventually faded to an occasional hiccup and a series of soft, throaty gurgles.

He'd succeeded where she had failed.

"Yes, that's it, sweetheart," he cooed, gazing into the tiny face with the most tenderness and patience Kaya had ever seen in a man. "Uncle Bryce knows just what you need, doesn't he?"

He settled her against his wide chest, his enormous hands supporting her back, his long brown fingers wrapping around the perimeter of her body. Kaya would never have dreamed a man holding a baby could look so irresistible. Especially a man she didn't trust with that very same baby.

"That's my baby," he said as Anastasia blew out a bubble and gurgled at him. "You miss your mommy and daddy, don't you? I know, darling. I miss them, too. But Uncle Bryce is home now.

He'll take good care of you, little Stasia. I will always be here for you. I promise from the bottom of my heart."

He came to a halt in front of Kaya, sending a pleasant combination of masculine odor and baby powder up her nostrils. "You're not taking these children out of Granite Falls," he warned in a low, gruff tone. "This is their home. It's where they belong and it's where they'll stay. Why don't you make it easy on everyone, Kaya, and just sign them over to me? I know what they need."

"That's not what their parents wanted, Bryce. They named me legal guardian in their will."

"Where there's a will, Miss Brehna, there's always a way to break it."

Kaya folded her arms and stared up at him, not knowing whether he was referring to her heart's will to take the children to Florida, or the legal document that gave her custody of them. Perhaps a little of both. "I don't want to argue with you again, Bryce. At least not today," she added, remembering what Libby had said, or not said about the "something awful" in his past.

"We don't need to argue at all, Kaya. Just do what you know is best for them."

Kaya strode to the east window overlooking the snow-covered hills of the White Mountain National Range. Apart from an immediate abundance of love and patience, she had no idea what was best. It took a lot of money to raise kids. She could remember her mother's constant complaints about not having enough money for one thing or the other. And Nadine only had one child, plus she was receiving a monthly child support check from Kaya's father.

She, on the other hand, had just inherited three. With formula, diapers, after-school, and daycare added to her rent and car payments, not to mention the emergencies that were sure to pop up every so often, Kaya knew that life as she'd known it was over. No more exclusive clothes and pricey shoes. No more eating out at expensive restaurants. No more weekend getaways. It was work, work, and more work from here on in.

She'd have to take on more customers and work longer hours. Her career required that she live in a big city where she had access to an infinite number of wealthy people and thriving businesses. Granite Falls was a wealthy, thriving town, she had to admit, but it was small. There wasn't room for expansion up here in the mountains, and it was bitterly cold. Even if she sold her father's jewel and stayed in Granite Falls, the money would run out eventually, and she'd be back to square one.

Florida was her only choice. She had to make Bryce understand the position she was in, and at the same time, find a way to establish a friendship with him for the children's sake.

CHAPTER THREE

"W here are Jason and Alyssa?"

Kaya turned around as the anticipated question broke into her thoughts. "Libby took them into town to see Ethan and Courtney. They needed some fresh air. I hope you don't mind that they aren't here."

"Not at all. Freed me up for this little one. She needed special attention." He smiled at the baby before looking Kaya up and down, quizzically. "Why are you wearing Lauren's clothes? Don't you have any of your own?"

Kaya pushed the oversized sleeves up her arms. "Since Anastasia's been crying so much, Adrianna Bennett suggested I wear Lauren's clothes to give Anastasia a sense of Lauren's smell. She said it worked for her mother when she babysat her children."

"Did it work for you?"

"Did it look like it was working when you barged in?" The mockery in his voice and eyes fueled her exasperation. "How did you get into the house, anyway? I know I locked the doors after Libby left."

"I have a key. Mike and Lauren allowed me to go and come

as I please. Do you have a problem with that?"

Kaya shrugged. "It's your house."

He closed the distance between them and glared down at her, his mouth taking on an unpleasant twist. She was quite taken aback when instead of delivering some curt remark, he merely held the baby out to her. "Would you like to hold her? Experience the feel of a happy baby in your arms?"

Kaya took a swift glance at Anastasia, who seemed quite content to remain where she was. "She might start screaming again. Maybe she's allergic to me."

He sat down on the wide window seat. "She just misses her mommy and daddy. You have to learn how to calm her." He put his thighs together and placed Anastasia on her back, her head resting on his knees and her legs toward his belly. He began to rub her tummy in slow, circular motions. "She likes this position. It's her favorite."

What's your favorite position, Mr. Fontaine?

Kaya shook her head, shocked as the question formulated in her mind. What was wrong with her? She'd never had these scandalous thoughts about any man before. Ever since she'd met Bryce this morning, he'd been making her feel things, want things that were foreign to her. And she didn't even like the man.

The sight of his long fingers making circular motions on the baby's tummy made Kaya's knees weak. With a shudder, she dropped down on the windowsill, being careful not to sit too close to him. She couldn't handle another surge of current ripping through her. The man exuded enough bolts to short-circuit her heart. "She seemed to like that lullaby you were singing to her," she told Bryce. "I've never heard it before."

"You wouldn't have." The sharpness in his black eyes dimmed a notch, and for a split second he looked as if he'd been transported back into a dark time in his life.

Did he lose a child? Kaya wondered. Was that the bad

experience Libby had mentioned? If he'd lost a child, where was the mother? Had he lost her, too? Was he married? Her heart skipped a beat. *No.* If he was married, he would have a ring on his finger, and his wife would be in the pictures he'd taken with Lauren and her family. *He wasn't married.* She knew she couldn't ask him anything without giving Libby away, so Kaya tucked her questions away for another time. "It's a beautiful song," she said with a bright smile. "And Anastasia thinks so, too. Look at her, gurgling and happy."

"Here, hold her," he offered again, gathering Anastasia into his arms.

Still reveling in the peaceful moments, Kaya put up her hands to stay him. Once she learned that song and mastered the art of baby-tummy-rubbing, she would have plenty of time to enjoy a quiet baby, whereas his time with her was limited. "You seem to have a way with her. Or maybe you just have a way with all women, no matter the age, Mr. Fontaine."

"I'll let you be the judge of that if you stick around long enough, Miss Brehna."

"Then I guess I'll never know. The children and I are leaving for Palm Beach next week." The moment the words left her mouth, she regretted them. He'd just saved her day. She could be a little more understanding, a bit more sympathetic to his feelings. "I'm sorry, Bryce. I shouldn't have said that."

He graced her with an unexpected smile. "It doesn't matter, Kaya. *You* may be going back to Palm Beach, but these kids aren't going anywhere."

"You seem so sure of—" Kaya stopped at the sound of feet thundering down the hall. Jason and Alyssa were screaming Bryce's name as they raced each other to the nursery.

"Here, you *have* to take her."

She got Anastasia out of his arms mere seconds before two excited kids burst into the room and threw themselves at him.

"Oh, boy." He fell to his knees and wrapped them in a big hug. "I'm glad somebody's happy to see me."

Kaya mouthed a thank-you to Libby, who waved a goodbye from the door before hurrying away.

"Did you bring me a present, Uncle Bryce? You promised you'd bring me a present," Alyssa said.

"You sure know how to deflate a man's ego, darling Alyssa."

Kaya smiled as Bryce sat on the rug and settled the little girl on one thigh while Jason perched on the other, their arms linking around his shoulders.

"What's an ego, Uncle Bryce?" Alyssa asked.

"Something you don't have to worry about for a long, long time, my sweet." He tweaked her nose between his thumb and forefinger.

"So, did you bring me a present?" Alyssa rocked impatiently back and forth.

"Am I merely a *present* uncle to you, Alyssa? Is that all I'm good for?"

"I'll give you a one hundreds of kisses." She slapped her hands on his cheeks and lathered his face with noisy smooches.

"Okay. Okay. Hold the saliva. I brought you a new doll. It's in your room."

"Cool. Wicked cool." She skipped out of the nursery.

"Such a little manipulator." He wiped at his wet face, his broad smile softening his dark features. "That one would do anything, say anything, to get what she wants."

"I know. Last night she justified getting into my makeup by claiming she wanted to be pretty like me. She's mischievous, but so adorable. You can't help but love her."

Bryce chuckled.

Kaya laughed out loud. It was endearing to see this jovial side of him brought out by the antics of a four-year-old girl. He reminded her of her father and the fun times they used to have before he disappeared from her life. She was just a few months older than Alyssa the last time she saw him. So young to lose the most important man in her life. It saddened her to know that Alyssa had to experience a more permanent loss, but she was consoled that her niece had her uncle Bryce to fill the void Michael's absence had created.

Yes, there was a definite bond of love and trust between Bryce and his godchildren, she thought, easing into the big, comfy chair near the crib and arranging Anastasia on her lap as she'd seen Bryce do. If she took these children away from him, they would see her as the mean old dragon for breaking that bond, just as she'd thought of Nadine for driving her father away.

You're nothing like Nadine. You would never hurt these kids. The fact that you are willing to fight for them proves you're different.

"I brought you a present, too, Jason." Bryce's voice reclaimed Kaya's attention.

"What?"

"A set of skate skis and a snowboard. They're the fastest and most popular on the market. All the kids in Europe are going bonkers over them. They're black and chrome. I think that's the color you wanted."

"Yes, it is. Thanks, Uncle Bryce. You're the best." He wrapped his arms about Bryce.

Bryce hugged him close, but the grim look on his face told Kaya that he dreaded the next few moments.

He cleared his throat. "So how are you, son?"

"I'm fine. Why didn't Mommy and Daddy come home with you? Are they having too much fun on the Alps?"

Bryce inhaled deeply and sharply.

Kaya shuddered. Jason's heart was about to be broken.

"Jason, your parents didn't go to Switzerland with me."

"Yes, they did. Daddy said he and Mommy had such a good

time when we all went before that they were going back again. I know they're still there. You left them there, like you left us the last time when you had to come back home for business. Right?"

Bryce hesitated, swallowing, as if fighting his own affirmation, as if trying to find the right words for the little boy who wanted so much to believe the impossible.

He took Jason's hands in his, and stared into his eyes. "Jason, listen to me. Your mom and dad didn't go to Europe with me this time. And I didn't leave them behind. They were in a terrible car accident two days ago. They died, son. They died."

"Noooo." Jason shook his head, his eyes wide with negation. "Noooo. Why are you lying, Uncle Bryce? Mommy and Daddy aren't dead! They wouldn't ever leave us. They promised. They promised they would never leave us."

"Have I *ever* lied to you, Jason?"

He shook his head.

"Then believe me now, son. Your mom and dad are really gone. They didn't want to leave you and your sisters. They didn't want to break their promise to you, but it wasn't their fault. They're not ever coming home, Jason," he reiterated.

Jason closed his eyes and his lips trembled as the words sank into his heart, crushed his young soul. "Why?" he wailed, trying so hard to make sense of a loss he didn't understand and couldn't accept. "Why did *they* have to die? Did me and Lyssa and Stasia do something wrong?"

"No! You didn't do anything wrong."

"Then why did God take them away from us? Why did He take the two of them? Couldn't He have left us just one?"

"I don't know, son? I *don't* know." Bryce's voice trembled with his own anguish and helplessness.

Tears rolled down Kaya's face as Bryce hugged the child to his chest. Jason's astute questions rang in her ears. *Why did God take both of them?* He *could* have left them one. She had wondered the same thing. *Why did they both have to die?*

"It's not fair." Jason's body rocked with sobs. "It's not fair. I want my mom and my dad back, Uncle Bryce. Please, bring them back home."

"I wish I could, Jase. I really wish I could."

"I hate God. I hate Him for taking them away from us."

Bryce pulled the boy's hands from around his neck and stared into his face. "Jason, I never want to hear you say that again. Promise me you won't."

Jason swiped the back of his hand across his nose. "You told Daddy you hate God for taking Aunt Pilar from you. I want to be like you, Uncle Bryce. I want to hate Him, too."

"No, you don't. You don't want to be like me. You cannot hate God. You hear me. You cannot hate Him."

Jason ran out of the room, sobbing.

Kaya stared at Bryce. His face was contorted, and his hands were pressed against his temples as if he were trying to muffle noises in his head.

A cold knot formed in her stomach. Pilar was Bryce's horrific experience.

Who was she? His sister? Lover? *Wife?* Whoever she was, her death had caused Bryce to hate God. He must have loved her deeply.

That's why Michael and Lauren had left the children to her. As much as they loved Bryce, and as much as he loved them, they couldn't leave their children to a man who hated a God they evidently believed in. Not that she was any better when it came to religious matters. She didn't even attend church. She probably knew less about God than Bryce did, but she didn't hate Him. She wasn't that stupid to alienate the Almighty Power and bring His wrath down upon her.

With a shake of her head, Kaya pulled her wits together.

Whatever had happened in Bryce's past was his business. It was none of her concern. Her concern was that little boy who'd just declared that he wanted to be like his Uncle Bryce, the man he adored, the man who may very well replace his father in his young malleable life.

The man who hated God.

"Go on, say it." Bryce was on his feet, glaring down at her.

"Say what?"

"That I'm an ungrateful rebel for hating God. I mean look at me. I've been blessed with more wealth than any one man should have a right to, and I still can't enjoy it. Tell me I'm a horrible person. It's what you're thinking, isn't it?"

"No," she answered, meeting his stormy gaze. "If you're a rebel, you probably have a cause. As to you being ungrateful, I don't know you well enough to make that assumption. You're obviously hurt, angry—stuck in neutral, maybe. But I do know that you're not a horrible person, Bryce Fontaine. These children love you. If you were as bad as you think you are, they wouldn't give you the time of day. Children are like that. They instinctively shun the bad and embrace the good."

"What are you, some kind of shrink?"

No, but I've spend enough time with one to know what she would have said. "I'm just very worried about Jason," Kaya said in an attempt to steer the topic of conversation away from Bryce. She hadn't come to Granite Falls to fix his problems. She had her own. "I knew he'd be upset when he heard the truth. I didn't expect this outrage."

"He's in shock. He doesn't really mean what he said." Bryce wiped his hand over his short crop of black hair. "I should call Samantha."

"Yeah, that's a good idea. She said to call her after you talked to him."

Anastasia began to whimper again. Kaya rubbed her tummy

the way she'd seen Bryce do. It didn't help. Her whimpers grew louder.

"What's wrong with her now?" he asked, looking at the infant with a bit of impatience.

"I think she's hungry."

"Then feed her."

"That's the problem. She misses being nursed. She doesn't take the bottle well. Or maybe it's the formula she doesn't like. I — I called her pediatrician—"

He glanced at the half empty feeding bottle sitting on the dresser. He picked it up and pinched the nipple between his thumb and forefinger.

Kaya inhaled sharply, and to conceal her response to his actions, she gathered Anastasia and hoisted her over her shoulder.

"Did you try a different kind of nipple?" he asked.

"Huh?"

"Of course, what would you know about babies and bottles and nipples? Rearranging furniture is your specialty." He set the bottle back on the dresser.

"There are different kinds of nipples? A nipple is a nipple, isn't it?"

"No, Kaya. A *nipple* is never just a *nipple*. *Nipples* come in different colors, shapes, sizes, and textures."

The slow, seductive sound of his voice, especially when he said "nipple" coupled with the sensual flame in his dark eyes, caused Kaya's own nipples to tingle and harden beneath her lacy bra. She was so happy she was wearing one of Lauren's bulky sweaters.

When his eyes shifted from her face to her heaving chest, then back to her face, she knew that *he* knew that *she* knew they'd moved beyond discussing the nipple on a baby bottle. Heat and moisture gathered at the junction of her thighs. Her throat became dry, and she had no power to stop the soft moan that escaped her.

"Babies get attached to the feel and texture of their mothers."

God, he wasn't done. If he said that word one more time…

"What you have to do is find a *nipple* that matches the shape—"

"Okay! I got it." *Just shut up, already.*

A satisfied smile curved his lips.

She wanted to smack him. Again. Twice in one day.

Maybe seduction was his way of convincing women to yield to his desires. If he thought he could just sing her a lullaby and she'd lie down beneath him, he'd better think again. She had to remember that they were still at odds when it came to the future of the children. "How do you know so much about babies? You don't even have kids of your own. Or do you?"

"Kaya, as far as I'm concerned, these kids are just as good as mine."

Just the answer she was expecting.

He pulled his cell from a case at his waist and strode out the door on his Viking legs, leaving her just as he'd found her—in the middle of the nursery, holding a fussy baby in her arms.

"They've been up there forever," Kaya said as she walked into the kitchen from the playroom where she'd just put on a movie for Alyssa, Snoopy, and her dolls.

"It hasn't been that long," Bryce replied from the chair where he'd just sat down to feed Anastasia.

"It feels like it." Kaya stared at the mess of bottles and nipples of varying sizes, textures, and colors scattered on the counter top. There were nipples made from latex and some from silicone; there were angled, orthodontic, and vented-shaped nipples; there were small, medium and large nipples with varying ranges of flow speeds. And then there was a huge variety of bottle textures and shapes to chose from.

There was definitely an acute science to this bottle and nipple amalgamation, Kaya thought as she watched Anastasia suckling greedily from the "nipple she had chosen" according to Bryce—a latex, orthodontic, medium-flow nipple. They'd tried several until she latched on to that one, which Kaya supposed most closely resembled her mother's.

Kaya finally took Bryce seriously when he said that he was close to the children and knew how to take care of all their needs. He'd called someone who owned a baby store in downtown Granite Falls, and instructed her to deliver one of every baby bottle and nipple she carried. The man didn't even have to go out. He called, and the town came running. That was how powerful he was around here. Did she really want to go up against such force?

No, but she would do it for her new family—especially Jason, who she still had to win over. The timing of her return to Palm Beach hinged heavily on his psychological and emotional demeanor, and from what she'd witnessed in the nursery, plus the amount of time he was now spending with Samantha, Kaya knew it would be a while. The thought of spending too much time in Granite Falls filled her with anxiety. The longer she stayed, the stronger the bond between Bryce and his godchildren would become. They might realize that they didn't need her at all. But she needed them.

"Do you think Jason will be okay?" she asked Bryce grudgingly.

He raised his head. Sorrow and antipathy mingled in his glance. "I don't know, Kaya. Would you be okay if you'd just lost both your parents?"

"I guess not." She was never okay after the day she last saw her father.

"I trust Samantha. She knows how to help people through tragedies such as this," he remarked in a more amicable tone.

So how come she hasn't helped you through yours? She pulled out the chair at the far end of the table and sat down.

"Jason is a very quiet and sensitive boy. Not the average nine-year-old who's ashamed to kiss his mother in front of his friends. He and Lauren were very close. They shared a very special kind of love. Maybe it's because he was her first child and only son. I don't know. Some people accused Lauren of babying him. Losing her wouldn't be easy for him."

"Nor for you." He was grieving for his friends while trying to stay strong for the children, and still obviously dealing with a loss of his own. It couldn't be easy for him. The torment in his eyes when Jason had mentioned Pilar in the nursery was embedded into Kaya's mind forever, and in spite of her protest, her heart took on the weight of his pain. "I'm sorry about the way I acted in Steven's office, Bryce."

"I wasn't that kosher, either. I said some pretty unpleasant things to you."

"I should have been a little more sympathetic to your grief and more understanding about your close relationship with your godchildren." She picked up a bottle ring and twirled it around on her finger. "It's just that, I fell in love with these kids the moment I saw them. They're family—"

"If you feel that strongly about family, why didn't you ever come up to visit Lauren?"

Kaya dropped the bottle ring on the table and watched it spin to a stop. *Because I was jealous of her. She had the father who'd abandoned me.*

She raised her head to find Bryce studying her. "I guess I was too busy building my career. You know, climbing my way to the top of that corporate ladder of success."

"Touché, Miss Brehna."

Despite their estrangement, there were details of her sister's life Kaya wished she knew. Simple things like... "How did Michael and Lauren meet?" she asked, verbalizing her question.

Bryce seemed to enjoy a slow smile before answering.

"They met when Lauren came to Granite Falls to compete in a skiing tournament. She beat Michael's prized student and took home the gold. Michael was so impressed he offered her a job as an instructor at his school. She returned to Granite Falls after she lost her mother to breast cancer. A mother who until today, I assumed you both shared."

Kaya was too embarrassed to admit that she didn't even know when or how Lauren's mother had died. She'd only met her sister once, and it wasn't under pleasant circumstances. Then shortly after their father died, Lauren and her mother moved to a town in the Pocono Mountains of Pennsylvania.

"It was love at first sight," Bryce continued, obviously happy to relate the heartwarming tale. "I was very skeptical of Lauren at first. She was barely an adult, but she soon proved that age was just a number, and that love knew no boundaries."

"Michael was a lot older than her," Kaya said of the salt and pepper-haired, distinguished-looking, silver-grey-eyed man she'd seen in the family pictures.

"Quite a bit." Bryce brushed the pad of his thumb back and forth across Anastasia's cheek. "Michael was a kid at heart, though. Perhaps that's why he gravitated toward the younger generation."

"How long had you known him?"

"Hmm. About twenty years. I signed up for ski lessons at his school. He was the best instructor in both alpine and Nordic skiing around here. Michael took one look at me and said, 'Son you have a better shot at making a profitable career in football or basketball. Why waste your time and talent on skis?'"

"I'm sure it's not just because of your quarterback size, but more precisely because you're black?"

"Yep. Michael was prejudiced and he didn't even know it."

"Well, he must have changed. He married Lauren, and she was black."

"That was the best decision he ever made in his miserable life. They were perfect for each other."

Kaya smiled. "I believe that."

He gave her a quizzical look. "You're bi-racial."

"Yes. My mother is Caucasian. Are you originally from Granite Falls?" she asked to keep the conversation away from Nadine. *That* topic was off limits.

"I'm from Queens, New York, actually."

"A city boy, huh? What brought you to Granite Falls?"

"Boarding school. I fell in love with the natural landscape— the mountains, lakes, rivers, and the people." He looked out the wall of glass, to the four-season porch and the line of evergreen trees bordering the lake. He smiled like a man who knew he was home and was happy about it. "I had no desire to return to an overcrowded city after this."

"But Granite Falls is a buzzing city, too," Kaya remarked. "I was totally surprised when I drove through downtown the first time and saw skyscrapers towering against the snow-covered mountains, and the beautifully restored mill buildings that housed department stores and elite boutiques. Who would think there was a little mecca like this buried in the foothills of the White Mountain National Range? Nobody."

"Shh. We try to keep it quiet."

Kaya giggled like a schoolgirl. He did have a sense of humor. "Do you have any other family?"

A frown settled between his brows. "Just my parents. They

live in New York. But they like to spend the winters in warmer climates. They're in Cambodia right now. Last time I heard, they were teaching Cambodian children English at a monastery. I've been trying to get them to move here, but they keep putting it off."

He's lonely, Kaya thought with a thud in her heart. "How did you finally convince Michael to teach you how to ski?" she asked to brighten the mood.

He chortled. "Michael liked to go off on his own at the end of the day. One afternoon, I followed him out on a pond and he happened to fall through a crack in the ice. I helped him out on the promise that he'd give up his archaic notions about black people and teach me how to ski."

"So you both got what you wanted?"

"You could say that."

"Was that when you began honing your negotiating skills?" His reputation as a relentless negotiator preceded him. He'd given her a taste of his shrewdness this morning in Steven's office, and then later in the nursery when he'd tried to manipulate her with seduction.

The corners of his eyes crinkled on a smile. "Probably. I learned that if people want something badly enough, they're always willing to make a deal."

"Your tactics work. Look at what you've accomplished in such a short time. This is probably the most beautiful house I've ever set foot in. And I should know. I've been in some of the grandest on the East Coast."

His countenance suddenly turned somber and he dropped his gaze to the baby in his arms.

Did speaking about the house bring back unhappy memories for him? Did it have anything to do with Pilar? Did he build the house for her? Did they live here together before she died? Questions swirled around in Kaya's head. Questions she dared not ask.

They'd only met a few hours ago. She had no right to probe into his private life. The lives of her sister and brother-in-law, however, were open for discussion. She had a right to know how they came to financial ruin, and the reason her whole life had changed overnight at their deaths. "Why were Michael and Lauren living in your house, Bryce?" she asked.

He gazed up through thick, dark lashes. "Lauren never told you?"

She shook her head. "No."

"Have you noticed the small scar over Alyssa's left eye?"

"Yes. But what has that to do with anything?"

"Everything. About a year ago, Alyssa fell and hit her head on the bathtub. She got a nasty cut and Lauren had to rush her to the hospital. Jason was at school and Michael was at work. While they were out, the house exploded."

Kaya grabbed the locket around her neck. "Oh my God. What happened?"

"A gas leak Michael thought he'd fixed. Lauren had left a fire going in the fireplace. They lost everything, except Snoopy, who was with Alyssa."

Kaya swallowed back a sob. If Alyssa hadn't fallen, she and Lauren would have perished in that explosion, and Anastasia wouldn't be here today. Only Michael and Jason would have survived. As bad as this present loss was, Kaya knew that one would have been worse. She couldn't imagine a world without Alyssa and Anastasia in it.

Now that she thought about it, it was around that time that Lauren began writing to her, sending her pictures of her family. That accident had brought Michael and Lauren face to face with their own mortality. It had motivated them to make plans for their children's future care.

"Michael was having some health issues with his heart,"

Bryce said. "He couldn't work as much. Lauren tried to help between taking care of him and the kids. Then his business failed due to lack of snow for three consecutive winters. Pride kept him from accepting my help." He paused and sighed. "Anyway, after the explosion, I insisted that they move in here until they got back on their feet. He couldn't refuse. They had nowhere else to go."

Kaya gazed at Bryce, moved by his kindness and altruistic nature. She now saw the good man Libby said dwelled beneath his hard exterior. He was kind to the people he cared about, and even though that did not include her, Kaya was happy her sister had known him. "It was really nice of you to let them live here, Bryce. But why would you build such a magnificent home and not live in it yourself? Is it because of Pilar?"

Like shades pulled against the glare of the sun, an impenetrable mask descended on his face. He got up and brought Anastasia to her, transferring the infant into the crook of her arm without breaking the feed. "Your twenty-twenty question session is up, Miss Brehna," he said and strolled to the sliders.

CHAPTER FOUR

Bryce stared out at the snowflakes drifting down from a cloudy sky to form a pristine white carpet across the frozen lake. This was the season when he felt closest to Pilar. He missed sharing meals with her in front of a roaring fire, then making love on the floor until the embers died out. He missed waking up next to her on cold wintery mornings, making love again, sleeping in, breakfast in bed, and sometimes lunch.

Those who were close to him knew not to question him about the few precious months he had with Pilar, and of the years of happiness they should have had in this house. His close friends and family understood his need for privacy when it came to Pilar. Kaya was neither friend nor family. She was a stranger Michael and Lauren had appointed guardian of their children.

He wanted her gone by the end of the week, either voluntarily or by coercion. He already had a private detective on her case. He needed something to use against her. Even an unpaid parking ticket could make her seem irresponsible. She'd already alluded to a somewhat unpleasant past, some loathsome secret she and Lauren had shared. Perhaps the threat of exposing "it" would be enough to persuade her to quietly hand over the children and return to her life in Palm Beach.

He had no desire to hurt Kaya, or Lauren's memory if the secret they'd hidden all these years turned out to be monumental, but he was willing to do anything, even resort to blackmail if that was what it took to keep the children where they belonged.

He'd be remiss in his role as a godfather if he did nothing to stop Kaya's plan.

"Uncle Bryce."

Bryce turned at the sound of his name. His heart trembled with joy and fear as Alyssa raced across the floor toward him, Snoopy under one arm. She wrapped her free hand around his legs. He couldn't bear the thought of going through life and not hearing her calling out for her Uncle Bryce.

"Yes, baby. What is it?" He stroked her hair away from her face.

"Can we go for a sled ride on the lake?"

"Maybe tomorrow, sweetheart."

"Why can't we go now? It's not dark yet."

"I know, baby. It's just that I—" He took a quick glance at Kaya who was still feeding Anastasia. She had that enraptured smile adults got when they stared into the innocent face of a child. She was bonding. He knew the feeling well. There was no way in hell he was going to leave her alone with Samantha. She would have zero opportunities to cut him out of any decisions about the children.

He returned his attention to Alyssa. "I have to talk with Miss Samantha when she's finished with your brother."

"But they've been talking for a one hundreds of minutes already. Is Jason bad? Does he have a timeout?"

Bryce crouched down to her eye level and held her hands. "No. They're just talking about some very important stuff."

"Like what?" She shrugged her shoulder.

Bryce studied her face. She seemed unaffected by her parents' absence. She hadn't even asked for them since he'd arrived. Where did she think they were?

Bryce stood to his feet as Alyssa stuck her thumb into her mouth and walked over to Kaya. She stared at her baby sister then announced around her thumb, "That's not the way Mommy feeds her."

"No? How did your mommy feed her?" Kaya asked as she finally pulled the empty bottle from Anastasia's mouth.

"With those." Alyssa poked a finger into Kaya's breasts, one at a time.

She flinched, twice, then stated with a stiff upper lip, "Well, this is how *I* feed her."

Bryce watched on, curiously amused as Kaya's cheeks turned a bright pink. She kept her head down, not daring to glance his way. She had the same uncomfortable look as before when they'd discussed nipples in the nursery. she that inexperienced? That innocent?

"Why don't you use those?" Alyssa jabbed her again.

And again she flinched. "Because I'm an aunt and not a mommy. Only mommies feed babies that way."

Her voice was as unstable as the rhythm of his heart.

"When is my mommy coming home?" Alyssa asked.

Finally. Bryce held his breath as he looked on silently.

She took a moment to hoist Anastasia over her shoulder before she responded. "Alyssa, remember we talked about your mommy and daddy being in heaven on vacation?"

So that's where she thought they were.

"Uh-huh, but when are they coming back?"

"Not for a long while."

"Why? Don't they love me no more?"

"They love you. They love you a lot. They didn't want to go to heaven just yet, but they had to."

"Why?"

Kaya finally glanced his way, her large brown eyes pleading for help as she tried to coax a burp from the baby. He couldn't help her. What was the point of prolonging the inevitable?

"Because God wants them to spend some time with Him," Kaya told Alyssa.

Bryce rolled his eyes. *Yeah, sure, bring God into it.*

"'Cause He loves them?" Alyssa asked?

"Yes. Because He loves them."

Lauren and Michael had never spent a day away from their children, so Bryce understood the look of confusion on Alyssa's face at the idea that her parents would go to heaven on vacation without her. Bryce wanted to go over and tell the child that her father and mother weren't coming home—not because God loved them, but because her father had been too damned proud to accept his help. There, he'd thought it.

According to Steven, Lauren had gone to pick up Michael from the lodge when his truck wouldn't start. The authorities speculated that while on their way home, Lauren's SUV might have hit a patch of black ice and careened off Route 80 into a deep ravine.

They were still waiting on the coroner's report for the causes and times of death.

Bryce balled his hands into fists. In the past two months, Michael had called him four times for a jumpstart—twice at the ski lodge, once at the supermarket, and once when he'd gone to get Alyssa from ballet. For his birthday, just a week and a half ago, Bryce had bought Michael a brand new truck. But his friend refused to accept it. It was too much, he said.

Bryce wondered if his scripture-quoting friend's last thoughts were "pride goes before a fall." Damn him for causing his children so much heartache.

He was mad at himself, too. If he hadn't allowed the small-town paparazzi to chase him into the Alps after his recent breakup with his latest lover, he would have been home to respond to Michael's call for help. He would have gladly laid down his life for these children.

"I'm hungry, Auntie Kaya. Can I have a cookie?"

Bryce walked over to the table, and taking Alyssa by the hand, he sat down and lifted her onto his knee. "How about Uncle Bryce order some pizza?"

"I just want a cookie." She pointed to the loon-shaped ceramic cookie jar on the counter.

Lauren kept it filled with homemade cookies. She always baked an extra batch for him. Many times in the past five years, he'd drowned his pre-dawn nightmares in a glass of milk and chocolate chip, or oatmeal-raisin and walnut cookies. "You can have a cookie after you eat some pizza," he told Alyssa.

"Okay. Can I have extra cheese and pepperoni?"

"You can have whatever you want."

"Can Snoopy have sausage? He doesn't like pepperoni. It makes him burp. Right, Snoopy?" She nodded the beagle's head.

Bryce chuckled. "Okay. Sausage for the dog."

Alyssa wrapped her arms around his neck. "I love you, Uncle Bryce."

Bryce held her close and closed his eyes as he drew comfort from her warmth, her trust, her innocence. He knew he shouldn't have favorites, but this little one held a very special place in his heart, perhaps because if his own child had been given a chance at life, he or she would have been the same age as Alyssa. They would have cut their first teeth together, taken their first steps around the same time, started preschool this very year. If only he'd protected his family... *If only...*

"Bryce."

Bryce opened his eyes to find Samantha watching him. From the empathy in her eyes, he knew she'd picked up on his thoughts. She was the only person who understood his special affection for Alyssa.

Four years ago, when his loss was still very fresh, Samantha had encouraged him to deepen his bond with the newly born Alyssa. Surprisingly, it had eased his grief over Pilar's death. He'd trusted Samantha then, and he trusted her now to help Jason through his pain. He set Alyssa on the floor and stood up. "Go ask your brother what he wants on his pie, sweetheart?" he said, smiling down at her.

"Okay, Uncle Bryce."

Bryce pulled out a chair for Samantha. "Can I get you something to drink? Tea, coffee, water?"

"I'm fine, Bryce. Just sit."

Bryce reclaimed the chair he'd vacated. "So, what's your prognosis on Jason?" He was never one to beat around the bush.

"The pain for a young child losing a parent is horrendous," she began. "Jason has lost both, and he's finally accepted that they aren't coming home. It's a start in the healing process. The next few days are going to be volatile. He may cry a lot. He may become distant, or he may have sudden outbursts of anger. It's different for each child. But given Jason's strong psychological and emotional background, I have no doubt that he'll eventually adjust to life without his parents." She looked from Kaya to Bryce. "You two have to be there for him."

Bryce's gazed locked with Kaya's across the table. Was that a hint of uncertainty he saw lurking in her eyes? Her hands seemed a bit unstable as she rubbed Anastasia's back. She was displaying the same nervousness as she did this morning in Steven's office when she talked about Jason. What had gone down between the two of them?

"There are some issues that need to be addressed immediately," Samantha said, placing a pair of reading glasses on her nose. She pulled a pen and an appointment calendar from her tote bag.

"What kind of issues?" Bryce asked.

She opened the calendar. "I'd rather not discuss them now. I would like to see you both in my office in the morning. Uh… around ten. Is that possible?"

They both nodded, their eyes locking in silent combat.

"Good." Samantha glanced at the empty feeding bottle. "She's eating."

Just then Anastasia burped loudly, pulling chuckles from all of them.

"Well, there's my answer." Samantha reached over and ruffled Anastasia's head of curly black hair. "At least this little darling is spared the pain of grief. One day you'll have to tell her about her parents."

"I'll do that," Bryce said, his gaze capturing Kaya's again. "I knew them better than anyone else. I will fill the void Michael's absence has created."

"I can't think of anyone who's better suited for the job. They're lucky to have you, Bryce. And you too, Kaya." Samantha sighed. "Well, I think I've done all I can here for the night."

"Thanks for the house call, Samantha." Bryce rose to assist her.

"No need to thank me, Bryce. I'll do anything to help these little ones cope. Their parents were faithful members of our church." She picked up her tote and slid it over her shoulder. "Oh, I forgot to tell you that I called in a mild sedative for Jason. The pharmacy will be delivering it shortly."

"A sedative?" Kaya exclaimed. "Is that wise?"

"I understand your concern, Kaya, but I'm a board-certified psychiatrist, and I did discuss it with the pediatrician who's covering for Dr. LaCrosse."

"I don't mean to question your qualifications. It's just that he's only a kid."

"I only prescribe sleep aids for children in extreme situations. This is as extreme as it gets. Jason hasn't slept in two days. He told me that whenever he closes his eyes, he pictures his parents in the ravine screaming for help."

"But didn't he think they were in Europe with Bryce?" Kaya asked.

"Ah, the mind is an intricate entity, Kaya. Jason knew his parents were dead. He knew how they'd died. He just didn't want to accept or believe it, at least not until he was with someone he felt comfortable with, someone he trusted as much as he trusted them, someone he knew loved him, and would be there to catch him when he fell apart." Samantha gave Bryce a knowing nod and a smile, though grim.

Bryce understood exactly what Jason was going through. He'd almost gone crazy the first few weeks after Pilar's death. He didn't eat. He was afraid to sleep because of the nightmares.

"We'll talk more tomorrow."

"I'll walk you out."

"No need, Bryce. I know my way. Go check on Jason."

All was silent in the kitchen after Samantha left. Bryce stared out as the last bits of light faded into darkness. Night had descended upon them. Figuratively and literally.

Kaya stood up with a sleeping Anastasia over her shoulder. "I'll put her down then take care of Alyssa while you tend to Jason."

Bryce watched her closely. Were those dark circles under her eyes and worry marring her brow? Maybe she'd back down now that she understood the magnitude of the responsibility that had been dropped in her lap. "I'll order the pizza," he said. "Anything special you want on yours?"

"I'm not hungry."

Neither was he. They were going through the motions, keeping their wits about them, and being tolerant and understanding of each other for the children's sake. But when all this was over, one of them would walk away with only a handful of memories.

❧

Kaya was finishing the laundry Lauren had started the night she died when the house phone rang. Recognizing Jack's number on the caller ID, she grabbed the receiver on the first ring. She'd asked him to call the house phone since she seemed to have misplaced her cell. She just hoped Bryce didn't pick up another extension in another room.

She pressed the receiver to her ears. "Hi, Jack."

"Hey, babe. Sorry for calling back this late, but I was held up at work."

"At this hour? It's almost midnight. I thought one of the perks of management was that you don't have to work late." She walked to the door of the laundry room and leaned against the frame with her face in the direction of Jason's room. She didn't want Bryce sneaking up on her like he'd done in the nursery that afternoon.

"I was busy," Jack said.

"You're too busy to call the woman you asked to marry you."

"Hey, I'm calling now. Quit badgering me."

"I'm not badgering you." Why was he so irritable?

"I'm sorry, babe. I guess I'm just tired. How are things going up there?"

"A little better." Before leaving to see Steven that morning, she'd brought Jack up to date on the children. He knew she had a half-sister because he'd met Lauren at their father's funeral, years ago, and she'd shared the contents of Lauren's recent letters with him. "Jason just met with his therapist and Anastasia is eating, finally." She refrained from mentioning Bryce, that he was the children's godfather, or that he played a crucial role in their lives.

"When are you coming home?"

"The funeral is on Saturday, so maybe in a week or two." She crossed her fingers.

"Okay. That should give me enough time to move my stuff into your place. It doesn't make sense for us to continue paying rent on two places. Since you have a two-bedroom apartment in a nicer area of town, I think it makes sense for us to live at yours. Don't you think?"

Kaya swallowed back the bile that rose to her throat. She pressed the receiver to her chest and closed her eyes, searching for the right way to tell Jack that she was a mother. That marrying her would be a package deal, and not to pack his stuff up just yet since they would have to find a bigger place to live. She took a deep breath and put the phone back to her ear. "Jack, my sister made me legal guardian of her kids. I'm bringing them to Florida with me." There she'd said it.

A long silence ensued, during which a numbing sensation settled in Kaya's belly. "Jack, say something."

"Do they come with money?"

"What?"

"A trust fund, an insurance policy, an inheritance?"

"No, Jack. They have no money. Their parents died bankrupt."

There was another long silence. "So how are you going to take care of three kids, Kaya? Do you know how much money kids cost these days? You have a good career and all, and it would be enough for both of us, but taking on the responsibility of three more mouths to feed—"

"They're my sister's children, Jack. They're my family."

"Look, Kaya, one of the reasons I asked you to marry me is

because you said you never wanted kids. Now, we had a deal. No kids. So make a choice. Them or me."

Kaya gasped at his cold cruelty. Was this the man she was contemplating marrying? "Jack, I'm not going to abandon them."

"Then you'll have to find yourself another sugar daddy."

Sugar daddy? Was he serious? The man couldn't even afford to buy her an engagement ring. He worked at a tire warehouse for crying out loud. "Jack—"

"Look, babe, I gotta go. Think about what I said. It's me or them. I don't want my own kids, and I'm sure not going to bust my ass trying to raise somebody else's."

Click.

Kaya slid to the floor, hugging her knees to her chest. She couldn't believe Jack had just blown her off so heartlessly. She knew he never wanted kids of his own, but when you love someone, you go to hell and back for them. You do things you wouldn't ordinarily do. You change your mind and your rules for them. You support their decisions, even if they don't correspond with yours. You sacrifice.

How could she not have seen this side of Jack before? She'd known him for most of her life. Had he been that good at hiding his true self, or had she been too naïve to see the real man behind the mask?

One thing became crystal clear to Kaya as she hunched in the quiet darkness of the laundry room: Jack Grainger never loved her. She'd always been alone. Truly alone.

"Stay where you are, or I'll blow her brains out!" The woman aimed the gun at him for a split second then jammed it back to Pilar's head.

Her petrified whimper ripped at his heart. Stark fear glittered in her green eyes.

Big drops of sweat raced down his armpits; his hair stood on end. "Victoria, give me the gun." He reached out his hand.

"Tell her that we're in love, Bryce. Tell her you're divorcing her. You promised we would always be together."

He swallowed a mouthful of anger. "I never promised you anything, Victoria."

"Shut your mouth! Shut your lying mouth!" She pointed the gun at him again.

Good! If he could just keep her wrath centered on him..."You're a deranged psychopath, Victoria. I wish I'd never met you!" He began walking cautiously toward her as he spoke. "You are crazy, and sad. Pathetic..."

Victoria played into his game and released Pilar to steady the gun with both hands.

With his head, Bryce motioned for Pilar to get out. He willed her not to bolt and spook Victoria.

She stood frozen to the floor, staring at him, all the love he would ever need in this world, rushing across the distance between them. He implored her with his eyes, even as his heart longed to run to her, to hold her, to tell her how sorry he was to have let this happen.

As Pilar began inching away, he returned his attention to Victoria's icy stare. He prayed she'd miss if she fired at him. "I never loved you, Victoria—"

"One more word and I'll blow a hole in your heart!"

He raised his hands to distract her attention from Pilar as the love of his life eased around a table laden with crystal ornaments. Any moment and she'd be safely out the room.

"I'm sorry if I misled you, Victoria. I never meant to hurt you." He changed his tactic and pacified her now that all he had to worry about was his own safety, his own life. Pilar would live.

"Does she know we were together in Seattle just weeks after your

wedding? Does she know we spent the night making love, and that's why you didn't call her? Does she know, Bryce?"

A gasp echoed in the air. Glass shattered on the tiles. The chilling blast of a gunshot ricocheted in his ears. A body slapped to the floor. Blood splattered against the walls.

"No! No! Nooo…"

CHAPTER FIVE

Bryce bolted up in bed, his convulsing body soaked in cold sweat. Pressing his hands against his temples, he tried to stop the explosions in his head while he took desperate gulps of air into his lungs.

When his breathing finally slowed to a normal pace, he wiped the moisture from his eyes and checked the Rolex on his wrist. 3:45 a.m. He'd been asleep for a little over two hours. That was all he'd get tonight.

As usual, his gaze switched to the nightstand and the picture of Pilar in her wedding gown. The happiest day of his life was when she stood beside him in church and pledged to love him for the rest of her life. He had no idea it would've been so short. He picked up the photo, holding it against the sliver of moonlight streaming through the windows, his mind rewinding to the worst day of his life.

"Hold on, baby. Hold on. Don't leave me." He ripped off his shirt and *stuffed it against the bullet hole, trying desperately to stop the river of hot sticky blood that slowly seeped from her chest to the floor.*

"God, help me! Please help me! Don't take her. Don't take my wife."

"Bryce, I— I—" She choked on a mouthful of blood, her nails digging

into his flesh as she clutched to him, to life.

It looked bad. She looked bad. Ashy, like the angel of death had already spread his wings over her.

"The paramedics will be here soon, baby. Don't try to talk. Just look at me. Draw life from me. Stay with me, Pilar." He held her head in the crook of his arm and brushed her long chestnut hair away from her face.

"I— for— forgive— you."

The love in her sapphire eyes flooded his soul. "There's nothing to forgive, Pilar. I was never unfaithful to you. Never." Tears poured out of him, landing on her face, mingling with hers. He dabbed at them with his knuckles.

"I— I— we— ba— ba—by." She managed a weak, pain-filled smile and touched his lips with her bloodstained fingertips. "Ba—by," she whispered again before her hand dropped lifelessly to her stomach.

"You can't leave me, Pilar. I'm nothing without you. I love you. I love you."

With a deft jerk of his head, Bryce stopped the cerebral tape and gazed at the white-gold ring on his finger. He only wore the band in the privacy of his home. He'd grown tired of people asking about his family, and of having to explain that his wife was dead when she was still so very much alive in his heart.

Sliding his fingertip along the glass frame, he traced the image of Pilar's face, his heart aching with emptiness, his soul caving under the guilt.

He should have known what Victoria was capable of doing. She was disturbed. He'd had several warnings, but he'd ignored them. Victoria had indeed put a hole in his heart as surely as she'd put one in Pilar's.

Bryce jumped as a barrel of black fur landed on the bed and a pair of bright yellow eyes stared into his. Settling the picture of his wife on the nightstand, he folded the cat in his arms. "Come here, you." He stroked the animal's thick, sleek fur.

Webster purred and burrowed deeper into his embrace, his

long, bushy tail tickling Bryce's face.

"Okay, boy." He set Webster on the bed and pulled the ring from his finger. "Until tonight, darling." He kissed the ring and placed it next to the picture.

He shrugged into his bathrobe, grimacing as the cold silk clung to his clammy flesh. Swinging his feet over the side of the bed, he made his way downstairs with Webster trotting at his heels.

It had been a while since he'd had that nightmare, but considering the circumstances, he'd been expecting it. That is why he'd left *L'etoile du Nord*, even though Jason had begged him to stay. He didn't want to scare the boy awake in the middle of the night. Nor was he in any mood to explain away his midnight screams to Kaya Brehna.

In the kitchen, Bryce warmed up a bowl of milk for Webster and a glass for himself. Then he set about making a pot of coffee to take to his den. As his grandmother's old coffee maker groaned and sputtered, he raised the lid of a cookie jar on the counter and reached inside.

His heart lurched when his fingers grabbed a handful of air. He dropped the lid as a numbness settled in the pit of his stomach. There would be no comfort treats tonight. Bracing his hands against the counter, he fought off the feeling of dread that threatened to paralyze him yet again.

Five years ago, he'd lost his wife and an unborn child he didn't know about until after it was dead. Two days ago, he'd lost his best friends. And now he was about to lose his three godchildren to Kaya Brehna and her fiancé.

Bryce slammed his fist against the cupboard.

When the phone rang at *L'etoile du Nord* last night, he'd picked up the extension in Jason's room at the same time Kaya had picked up another somewhere in the house. Ethics had told him he should hang up the phone when he heard Kaya accuse some man of being too busy to call the woman he'd asked to marry him. When Jack told her that he missed her and to hurry home to plan their wedding, Bryce knew he'd had enough.

She was getting married, yet she didn't think it important enough to inform him that some other man, another total stranger, was about to be added to the mix.

Bryce dumped his glass of milk down the drain. When the coffee maker ceased its sputtering, he picked up the whole pot, grabbed a mug, and took them to his den. He had a lot of thinking to do. Choices to contemplate. Decisions to make.

He was sitting on the sofa, watching the night grey into dawn through the window when his cell began to ring. Thinking it might be the private detective whom he'd instructed to call him the minute he found something on Kaya, Bryce rushed to his desk and grabbed the phone. It wasn't the detective. It was Michael's cell number flashing across the caller ID.

Bryce's heart leaped for a split second, then he closed his eyes and let reality sink in. He took a deep breath and raised the phone to his ear. "Yes."

"Uncle Bryce, did I wake you up?"

"No, Jason." Realizing that his voice conveyed his disillusionment, he grimaced. "You know you can call me any time, night or day, don't you, son?"

"I know."

It was a halfhearted response, filled with questions and negations. Bryce picked up the empty mug and coffee pot and took them into the kitchen. "Is everything okay over there? Are your aunt and sisters up yet?" Anything to avoid the obvious.

"I don't know. I just woke up."

Wonderful. He'd slept through the night. Bryce set the dishes in the sink and glanced at the range of snow-covered hills outside his two-story penthouse suite in *Hotel Andreas*. The slopes would soon be teaming with skiers and snowboarders—favorite sports

Michael and Lauren would never again enjoy with their kids. He walked toward the stairs. "Did you sleep okay, buddy?"

"I miss them, Uncle Bryce. I miss Momma and Daddy so much. Why did they have to die?"

The sobs and the pain in the boy's voice tore at Bryce's heart. He collapsed on the stairs like a beaten-down soldier returning from battle, incapable of taking another step with the unbearable weight of war on his shoulders.

If things had been normal, at this exact moment, Lauren would have been waking up Jason for school, and Michael would be cooking breakfast for his family. Michael believed a child should start the day with more than a bowl of cold cereal, especially in the winter. Jason and Alyssa always looked forward to the Mickey Mouse or Garfield-shaped pancakes swimming in hot maple syrup, delicious omelets, or whatever Michael decided to prepare that day. Many times, Bryce had stopped by for breakfast unannounced before going on to his office at Fontaine Enterprises. They were such a happy family.

"Uncle Bryce? Are you still there?"

Bryce stifled a moan. "I'm here, Jason. I'm here."

"Can you come over? Please, Uncle Bryce. I need you."

"I'll be there, son. I'll be there as soon as I can."

"I want oatmeal."

"I'll make you some as soon as I finish feeding your sister, Alyssa." Kaya glanced at the pouting child. She'd poured her a bowl of cold cereal, but Alyssa had knocked the bowl to the floor. She had turned into the little girl with the curl in the middle of her forehead who when she was good, she was very, very good, but who when she was bad, was horrid. Alyssa wanted oatmeal, and that was final.

Kaya knew Alyssa's behavior had little to do with the oatmeal and everything to do with the prolonged absence of her parents.

"You love Anastasia more than me, Auntie Kaya."

The unshed tears in her eyes tugged at Kaya's heart. "That's not true, Alyssa. I don't love Anastasia more than I love you."

"Then why can't you make me some oatmeal? Daddy makes me oatmeal. I want my daddy. I don't want him to be in heaven no more. I want him to come home and make me oatmeal." Alyssa dropped her head on the table and began to sob.

Kaya knew it would get worse before it got any better. Anastasia had awakened screaming at the top of her lungs, and Kaya had brought her downstairs so she wouldn't wake Jason.

She'd just popped the bottle into the screaming infant's mouth when Alyssa sauntered into the kitchen, demanding oatmeal. She had to choose between making Alyssa wait, or have Anastasia cry herself into a fit. Had she made the wrong choice?

One child was hostile, one was demanding, and the other was totally dependent on her. Her eyes itched from sleeplessness. Her mind burned with worry. And her body ached from fatigue. She couldn't remember ever feeling this haggard. Is this what being a mother was all about?

"Sweetheart, what's the matter?"

Kaya tensed at the deep, masculine voice, and turned to see Bryce heading toward Alyssa. He set a brown shopping bag on the table then knelt on the floor and gathered Alyssa into his arms.

"I want oatmeal." Alyssa sniffled into his neck. "And I want my daddy and my mommy, Uncle Bryce. I don't want them in heaven no more. Can you tell God to send them home?"

"I would have made her oatmeal," Kaya stated when Bryce pinned his dark gaze on her. "But I had to feed Anastasia. You know how she screams when she's hungry."

His features softened as he gazed at the suckling infant.

"Michael made them a hot breakfast every morning. They aren't used to cold cereal or a single-parent home." He picked up the bowl Alyssa had knocked to the floor. "Change is never welcomed, and patience is a learned art." He scooped Alyssa from her chair and strolled to the walk-in pantry. "Get your stuff, darling. We'll do it just like you and daddy used to."

Alyssa grabbed the container of oatmeal, a small box of raisins, a bottle of honey, and some cinnamon. She stacked them on Bryce's chest then hugged her arms around his shoulders to keep them from falling to the floor.

Kaya assumed that was exactly how she and Michael used to do it. She had so much to learn about these children—their likes, dislikes, the routine of their daily lives.

"Can I help, Uncle Bryce? Daddy let me help." Alyssa beamed, happy again.

"You don't think I'm going to do all the work, do you?" He kissed her forehead, then set the ingredients on the counter and Alyssa next to them. "Don't move," he warned, as he began collecting pots, dishes, and utensils from the cabinets and drawers, and milk from the fridge.

Excitement replaced Alyssa's blues as Bryce helped her measure oatmeal and milk into the measuring cup then poured them into the pot he'd placed on the stove.

"Can I have more *cimmamon*?" Alyssa asked.

"Just a little bit. 'Too much of one thing is good for nothing', my mommy always says."

"Okay, Uncle Bryce." She shook a little bit more of the brown powder into the pot. "Is that 'nough?"

"Perfect. I'm going to turn on the stove, and you know you can't touch the pot nor put your hands near the flame, right?"

"I know. Daddy tells me a one hundreds of times."

Bryce placed a wooden spoon in her hands then placing one of his over hers, he began to stir the pot.

Alyssa grinned. "This is gonna be yummy in my tummy."

Kaya couldn't help but smile as she watched the huge man and the little girl work together. Bryce's tenderness amazed her. He attended to Alyssa as if she were his only concern in the world. It was the same attentiveness he'd portrayed with Anastasia yesterday. Then last night, he'd given his full attention to Jason when the boy needed him.

He would make a wonderful father and committed husband, she thought, admiring his Herculean physique, dressed in perfectly fitted jeans and a pale yellow sweater that accentuated his broad, strong shoulders.

Any woman who captured and managed to hold his attention would have no doubt that she was loved. He would devote his heart and soul to her one hundred and ten percent. She was certain he'd been like that with Pilar—whoever she was.

"Air will give her gas, you know."

"Huh?" Kaya caught his gaze in the mirrored wall behind the stove. She glanced down to find Anastasia's bottle was empty. She pulled the bottle from her mouth and hoisted her over her shoulders.

Bryce had been watching her while she'd been studying his physique from behind. How embarrassing could that be? Color crept into her cheeks as she became acutely conscious of her flannel pajamas and uncombed hair haphazardly pulled back into a ponytail. She hadn't even had time to wash her face before she'd rushed a wailing Anastasia downstairs.

She must look a sight.

She hadn't expected Bryce this early in the morning. In fact, she hadn't expected him at all. They'd agreed to meet at Samantha's office. If she'd know he was coming by, she would have gotten up earlier and showered and dressed before coming downstairs.

Anastasia expelled a long, loud burp that would make a sailor blush.

Unable to help herself, Kaya burst into giggles.

"Hard to believe something that gross could come out of something so small and sweet," Bryce said, turning with a grin on his face.

"Yeah, I was thinking the same thing," Kaya replied, transferring Anastasia to the crook of her arm and wiped the spit-up from the corners of her mouth.

"How did she sleep last night?" He opened the box of raisins and handed it to Alyssa.

"She awoke around two for a feed, then slept until early this morning. So, I'd say, well."

He gave her a swift once-over. "What kept you awake, then?"

Kaya averted her gaze. She must look far worse than she thought. "I—"

"Uncle Bryce, I think it's done," Alyssa announced.

"I think you're right, pumpkin." He turned off the stove and poured the porridge into a bowl. Then, scooping Alyssa up, he took the porridge to the freezer, placed it inside, and set the built-in timer on the freezer door. "You were saying," he said, walking back to put Alyssa into her seat.

"What's in the bag?" Kaya changed the subject, not wishing to be the topic of conversation. Thinking about the way Jack had dumped her and trying to figure out how she was going to take care of the children on her own had kept her awake last night. But since Jack had removed himself from the equation, there was no need to tell Bryce or anyone else about him.

"Coffee, fresh donuts, bagels, and cream cheese from Mountainview Café."

"Libby told me about that place. Ethan's grandmother owns it."

"It's the best coffee and bakery shop in town. The bagels are still hot from the oven. I don't know what you like, so I brought one of everything. Last night, I noticed the scarcity of food in the house, so I also went ahead and ordered a variety of luncheon dishes from Andreas. They'll be delivered around the same time we get back from Samantha's."

"Thanks, Bryce." She was warming to the thoughtful man underneath the hard exterior. "What are you doing here, anyway? We were supposed to meet at Samantha's office."

"Jason called me. He's not doing well."

"I didn't even know he was up."

He glanced over his shoulder at Alyssa, who was busy talking to Snoopy. "What's going on between you and Jason?" he asked in a lowered voice. "Yesterday afternoon, you avoided each other like the plague. And last night when you offered him a slice of pizza, he almost bit your head off. Did you say something to upset him?"

"What could I have said, Bryce? He just lost his parents. He doesn't understand why. He's mad at the world. Can you blame him?"

"Actually, he's only mad at you, Kaya."

The implications in his tone told her he was all too eager to point out the obvious. "I guess that's why we're going to see Samantha. Maybe she can shed some light on his attitude toward me."

"I know these kids better than anyone, Kaya. Samantha included. I know what they need." He looked her over from her rumpled curly head to her fluffy-slippered feet. "I don't need a psychiatrist to tell me how to take care of them."

"I know, Bryce. I appreciate all that you're doing for them—"

He lifted an eyebrow. "You appreciate all I'm doing for them? How big of you." He paused. "I may as well tell you now that I've made a decision about the children's future."

She balked. "*You* made a decision?"

"Yes, for you and the children. I've decided that you—"

"Hi, Kaya. Boss? I didn't know you'd be here."

Bryce's mouth tightened into a grim line. Kaya looked past his imposing stature to smile at Libby, who'd snuck in undetected.

"Boy, it's cold out there." Libby rubbed her hands together. "The road is one long sheet of ice."

The timer went off, and when nobody moved, Alyssa shouted, "Can somebody get my oatmeal from the freezer, please?"

Another silent moment dragged by before Libby responded to the child's request. "Well, it seems I came just in the nick of time." She got the bowl from the freezer and placed it in front of Alyssa.

"Can you please put some honey in it, Miss Libby?"

Libby squeezed a spoonful of honey into the porridge. "Looks yummy. Can I have some?"

"No-ah." Alyssa grabbed her spoon and stirred the oatmeal. "Me and Uncle Bryce made it. Only he can have some. You want some, Uncle Bryce?" she asked around the first spoonful, bits of oatmeal flying from her mouth.

He turned, his face softening only for her. "It's all yours. Enjoy it."

"We'll finish this later," he said to Kaya. "You should get dressed. You heard Libby. The roads are bad. I suggest you plan on driving into town with me," he said on his way out.

"What was that about?" Libby whispered, rescuing Anastasia from a dumbfounded Kaya. "The tension in here is as thick as cheese. Is he upset about something other than—you know, you taking them to Florida?"

Kaya stood up. "I have no idea. The man's moods change like the wind."

"Did he do that?" Libby pointed to the spilled milk and cereal on the floor.

Kaya chuckled at Libby's sense of humor. She grabbed a roll of paper towels and some cleaning fluid and got down on her hands and knees. "I wish all the mess in my life could be cleaned up this easily."

"Come on. It can't be that bad."

Oh yes, it can.

A sister she'd only met once was dead. She'd inherited three penniless children whose wealthy godfather's new mission in life was to make hers miserable. Her career was in jeopardy, her fiancé had dumped her, and Bryce was making decisions about her life.

It was that bad!

Kaya dumped the soggy paper towels into the garbage, washed her hands, and pulled a cup of coffee from the bag Bryce had brought. "You heard the man. I should get dressed. Help yourself," she added, pointing to the bag. "Compliments of your boss."

"So, when were you going to tell me about him?" Bryce suddenly asked.

Oh, so now he wanted to talk, Kaya thought after several attempts to engage him had failed. They'd driven along Route 80 West for at least twenty minutes, most of which Kaya had spent gazing out in silence upon the white hills and thick forests that made up the White Mountain Range on the right side of the road and the skyscrapers of downtown Granite Falls on the left.

"Kaya?"

Kaya turned and caught his gaze. "Tell you about whom?"

"Your boyfriend, or should I say *fiancé?*"

Kaya cleared her throat. She was surprised his answer hadn't sent her into a panic. Instead, she felt somewhat relieved that he knew about Jack. Yep, just as she expected, he already had a private investigator on her tail. "How do you know about Jack?"

"He called you last night."

"You were eavesdropping on my conversation? Of all the lowdown dirty rotten tricks I expect from you, I never thought you would eavesdrop on my private conversation, Bryce."

"First of all, I was not eavesdropping on your conversation. And second, I could not care less whether or not you have a boyfriend."

"Then why are you getting so worked up?" If the veins in his neck got any fuller with blood, they would pop.

He crossed the Aiken River Bridge and turned left onto Industrial Drive. "I'm worked up, Kaya, because you're planning to raise my children with some man you haven't even mentioned."

"They're not your children, Bryce. And besides, Jack and I —" She stopped herself. If he'd heard the entire conversation last night, they wouldn't be having this one today. She sighed, grateful he hadn't heard Jack ceremonially dumping her. That would have been humiliating, and it would give him another reason to force her to give up the kids.

"Who is he?"

"Nobody."

"You're marrying a nobody? That's just fantastic. *Nobody* is going to be a father figure to my children."

"Jack isn't—" Kaya clammed her mouth shut again. What was the use of explaining anything to him? He was determined to fight her tooth and nail for the children, whether or not Jack or any other man was part of her life. It didn't matter what she did or what she said, she couldn't win with him.

He shot her a lethal glance. "Jack isn't what?"

Kaya sighed as they passed Fontaine Conference Center on the left and Andretti Industries on the right, two monstrous skyscrapers that occupied entire blocks. From the center of the town, the steeple of Granite Falls Community Church loomed above the skyline like a beacon of hope to the residents and visitors of the area. Libby had told her that the church was as old as the town, but that it had recently undergone a complete renovation and expansion. Compliments of Fontaine Construction.

The man was an enigma to Kaya. He'd built a house he didn't live in, and he'd renovated a church he didn't attend.

"What about Jack, Kaya?"

Kaya turned her head. "I don't want to talk about Jack. Right now, my main concern is Jason and what Samantha has to say about him. That should be your main concern as well."

He made a right turn, cruised around the Esplanade, and parked in a space in front of the row of red brick buildings that lined the riverfront. He shut off the engine and grabbed her arm, his rapier glance penetrating deeply. "Why so secretive, Kaya? What are you hiding? Nobody in this town knows anything about you. Yet we're supposed to trust you with three children we hold dear to our hearts."

Kaya lowered her gaze to her arm where he held her firmly. Even through the thickness of her sheepskin jacket she could feel the heat from his touch. They'd been at odds since the moment they met, and she was so tired of it. Why couldn't he just accept that Michael and Lauren had chosen her over him? Maybe if he tried to be nicer to her, more understanding of her feelings as she has been of his, he might get somewhere with her. "Their parents trusted me. Shouldn't that be enough, Bryce?" She yanked her arm from his grasp and opened the car door.

The instant her foot hit the pavement, she knew it was a mistake. She felt herself flying and fumbled for the door handle. She missed.

"Damn stubborn woman."

Kaya let out a gasp as two strong hands closed around her waist and lifted her back into the car. Her body collided with a wall of hard, warm muscles that smelled intoxicatingly male. She remained in the strong prison of his arms for a few breathless moments until her heart returned to its normal pace. Swallowing her pride, she gazed up into his face. "Thank you."

His eyes bore into hers and the sad mystery in their obsidian depths beckoned to her irresistibly. The strange surge of affection Kaya felt for Bryce in that single moment alternately thrilled and frightened her so much, she shuddered outwardly.

His arms tightened about her, his lips parted slightly, and Kaya swore his head started to descend, before he caught himself and abruptly pulled his arms from around her. He placed his hands on the steering wheel and looked straight ahead, his body stiff and motionless.

Kaya took the cue and slid back to her side of the car. Whatever magical connection they'd shared in that moment was over. She pulled her coat about her as the frigid cold from the open door seeped under her skin.

"Stay where you are if you don't want to break your pretty little neck," was all he said before hopping out of the car and coming around to her side.

Kaya took his arm and let him help her across the slippery sidewalk. She paid little attention to the passersby and spectators, looking out from the restaurants and cafes, who'd obviously witnessed her mishap a few moments ago. She hadn't fallen, but she was embarrassed nonetheless. She clutched Bryce's arm a bit tighter as he led her up the steps to the main entrance of the building.

He said nothing, nor did he look at her. He just kept her close to his side, letting her know he was there to catch her if she stumbled.

At least he thought her neck was pretty enough to save.

CHAPTER SIX

Samantha ushered Kaya and Bryce into her office and closed the door. "Please." She pointed to a sofa on one side of the small, but sunny room.

Kaya sat at one end of the sofa while Samantha took a seat in a chair opposite her. Bryce took up vigil near a window, leaning stiffly against the frame, obviously still perturbed about their argument over Jack and that tense moment they'd shared after she almost cracked her skull on the icy pavement.

"I might as well get to the reason I asked you here." Samantha picked up a pen and a notepad filled with notes from the coffee table, and donned her reading glasses. "As you might suspect, it's primarily about Jason's attitude toward Kaya."

Kaya's hands twisted nervously on her lap.

"There are two reasons for his behavior." Samantha offered her a soft smile then consulted her notes. "First is an unconscious fear of betraying the love he has for his mother."

"I'm not trying to take his mother's place," Kaya said. "I'm just trying to—" What was she trying to do? She wasn't his friend. She wasn't even his aunt in the true sense of the word.

She was a stranger who'd shown up on the worst day of his

life, expecting him to welcome her with open arms. Perhaps if he'd grown up like her, devoid of love and attention, he would have eagerly soaked up the affection she offered. But he'd had the real thing. *Genuine love.* He wanted the mother he'd lost, not some bumbling, substandard substitute.

"It's not personal," Samantha stated. "Jason would have the same reaction to anyone who assumed his parents' roles."

"Then why doesn't he react that way toward Bryce? He's assuming Michael's role as father."

"He knows me." Bryce eyes flashed imperiously.

"Bryce is right. He's always been a part of Jason's life. Jason knows what to expect from him. He's not a threat."

"Are you saying I'm a threat to Jason? I will never hurt him, Samantha."

Samantha removed her glasses and laid them on the coffee table. "Not intentionally, Kaya. Bryce isn't a threat because he doesn't have custody of the children. He will always be exactly who he is, Uncle Bryce. You, on the other hand, are their legal guardian, their mother by default. From now on, every decision you make about *your* life will have a huge impact on *theirs.* Jason is scared of more changes, and rebelling against you is the only way he thinks he can keep you from destroying the rest of his world."

"Jason was able to perceive all this in his little nine-year-old mind?" Bryce asked, his voice rich with skepticism.

"I wish I could give him credit for insightfulness. The truth is, he overheard Kaya telling Libby about her plan to take them to Florida."

"Oh, no." Kaya's hand crept to her throat.

"I knew you'd done something to upset him," Bryce said.

"Let's not start throwing blame around," Samantha warned. "I understand Kaya's position. She's just as scared as these children, Bryce. She had a life of her own before all this happened. And from what I've heard, she wasn't even aware that

Michael and Lauren had made her legal guardian until after they were gone. If I were in her shoes, I'd be thinking along the same lines. She's responsible for those children, and in order to provide for them, she feels she has no other alternative but to return to her comfort zone, her career, the life she knows."

Finally, somebody understood her. Kaya looked up to find Bryce watching her with a hint of speculation in his eyes, as if he were assessing her, measuring her against something, or someone. It was the same look he'd given her in the car just before the "almost" kiss.

"I never saw it that way," he drawled. "I suppose it's only fair to consider her position."

Was that an apology?

"Great," Samantha exclaimed. "Showing consideration for each other is a good start. There's a lot of tension between the two of you. I felt it last night. I feel it now. Children have high sensors for discord."

Samantha's eyes fixed on Bryce. "Jason looks up to you, Bryce. He respects you and he loves you. He'll feed on any negative vibes you send Kaya, making it more difficult for her to form a relationship with him. You have to be careful how you relate to her when you're both in his presence. Do you understand what I'm asking?"

"Yes. I'll try to be nicer to her," he grumbled, clearly annoyed at being told to curtail his feelings.

"That shouldn't be too hard," Samantha said. "Now, Alyssa."

"Alyssa? Alyssa seems to be the only one who's dealing well considering—"

"Come on, Kaya. She thinks her parents are in heaven, on vacation." Bryce stated, making quotation marks in the air at the word "heaven". "She's been asking when are they coming back. I'm no psychologist, but I know it's not healthy to avoid the truth just because it's painful."

"Bryce is right, Kaya. When children this young suffer such a traumatic loss, the brain protects itself from the idea of permanent departure and the lack of stability and security by asserting that the separation is temporary. Alyssa's stuck in what we call a "frozen block of time" where the grief is on hold or non-existent. She's separated from her true emotions, and merely existing in a state of emotional suspension. She won't be able to move forward until she understands that the loss is real and permanent."

Kaya stirred in her seat, feeling even more ill-equipped to undertake her new responsibilities. When she walked into Samantha's office, she thought she only had one child's emotional state to worry about. But now Samantha was telling her Alyssa was also in trouble. "What can I do?" she asked in a choked voice.

"There's only one thing to do," Bryce said, moving away from the window. "Tell her the truth."

"Right again, Bryce. You have to explain the accident, using an analogy that explains the meaning of death. You know her best. There must be some experience you shared together that would help her understand. Then offer her the choice to say goodbye to her parents."

"You— you want us to take her to the funeral home?" Kaya asked.

"Both she and Jason should be given the choice to see them. It's the only chance they'll have. It will help them to accept the loss, which is the first step toward healing. If they decline, that's okay. Encourage them to do something else to help bring closure."

"Like what?" Bryce asked.

"Children Jason's age like to pick out the burial clothes, or write a poem or letter to a departed parent. It makes them feel important."

"And Alyssa?" Kaya could scarcely get the words past the constriction in her throat.

"Children Alyssa's age like to draw or color pictures to place in the caskets. Some leave parts of a special toy, like a puzzle piece, or one of a pair of something, so each time they look at the part they kept, they'll have a sense of eternal connection."

Kaya closed her fist around the locket against her sweater. *Her bond to her father.*

"The bottom line is, Alyssa needs to know beyond the shadow of a doubt that her mommy and daddy aren't coming home, that they're in heaven forever."

Kaya dropped her head in her hands. She remembered her childhood hopes that her father would walk through the door one day, pick her up and tell her that he loved her, that he would never leave her again. But he never came, and the next time she saw him, he was stretched out in a casket, stiff and cold. Then, and only then, did it sink in: her daddy was never coming back for her. He had truly abandoned her.

Perhaps she should have been happy she had a sister—half or not—someone she could share her pain with, since Nadine didn't care one way or the other that her father had died. But how could she have honestly, in her twelve-year-old mind, accepted Lauren when her father had chosen his other daughter over her?

He'd walked out of her five-year-old life to build one with Lauren and *her* mother. And now here she was, twelve years later, contemplating ruining her life, putting the security she'd built for herself into jeopardy to raise Lauren's children.

How was she to keep Jason's world intact when hers was falling apart? Where was she going to find the strength to burst Alyssa's happy bubble and tell her the truth?

Kaya was powerless to stop the tremor in her lips or the tears stinging her eyes. She was suddenly aware of Bryce sitting next to her, his strong arms enfolding her. Again.

"It's okay, Kaya." His warm breath fanned the top of her head. "We'll get through this together."

Kaya dropped her cheek on his chest and drank in the comfort of his nearness, the strength of his masculine support, wrapping her in a cocoon of physical warmth like she'd never had before.

His firm hands massaged away the tension in her back and shoulders. The steady beating of his heart beneath her cheek soothed away the longing in her soul. This embrace was so much more affectionate, more meaningful than the one they'd shared in the car. He was her gentle giant—her rock.

She pulled out of his arms, embarrassment and frustration added to the turmoil in her heart. No matter how hard his tenderness hammered at the wall of her defense, she had to stay strong. They were still at war; he'd made that absolutely clear when he'd turned away from her in the car. She wouldn't put it past him to use her weakness against her, to try to convince her once again to give him the kids and return to her happy childfree life in Florida.

He pulled a tissue from a box on the center table and handed it to her. His countenance had changed from concern to indifference. He pushed to his feet and moved away as if being near her, holding her in his arms again, was a terrible mistake.

Perhaps it was a mistake for both of them, for she'd experienced a side of him that made her hunger for more. She didn't want to depend on Bryce Fontaine for anything, least of all comfort.

Kaya turned to Samantha. "I'm sorry. It's not like me to fall apart like that. It's just that this— this whole situation is new, moving way too fast, and is so overwhelming. Three days ago, I had only myself to think about. Now I have three children whose lives will be affected by every decision I make from now on." Kaya shook her head as a new batch of tears welled up in her eyes. Damn Jack for leaving her at a time like this.

Samantha gave her a sympathetic nod. "That's parenthood, Kaya. It's perfectly normal for you to feel this way. Every new parent experiences the same doubts, fears, hesitations, and feelings of inadequacy you're going through. But I'm glad to hear Bryce say that you'll do this together, because the children need you both. You have full legal custody, but Bryce has deep emotional ties that are far more powerful than any will or therapy can provide. It is imperative that they maintain that connection.

"You have to decide, mutually, on what's best for everyone," Samantha added, rising from her chair. "Consider all the pros and cons then agree on an approach to return some form of stability to the children's lives. I would advise that you wait until after the funeral. Right now, your main priority is to prepare Jason and Alyssa to say goodbye to their parents. After that, one of you will have to make a monumental sacrifice."

Kaya glanced over at Bryce. He was staring out the window, lost in his own time and space, as if she and Samantha weren't even there.

Bryce took a swift glance at Kaya, huddled in her corner of the car with her coat wrapped tightly about her. They hadn't spoken since they left Samantha's office. What was there to say, anyway? Samantha had given both of them a lot to think about, and he supposed that was exactly what Kaya was doing—thinking about her future.

He, on the other hand, had embarked on a journey into his past even before they left the therapist's office. Kaya's tears and

Samantha's speech about doubts, fears, and feelings of inadequacy had hurled him back to the day he'd met Pilar, the day he'd promised to love her and protect her, and the day he'd failed her. Holding Kaya in his arms while she cried had reminded him of the reason he stayed clear of women who were prone to tears.

Like a gallant knight, he'd responded to a female's call of distress—twice in one day. When it came to women, there was only one call Bryce responded to: the mating call.

And from the moment he'd seen Kaya in Steven's office, Bryce had wanted to mate with her. He'd been envisioning them entangled in carnal sexual exploits, their damp, naked bodies slapping against each other until they were both satiated with lust. What he liked most about that fantasy was that Kaya's antagonistic attitude toward him would make it so easy for him to walk away, unaffected, when it was all over.

But today, she'd let her guard down and revealed a side of herself that he despised for no other reason but that it took him back to a specific moment in time, a time he'd vowed never to revisit. Bryce wished he'd never gotten that close to Kaya. He wished he'd never touched her.

He took another glance at her. This time she turned her head and met his gaze. His heart jolted at the misty torture in her brown eyes.

"You can rub my face in it if you want," she said.

Bryce turned his concentration to the road as he navigated his way along Route 80 East. Even though it would make his task of crushing Kaya a lot easier if she continued to distrust and dislike him, he really had no desire to continue this battle between them. Through no fault of her own, Kaya had been dragged into this situation. They were facing some difficult decisions, and like it or not, it would be better if they joined forces and worked together for the children's sake instead of trying to beat each other down. "What am I supposed to rub your face in, Kaya?"

"Like you, Samantha thinks it would be a mistake for me to uproot the children from their home. She's the expert, so she should know. At least now I know why Jason hates me."

"He doesn't hate you, Kaya. He's just a scared little boy."

"I'm surprised he didn't tell you what he'd overheard."

Bryce chuckled as he exited the highway and turned unto Crystal Lake Road that ran the perimeter of the lake. "He probably thinks he would get into trouble."

"Get into trouble with you? That's a surprise."

"Michael and Lauren had a big problem with him. He's a little eavesdropper."

"Like his Uncle Bryce?"

A muscle quivered in Bryce's jaw. He needed no reminders that she had a fiancé waiting for her in Palm Beach. He spoke only when he thought his voice would not betray him. "It's my house, Kaya. The phone rang. I picked it up. I hung up when I realized it was for you. If you wanted secrecy, you should have had your boyfriend call your cell."

"I seem to have lost my cell phone," she said without emotion.

"Well, I'm not going to apologize for doing something completely normal in my own home, so let's stop wasting time on something so petty when we have far more important issues to deal with."

She pressed her lips together and gave him an indignant flash of her eyes—one he thought was well deserved for his caustic tone, but he had no intentions of apologizing for that either.

"Since we're on the subject of important issues, what were you about to tell me this morning before Libby came in?" she asked.

Bryce pondered her question. He didn't know how she felt

about her fiancé, how deeply she loved him. This morning he was going to suggest that she break off her engagement with Jack and move to Granite Falls permanently.

It was quite presumptuous of him, and of course he had ulterior motives, especially after finding her in such a disheveled state in the kitchen. She exuded sensuality from every pore of her sexy little body, from her curly, tousled hair to her fluffy, pink slippers. And the most arousing thing was that she didn't even know it. She had no idea that his head had been spinning with lascivious thoughts as they stood there warring—thoughts of slowly undoing the buttons of her flannel pajama top, one at a time, of pushing it off her creamy shoulders, of kissing every inch of her smooth skin as it came into view, of feeling the weight of her voluptuous breasts in his hands. He'd wondered about her nipples—the shape, size, and texture of them. He'd imagined his tongue gliding across...

"What were you going to tell me, Bryce? What decision about my future have you made?"

Bryce shook his head, bringing his salacious thoughts to a screeching halt. "I was going to—" He stopped himself. He couldn't ask Kaya to move to Granite Falls, not after Samantha had advised him to consider her feelings and the position she'd been placed into. Before all this happened, Kaya had a life in Palm Beach. She had plans to marry Jack and spend the rest of her life with him. She was obviously the marrying kind of woman, and since he could never offer her the joys of married bliss, it would be best to let her return to her life with Jack. By the time she had a baby or two with the lucky guy, she would have forgotten about these three she'd left behind in Granite Falls. "It doesn't matter anymore," he said in a tone that held a bit more ice than he would have liked to reveal.

Her eyes swept his face curiously before she pursed her rosy mouth and shrugged.

Bryce sighed as the white facade of his house came into view. The house he and Pilar had spent months planning. The house she never had a chance to make into a home for the family they almost had.

"I have a question for you," Kaya said after a few moments of silence had elapsed.

"Yeah," he answered cautiously.

"Back in Samantha's office when I started crying, you held me in your arms, but then you withdrew so abruptly, as if being near me upset you. Did holding me bring back unhappy memories?"

The woman was too damn discerning. Another thing he disliked about her. The last place he wanted her was in his head. Women were only allowed in his bed. Never in his head.

"Who was she, Bryce? Who was Pilar?"

Bryce's gut twisted into a painful knot. *Who was Pilar?* She was everything. *Everything to him.* He met Kaya's wide, questioning gaze, and he knew if he didn't tell her now, she'd ask again. "Pilar was my wife."

A look of shock swept across her face. "Oh. I thought she was a serious girlfriend or a fiancée. I didn't know you'd been married. I didn't know you're a widower. I'm sorry."

She didn't know a lot of things. "Pilar was never any of those. She became my wife the instant I met her."

"Love at first sight," she stated. "I've never met anyone who it happened for."

"It happened for us. We loved each other the moment our eyes met. I knew instantly that I wanted to marry her." Bittersweet memories churned inside Bryce. He'd often wondered if Pilar would still be alive if he hadn't met her, hadn't married her. What would her life, his life be like if he hadn't stepped onto that elevator in Chicago six years ago and found her crying? If they'd never met, would they have been married to other people, made babies with other people? Were they destined to meet, to fall in love, to marry? Was she destined to die such a senseless, violent death? What was the point of him loving her then losing her in such a short timespan? *What was the point?*

"And now she's gone. How did she—"

"You have an incoming call from Libby Parker. Would you like to accept?"

Bryce exhaled a sigh of relief as the message alert came through the car's stereo system. "Yes," he said upon pushing the connect button on the steering wheel. "What is it, Libby?"

"Where are you guys? Are you almost home?"

"Why?" Kaya asked. "Is something wrong?"

"It's Alyssa. She's been crying hysterically and running around the house calling for her parents and you. I can't get her to calm down. She thinks you went to heaven on vacation, too."

Bryce put pressure on the gas pedal. "We're almost home," he said, and ended the call.

He glanced warily at Kaya. There was no need for them to say anything. They knew what needed to be done.

❧

Kaya studied Jason as he and Anastasia played on the floor in the sitting areas of the second-floor balcony. He was making funny faces and noises, and Anastasia stared back at her big brother, kicking her little arms and legs and trying to mimic his sounds. It was such a sweet picture, one Kaya wished she could capture and replay over and over again. It was the happiest scene she'd seen since she arrived in Granite Falls, and a welcome change to the one she and Bryce had come home to a few hours ago.

They had found Alyssa in her parents' bed, hugging Snoopy, and sobbing her little heart out. It was a pitiful sight. The child's heart-wrenching sobs and questions about the whereabouts of her mommy and daddy had brought tears to Kaya's eyes. Heeding Samantha's advice, Kaya had been ready to tell Alyssa the truth about her parents, but Bryce had stopped her. He thought it best if she heard it when she was in a calmer and more receptive state of mind. Kaya didn't argue with him, since he was the expert when it came to the children's emotional needs.

Bryce's promise to take Alyssa for a sleigh ride on the lake after lunch had gotten her out of bed and down to the kitchen to have some of the delicious lunch he'd ordered from Andreas.

After lunch and Libby's departure, Bryce had taken Jason aside to discuss the conversation he'd overheard between Kaya and Libby, and about going to say goodbye to his parents. Kaya wasn't privy to that conversation, but when he and Bryce returned from Jason's bedroom, the boy's attitude toward her had changed. He was more tolerant and civil. He'd even responded politely when she tried to strike up a conversation with him. They weren't friends yet, but they weren't enemies anymore. Bryce could have maligned her to Jason. But he hadn't. She hadn't yet figured out if his influence on Jason was good or bad for her in the long run.

With Jason temporarily in a better frame of mind, Bryce had turned his full attention to Alyssa. They'd been out on the lake for about forty minutes and probably should be coming in soon. It was below freezing out there—a fact that neither of them heeded when she'd pointed it out. They were true New Englanders. Kaya shuddered at the very thought of being out in that kind of weather for such a long time.

Kaya stilled when Jason suddenly turned and glanced over at her. For a few seconds, all that was audible in the room were the crackling sounds coming from the fireplace.

"You look like Alyssa," he said, a mild curiosity in his silver-grey eyes.

Kaya chuckled. "I think she looks like me. You have your

dad's eyes," she added, pushing the envelope just a tiny bit. "But you have your grandpa's ears."

He cracked a shy smile. "His big ears. Mommy used to tell me that all the time." He broke their gaze and looked off into the crackling fire, his smile replaced with a sheet of sadness. Kaya's heart went out to him. She was about to get off the sofa and join him on the floor when Anastasia kicked him in his stomach and gurgled. That pulled him out of his funk. He ducked his head and let Anastasia grab one of his big ears.

Kaya broke into a grin. When she used to tug on her father's Dumbo ears, he'd toss her high in the air in retribution. She was never afraid because she knew he would always be there to catch her. He never let her fall. What she wouldn't give to have those years back, to have those thick arms wrapped around her, protecting her, comforting her.

Pushing the memories aside, Kaya turned and gazed out the glass wall overlooking the back of the house. A single sleigh trail led away from the pier near the boathouse and further into the lake. From there, it turned into a maze of circles, and then again into one trail that disappeared around the pine tree line.

She wasn't looking forward to telling Alyssa about her parents when she and Bryce eventually retuned. Kaya wished she had the power to fast-forward into the future to a happier time and place.

Dread pushed her off the sofa when she heard voices downstairs. She went to stand at the railing, her heart pounding against her chest as she watched Bryce climb the stairs with Alyssa in his arms. Alyssa's arms were locked about his shoulders, her face buried against his neck, and Snoopy trapped between them.

He was so predatorily male, Kaya thought, captivated by his large frame, straight back line, and long, well-muscled limbs.

There was nothing insubstantial about this man. He was born to conquer, to rule.

A hot flash of desire settled between Kaya's thighs. How could she be feeling this mesmeric fascination with him at a time like this? They were in the wake of a tragedy with the air around them saturated with the stench and chill of death, yet her body constantly ached to be near him, to be touched by him, even when she was mad as hell with him.

She couldn't shake the undeniable web of attraction that had been building between them since she first saw him in Steven's office. Even before she'd turned around and encountered his yard-wide shoulders and powerful, bronzed physique coming through the door, her heart had already turned over in response to his voice. She'd trembled from his first gaze, burned at his first touch, and she was certain that Bryce had picked up the scent of her pheromones as she'd picked up his. But alas, it was just lust. What else could it be since he'd turned into a raging bull just minutes after the sparks had flared?

What Bryce had with Pilar was love. *Simple and real.* Kaya wondered about that feeling of instantaneous knowledge of a soul's recognition of its counterpart in another. She definitely never had that with Jack or any of the other men she'd dated. Would she ever know it? Should she wait for it?

Kaya's breath caught in her throat as Bryce walked across the landing toward her. Her heart drummed harder at each step he took. Even from a distance, she could feel the threat of excitement pulling tighter between them. There was no denying that they shared an intense physical awareness of each other. But neither was brave enough to explore it. It was not the right time, she thought when Bryce stood beside her, tall and straight like a towering spruce.

As she gazed up at him and detected the explicit sadness lurking in the perimeter of his dusky eyes, Kaya realized that they might never have a chance to explore the attraction between them.

She wondered how much of the sleigh ride he'd actually enjoyed. She knew that like her, he dreaded the next few moments when they would tell Alyssa about her parents. He'd already lived through the horror of losing someone he loved, and here he was doing it again. This time his pain was doubled, his grief threefold, because he had to absorb the loss of three children he loved.

He turned his head as Anastasia's happy gurgle broke the spell. "How are you and Jason?" he asked in a lowered voice.

"We're good." Kaya smiled, thankful for the small blessing.

"Have you spoken to him about what he overheard?"

She crossed her arms over her stomach. "Not yet."

"You know you have to. I tried to explain your reasons to him, but he needs to hear them from you."

Kaya nodded. "I know. I will. I will talk to him."

"Can I go play with Jason and Stasia?" Alyssa asked, pointing at her siblings.

"In a little bit," Bryce said.

On unstable legs, Kaya preceded him into the center of the room and dropped down in the middle of one of the three sofas.

Bryce eased down beside her, unwrapped Alyssa's hands from around his neck, and sat her between them. He took one of her small hands in his giant one and dropped a kiss on her head. "Alyssa, you remember I said that your Aunt Kaya and I need to talk to you about something important?" he asked in a voice that was gentle yet tight with emotion.

Alyssa wrapped her arm about Snoopy and rested her chin on his head. "Was I bad?"

"No. Never." Kaya took her other hand and squeezed the tiny fingers. She was still such a baby. Kaya wanted to spare her the truth, but she knew she had to face the pain before she could heal and move on.

"Then why can't I go play with Jason and Stasia?" She pointed at her siblings.

Kaya noticed that Jason had stopped playing with Anastasia. He was sitting up, his back against a club chair and Anastasia on his lap, but his full attention was centered on his other sister. He seemed to be vacillating between staying where he was and coming over to join them.

"Because we have to talk about your mommy and daddy," Bryce answered.

Alyssa's eyes brightened as she gazed up at Bryce. "Are they coming back from heaven? Are we going to pick them up at the *aeroport*? Are they gonna come out of your big plane, Uncle Bryce?"

Kaya stifled a sob. "No sweetie, your mommy and daddy can't ever leave heaven. They can never come home, Alyssa."

"But you said they're just on vacation. Why can't they come home?"

"Because— because they're—" She couldn't tell this child that her parents were dead. It was too harsh. *Too final.* Kaya was twelve years old when Eli died, and she'd still fallen apart at the death of a father she hadn't seen or spoken to in seven years. Alyssa was only four, and up until three days ago, her parents were very much a part of her daily life. How could anyone explain the meaning of their absence in a way that would make sense to her?

"I'll take it from here." Bryce lifted Alyssa onto his lap and began to brush his fingers through her brown curls. "Alyssa, do you remember last summer when you and I went for a walk and we found a squirrel lying on the side of the road?"

She thought for a moment then nodded. "He got dead 'cause he came out too fast from the bushes and a car ran over him. He didn't look both ways, Uncle Bryce. But I look both ways. See, like this." She turned her head one way and then the other.

"That's a good girl." Bryce shifted and braced his back against the cushions. "Do you remember what Uncle Bryce said about what it means to be dead? Why the squirrel couldn't go home to his family?"

"It means his heart don't work no more."

"That's right."

"Well, sweetheart, your mommy and daddy are—" He pulled her closer, propping his chin on the top of her head. "What I'm trying to say, Alyssa, is that your mommy and daddy— They— they died, baby."

Alyssa's brows knitted tighter together. "They didn't go to heaven to see God?"

"Yes, Alyssa. They— they are in heaven," Kaya said, picking up the baton. "That's where people who love God go when they die."

"And your mommy and daddy loved God very, very much," Bryce added, smiling into her perplexed face.

Anastasia whimpered, drawing Kaya's attention to the other side of the room. Jason was shaking and tears were streaming down his face. She immediately went to rescue Anastasia from his loose grip. She wanted to sit with him, hold him, but was unsure of how he'd react to her.

"But I didn't see them dead," Alyssa said. "How did they get dead, Uncle Bryce? Did they run across the street and didn't look both ways?"

Bryce inhaled sharply. "Not exactly, honey. Your— your daddy's car broke down. And your mommy— she went to bring him home, but—"

Kaya could tell he was trying to control his anger at Michael for not accepting the new truck he'd bought for his birthday. Bryce had relayed that bit of information to her earlier today. He blamed Michael for turning his children's lives upside down, not to mention his own and Kaya's, too.

"It was snowing," Bryce continued after a long pause, "and your mommy's car, well, it skidded off the road. There was no one around to help them. It was very dark and cold. Their hearts were hurt really badly and— um— and they just stopped working."

"Did you dig a hole like we dug a hole for the squirrel and put them in it, Uncle Bryce?"

Kaya held Anastasia close to her chest as Bryce explained about the grave they would be digging in the spring for Michael and Lauren, because the ground was frozen over now. While others would be planting flowers and seeds for a season of new life, she would be burying her sister and her brother-in-law.

This darling little baby she held in her arms would never remember the feel of her mother's cheek pressed close to hers. She would never hear the anxious sound of her father's voice calling her back from danger.

"I don't want my mommy and daddy to be dead, Uncle Bryce," Alyssa said. "I want them to come home."

"I know, darling. I wish they could, more than anything in the world."

Her little mouth quivered, and moisture shimmered beneath her long, dark lashes. She dropped her head against Bryce's chest. "I want my mommy and my daddy to come home. I don't want them to be in a hole." She clutched Snoopy closer. "I want them to come home."

"I know, baby. I know." Raw pain hummed in Bryce's voice as he hugged the whimpering child. The moans erupting from his throat, the tears streaming down his tortured face ripped at Kaya's heart. His sobs were old, tired, too long repressed. He was crying for more than Michael and Lauren and these three little children he loved.

He was crying an old hurt for the wife he'd lost. The wife whose death Michael and Lauren's had resurrected.

"Uncle Bryce?"

Desperation edged Jason's voice. He ran to Bryce, fell on his knees, and wrapped his arms about him and his little sister. He'd probably never seen Bryce cry before, Kaya thought. He looked as frightened as she did the day she watched her father cry for the first time before he walked out of her life, never to return.

Cradling Anastasia in one arm, Kaya sat beside Bryce and draped her other arm around his shoulders. It was her time to lend a shoulder to cry on. But as the sobs of the man and the children filled the room, Kaya's own dam of pent-up emotions broke.

Kaya wept for the sister she hardly knew, the brother-in-law she never met, and the tragic way their lives had ended. She wept for the precious children Michael and Lauren had left behind, and through whose souls she would learn about the parents they'd lost. Then she wept for Bryce and the pain that kept him shackled to his painful past.

Long after the sobs had ceased, the five members of this singular family that fate had fitted so perfectly together, like the interrelated pieces of a jigsaw puzzle, continued to huddle close, drawing solace from each other.

They had accepted the simple fact that they needed each other.

Then life outside intruded in the ringing of the phone.

"I'll get it." Jason jumped up from the floor, seemingly anxious to escape the awkward circle of solace they'd formed.

Kaya gazed at Bryce. The austere business mogul who portrayed an aura of strength and validity to the world had just broken down in front of her. She'd seen him at his weakest.

That could not be good for him.

But then he smiled, and the light in his eyes assured her that he was okay with her. He seemed grateful that she'd been there for him. *It was easy.* He'd come to her rescue twice today.

"Uncle Bryce." Alyssa stared up at him. "I don't have a mommy anymore."

"That's why I'm here, Alyssa." Kaya smiled at her. "Your mommy and daddy asked me to take care of you, and Jason, and Anastasia."

"But you're not a mommy. You're my Auntie Kaya."

"We can pretend I'm a mommy." Kaya wiped a lingering tear from Alyssa's cheek. "I'll do all the things your mommy used to do with you."

"Like play dolls, and hide and seek, and take me to ballet?"

"Uh-huh," Kaya said of the short list of things that were most important to her.

"And I'll be your pretend daddy, if you'd like, Alyssa. We can do all the things you and your daddy used to do together."

"You'll make me oatmeal for breakfast, and take me skiing and for a sleigh ride on the lake, and dance with me and twirl me around and around?"

"I'll do all that, and more, my baby. I love you, and Jason and Anastasia very, very much."

Alyssa laid her head on his chest. "But my heart is broken, Uncle Bryce. I'll never see my mommy and daddy again."

Bryce stoked her hair as a fresh batch of tears gushed down her face. "You'll be sad for a very long time, Alyssa, but your Auntie Kaya and I will always be here for you. We'll take care of you."

"Promise?"

"We promise," they said in unison as their gazes met and held over Alyssa's head.

They were making promises they both knew were impossible to keep. Kaya hadn't crossed Palm Beach off her list, and Bryce was still determined to keep them in Granite Falls. How could they make such a promise when they lived on opposite sides of the east coast?

"It's for you. Somebody named Jack." Jason shoved the cordless receiver into her face.

She watched the muscles in Bryce's jaw tighten and his eyes darken like an angry storm cloud. She understood his rage. Jack's timing couldn't be worse. *What did he want?* He had some nerve calling her after the way he'd treated her last night.

"Who's Jack?" Alyssa asked.

"Your Aunt Kaya's fian— friend." Bryce set Alyssa on the floor and stood up. He took the phone from Jason and pressed it into Kaya's hand. "Talk to Jack. I'll take care of the kids."

The threat in his voice and the hardening of his eyes told her he wasn't just talking about the moment, but from here on in. Since they'd returned from Samantha's office, he'd been nice to her. Jack's call had changed his attitude.

The formidable Bryce Fontaine was back.

He bent down and took Anastasia from her. "Come on, kids. Your aunt needs some privacy."

"Bryce, wait. There's something you should—"

He silenced her with a menacing stare and stomped down the corridor with Alyssa and Jason tailing behind him.

Kaya slumped back against the cushions, swallowing the scream of frustration that rose to her throat. The inopportune timing of a stupid phone call had just shattered all the progress they'd made today.

As she watched Bryce and the kids disappear into the nursery, Kaya felt as if she'd just lost her best friend before she had a chance to get to know him.

CHAPTER SEVEN

"You okay, buddy?" Bryce asked Jason as they drove toward Elliot's Funeral Home.

Jason nodded and fidgeted with the gold statue of a skier he'd won in a downhill competition last winter.

Michael had coached him for months while Lauren complained as usual that he was pushing Jason too hard, that he expected the boy to live his own dream of becoming an Olympic skier.

Bryce recalled the pride on Michael's face as he watched his son steal away from his two most competitive opponents in the last fifty yards to swipe first place. It was worth all the hard work.

"That boy is gifted," Michael said as they enjoyed a cup of hot chocolate at the resort café afterwards. "I've taken him as far as I can. I just wish I had the means to have him professional trained for the Olympics."

"He can still be," Bryce assured his friend.

Michael chuckled. "Sure. Do you have any idea what it cost to train for the Olympics—private teachers, private coaches, proper clothing and state-of-the-art equipment? He'll be away from home, so there's room and board."

"I'm pretty sure I can afford it," Bryce responded. "Fontaine Enterprises sponsors a lot of athletes and hands out scholarships to a host of college

students. I would be honored to sponsor my godchild as long as it's Jason's dream and not yours."

"I can't let you do that. You've given us so much already."

"All the more reason I should do this for Jason, if that is what he wants. If it weren't for me, he wouldn't be here."

Michael frowned over the rim of his mug. "How do you figure that?"

"Think about it. If I hadn't pulled you out of that half-frozen pond that day, you would be pushing up saplings by now."

Michael nodded in agreement. "You have a point there. Each person we meet in this life is put there for a specific reason. You hounded me for weeks trying to persuade me to teach you to ski, and I kept ignoring you until that fateful day. If it weren't for you, I would never have had the chance to meet my sweet Lauren, and make three beautiful babies with her."

"Three! Lauren is pregnant again?" Bryce exclaimed.

"Yep," Michael said with a sly grin. "We just found out."

"Well congratulations, my prolific brother." Bryce reached across the rugged table and slapped him on the shoulder heartily.

"This is the last one," Michael said. "Alyssa has already shaved ten years off of my life. That child is so full of energy. I can't keep up with her. I'm too old for this, Bryce. It's your turn."

"My turn for what?"

"We already know why you were placed in my life. Question is, why was I placed in yours? There must be something in it for you. Maybe you'll meet your next true love through me, and stop chasing after the wrong women. Have a second chance at love."

"I like chasing the wrong women," Bryce responded truthfully.

"I understand. You don't want to be hurt again. I love you like a brother, Bryce, but I can't let you go on pretending that my kids are yours."

"Michael, I don't——"

"Don't get me wrong," Michael interrupted. "I appreciate everything you do for them, and it warms my heart to know that if anything should happen to me, you'd be there for them, and Lauren. Pretending they're yours is good for them, but it's not good for you. You need your own brood to carry

on your family name. My children are Rogers. They will never be Fontaines."

"Did you see them already?"

Screech!

Bryce pulled into the driveway of the funeral home. He parked in a space close to the door, engaged the emergency break, and unbuckled his seatbelt before responding to Jason. "Yes. I've seen them." He'd come by the day he'd returned home, just to make sure Kaya wasn't a figment of his imagination, and that he wasn't caught up in another unending nightmare.

"How do they look?"

"Peaceful."

"Like they're sleeping?"

He nodded.

Jason fidgeted with the trophy he would put in his father's casket. He'd written a letter to his mother and sealed it in a purple envelope—Lauren's favorite color. It was inside the pocket of his jacket, close to his heart.

Bryce looked up as an SUV parked next to them and a family of three generations piled out of it. A young girl was carrying a wreath with a white banner that read, "Goodbye Grandpa. We love you."

That was the order of things.

No young child should ever have to say goodbye to a parent. And this child had to say goodbye to both. Where was the justice in this world?

Jason unbuckled his seatbelt and scooted across the seat. Bryce wrapped the boy in his embrace as they sat quietly for a few precious moments. Bryce knew he was stalling, putting off the moment when he would see his parents lying in death. His heart bled for him.

"Do you dream about Aunt Pilar every night, Uncle Bryce?" Jason broke the silence.

Bryce swallowed the lump in his throat. Last night Jason had begged him to stay at *L'etoile du Nord*, but for obvious reasons, he'd taken him to his penthouse suite at Hotel Andreas instead. Fearful that Jason might hear his screams, Bryce had brewed a strong pot of coffee and retired to his den to work on the eulogy for Michael and Lauren.

He'd dozed off and the dream had come. He'd awakened to Jason shaking him awake. Bryce wished he could erase the memory of his screams from the boy's mind. "Not every night." He rubbed his chin in Jason's soft, straight black hair. "Only when something happens to remind me of what happened to her."

"Like Mommy and Daddy dying?"

"Yes."

"Why do you hate God, Uncle Bryce? Don't you want to go to heaven to see Aunt Pilar and Mommy and Daddy again?"

Bryce inhaled deeply. He would love to see his wife again, even if were just to tell her that he was sorry. He blamed himself for not protecting her. He was angry with God for not sparing her. But he didn't hate Him. "I don't hate God, Jason."

"But you told Daddy you did."

"I know what I told your dad. When Pilar died, I was very hurt and angry. When we're hurt and angry, we say things we don't mean. Did you mean it the other day when you said you hate Him?"

"No. I was hurt and angry, too. I still am."

"I know." He paused. "It's okay to have those feelings, but eventually we have to learn to deal with our pain and our loss in a different way."

"Daddy said you deal with your loss by chasing after the wrong women."

The words pulled a cynical chuckle from Bryce. "Your daddy

said a lot of things. He was very wise like that." *I wish he'd been wise enough to accept the damn truck.*

"I hope they like the clothes I picked out," Jason said, crawling back across the seat.

"I'm sure they will, son." Bryce swallowed back another lump and willed his heart to be still.

Jason thought his parents should be buried in their best ski outfits with poles and skis in tow, just in case it snowed in heaven. Bryce couldn't think of anything Michael and Lauren would enjoy more than spending eternity on the slopes, hand in hand. That is, if it snowed in heaven.

❧

Bryce had just put Anastasia down for a nap and was on his way back downstairs to rejoin the guests who'd gathered from the funeral service when the house phone rang.

He hurried to the nearest connection—the sitting area of the second floor and picked up the cordless extension. He froze for a moment as he recalled his conversation with Alyssa in this very spot, two days ago. Besides burying his wife, telling Alyssa that her parents were dead was the hardest thing he'd ever had to do. He'd broken Alyssa's heart. The memory of her tears and the sounds of her sobs would haunt him for a very long time. He hoped that in time he'd find a way to put the shattered pieces of her little life back together.

Bryce straightened up, pressed the answer button, and raised the receiver to his ear. "Hello?"

"Who's this?"

"Who's this?" Bryce was taken aback at the question, even as he recognized the voice.

"Jack. Kaya's fiancé. Can you grab her for me?"

Bryce sucked in a sharp breath and walked to the railing

overlooking the spacious first-floor parlor where people stood or sat around in small groups, talking. The air was still pulsing with life—music and chatter—because that is what Michael and Lauren wanted. No mourning, they'd instructed, just laughter and cheer. And laughter and cheer is what Bryce had given them. He'd invited the funeral attendees to *L'etoile du Nord,* and hired Andreas to cater the event.

It was getting late, and the important guests, like Pastor Kelly, Samantha, and the faithful members of Granite Falls Community church had already made their judicious departure. He was quite anxious for the rest to scoot, most of whom were a bunch of free-loaders who'd jumped at the opportunity to see the inside of his home and feast on Andreas' cuisine for free.

Bryce's gaze zeroed in on Kaya. She was among a group of four women who were sitting on the cushioned steps leading up to the fireplace. Alyssa was straddled across her lap, nibbling on a piece of chocolate cake. There was no doubt in Bryce's mind that Kaya was the most beautiful woman in the house. She looked poised and sophisticated in a lovely black and white silk dress, and she didn't seem to mind that Alyssa was smearing cake all over the front of her dress. She was the perfect picture of a devoted mother who would put the needs of her children ahead of hers. Bryce liked that about her. A lot.

Libby was at her side, he noted with relief. Bryce had overheard a few hushed conversations among the young women as he moved through the groups, so he'd commissioned Libby to shadow Kaya to deter the town gossipers from filling her head with rumors about him and the other members of the Billionaire Club—a club that comprised of himself, Erik LaCrosse, who was also the children's pediatrician, and the Italian cousins Adamo Andreas and Massimo Andretti, all of whom were presently out of the country on personal and business affairs.

Except for Erik, who had recently remarried, all of the

members of the Billionaire Club had notorious reputations with women. It was a small town, and for some undetermined reason, Bryce did not want Kaya's opinion of him influenced by embellished tales of his sexual dalliances.

"Hey, did you hear me? I asked you to get Kaya for me."

Bryce started. He'd totally forgotten about Jack. "Kaya is busy," he said in a clipped tone.

"Busy doing what?"

Bryce stifled a grunt. "We just returned from a funeral, Jack. Perhaps you should call back after our guests leave. Goodbye."

"Hey, wait a second. That's why I'm calling. To see how the funeral went."

"It went as funerals go." *If you're so concerned about Kaya, why aren't you here with her?*

"Is this Bryce? Bryce Fontaine?" Pause. "Of course. Who else would be answering the phone but the man of the house? Hey, brother, I'm sorry about your friends, and those poor little kids… your godchildren, right? I can't wait to meet you."

"You seem to know a great deal about me, *Jack*, when Kaya hasn't even mentioned you." If he hadn't overheard that conversation the other night, he probably still wouldn't have known of Jack's existence.

He was beginning to understand why Kaya had kept him a secret. Nothing to boast about. Thirty seconds on the phone and Bryce was ready to swat Jack like the annoying little bug he was. One look at the scrawny, squinty-eyed man from the pictures the private detective had faxed him yesterday, and Bryce knew he was a loser. He still hadn't read the report on Kaya's past he'd also received. He wanted Michael and Lauren buried before he and Kaya began their next round of attack, whatever it was.

"Well, you know how it is," the bug spoke again.

"No, I don't know how it is. But I know this much," Bryce stated, his eyes drinking in the delicate softness of Kaya's heart-shaped face, his heart racing with the memory of her comforting arms when his own grief had overwhelmed him, "if Kaya were my fiancée, I would be with her at a time like this."

"She's fine, isn't she? Just remember, she's mine. Don't you forget that while you guys are up there playing house," he added with a snicker.

The tone of his voice and the implication of his threat sent a cold chill up Bryce's spine. "Is there a specific message you would like me to relay to Kaya, Jack?"

"Yeah, brother, tell her I'm flying up tomorrow. I mean, since we're getting married, the children should meet their new daddy, don't you think?"

Bryce's fist curled so tightly around the ivory railing, it hurt. "Kaya is free to marry you if that's her wish. As for my godchildren, you'll be their *daddy* over my dead body. Don't *you* forget that, *Jack*. And one last thing, don't call me, *brother*. As a matter of fact, don't ever call here again." Bryce marched to the table and slammed the receiver into the cradle.

He stood in the center of the room shaking, having no idea what infuriated him more: Jack's assumption that he would become the children's new daddy or his claim that Kaya was his.

He tried to curb his anger as he strode toward Jason's bedroom. The door was closed, but he could hear voices coming from inside. He'd noticed Jason and Ethan heading into Jason's room a while ago. Over time, a handful of other children from Jason's school and church had sneaked up the stairs to join them. At least, for a time, the boy could think about something other than the fact that he'd just lost his parents.

The support of his trusted friends was the best medicine for Jason, Bryce thought as he continued downstairs.

Michael and Lauren weren't here to fix the problems their deaths had caused. They had no idea what was best for their children. He didn't give a damn what their will stated, or what their last wishes were. It was time Kaya made a decision.

Negotiations were off the table—not that they were ever on it, anyway.

From the bottom of the stairs, Bryce took a derisive glance at the crowd scattered around his house. Having no desire to rejoin them, he took a left turn under the stairwell and stole away to the library. Once inside the sound proof room, he lit a fire in the fireplace then removed an original van Gogh painting from a wall to reveal a hidden safe. He deftly punched in the security code and retrieved a large envelope.

Comfortably seated in a chair near the fire, Bryce ripped the envelope open.

With a glass of scotch in one hand, Bryce stared out the Palladian window into the cold gloomy night hovering above the lake. It was hours since the last guest had left and the children had been put to bed. The house was quiet. Quiet enough for him to hear the ghosts lurking in the shadows.

His eyes scanned the room, decorated with an array of original fine art and collections of sentimental ornaments that had once adorned the hillside villa he'd shared with Pilar. This was the only room in the house that was off limits to the children —all but Jason, who was old enough to appreciate and respect the value of the contents within it.

Bryce downed the last mouthful of scotch and grimaced as the rich, spicy liquor scorched the back of his throat.

Soon after his friends left, he'd checked on Jason, only to find him weeping on his closet floor, a picture of his parents clutched to his chest. Bryce had picked him up and carried him to his bed. He'd said nothing to Jason, because there was nothing he could say to mend the boy's heart. He couldn't tell him that he understood, because he didn't understand a nine-year-old boy's pain of losing both parents in a tragic accident. Bryce had simply lain next to Jason and held him until his sobs ceased and he'd drifted off to sleep.

Bryce could sure use the support of his friends and family right about now. But his parents were on a charitable mission in Asia, the Italian cousins, Massimo and Adam were in Africa, and Erik and Michelle, who'd grown close to the Rogers family since they became neighbors last year, were in the Seychelles Islands. Bryce saw no sense in overshadowing their honeymoon with such sad news.

They would all have the chance to say their goodbyes to Michael and Lauren during the private ceremony Bryce had arranged to take place in late spring when they would be laid to rest. The service today was strictly for the children's sake, and his and Kaya's, too. They needed closure before they could begin to rebuild their lives, either together or separately. Whether they chose the latter was up to Kaya.

Bryce walked to the minibar and poured himself another scotch. According to the report he'd received from the private investigator, little Kaya Brehna had lived in foster homes most of her teenage life, and she'd spent time in juvenile detention. She wasn't as sweet and innocent as she pretended to be. The records were sealed because of her age at the time of the crime, so he didn't have all the facts yet.

Tonight he would give her the chance to choose between staying in Granite Falls permanently or signing the kids over to him and returning to Palm Beach alone. He didn't relish the idea of digging into her past; he really didn't care to know what she'd done. It wasn't his business, but he wasn't above resorting to blackmailing her, either.

Before he fell asleep, Jason had begged him not to let his aunt Kaya take them to Florida.

Bryce was not about to break that promise.

"Bryce?"

Bryce's heart skipped a beat at the sound of his name. He set his half-empty glass on the bar and looked up at Kaya standing at the door. She was wearing a pair of white sweats, and her damp hair fell in curly tendrils down both sides of her face and disappeared behind her shoulders like a thick dark, drape. She was a delicate woman, with a childlike innocence about her. But Bryce knew she was no child, nor was she innocent.

She'd been in trouble with the law, and she was old enough to have a lover. Jack may be an ass, but of all the men in Florida, Kaya had chosen to spend the rest of her life with him. Jack knew the pleasure of touching her in the most intimate way a man could touch a woman.

If he were in Jack's shoes, Bryce knew he'd be possessive of Kaya, too. He'd put tabs on her. Every second she was not in his line of vision, he'd know where she was, what she was doing, and with whom.

If he'd kept tabs on Pilar, he would have known that Victoria had befriended her. He would have been able to protect her. She would be alive today. "Come on in, Kaya," he said.

She advanced into the room, a frown of confusion on her flawless brow. She had no idea why he'd asked her to meet with him. Bryce indicated a chair near the fireplace where the flames danced with enthusiasm in the marble hearth.

She stifled a yawn and drew her bare feet up under her. "What's so important that we have to discuss tonight? Can't it wait until tomorrow? I'm really tired."

Bryce felt awful for dragging her back downstairs at such a late hour. He'd intended to delay this discussion for a day or two, give her time to recuperate after the stress of facilitating the funeral and entertaining today, but his conversation with Jack this afternoon had forced his hand. What was an intelligent woman like her doing with a character like Jack? She could do so much better, despite the fact that she had a blemished past.

"Did you get a chance to talk to Samantha about Alyssa wetting her bed and clinging to us since we told her about her parents?" he asked, easing into the conversation.

She nodded. "She said it's normal behavior for a child in this situation. She said Alyssa's afraid that you and I will disappear from her life, but that her fears will gradually cease with a lot of patience and attention from both us. We both have to be there for her," she added as if it were a death sentence to be in cahoots with him.

God, please let her choose to stay. Alyssa was so in love with her already. He couldn't bear breaking the little girl's heart again, or Kaya's. He knew she was already attached to the kids—even Jason who still kept her at arm's length.

She tucked a handful of hair behind one ear and offered him a bland smile. "That was a nice eulogy. Everyone was talking about it."

"It was the least I could do. Lauren gave the eulogy for…"

"Pilar?" she finished when his voice trailed off.

CHAPTER EIGHT

Bryce braced himself against her sympathetic eyes. Being in that church had evoked memories of saying goodbye to Pilar. One tragedy had kept him away and another had taken him back. It was Kaya who had kept him grounded during the funeral service. Each time he glanced at her, her smile had eased the stagnant pain in his chest.

"Um, could we not talk about Pilar?" Her curiosity about his deceased wife was understandable. Perhaps one day, if she stuck around, he would fill her in, but not tonight.

"I understand," she said.

How could she understand? What love of her life had she lost?

"I want to thank you for hiring a baby nurse to take care of Anastasia tonight."

"You deserve a good night's sleep after the way you've been running around all week." Bryce kept telling himself that his concern for Kaya was a result of his concern for the children since she needed to be physically and emotionally fit to take care of them. But a couple major organs of his anatomy kept trying to prove him wrong. Kaya was forging her way inside his head and his heart—the two sacred places women weren't allowed.

"How's Jason?" she asked. "I haven't seen him since earlier today." Her hands twisted nervously on her lap. "Then after everyone left, I was busy with Alyssa."

Bryce eased into the chair next to her, his chest tightening significantly. "Jason isn't well. He has regressed since this afternoon."

"I'm sorry to hear that."

"After his friends left, he locked himself in his bedroom. I had to use the master key to get in. I found him on his closet floor, crying."

She wiped her hands down her face. "The poor kid. He was in such a good mood when last I saw him with his friends. I should have known it wouldn't last."

"We can expect this emotional ebb and flow to continue for a while," Bryce said from experience. He leaned forward and covered her hands with his. She tensed, relaxed, and tensed again, before settling down and allowing him to hold her.

"You have to make a choice tonight, Kaya. I don't want the uncertainty of your indecision hanging over our heads any longer."

She pulled her hands from under his and stiffened her back in defiance. "We decided to discuss my plans after the funeral."

"The funeral is over, Kaya. What are your plans concerning the children? I need to know so I can begin making some of my own. It doesn't matter whether you stay or leave. I still have to make decisions about their future."

"What's the rush, Bryce?" She passed her hands down her face again. "I'm tired, and clearly not capable of making any decisions tonight. Can't we talk tomorrow?"

He studied her face. Shower gels, bath salts, and water couldn't wash away the dark circles beneath her eyes. Only sleep would cure her fatigue. But neither one of them was leaving this room until she made a choice.

"Your fiancé is coming to Granite Falls tomorrow, Kaya. Just know, the children aren't going to Florida with you, so if you decide to return to your life there, you'll have to sign their custody over to me," Bryce said in a cold, exact tone. There was no need to be subtle about the situation.

Her forehead furrowed in deep confusion. "My fiancé?"

"Yes, Jack. The man you promised to marry. Remember him?"

A shaky hand crept to the golden hollow of her throat. "Where did you get such a crazy idea?"

"Straight from the horse's mouth." He wanted to say from the jackass' mouth, but he restrained himself. He didn't want to insult her. It was her prerogative to marry the jackass if that was her desire.

"You— you talked with Jack?"

"He called this afternoon while you were entertaining. He asked me to let you know that he's flying up tomorrow to meet the children since he'll be their new daddy. I told him that would happen over my dead body."

She shook her head back and forth, her eyes darting around the room as if she expected Jack to float down from the ceiling.

"Are you afraid of this man, Kaya?"

"No, not really. He has become a bit possessive after I agreed to marry him. But we're not getting married."

"You're not?"

"He broke off the engagement."

His heart danced a jig. "He did?"

"We weren't really engaged to begin with."

"You weren't?" He felt like an idiot asking a string of stupid two-word questions. "I've wondered why you aren't wearing an engagement ring."

Leaving her chair, she took a few unsteady steps toward the fireplace and stared into the flames. "Jack asked me to marry him, and I kind of said okay," she began in an unemotional tone. "He never gave me a ring, so I never really thought of him as a fiancé, just a boyfriend who I may one day marry."

He scolded his heart for flipping a somersault. There was absolutely no reason for her to return to Florida.

"When I told him that I'd inherited the children," she continued, folding her arms about her, "he took back his proposal." She braced a tired smile. "That was the night you picked up the extension. You didn't stay on long enough to hear him dump me."

"Why didn't you tell me before? I would have handled him differently this afternoon."

"I was too embarrassed. And I didn't know what I was going to do. I was banking on Jack helping me with the kids." She shrugged. "It's for the best, anyway. I've known him since we were kids, but I've never loved him, and marrying him would have been a mistake."

Was he the one who'd led her astray, gotten her into trouble with the law? Jack struck him as the type of jerk who'd use a young girl for personal gains. How could she be with someone like that? She seemed intelligent enough to know better, to make better choices.

Bryce balled his hands into fists. "Then why is he coming to Granite Falls?"

"I don't know. The other day when he called, he said he was sorry about the way he reacted to the news of a ready-made family. He said I caught him at a bad time and that he still wanted to get married and help me raise the kids."

"Did you tell him anything about me? That I am their godfather?"

She shook her head, causing her soft curls, now dry and springy, to bounce off her delicate shoulders. "*He* brought up your name. Apparently he'd heard about your relationship to them. He knew stuff about your history with them and their parents that I didn't even know. He offered to move up here if it would be easier on me."

Bryce pushed to his feet, shaking his fists in the air. "Opportunistic little parasite! He dumped you when he thought he'd have to dig deep into his measly pockets to support the children. Then when he learned of my relationship to them, he saw a meal ticket to an easy life." Bryce closed the distance between them. "You are their legal guardian. If he married you, he'd benefit from any financial support I give you."

"Support me?" An eyebrow raised in amused contempt. "I don't need your support."

"It doesn't matter if you need if or not. You will have it. But only if you stay in Granite Falls."

She took a step back to better glare up at him. "And if I don't?"

"Then you may as well pack your bags tonight. I will not allow you to get any closer to those kids only to break their hearts."

"What are you talking about? How will I break their hearts?"

"When you have to leave them here and return to Florida alone. Alyssa is too attached to you already."

She slapped her hands against her temples. "Oh my God, you're planning to fight me for them."

"I'm planning to fight for them."

She flared her hands in the air. "Semantics, Bryce! Like you said, I'm their legal guardian. I have a contract that gives me full authority over them."

"A contract that will soon expire if you don't make the right decision."

Loathe and disbelief sprang from her eyes. "I can't believe I thought you were…"

"You thought I was what?"

"Kind. But apparently I was mistaken."

Kind! She thought he was kind. He almost laughed out loud.

Bryce's eyes shifted back and forth between her mesmerizing eyes, stormy with passion and her plump, lustrous lips that resembled two halves of a ripe juicy peach. He wanted to bite into her, taste her sweet juices on his tongue, feel her soft flesh melting under his touch. Nothing aroused him more than when a woman he'd set his sights on dared to challenge him.

A log crackled in the hearth, sending a deafening blast and auburn sparks shooting into the air. Kaya jumped and grabbed the front of his shirt with both hands, momentary fear sparkling in her eyes. He clasped his hands on the slender portion of her upper arms, offering her security.

Two things happened to Bryce the instant Kaya grabbed him. One: he felt an overpowering need to protect her. Even though the threat of danger had come in the harmless pop of a vaporized log shifting in the fireplace, the fact that Kaya was afraid sent adrenaline rushing through his body. Two: his erection throbbed against his thigh, reminding him it hadn't been fed in weeks.

He continued to hold her gaze as his hands slowly crept up her arms. He paused at her shoulders and threaded his fingers through her bouncy curls, loving the feel of the silky strands against his fingertips. He cradled her small face in his palms.

She inhaled sharply and made a reflexive attempt to break free.

Bryce tightened his hold as she pushed against his chest. She wasn't getting away that easily. She'd subtly enticed him into the web of her allure. If she wanted him to stop, she would have to be more direct. He used the pad of his thumbs to massage the soft skin of her throat, her chin, her cheeks, and the outline of her small, sexy mouth, all the while watching the emotions in her eyes shift from surprise, to doubt, to reluctance, and then finally desire.

Her pupils were enlarged, and the amber specks around her irises burned a bright orange glow. She began to tremble like an autumn leaf about to be shaken from its branch at the slightest wisp of wind. He increased the pressure of his strokes, deliberately arousing the fervor in her, watching her burn.

Her fingers tightened around his shirt, causing his heart to somersault in his ribcage. Her chest rose and fell with her shallow breathing, and the thunderous beating of her heart echoed in Bryce's ears. He crouched down, way down, aligning his face with hers, his mouth just inches from hers. He felt the live energy sizzling in the tight space that separated their lips. With deep breaths, he savored her fresh, clean woman's scent mingled with the faint odor of baby oil and powder. She was beginning to smell like a mother, and he loved it.

He angled his head and closed the distance. His lips trailed down her cheeks and lingered at one corner of her quivering mouth. Because he knew he had control, Bryce hesitated, giving her time to protest, to pull free and run. He was certain of what he wanted from her, but doubtful of what she expected from him.

The wild pounding of her heart and the erratic rhythm of her breathing echoed in his ears. He closed his eyes and waited, still giving her time to back out, but then a weak moan escaped her throat, and Bryce knew the battle was over. They'd trespassed into each other's forbidden zones and forfeited their rights to resist one another.

With a harsh groan, Bryce drew her into his body and, circling his arms about her lithe frame, he covered her soft mouth with his.

He groaned again when she reached up and linked her arms around his neck and curled her body into his. A shiver touched his spine when her tongue timidly emerged from the dark recess of her mouth and danced around his in a slow, dreamy waltz. It was the only encouragement Bryce needed. He kissed her softly, lingeringly, cherishing the aroma of her warm breath, the softness of her moist flesh, the timid smoothness of her tongue, and the dreamy intimacy of the moment.

With their mouths and limbs locked together, Bryce picked Kaya up and stumbled towards the chair she'd previously occupied. It was a large chair, with a sturdy back, and the right height for a man of his giant stature to fit perfectly with a woman seated upon it.

He set Kaya on the smooth leather surface and positioned himself between her parted thighs, his inflamed erection pressed against her feminine softness. He could feel her heat, her moisture through the thick material of their clothes. He wrapped her legs around his waist, and his arms around her body. He caressed her shoulders, her back, her hips, and the round rump of her derriere as he rocked against her slowly, boldly simulating the delirious act of copulation. When Kaya's limbs tightened up around him and a series of shivers rippled through her body, Bryce deepened the kiss, sucking, nipping, and licking at her warm sweetness.

His mouth left hers to nibble at the delicate skin at the base of her neck. The sexy whimpers from the core of her belly and the pheromones seeping from her skin lulled him into a lustful stupor. He licked at her as his hands stole under her sweat top to find her bare beneath it. His palms glided around her sides and up along her flat belly until his fingers grazed the underside of her breasts.

She moaned into his mouth.

He sucked in his breath and hers as his hands closed over the mounds of her breasts. They were the breasts of a goddess—full, firm, and ripe for plucking. His mouth watered as he molded them in his palms.

One hand grudgingly released a breast to seek out the waistband of her sweat pants. Hooking a finger inside, he proceeded to pull it down past the curve of her hips. She bucked and slammed into him when his fingertips grazed the round fullness of her derriere. He rocked against her, slowly, boldly, showing her exactly what he would love to do to her. His cock grew harder with hope, wishing to be freed from the constriction of his trousers and feel something warm, soft, and wet clamped around it. It was hungry. *He was hungry*.

His hands glided around to the front of her body, his fingers just inches from her moist heat.

Bryce swore and stopped in mid thrust as his cell phone chimed.

Kaya ripped her mouth from his, breaking the spell. With a firm thrust, she pushed him backward, jumped down from the chair, and automatically pulled her sweat pants back up and her top down. She pressed her fingers to her bruised lips, her pupils dark with desire as she gazed at him. "I'm not that easy," she said.

Bryce gazed down at her, his heart pounding against his chest so urgently it caused him physical pain. He silenced his phone without taking his eyes from hers. "I don't think you're easy at all, Kaya. We got caught up in the moment. But don't act as if you didn't want it, too. You were enjoying me as much as I was enjoying you. Passion still shimmers in your eyes; your heat still burns through my skin. You can't deny that."

In an attempt to hide her telling eyes, she dropped her gaze, only for it to land on his crotch. He felt the heat of her eyes in every engorged inch of his erection straining beneath the restrictive material of his trousers. She gasped and stepped back as if she'd stumbled upon a cobra, poised and ready to strike.

He could turn around to save her further embarrassment but he refused to oblige her. She had made him hot and hard and achy. Let her deal with it. Let her fantasize about him thrusting in and out of her tight little body, exploding inside her womb as she crumbled beneath him, or above him. Either way, they'd be coming together.

She sped past him in a flash and headed for the door.

Yes, you better run, little Kaya. If you let me catch you, there's gonna be hell to pay.

Bryce checked his phone and when he didn't recognize the number, he slid it back into its clip. How far would they have gone if the damn phone hadn't interrupted them? Would she have let him take her? Would he have gone the distance? She wasn't the "wrong kind of woman". So why wasn't he avoiding her?

Bryce turned and his body ached for Kaya even more when he saw the shiny spot on the back of the chair where her juices had leaked from her body. He passed his palm across the warm spot and brought it to his nose. Her scent was intoxicating. He rubbed his thumb across his lips, tasting the remnants of her essence in his mouth. He could easily develop an addiction to her. Perhaps he already had, he thought, as her scent lingered in his nostrils.

Bryce sighed, knowing nothing but a different kind of pain would ensue if he'd made love to Kaya. Sex complicated matters in any relationship, except marriage where it was expected—the strings were already attached. But sex also relieved emotional pain, even if it was just a temporary fix. He and Kaya were experiencing the same loss. They had clung to each other like two shipwrecked souls, lost in a black sea of grief, searching for something, anything that offered an inkling of hope, of light, and refuge from the tumultuous storm that had cast them together.

For the past few years, sex for Bryce had been all about

physical release—nothing more, but tonight as he held Kaya in his arms, he knew he wanted more. He knew he'd never be satisfied with the possession of her body alone.

She was different.

She was also vulnerable in too many ways. She'd just inherited three children who didn't have a penny to their names, and she'd just learned that the man she'd agreed to marry was nothing but a bloodsucking parasite. It was enough to drive her into his arms, even though those arms belonged to the man who had threatened to take the children away from her.

Had she seen through him? Did she really believe he was kind?

Bryce walked over to the safe and pulled out the envelope that contained the report on Kaya. With one flip of his wrists he tore the envelope and the contents into halves, then went to the fireplace, removed the glass door, and tossed them inside.

"This isn't the way," he murmured, as he watched the pieces of paper curl from the heat of the flames and disintegrate into ashes. He set the door firmly in place and shivered at the memory of Kaya's eyes staring back at him with hints of fear and susceptibility when she'd spoken of Jack's possessiveness.

That image, and the threat in the man's voice today had propelled Bryce into action. He hurried out of the library, across the foyer, and into the garage that housed his Bentley.

"Call Hector," he said as he climbed behind the wheel and backed out of the garage. "Hector, meet me at the airport in twenty," he ordered the minute his pilot picked up the other end.

"Mr. Fontaine, it's past the normal hours of operation. The airport is closed. The general manager—"

"Leave the general manager to me. I built that airport. It closes when I say it's close."

Bryce's nostrils flared with a mixture of fear and fury as he sped down Fontaine Harbor Road toward Crystal Lake Road.

Six years ago, he'd failed to respond to a threat that seemed harmless at the time.

He was still suffering the consequences.

He'd be damned if he was going to stand idly by and let it happen again.

CHAPTER NINE

Kaya's eyelids fluttered before fully opening to the rays of a new day forcing its way through the unclothed window. Squinting, she rolled over to escape the sunlight, but immediately sat up when her cheek landed on a cold damp spot on the mattress and a rancid smell wafted up her nostrils.

Did she wet her bed last night? She felt for the signs of wet clothes under the white cloud of a duvet, only to find that she was naked. *Why was she naked?*

Fully awake, she pushed scattered curls from her face and glanced at the clock on her nightstand. It was twenty-one minutes past noon *Goodness*. She'd slept half the day away. From the corner of her eyes, Kaya spotted a pair of pink PJs in a damp pile near the door.

Alyssa. She must have crept into her bed last night. *Had she slept that soundly?*

Panic propelled Kaya out of the bed, but as her feet landed on the lambskin floor rug, she remembered that Bryce had hired a baby nurse for the night. Exhaling a deep sigh of relief, Kaya flopped back down onto the bed, but was sitting up again at the thought of Bryce.

She was turning into a human yo-yo.

She touched her lips as memories of the passionate moments came back at her full force. She'd let Bryce kiss her, and touch her in her most intimate places. She trembled as she recalled his demanding mouth on hers, his tongue boldly stroking the sensitive interior of her mouth, swirling around hers, sucking base, unrecognizable sounds out of her. Her skin burned at the memory of his warm hands crawling along her bare back, across her sides, up her belly, and finally cupping her breasts, molding them, shaping them in his palms. The feel of his erection pressing between her thighs was like nothing Kaya had ever experienced before.

Bryce had lit a fire inside her. He'd awakened a wanton tigress Kaya didn't know inhabited her being. Oh God, she's craved him like she'd never craved anything in her twenty-three years of life. She hadn't cared that they were enemies—that moments before she was locked in his arms, he'd threatened to take her to court to win custody of the children.

The only thought in her head last night was to have Bryce undress her and make love to her on the back of that chair, quench the fire he'd ignited inside her. Men like Bryce Fontaine who could make a woman want to shed her clothes and lie down with him, even after he'd just declared war on her, were dangerous.

Kaya walked into the bathroom. "That's why I'm naked," she exclaimed, as the pile of clothes on the floor reminded her of the cold shower she'd taken after leaving Bryce.

She could say that she'd been too tired to fight Bryce, that he'd taken advantage of her vulnerability, she argued as she turned on the shower and punched in a number to set the desired temperature. But she'd be lying. The stories she'd heard about him and the other members of Granite Falls Billionaire Club had roused her curiosity.

She knew Bryce had stuck Libby on her tail yesterday because he was afraid she'd hear about his infamous reputation from the town gossipers, but by then it was too late. Yet, learning that he swept through women like nor'easters, and that he'd broken off his latest affair with a French model, only three weeks ago, she'd allowed him to seduce her last night.

She'd never been this impetuous with men.

At the thought of what could have happened if Bryce's cell hadn't interrupted them, Kaya grabbed a bottle of gel and her loofa brush. She scrubbed her body as if she could erase the feel of Bryce's touch, his smell, the spicy taste of his breath from her memory.

What should have been foremost in her mind last night was the future of her sister's children. They were her top priority. She couldn't afford to let Bryce derail her again.

Kaya stepped out of the shower and slipped on a white terry velour robe and wrapped a towel around her wet hair. She was back in the bedroom stripping the soiled sheets from the mattress when she heard a knock on her bedroom door. She stared at the door, wondering if it was Bryce. Alyssa would have barged right in, and Jason, well, he wouldn't be seeking her out. She wasn't ready to face Bryce just yet. Maybe if she kept quiet, he'd think she was still asleep and go away.

"Miss Kaya?"

Kaya chuckled. Now there was a name she's never been called by until last night when Mrs. Hobbs showed up on the doorstep. She dropped the sheets on the floor and hurried to open the door. "Good morning, Mrs. Hobbs," she said on a bright smile.

"Good morning, Ms. Kaya. You look rested," the middle-aged woman said, smiling back.

"I feel rested, and a little guilty for sleeping so late." She tightened the towel around her head. "I must have been really tired."

"No need for apologies. Mr. Fontaine told me that you have been working hard all week, and he insisted that the children not disturb your sleep, although I couldn't keep little Alyssa from sneaking into your bed last night. I hope she didn't keep you awake."

"No. I didn't even know she'd slept with me until I woke up to a wet spot on the mattress. She's been wetting her bed since we told her about her parents."

"Yes, Mr. Fontaine warned me about that. I found her in the playroom, naked as the day she entered the world."

Is there anything Mr. Fontaine hasn't told her?

"I came to tell you that I'm leaving," Mrs. Hobbs said.

Although she felt like her old self again, Kay couldn't shake the anxiety of being alone in this big house with the children. There was always somebody around this past week to help out with the funeral arrangements, but now that the funeral was over, people had gone back to their lives—everybody but her and the children, and of course Bryce.

The last chapter of their old lives had ended last night. A new one was beginning today.

"You sure you can't stay the rest of the day?" she asked Mrs. Hobbs, the thought of being alone with Bryce causing her heart to race. "I'll pay you."

"That's very sweet of you, dear, but I have another commitment, another family to get to. I'm a fill-in from a nanny agency."

"Oh," Kaya said. "Can you at least stay with the children until I'm dressed? I won't be long."

"Take your time, Ms. Kaya. The children aren't here."

Kaya felt as if a hand had closed around her throat. "What do you mean they're not here? Where are they?"

"Mr. Fontaine came and took them this morning."

"Took them where?" She tried to control the spasm inside her.

"Out. He said you need time to talk."

"With whom?" *Oh God. Was Jack in Granite Falls?* If her mind hadn't been so preoccupied with Bryce last night, she would have remembered to call and make it perfectly clear to Jack that they were over. That she wanted him out of her apartment and out of her life.

"The little boy," Mrs. Hobbs replied.

The constriction around her chest eased. "But you said Mr. Fontaine took the kids out."

"Just the girls. He left the boy."

So they could talk. Kaya shook her head, unable to wrap it around the man's intentions. Why would Bryce hire a nanny for the night so she could sleep? Why would he take the girls to give her uninterrupted time with Jason? What would he gain if she made peace with the boy when he was determined to take him away from her? She didn't understand the man.

"He wasn't happy about being left behind," Mrs. Hobbs continued, clearly oblivious of the turmoil in her head. "He's been in his room since Mr. Fontaine left with the girls. He didn't even come down for lunch."

She could only imagine how Jason felt when Bryce left him behind. She sighed. "Thanks for all your help, Mrs. Hobbs."

"Goodbye, Ms. Kaya."

Kaya went back into her bedroom and took her time getting dressed. Only now did she feel the weight of the responsibility that had been placed on her shoulders. She'd spent the week preparing the children to say goodbye to their parents. It was time to prepare them to live without them.

God, help me to help them, Kaya prayed as she left her bedroom and headed in the direction of Jason's.

She knocked on his door. There was no response. "Jason." She repeated the knock, hoping he hadn't locked himself inside again. She had no idea where the master key was.

After the third futile attempt, Kaya turned the doorknob, relieved to find it unlocked. She stepped inside. Jason was sitting on the foot of his rumpled bed, still wearing his pajamas.

The room was a mess. Clothes, action figures, video game jackets, and half-eaten plates of food were scattered about. The cleaners hadn't been able to get to his room last night because he'd locked himself inside it. This was the least of her worries, Kaya thought, picking her way through the chaos. An untidy room she could clean. Convincing a hurting child to trust her was an uphill challenge.

"Is it okay if I sit here with you?" she asked, dropping down beside him before he could refuse.

He pushed his hands under his thighs and turned his face away, squaring his shoulders in defiance. He was clearly sending her a message.

"Jason," she said, determined to send him her own message. "You may not believe this right now, but I do love you. All I want is what's best for you. You were blessed with a wonderful mother and father who loved you very much. Everyone talks about the special connection you and your mom shared. I want you to know that I would never do anything to interfere with that bond."

He drew his shoulders tighter together.

"I know you overheard me telling Miss Libby that I was moving you and your sisters to Florida," she continued. "I can only imagine how scared that made you feel." She cleared her throat. "This is all new to me, you know. I've never had to take care of anybody but myself before. I was doing what I've always done, which is thinking about my needs. I expected you and your sisters to fit into my world without even considering the possibility of me living in yours."

He turned his head and gave her a piercing stare. "Are you taking us to Florida?"

"I don't know what I'm going to do, Jason. But—"

"I'm not going with you."

"Jason—"

"If you take me away from Uncle Bryce, I'll run away. I swear I'll run away and you'll never see me again."

"Okay, Jason. Okay." The words ripped out of Kaya before she had a chance to analyze them. She said she'd do anything for them, and the thought of Jason running away and living on the streets of Florida was a gamble she wasn't willing to take. She'd been there and done that. The streets were nowhere for a child to be. "I wouldn't force you to move to Florida. I'll stay in Granite Falls. I'll stay here with you." At least for now until he learned to trust her.

His chest rose on fell on two hard breaths. "Forever?"

"Jason, forever—" Kaya paused on a deep breath. She was going to say that forever was a long time, and that they should take it one day, one week, one month at a time. But this child needed much more than an ephemeral promise that could be gone with the closing of a door. She had to prove that he could trust her to keep the rest of his world together, that he needn't be afraid of more losses, of more changes.

Kaya had no idea how this change would affect her or how she would manage financially. All that mattered was that this little boy and his sisters were happy and safe. They were happy and safe in Granite Falls. She could make it easy on everyone by handing them over to Bryce and returning to her life. But Kaya knew that she would be miserable if she went back to Florida without them. She couldn't live without them now.

She smiled through her fog of uncertainty. "Yes, forever,

Jason." The pulse-pounding admission was dragged from the place deep inside her where her own soul cried out for love and acceptance.

For so many years, her career had been a substitute for human intimacy. By day, she threw her passion into her work, brightening the homes of her clients. But at nights when she went home to her empty apartment, the loneliness devoured her inch by inch, piece by piece.

Even her relationship with Jack had been a crutch. She'd needed someone to care about her, someone she knew she could never love, knowing that if he ever walked out on her, her heart would remain unaffected.

She'd played it safe until the moment she'd stepped into these children's lives and found she'd been forced out of her comfort zone. The love she felt for Jason proved that she was capable of loving someone, even if he didn't love her back.

She wasn't afraid of love anymore. If only she'd found this out when Lauren was still alive.

"Did you and my mom have a fight? Is that why you never came to see us? Were you mad at her?"

Kaya shook her head. "No. I wasn't mad at her, Jason. I guess I just thought she would always be here and that some day we would have gotten together eventually. I regret—"

"My dad says it's a waste of time to regret things you should have done." Jason shot off of the bed and kicked his way across the floor. "You never came to visit Mommy and now it's too late. Regretting it isn't going to make it happen. It wouldn't change anything. You missed your chance to get to know her."

The boy was intelligent, and she deserved that scolding. "Your dad was right, Jason. I wouldn't spend my time regretting what I should have done, but you have to know that I did love your mom. *Yes*, I did love her," Kaya repeated on a tremor.

She loved her sister. She'd been so happy when Lauren had

started writing to her. Every day she would hurry home hoping they'd be a letter from her. Even though she never responded, Lauren had kept writing. It was as if Lauren knew why she couldn't write back—except when she'd agreed to come up for Michael's birthday—and had not held it against her. Why hadn't she been able to let go of her foolish jealousy and reach out to her sister? They had both been robbed of a close relationship by their parents. She should not have taken out her jealousy on her sister.

"I hope to get to know your mom through you, Alyssa, and Anastasia," Kaya said, joining Jason at the window.

He stood rigidly, staring out the pane, looking very lost and sad.

"Your mom and dad will always be close to you," Kaya told him. "You're a part of each other forever. Just because you can't see them, doesn't mean they're not with you. You carry them in your heart, and in your blood, Jason."

Jason placed his hand over his heart, his face twisting with grief. "Why does it hurt so bad, right here?"

"Because that's where love lives. When we lose someone we love, our hearts hurt because there's a big, empty hole where all the love used to be."

"Is it going to hurt forever?"

"No, honey. Over time, the pain will fade, and as you remember all the wonderful things about your mom and dad, you'll be able to smile with the memories."

"How long is it going to take?"

"It's different for everybody. But you can take as long as you want. And when you're ready to trust me, I'll be right here." Kaya dared to place a hand on his shoulder. He flinched, but didn't shake her off.

He gazed at his fist. "Do you know your heart is as big as your fist?"

"Yes," Kaya whispered on a sob, knowing where he was going. She reached up and clasped the locket at her chest.

"Mommy used to say that she— that she—"

"That she has a fistful of love for you." She imagined her father must have said those words to Lauren every day, just as he used to say them to her before he walked out of her life forever.

Fat tears rolled down Jason's cheeks. "I don't want my heart to hurt, Auntie Kaya."

Kaya pulled him into her arms, her heart filling with his pain.

"No." He struggled to break free from her.

"I love you, Jason." She held him fast.

"I don't want you to love me."

She cupped one hand under his chin, raising his face to look into his tear-filled eyes. "It's okay, baby. It's okay."

"It's not okay. I'm not your baby. I don't want you to love me," he cried in a hoarse voice.

"I can't help it, Jason. I just do."

"I hate you!" He pulled back and punched her in the stomach.

Kaya winced, holding her breath and his ambivalent glare. She'd thrown the same words at Nadine. If her mother had only taken the time to look beyond those three words, she would have found a heart flooded with love for her, aching to be loved by her.

Jason punched her again. "You're not my mother. You *can't* be my mommy."

"I know, Jason. Just let me help you get through the hurting." She pushed the words through the pain in her stomach his fistful of love was inflicting. "Just let me love you, honey."

"I don't want you to love me. I don't. I want my mom. I want her—"

He punched her one last time, then collapsed against her, sobbing.

His agony pulled Kaya back into her own childhood

memories of crying herself to sleep every night, calling for her daddy, wondering where he'd gone and why he didn't love her.

All she'd ever wanted was a safe home where she was loved, for someone to take care of her. She still wanted it. Perhaps fate was giving her a second chance to build that home with Jason, Alyssa, and Anastasia. As long as they stayed together, she knew they would be just fine.

"Auntie Kaya, why's Jason crying?"

Through her tears, Kaya peeked at Alyssa standing in the middle of the room with her hands on her hips.

Jason pulled away and, turning his back on his sister, wiped at his tears.

Kaya blocked Alyssa's view from him, giving him time to regain his composure. "He's just— Where's Uncle Bryce?" No need to start Alyssa thinking about her parents. She seemed to be in a good mood.

"He's downstairs. Jason, guess what?" She ran over to her brother. "Webster's here. He's gonna live with us."

"Who's Webster?" Kaya asked.

"He's a cat," Jason yelled on his way out the room.

Kaya sent up a prayer of thanks for her breakthrough with Jason. She hadn't expected it so soon, nor had she expected to tell him she would stay in Granite Falls, either. As she walked the long corridor and passed the elegantly decorated sitting area with the fire glowing in the marble fireplace, one thing became clear to Kaya: she couldn't stay in Bryce's house. She had to find a place for her and the children as soon as possible.

Last night, Bryce had offered to support her, but Kaya wasn't prepared to pay the price for such luxury. If she'd had any doubts about what Bryce might want in return for his financial support, their heated encounter in the library had cleared them up.

As she descended the stairs, her locket bounced against her

chest. Kaya wrapped her hand around it. She would have to sell her gem. Perhaps Eli had seen the future when he gave it to her eighteen years ago. Maybe this was the reason she was destined to have it. It was a good thing she'd never told Jack about it. Judging from his recent behavior, she had no doubt that if she'd married him, he would have one day stolen it from her and disappeared.

You really don't know people.

Kaya stood at the entrance of the playroom and watched Jason and Alyssa on the floor, thoroughly engrossed in petting a large animal with fur as sleek and black as sable.

She looked across the room at Bryce standing near a built-in bookcase with Anastasia over his shoulder. An empty feeding bottle sat on one of the shelves, and from the motion of his right hand under the blanket that was draped across Anastasia, Kaya guessed he was trying to coax a burp out of her.

"So this is Webster," she said, strolling into the room.

Bryce shot her smile. "Yes, this is Webster."

Kaya was surprised that the tension she'd anticipated at being alone with Bryce had all but dissipated. The children's presence was the buffer between them. She would have to make sure that at least one of them was always around when she was with him. *But of course, silly. What other reason would you have to see him?*

Kaya felt a touch of sadness at the thought of not having Bryce in her life, not being alone with him like they'd been last night. She'd run from the library—not because she was afraid of him, but because she was afraid of what she was feeling for him. It was a feeling she had to resist.

"Isn't he pretty?" Alyssa asked, with an animated smile on her face.

"Boys aren't pretty," Jason stated.

"Uh-huh. Uncle Bryce is pretty. Right, Auntie Kaya?"

The mockery in his eyes dared her to agree with Alyssa.

"Yeah, he's pretty. Pretty thoughtful," she said, thinking of all the wonderful things he'd done for her sister and her family over the years, of how he'd hired a nanny so she would get a good night's sleep last night, and of bringing his pet over to take the children's minds off of the absence of their parents. He was pretty thoughtful.

She came to a stop beside him, and gazed up at him. He looked haggard, as if he hadn't slept all night. The tight skin of his jaw and chin was shadowed with morning stubble, and he was still wearing the tux he'd worn to the funeral yesterday. He exuded a raw masculine scent she wouldn't mind waking up to in the morning. Kaya shook her head, squelching the vision of waking up with Bryce's arms around her, his muscular thighs pinning her slender ones to the bed. "It was nice of you to bring them your cat," she said.

"It was my mother's idea. She said the quickest way for someone to get over a loss is to fill the void with something or someone else."

Kaya wondered if that was the reason he'd gone through so many women since Pilar's death. Was he trying to fill the void she'd left in his heart? "I must remember to thank your mother if I ever have the opportunity to meet her."

She glanced over at the children. Webster didn't seem to be having any fun, but had the look of a trapped cat, desperately looking for a way of escape. His temporary discomfort was a small sacrifice for the joy Kaya saw on Jason and Alyssa's faces. Alyssa hadn't even hugged her since she came home. She felt like an old doll that had been tossed aside at the novelty of a new one joining the brood.

She would never have guessed that Bryce was the feline kind of man. He looked more like the canine type. German Shepherd or Doberman. Something large, powerful, and fearless like him. "How long have you had Webster?" she asked.

"He was Pilar's cat."

She took a moment to let that information register. "Then you're going to miss him a lot."

"Not really. I imagine I'll see him every day. There's a lot more roaming room here than in my penthouse."

The steely edge in his tone indicated that he was still determined to keep the children in Granite Falls. She wondered if he would abandon his threat to take her to court if he knew she'd made the decision to stay. Would that be enough for him, or would he want more?

"You're not allergic to cats, are you?" he asked with a hint of anxiety in his voice.

"No. Why do you ask?"

"Lauren had a terrible allergy to animals. She couldn't be anywhere near them."

"Well, it happens that I like cats," Kaya said.

"Good, then it's settled," he announced with a satisfied grin. "Webster has a new home here with the kids."

Now would be a good time to tell him that she was staying in Granite Falls, but that she was moving the children out of his house. "Bryce—"

She was interrupted by Anastasia's infamous burp that made everyone chuckle, even Jason and Alyssa.

"I hope she grows out of it," Kaya said when the laughter died down.

"Who knows," Bryce stated, humor lingering in his voice, "maybe she'll meet a boy who finds burping like a pirate an attractive trait in a girl." He moved the baby into the crook of his arm and wiped her mouth with the edge of the blanket.

"That'll be the day. Men are so— What are those?" Kaya stared at a cluster of bruises on the knuckles of Bryce's right hand. She took his hand in hers and inspected the area closely. "These weren't here when last I saw you. What happened?" She gazed up at him, surprised that an injury that small could trigger such concern for him.

His eyes narrowed as he met her gaze. "I banged it against something."

"That must have been a pretty hard bang. Looks to me like you were in a fight."

He winced when she touched her fingertip to the raw wounds.

"Your knuckles are swollen. You might have broken a bone. You should have it looked at right away."

A muscle twitched in his jaw. "I'm fine. I've already iced it, but if it'll make you happy, I'll ice it again." He pulled his hand free, and his eyes softened as they roamed down her body. "You look better today," he said, his lips parting on a smile.

"Gee, thanks."

"What I mean is that the bags under your eyes are gone. You look refreshed, like you had a good night's sleep."

Even at the height of her concern for him, Kaya felt color rise to her cheeks at the simple compliment. "I did. Thanks." She wished she could say the same about him.

"Even though Alyssa joined you?"

"I didn't even know she was there until I woke up in a bed, damp and rancid with pee."

He sighed and glanced over at the children. "Samantha will be stopping by later this evening to check up on her and Jason." He paused. "How did your talk with him go?"

"Better than I expected. He did a complete three hundred and sixty after I told him I'm staying in Granite Falls."

His mouth opened in shock. "Really. For how long?"

"I told him I'd stay forever."

"Wow. Of all the things I was prepared to hear, this wasn't one of them. What caused you to change your mind so quickly?"

"You."

"Me?" He cleared his throat and said in a lowered voice. "Kaya, I hope you're not taking what happened between us last night as—"

"Oh don't be so conceited, Bryce. My decision has nothing to do with *that*."

He let out a breath of relief.

He could have at least pretended to be hurt by her negation that what happened between them was not that important to her. "Jason needs you, and he needs his friends. I made the decision for him and his sisters. I just want them to be happy, and if that means staying here permanently, then that's what I will do."

"Uncle Bryce, can we take Webster upstairs?" Jason called from across the room.

"You don't have to ask. This is Web's home now. He's allowed everywhere."

Jason scooped up the cat.

"I wanna hold him," Alyssa whined, trying to take Webster from him.

"You just had a turn."

Webster snarled and struggled to make a break for it.

"Hey," Bryce growled. "I don't want you fighting over Webster. If you can't learn to share him, I'll take him back home with me."

One pair of grey eyes and one pair of brown stared at Bryce then at each other.

"You can have him, Jason." Alyssa released her hold on the cat's front paws.

"No, you hold him."

A very pleased Alyssa took Webster. "Let's go show him our rooms."

"Mine first."

"No, mine—"

Bryce cleared his throat.

"Okay, yours first," Jason said, trudging behind Alyssa.

"You're good with them," Kaya said. "I would not have known how to settle that spat."

"It comes with experience. I watched their parents for years. I never saw Michael nor Lauren raise a hand or voice to either of them, yet they are the best behaved kids in town."

Kaya wondered what it was like to have loving parents. She had grown up fearing her mother's backhand. Even when she was good, Nadine would find a reason to slap her. She slapped her just for being. "I hope I can walk in their footsteps," she said, forcing the unpleasant memories back into the chapters of her past where they belonged.

"I'm sure if Michel and Lauren had any doubts about your capabilities as a parent, they would not have made you legal guardian of their children. Jason is not a boy who's easily persuaded, but you got him talking to you. Alyssa loves you, and this little one," he added, gazing into Anastasia's face, "you are the only mother she'll ever remember. You are part of the children's lives now. You're just as important to them as they are to you, Kaya. Always remember that."

Kaya blinked in bafflement at his kind words which were a far cry from his promise to take her to court, only hours ago, but the sudden chime of the doorbell delayed her computation and response. "I'm not expecting anyone," she said. "Are you?"

"Yes, I am." His dark gaze swept over her, making her tremble where she stood. "Remember what I said about your importance in the children's lives," he said, handing her the baby and heading into the direction of the front door.

"What is your uncle Bryce up to?" Kaya asked, caressing Anastasia's chin.

Anastasia cooed and blew bubbles at her.

"Yeah, that's what I thought." Kaya kissed the baby's cheeks and pressed her to her breast before placing her in her crib. She stood watching Anastasia until her long lashes crash-landed on her olive cheeks. "I love you," Kaya said, placing a blanket over the sleeping baby.

Feeling a sense of relief and contentment like she'd never experienced before, Kaya sat down on a sofa facing two pairs of French doors that led out to an enormous fenced-in playground, complete with every imaginable piece of play equipment a child would ever need. There was even a tree house and a mini replica dollhouse of *L'etoile du Nord* on opposite sides of the snow-covered playground.

So this was what being the progeny of Bryce Fontaine was all about. Kaya felt a mixture of longing and sadness as she thought of the life Bryce and Pilar had planned for their children. No wonder he didn't want to live in this house. The memories must still be unbearable.

Her heart ached for him, especially because she was moving his godchildren out of his home where he seemed to gather comfort from watching them enjoy the life his and Pilar's children would never have.

She had no choice. *L'etoile du Nord* did not belong to the Rogers or the Brehnas. It was Fontaine property. Kaya was sure that one day when Bryce healed enough to open his heart to love again, he'd find another woman with whom to share his dream in this extravagant home he'd built.

She just hoped…

"Kaya."

Kaya's entire being responded to the sound of her name.

She turned around. Bryce was walking toward her, but her eyes were fixed on the brunette lurking near the entrance of the playroom. She looked a little older than Kaya, perhaps in her late twenties or early thirties. She was attractive, with a toned, athletic body clad in jeans and a sweater.

Kaya felt sick to her stomach when she saw the overnight bag at the woman's feet.

Was she Bryce's new lover, or an old flame he was rekindling?

Was he moving her in?

CHAPTER TEN

The thought tore at Kaya's insides.

She sank into the cushions and closed her eyes.

"Kaya?"

She raised her lids to find Bryce standing over her with a pensive shimmer in his eyes. He got down on his knees in front of her and planted his palms on the sofa at her sides. He didn't touch her, yet her body felt warm and heavy at his nearness.

"Who is that woman? What is she doing here?" Kaya whispered in a voice shakier than she would have liked. "Is she the reason you were buttering me up, telling me to remember my importance in the children's lives? Is she moving in?"

His mouth ruffled as if he were weighing her questions in his mind, then he broke into a dazzling smile. "Yes, she's moving in, but—"

"Then it's a good time to tell you that the children and I are—"

His lips were warm and firm as they moved over hers. He kissed her slowly as if he were enjoying the delights of a succulent fruit. His tongue swerved into her mouth, seeking hers, stroking, probing, retreating, and advancing with increasing pressure that made the inner walls of her sex throb and contract as if seeking something hard and hot to hold on to—to satisfy the hot ached inside.

Kaya closed her eyes and moaned her pleasure into Bryce's mouth as a series of electrical shocks exploded inside her one after the other. Her crusted nipples throbbed painfully against the lace of her bra. Her heart hammered inside her chest as her body quivered uncontrollably for a few intense moments before a powerful wave of release crashed over her, lifting her up then pulling her under. She squeezed her legs together as a deluge of hot liquid gushed between her thighs, soaking her panties. She moaned her release into Bryce's mouth.

Only when she fell weakly against the cushion did Bryce drag his mouth away from hers. Still breathless and speechless, but considerably relaxed, Kaya stared at him. His lips were moist, his eyes glazed, but he seemed unaffected from the kiss when she was still trying to fathom the fact that he'd just brought her to a shuddering climax without ever touching her with his hands.

He was a wicked, wicked man.

She touched the tingling area around her mouth where the stubble of his beard had grazed her. Morning sex with him would be so tantalizing.

"Feel better?" he asked on a leisurely smile.

She did feel better. All the tension that had been building up inside her since last night was gone. Still unable to speak, she nodded.

"Great. Now, as I was saying, Haley is moving in, but not for the reasons you think. Pull yourself together before I call her over." He pushed to his feet in one fluid motion as if they'd merely been discussing dinner and he'd agreed to the seafood she wanted instead of his steak.

Kaya took in big gulps of air into her lungs and struggled to her unsteady feet. She still didn't know who Haley was, but at least she knew who she wasn't. Bryce would not have kissed her like that while his lover was around.

The high back of the sofa had protected them from Haley's view, but as Bryce motioned her over, Kaya wondered if the woman had heard the whimpers she'd been powerless to stop.

"Kaya, this is Haley Stiggins. She's the new nanny. Temporary, until she proves she can do a good job."

"It's nice to meet you, Miss Brehna."

"So when did Mr. Fontaine hire you?" she asked, shaking the hand Haley offered.

"Just this morning. She had brunch with the girls and me," Bryce answered.

"You've been quite busy, Bryce," Kaya said through clenched teeth. "I wish you'd filled me in on your intentions, since I have made decisions of my own."

"I'm well trained, Miss Brehna, if that's what you're worried about," Haley said. "I have lots of experience with young children. I wouldn't disappoint you."

"Excuse us." Kaya forced a sweet smile to her lips and grabbed Bryce's arm. He was tight and hard. "Can we talk in private?"

He didn't budge an inch when she tried to steer him away from Haley, but walked in the opposite direction toward the crib. He carefully picked up Anastasia and brought her to Haley. "You may as well begin your trial run," he said, placing the sleeping baby in Haley's arms. "Take her to the nursery." He pointed to a flight of stairs at the back end of the playroom. "Up those stairs and the third door on your left. Oh, and keep the other two children upstairs until I call them down. There's food in the kitchenette of the second-floor sitting area in case they get hungry. Ms. Brehna and I will be occupied for some time. We don't want to be disturbed."

"Yes, Mr. Fontaine. I understand."

Haley's slightly embarrassed expression told Kaya that she knew exactly what had transpired between her and Bryce a few minutes ago. It also carried the assumption that they were anxious to pick up where they'd left off.

He was never getting that close to her again.

"What are you doing?" she asked Bryce as soon as Haley was out of earshot. "I don't need a nanny."

"This is a big house, Kaya. You're not ubiquitous. You need help, especially because you're new at this. I've also arranged for a housekeeper to begin tomorrow, and a cook if you need one."

"Bryce, the children and I are moving out, so unless you plan to move in with a baby in tow, you'd better get rid of that nanny."

His forehead creased on a deep frown. "I thought you were staying."

"In Granite Falls. Not at *L'etoile du Nord.*"

"But this is the children's home."

"It's your house, Bryce, not theirs. I am their legal guardian, not you. I'm going to start looking for a place of our own, right away. One I can afford."

"Oh, Kaya," he groaned, brushing his hand across his short crop of black hair.

"What now?"

"There was someone else at the door. An attorney you need to talk to. It concerns Michael and Lauren's will."

Kaya threw her hands in the air. "You're still planning to fight for custody even after I told you I'm staying? I should have known that wasn't enough for you. You don't like to share, do you? You're the little boy who wants it all. You're such a selfish, ego—"

His eyes impaled her. "Perhaps you should hear out this attorney before you utter any more harsh words and start calling me names I may find hard to forgive and forget," he warned in a gravelly voice.

"I'm not talking with your lawyer or any lawyer without mine present. I'm calling Steven."

"Steven and Libby eloped to the Caribbean this morning. They're getting married today."

Her eyes widened. "But they're planning a June wedding."

His lips twisted ruefully. "People change in the face of tragedy, Kaya. In light of the recent events, Steven and Libby decided not to waste any more time apart. They'll have the big wedding in June to appease their friends and families, but they want to begin their lives together now."

Kaya couldn't say she blamed them, but Steven's absence made things more complicated for her. The fact that Bryce wanted her to meet with an attorney to discuss Michael and Lauren's will at the same time her attorney was out of the country reeked of control and sabotage—Bryce's specialty in the business world. She wasn't falling for that. "I'm happy for them," she said, "but all the same, I'll wait until Steven returns to discuss any details of the will."

He shoved his hands into his side pockets and peered down at her with softening eyes. "Kaya, the will Steven drew up for Michael and Lauren is null and void. They made a more recent will before they died. There are some changes. On your behalf, I emailed a copy to Steven. He responded that it's solid and legal. I will show you the email."

Kaya's heart dropped to the bottom of her belly. She crossed her arms to subdue the tight knots. "Am I going to lose the kids, Bryce?"

"Not necessarily," he said with a level of tenderness in his voice Kaya had only heard him use with the children. "I meant what I said. You play a major role in the children's lives. We both do. As long as we keep that fact foremost in our minds, we can't go wrong in any decision we make about their welfare. They need us both." He paused and sighed deeply. "Let's not keep Mr. O'Brien waiting."

Mr. O'Brien rose from his chair when Kaya and Bryce entered the library. He was a stocky, balding, middle-aged man wearing a faded black suit that looked as if he'd bought it at a yard sale. It had seen one too many funerals and or washes, Kaya thought.

"This is your lawyer?" she whispered. "I thought you could afford better."

"I never said he was my lawyer. Michael and Lauren hired him." He placed a restraining hand in the hollow of her back and propelled her forward.

He made quick introductions, and before Kaya could fully sum up Mr. O'Brien, she was seated at a table across from him and Bryce, perusing a legal document.

"I don't understand," she said, looking at the attorney. She really wanted to tell him that she didn't trust him, but Steven's email stated that she should. "Mr. Lynd was my sister and bother-in-law's attorney. He drew up their will that named me legal guardian over a year ago. Why are you just coming forward with this new will? Why didn't you come forward immediately after their deaths, like Mr. Lynd had done? He called me that same night. I was here the next day."

Why hadn't he come forward before she'd promised a little boy that she was abandoning her old life in Florida to start a new one in New Hampshire with him?

"Your questions are very apropos, Miss Brehna. But I was prohibited to come forward until the autopsy revealed the identity of the survival spouse. According to the simultaneous death clause in the will, since Mr. Rogers survived his wife, Mr. Fontaine has gained custody of the children. If his wife had survived him, you would have maintained custody. When I received the toxicology report yesterday, I immediately called Mr. Fontaine."

"You knew about this since yesterday?" Kaya flung the words at Bryce.

"It was Mr. O'Brien's call that interrupted us last night. In *here*," he added with emphasis. "I didn't answer because I didn't recognize the number. I learned about the new will when I called him back this morning."

"And you don't think you should have informed me *then*?"

"I came to the house to do just that, Kaya, but you were still asleep," he said in his defense. "Should I have awakened you?"

"I wish you had, because then I wouldn't have—"

"Are you telling me that if you knew that I had custody of the children, you would not have told Jason that you would remain in Granite Falls? That you would have packed your bags right after you heard the news and returned to Florida, forgetting that they even exist? Is that what you're telling me, Kaya Brehna?"

"No! I'm not saying that. I love them. I would do anything for them. But I don't have the right to them anymore. You do, Bryce. You have the power to kick me out of their lives if you want to."

"And you think I want to kick you out of their lives?"

"I don't know. I don't know anything anymore," she rasped on a ragged breath. "I don't know who to trust."

Kaya shot out of her chair and began to pace as anger twisted her guts into knots. How could Lauren have done this to her? How could she make her fall in love with her children and then take them away on a twist of fate?

Wasn't it enough that she had stolen their father's love and devotion all those years ago? Once again, she was left with nothing.

Overcome with an amalgam of old and new hurt, Kaya dropped her face in her hands and began to weep.

She relaxed into the wall of warm flesh as Bryce's arms closed about her. She let him lead her over to a love seat where he sat with her tucked tightly against him. The brush of his fingers through her hair and the gentle caress of his hands along her shoulders and back slowly eased the suffocating sensations in her throat. He held her even after she stopped crying her pain into his chest.

Opening her eyes, she raised her head and gazed up at him.

"You can trust me," he said, brushing her hair away from her damp forehead.

"That's easy for you to say now you have custody. Congratulations, Bryce. You won. You should be happy."

"There's nothing to be happy about, Kaya."

She looked around the library. "Where's the seedy little lawyer?"

"He broke your heart, so I threw him out."

"You're my hero."

"If you say so." His hands moved up and down her arms, still offering her comfort and warmth.

"What do we do now?" she asked on a shudder.

"We get married."

Kaya couldn't stop the bubble of laughter that erupted from her throat, but it quickly died as she held Bryce's steady and unflinching eyes. "You're serious." She tried to back out of his arms.

He drew her gently back in. "I am serious. We both love the kids and we both want to be part of their lives. Can you think of a better way to bring stability and security back to them? We are their parents now. We can be a family."

The images of their passion-filled moments in the library and in the playroom surfaced in Kaya's memory. If she married Bryce, he would expect more of the same. As his wife, she would be obligated to meet all of his needs in the bedroom. "Bryce, I can't marry you. I wouldn't marry you."

"Why?"

"You know why. Your reputation with women is—" She shrugged. "Well you know what it is."

"Oh, so you heard."

"Yes. By the time you called in Guard Libby, yesterday, it was too late. I'd already heard enough."

"What did you hear?" A curious smile curved his lips.

"That you love them and leave them."

"I leave them because I don't love them." His voice held no apology, no regret.

"Well, you don't love me, either." With her eyes, she challenged him to refute her claim.

"I'll never leave you," he simply stated.

Kaya dropped her gaze to the wet spot on his shirt that her tears had left. Marrying a man like Bryce would surely bring its share of troubles, and many reasons for her to cry in his arms more often than not. Would he be this understanding of her feelings when she accused him of infidelity? Would he be evasive, honest, or would he lie about his affairs? "How can I be sure of that?" she asked, wondering if she really wanted to know the answer. He could start lying right now just to get what he wanted. He wanted the children, and he wanted her. There was no doubt about that.

He slowly stroked a fingertip down one side of her face, hooked it under her chin, and tilted her face upward. "I don't abandon family, Kaya. I take my marriage vows extremely seriously. I will never be unfaithful to you. I will never mistreat you, embarrass you, or cause you harm. You can trust me to be there for you and the kids. Always and forever."

But don't trust me to love you, was the deep-seated promise Kaya read in the dark recesses of his eyes.

His phone buzzed between their joined hips. Kaya expelled a sigh of relief when he let her go to retrieve it.

"It's the nanny," he said, frowning as he touched the speaker icon. "Yes, Haley?"

"I'm sorry to disturb you, Mr. Fontaine, but Alyssa is crying for you and Miss Brehna."

Kaya jumped to her feet, happy to put some real distance between her and Bryce. "I'll go check on her."

"Ms. Brehna will be right up, and please send Jason down to the library, pronto." He ended the call, caught Kaya's hand, and pulled her back down next to him. "You haven't given me an answer."

Kaya licked her lips as her gaze fixed on his sexy mouth. She was too chicken to look into his eyes. "It wouldn't work, Bryce."

"We'll make it work, simply because we're doing it for the children. What am I to tell Alyssa when she awakes in the middle of the night and calls for you?"

Kaya didn't know what to say, or maybe she was just avoiding the truth, the inevitable. It was so hard to remain coherent when so close to him.

"It's the only way I will allow you to maintain contact with them, Kaya," he proclaimed, dropping the other shoe. "I'm the only man who will replace Michael in their lives. You need to decide if you'll be the woman who replaces Lauren. Marrying me is the only way it will happen."

"Do we have to decide now? Today?" Her hands clasped and unclasped on her lap.

He responded with a resounding, "Yes! I will not sit around and wait for you to hook up with someone else, bring another man, or men, into their lives."

"What makes you think I want to hook up with anyone?"

"You're young, gorgeous, smart, sexy. It's only a matter of time before some poor sucker under the guise of a genuinely good man falls for you, but no matter how good he is, no other man will ever love these kids more than I do." He put his finger under her chin and forced her to look at him. "Will you marry me?"

Kaya knew she may live to regret it, but Bryce was right. There was not another man out there who would care for them more than he did. Except for his brief and callous relationships with women—which he promised to abandon, and his egotistical personality—which she could curb, he was a decent man—kind, loving, thoughtful, and considerate. He had promised never to hurt her, or leave her. She didn't know why, but she believed him.

She could do worse. Far worse. Damn, she'd agreed to marry Jack, and he wasn't worth the spit-up on Anastasia's bib.

"Okay," she said, nodding. "Yes. I'll marry you, but if you think that—"

He cut her off by claiming her mouth. Only this time, he ended the kiss just as quickly as he'd started, but not before he'd sent her pulses spinning. "That's all I want to hear. We'll work out the details later. Go take care of Alyssa." He nudged her off the love seat and slapped her playfully on her jean-clad buttocks.

He thinks I'm gorgeous, smart, and sexy, was the thought in Kaya's head as she exited the library, walking slowly this time. The impact of his slap on her cheek caused a sweet tingling that left her craving for more.

She bit her lips in deep thought. *You're sexy, too, Bryce...*

"...And because your mom died before your dad, I now have custody of you and your sisters," Bryce said, bringing Jason up to date on yet another change in his young life. He prayed it would be the last for a long, long while. If he the adult was tired of the rollercoaster ride they'd been on this past week, he could only imagine how confusing it was for Jason.

It was time for stability. That's why he'd tricked Kaya into agreeing to marry him.

Yes, he could admit it now. He'd tricked her. He would never have prevented her from seeing the children, but the thought of Kaya with another man was something he wasn't willing to risk, not after…

"What about Aunt Kaya?" Jason asked, cutting short Bryce's reverie. "Is she mad?"

Bryce smiled inwardly at the trepidation in Jason's eyes. Jason was beginning to like her. "She was when she heard the news. And she was very sad, too, at the thought of losing you guys," he added. "Your aunt really loves you."

"But is she going back to Florida? She said she was going to stay, but that was when she had custody of us. She doesn't have to stay now." He dropped his gaze to his hands clenching and unclenching on his lap.

Just like Lauren and Kaya when they were nervous, Bryce thought with a wry smile. "No, Jase. She isn't going back to Florida. She's keeping her promise to you."

His head shot up, and a sliver of hope flashed across his face. "Are you moving in here with us?"

He hadn't thought of that. "I don't know yet. But there is something else I must tell you."

"What?"

"Your aunt and I are getting married."

Jason stared at him for a long while then asked, "Are you getting married because of us?"

Bryce sighed and leaned back into the love seat. He wasn't going to lie to the boy. His parents always answered his inquiries truthfully, and he was determined to keep that tradition going. "Yes. Your aunt and I care about you and your sisters."

"Do you love her?"

So this must be how suspects felt in the interrogations room. Bryce couldn't remember being this uncomfortable. Damn, sweat was running down his armpits, and it wasn't because of the fire in the fireplace. "No, Jason, I don't love her, but I like her. I like her a lot."

"Mommy said people should only get married for love."

"We both love you." Bryce deliberately twisted his words. "We want to provide a safe and happy home for you. We will be true to that promise."

"Then it's just a MOC."

Bryce cocked his head. "A MOC? What is a MOC?"

"A marriage of convenience."

"What do you know about marriages of convenience?"

"From TV. There's no sex involved."

"This conversation is over." Bryce shot to his feet and marched to the other side of the room. For once, he wished Michael and Lauren had been more conservative in their conversations with their children. He knew Michael had already given Jason the sex talk, because Jason had asked. While the rest of the world believed that "What you don't know *can't* hurt you" Michael's motto was "What you don't know *will* hurt you".

"I'm sorry if I upset you, Uncle Bryce."

Bryce gazed over at the puppy-dog face. He spread his arms.

Jason immediately ran to him.

Bryce hugged him close. "I'm not upset, but there are some things about your aunt's and my personal lives that are off limits. You understand?"

Jason nodded, and hooked his arms around Bryce's waist.

Bryce looked out the window at the snowcapped mountains in the distance. It was a gorgeous day with a bright sun, clear blue skies, and temperatures in the low to mid thirties. Perfect for outside activities. His eyes shifted to the Persian rug in front of the fireplace and thought that was perfect for inside activities, as well, especially because the room was soundproofed.

Bryce sighed and glanced at his watch. It was a little past two. He needed to get out of this room, the house, and clear his head of the evocative images of him and Kaya locked in each other's arms last night and that epic kiss they'd shared just recently in the playroom. He'd gotten a lot more than he'd bargained for. What a woman!

Bryce felt a wrenching pain in his gut as he recalled the insults about Kaya, Jack had hurled at him last night. He wanted to break his face. *Again.* Bryce returned his gaze to the window. He needed to blow off some steam. And there was nothing like zipping down a mountain at over sixty miles an hour with the wind lashing his face to make him forget about everything, but being in that timeless, thrilling moment.

"You want to go ski?" he asked Jason.

"Okay," Jason replied immediately.

Bryce smiled at the renewed vigor in his voice and the glow on his face.

"Go gear up, but we have to be back by the time Miss Samantha gets here to visit with you and Alyssa."

"Why's she coming? I feel better. I'm not mad at Aunt Kaya anymore."

"I get that, but losing someone we love affects us in ways that we would never imagine otherwise. It's good to have someone to talk to, someone who understands what we're going through."

"You understand. I can talk to you."

"Anytime, night or day, but you should still see Miss Samantha. She's trained to help you deal with issues that I can't. Will you do that for me? It will make *me* feel better."

Jason flashed a thin smile. "Okay, Uncle Bryce. Can I try out the new skis you got me?"

"Duh. I didn't buy them to sit in your closet. Let's get going before the sun sets."

After Jason left, Bryce remained where he was, staring off at the mountains, the place where the spirits of his friends would live on forever.

Why did Michael and Lauren change their minds six months ago and draw up another will? Why hadn't they informed Steven of the changes and have him destroy the one in his possession?

If the first will had been destroyed, Kaya would never have been brought into the equation. As things stood, there would have been no need to call her. She would be in sunny Florida this very moment, playing house with Jack, instead of upstairs in his home comforting a little girl who was experiencing the worst pain of her life.

Bryce trembled at the thought of never meeting Kaya. He'd only known her for a week, yet her sweet warmth was already melting the icecaps from around his heart, making him wish for the filial joys of life he'd been robbed of. He could have them again with the children and Kaya by his side, but Bryce knew deep down inside that it would never be enough.

He wasn't the kind of man who was content with what other people viewed as standard or customary. He wanted more. He has always wanted more. Wanting more was what had driven him to build his empire so quickly.

Michael and Lauren had left no letter of explanation for any of their decisions, but their actions, whether planned or accidental, had brought Bryce and Kaya together. Lauren had accomplished in death what she couldn't accomplish in life.

Bryce crossed his arms as he recalled various conversations where Michael had told him that there were no coincidences in life, and that every person we meet comes across our paths for specific and mutual reasons. Michael's reason for meeting Bryce had already been revealed when Bryce pulled him from the frozen pond. And now Bryce's reason for befriending Michael was unfolding before his very eyes. But it was much, much more than either one of them could have ever imagined.

If Bryce believed in predestination, he'd have to say that this was the best-laid plan he'd ever seen.

CHAPTER ELEVEN

"They're all asleep? Even Alyssa?" Kaya asked into the phone.

"Yes, Mrs. Fontaine," Haley replied.

"Alyssa didn't even ask for me?"

"Well, she did ask a couple times, but Jason and Precious always managed to get her engrossed in something else."

The fact that Alyssa had gone to sleep without her auntie Kaya's arms around her for the first time in weeks, made Kaya wonder if *she* was the one who'd grown dependent on the little girl's love. Tonight was the first night they'd been separated, and even though Kaya was happy that Alyssa was adjusting well to her new family, she couldn't help but feel a little despondent. Gone was her excitement when she'd stolen away from the crowd at the dinner table and snuck upstairs to check on her babies.

"The children are fine, Mrs. Fontaine. There's no need to worry about them."

I'm worried about myself, Kaya thought, fully realizing another dimension of love. Love wasn't merely about you loving someone unconditionally, but the joy of knowing that that someone needed you. "Thanks, Haley," she said with a tremor in her voice. "But if Alyssa wakes up during the night and cries for me, I don't care what time it is, you call me, okay?"

"Yes, I will call you if Alyssa wakes up."

"Goodnight, Haley."

"Good night, Mrs. Fontaine."

Mrs. Fontaine. What a crock, Kaya thought as she hung up the phone.

From the balcony, she stared down at the lively conversation still going on between her husband of four weeks and their dinner guests—Steven and Libby, the newlyweds, Erik and Michelle Lacrosse who'd recently returned from their honeymoon, and Adam Andreas.

For the past few hours, Kaya had been listening to the newlyweds and honeymooners recount their stories of loving moments under tropical suns and moons. Although she too was a newlywed, the only stories she could have contributed were tales of how well the children were doing. Since there was only so much of that topic she could talk about, she'd taken the opportunity to silently observe her circle of new friends.

From their interactions with each other, Kaya could tell that Erik and Michelle wished they were still in the Seychelles Islands totally enthralled with each other, although Michelle had said that she missed her kids—Erik's eight-year-old daughter, Precious, from his first marriage, and their own absolutely adorable nine-month-old son, Little Erik. Michelle's elated announcement earlier that she was three months pregnant with their third child made Kaya wonder if she and Bryce would ever experience their kind of marital bliss.

Kaya smiled as Adam began talking about his trip to Africa with his cousin Massimo who'd remained on the mother continent to venture out on a lone safari. Adam owned Hotel Andreas and Ristorante Andreas—exclusive hotel and restaurant chains. The restaurant was so élite that patrons made reservations with sizable, non-refundable deposits months in advance. There were no walk-ins at Ristorante Andreas.

"I hope Massimo is more careful this time. We don't want a repeat of the last solitary trip he took," Bryce said. "I have a new wife and family now and don't have time to run Andretti Industries for him."

Kaya had no idea what Bryce meant by that remark, but the high level of concern in his voice, and the grave expressions on the other men's faces indicated that it was something really serious.

"You know Massimo. I advised him to take along a guide, but he will do what he pleases," Adam said, knocking back a swallow of liquor.

"Don't we all?" Erik interjected. "We think our way is the only way, that everyone must conform to our rules until we wake up one morning and realize that we're just plain stupid and on the verge of losing what matters most to us. Thank God for loving women who forgive the errors of our ways and give us second chances," he added, glancing down the table to smile at Michelle.

Great insightfulness, Kaya thought, looking from one man to the next.

Libby had told Kaya that Bryce, Erik, Massimo, and Adam had known each other since high school and it was then that they started the Granite Falls Billionaire Bachelor's Club and sworn their loyalty to each other. Bryce was the anomaly. He was an outsider and the only one of the four who was not born into wealth. It was only after he graduated college and began working at Andretti Industries under the tutelage of Massimo's father, Luciano Andretti, that he began making his mark in the world. And what a mark he'd made. He was just as wealthy as the other men, who now sat at his table.

The Billionaire Bachelor's Club became simply the

Billionaire's Club after Erik, and then Bryce were married. It was coincidental that they both lost their first wives to tragedy. Erik's to a hit-and-run driver, and Bryce's—well, she was yet to learn how Pilar had died. She'd been tempted to Google it, but out of respect and loyalty to her husband, Kaya had opted not to probe into his past. She wanted to hear about it from him, and hoped that at some point he would feel comfortable enough to trust her with his innermost fears and hurts.

Kaya turned her gaze to her husband seated at the head of the dining table, clearly enjoying the company of his most treasured friends—all of whom had welcomed her into their exclusive circle with open arms.

The club met once a month. There was no talk of business during these get-togethers, just rich gourmet meals, lots of expensive liquor, and adult fun. Michelle and Erik, who live on the other side of Crystal Lake, had hosted the last party. That was a solemn gathering since much of the conversation had been centered on Michael and Lauren's deaths. They'd held back on the liquor, but had enjoyed some rich gourmet food prepared by Mrs. Hayes, Michelle's housekeeper—a sweet old lady who reminded Kaya of her last foster mother.

Kaya was hosting her first party tonight, and she'd prepared a four-course meal that began with crab-stuffed mushrooms, followed by a green salad with jicama and goat cheese, topped with vinaigrette. The main course was baked lobster tails with a side of grilled asparagus, and smashed garlic potatoes sprinkled with fresh rosemary. And for dessert, she'd served individual molten chocolate cakes with warm black cherry sauce.

She'd been receiving compliments all night—especially from Adam, who'd jokingly offered her a job in his kitchen at Hotel Andreas. Bryce had also been generous with his praise, and his pride in having a wife who knew her way around the kitchen was evident in his voice each time he complimented her.

As Kaya started down the stairs to rejoin her guests, she recalled Bryce's surprise the first time he'd joined her and the kids for dinner. He'd enjoyed several servings of her chicken and quinoa chili, and homemade sourdough rolls, and had even taken some leftovers to his penthouse. "Marrying you was the best business decision I've made in a long time," he'd said later when the two of them were cleaning up the kitchen. His cutting remark had reminded Kaya that their marriage was one of convenience.

"Are the kids okay?" Libby asked as she approached the table.

"They are. I'm a little let down because Alyssa went to bed without me. I'm so used to her falling asleep in my arms."

"You'll get used to it." Michelle chuckled. "It was a relief when Little Erik started sleeping through the night. It was nice to make love without having one ear cocked, ready to bolt. Soon you and Bryce will be able to enjoy each other without the fear of interruption."

Kaya felt heat rising to the surface of her skin. She took a sip of red wine and stared across the table at Bryce as he popped the cork on a bottle of whiskey and began refilling his friends' glasses while they argued about sports. It was three New Englanders against the New Yorker.

"They'll be wasted and completely stupid by the end of the evening," Libby whispered in her ear.

"I figured as much. Why make us dress up in fancy clothes and have a gourmet meal, just so they can ignore us and drink themselves into a stupor when they could have gone out to a bar or pizza parlor?"

"I guess we need to educate her about the sanctity of the clubs, tell her why our husbands have these special gatherings," Michelle said to Libby.

"Steven isn't even a member. They pay him well to attend these parties. His job is to keep them in check and see them safely home at the end of the night. That's why he's been nursing one drink all night. I'm only here because I'm his wife."

"Well, you're as important a member of the Billionaires' Brides Club, as Kaya and me, so you—"

"Wait a minute," Kaya exclaimed, throwing her hands up, her eyes darting between Michelle and Libby. "There's a Billionaires' Brides Club? Why don't I know I'm a member? And what's the purpose?"

The room got deathly quiet, and Kay could feel all eyes trained on her. *Damn*, she hadn't meant to be so loud, but she'd been shocked to learn she was a member of a club she didn't even know existed. Was she unsuspectingly inducted into a cult? Were these people swingers? She knew of couples that indulged in such dalliances. Is that why Bryce had insisted that Haley and the kids spend the night at the LaCrosse's? *Dear Lord.* Kaya took a deep breath and raised her lids to meet the intense, dark eyes of her husband.

He stared at her for endless moments then cleared his throat. "Yes, my lovely, reluctant bride. There is a Billionaires' Brides Club and you became a member when you promised to love, honor, and cherish me four weeks ago. The purpose for the club is for you ladies to support each other, and help each other become quintessential wives and mothers."

"Speaking of quintessential wives," Adam said, looking at Bryce. "Why are you still in my penthouse suite when you have such a gorgeous woman in your house? If Kaya were my wife—"

"She's not your wife, Adam," Bryce threatened in a low, steady voice. His eyes continued to burn into Kaya's. "And the reason I'm still living in your hotel is not open for discussion."

"Are you kidding me?" Adam planted his elbows on the table. "Since when is discussing your love life off the menu?"

"Since he got married. I'd imagine that it's one thing to share stories about your lovers, but once a man takes a wife, the rules change."

"That's my man," Michelle murmured on a chuckle.

"I don't like that rule. It's stupid and unfair." Adam downed the contents of his glass again and held it out for a refill from the fifty-year-old bottle of scotch Bryce had fetched from his underground cellar.

"Maybe you should take a wife and level the playing field," Erik suggested. "Think of the advantages of having a woman all to yourself every single night." He winked at Michelle who sent him a sexy smile as she blew a kiss at him.

"If it's one thing I know I don't need, it's a wife. I'm my own man."

"Your loss." Steven raised his glass to the women then placed it back on the table.

Relieved that they weren't swingers or member of some type of scary cult, Kaya watched in disbelief as the men continued to argue about rules of the games and wives and lovers as they emptied one liquor bottle after the other. One proposed that they make some new rules and commissioned Steven to record them on one of her white linen handcrafted napkins.

She turned to Michelle. "Do they always get like this during these gatherings?"

"I'm afraid so." Michelle ran her fingers through her short black hair. "You understand now why the kids can't be around these events? They can never see their fathers in such drunken states."

Kaya nodded, happy it wasn't for the reason she'd thought. "But why? What's the point?"

"It's an agreement they concocted to protect themselves," Libby responded.

"From what?"

Libby swallowed a bite of her cake. "They are powerful men

who come from powerful families, Kaya. They have seen what public inebriation can do to men like themselves."

Kaya had no idea what Libby was talking about. She'd seen some of her wealthy powerful clients make fools of themselves in public, but by the next day, their lives returned to normal.

"When Massimo and Adam were teenagers," Libby continued, "both their fathers got wasted at a business convention and inadvertently spilled the details of a highly secretive joint business deal. By the next morning, both Andretti Industries and Andreas International were in jeopardy."

"So these men made a pact never to become intoxicated in public," Kaya murmured, nodding with understanding.

"They trust each other with their lives," Michelle added. "They get wasted only once a month, and only with each other. It's a time for them to forget the stress of their professional lives, let their guards down and just be... *boys*. And for additional protection, they added the "no business talk" clause."

"Wow." Kaya stared at the men, laughing, arguing, and slapping each other on the shoulders as they filled and emptied their glasses. There was no mistaking the depth of their friendship.

Steven pushed back his chair and stood up. "Who's up for some pool?" He took control like a parent at a birthday party who wanted to move the fun along.

"I second that." Adam staggered to his feet and swatted strands of his extremely long black hair from his face with impatient swipes of his wrist. He blew at the stubborn strands that adhered to his cheeks and mouth.

Kaya chuckled at the comical picture he made, and of the others trying to steady themselves as they vacated their chairs.

"You need a haircut." Erik tried to help Adam with the errant strands of hair. "Men shouldn't have long hair. Don't you think?" He gazed cross-eyed at Steven and Bryce.

"Leave the man alone. It's his hair. He can wear them— uh, it— any way he wants. I think you have beautiful hair," Bryce said on Adam's behalf.

"They also defend each other, but when you cross one, you cross them all," Libby stated.

It was all Kaya could do not to burst out laughing when Bryce bent down, planted his hands on the table, and looked over at them, his eyes glazed and bloodshot, his mouth twisted as if it hurt to talk.

"La— ladies, you must execute— um, no—" He swirled an unsteady forefinger around and his eyes rolled back into their sockets as if he were searching for the right word. "Excu— excuse us." A loud burp erupted from his throat and he continued as if it were the most natural thing in the world. "We're off to the man cave to do man— manly stuff." He picked up an unopened bottle of liquor and swayed on his heels.

Adam draped one arm about Bryce's shoulders and the other about Erik's. "Lean on me, brothers." He threw his head back and hollered, "Mass! Massimo! Where's my cousin?"

"You left him in Africa," Bryce told him.

"Yeah, I did, didn't I? Why would I do such a thing? I love my cousin."

"Oh my God," Kaya exclaimed as the men staggered off, arm in arm, into the vicinity of Bryce's man cave—a soundproof room adjoining the library. It was equipped with everything a man would ever need—poolroom, bowling lane, mini-golf course, a complete bar, and an audio and video wall system Kaya knew was worth more than she'd made in three years. Each man cave was similarly equipped, as if they were trying to out-do each other.

"Unbelievable, isn't it?" Libby said, as they began to gather the dishes from the table and take them into the kitchen. "They would go to hell and back for each other, though."

"And for any woman they choose to be by their sides," Michelle added. "Once they fall in love and marry, they become fiercely loyal and protective of their wives."

"Bryce doesn't love me," Kaya said as she placed a plate in the dishwasher. She felt she could be honest with these women— her closest, newest friends, her sister billionaire brides, she thought with a smile. "He only married me to make a home for the children." *And for sex.*

"I've known Bryce for a long time. He could have come up with a thousand other ways to keep you in the kid's lives. He married you because he sees the possibilities of a future with you, Kaya," Libby remarked over her shoulder as she scraped some scraps into the trash disposal.

"He may already be in love with you, but fighting it tooth and nail," Michelle said. "I was Precious' nanny before I became the second Mrs. LaCrosse, and believe me, Erik fought his feelings for me because he was afraid to get hurt again. It's probably the same way for Bryce. He wouldn't show you how scared he is because he's a macho man; they all are. They wouldn't even let their mommas know when they are in pain. You're Bryce's wife, Kaya. You're the only woman who has the power to heal him. You can do that by loving him and by caring for him in words and in deeds."

Kaya's hands curled around the edge of the sink. No one had ever taught her about love, much less how to love a man like Bryce Fontaine. The only men she was familiar with were the losers her mother used to bring home. They were charming in the beginning. They took her and Nadine out to nice restaurants and some even bought Kaya a gift or two here and there. But once they got enough of what they were truly after, they split.

After her father left, she'd watched her mother try time and time again to find true love, only to be disappointed. Nadine had taken out her frustrations on Kaya, and blamed her for the reasons her boyfriends didn't stick around.

Kaya's knowledge about sex was even more limited. The little she knew, she'd heard from Isis—a promiscuous foster sister. Isis equated sex with love, and Kaya had lain awake many nights, listening to Isis cry herself to sleep when yet another boyfriend had dumped her.

Her father's abandonment, coupled with her mother's and Isis' relationship experiences, had caused Kaya to steer clear of men. She'd allowed Jack to get close to her because he'd been a good childhood friend, someone she thought she could trust. Sadly, he'd grown up to become as much a loser as Nadine and Isis' men.

The two men she'd ever trusted had abandoned her. How was she supposed to trust another man, much less love one? Even though that man was her husband and had promised to love her, and be faithful to her.

They had exchanged their vows in the library, on Valentine's Day, just five days after Michael and Lauren's funeral. Pastor Kelly had pronounced them man and wife with the children and Haley as witnesses.

Bryce had taken the family to Andreas to celebrate afterwards. Jason was relieved that they wouldn't be fighting over him and his sisters, and Alyssa was excited that Uncle Bryce was going to live with them. Jason had told his sister that she and Bryce had gotten married so that they could all live together as a family. Kaya didn't bother to inform them that Uncle Bryce was not moving in. Bryce had made that clear before the nuptials, and Kaya still wasn't sure how she felt about it.

On their wedding night, after the children and Haley were in bed, Bryce had knocked on her door. She'd thought he'd come to say good night before he went to his penthouse, but when she'd opened the door, he'd pulled her possessively into his arms, and without a word had begun kissing her, and caressing her through her nightgown. His arousal was evident through the silk robe he wore. She'd been weakened by his strength and his clean, just-showered scent, but when he lifted her off the floor and took her to bed, Kaya had put a halt to his advances.

Her warped experiences and eyewitness accounts about men, along with Bryce's reputation with women had made it easy for her to say no to him. Bryce had promised not to abandon her. And perhaps he wouldn't, physically. But what about emotionally? What if after he made love to her, he lost interest in her? What if he started treating her differently? *Indifferently?* She couldn't risk that kind of awkwardness between them. It wouldn't be good for the children. "Bryce and I haven't made love yet," she said, turning to face the women.

They both dropped their gazes to the floor at her announcement.

Libby spoke first. "That's a good thing. It proves he doesn't see you as just a sexual object."

"It's not him." Kaya pushed a handful of curls from her face. "He wanted to make love on our wedding night, but I said no. I told him I was reluctant to consummate our marriage."

"Oh," both women uttered, understanding why Bryce called her his reluctant bride.

"I haven't had good relationships with men, and Bryce's prior reputation with women isn't a good one. He uses them then walks away when he's done."

"They meant nothing to him. That's why it was easy for him to walk. I'm not condoning what they do as men, but these women enter the relationships with their eyes wide open. They aren't innocent, so don't waste your time feeling sorry for them. They get what they want from these men. Bryce married you because he wants you, Kaya! And he's willing to wait until you're ready." Michelle tapped her on the shoulder.

Kaya crossed her arms about her stomach. "It may be too late. He's lost interest in me. He avoids being alone with me. I only see him when the kids are around." *Wasn't that your wish?* She centered her attention on her hands clasping and unclasping in front of her. "Bryce isn't the kind of man who gives up easily. I thought he'd be banging down my door every night until he broke down my defenses."

"Gosh, we do need this Billionaires' Brides Club." Michelle steered Kaya over to the kitchen table and sat her down. "If it was only sex he wanted, that's exactly what he'd be doing. When a man truly cares about a woman, the worst thing she could do to him is reject him."

"Michelle's right. Bryce has a lot of pride. You hurt him, and he wouldn't put himself in that position again. If you want this marriage to work, Kaya, you have to make the next move."

"Don't make it tonight," Michelle advised her. "He's too drunk to perform or to remember anything in the morning. You'll want him to remember every second of it."

"He isn't sleeping here anyway. Steven is driving him back to Hotel Andreas."

"What you need to do is plan a grand seduction. I have some books and videos I can loan you." Michelle's eyes twinkled mysteriously.

"Books and videos?" Kaya's voice raised an octave.

"They'll teach you how to seduce a man, how to make him beg. They want us to be ladies in the ballroom but nymphs in their beds. I didn't have a lot of experience when I met Erik but I quickly learned what he needed, expected from me—and believe me, I crave him every second of the day and night. I know you and Bryce will get there. And once you start, don't limit it to the bedroom. Erik and I make love in the most unusual places. You have to keep them guessing or they'll get bored."

"Steven and I joined the mile-high club on our way from the

Caribbean," Libby said with a demure smile. "It was amazing. Mmmm!"

Kaya blushed. She didn't know sweet Libby who sang in the church choir was so wanton. Seemed as if everybody in Granite Falls was having wild sex—except her and Bryce.

"I think we're overloading her." Libby waved a hand in front of Kaya's face.

"It's a bit overwhelming, but honestly, I'm just tired." She'd been cooking all day.

Michelle glanced at the clock on fridge. "It is late, and I do have that book signing in Manchester tomorrow." She hugged Kaya. "Tonight was awesome, Kaya, and I look forward to the next time when I can sample another delicious meal from your kitchen. Where did you learn to cook like that, anyway?"

"One of my…" Kaya let her voice trail off. Nobody in Granite Falls knew anything about her. If she told Michelle and Libby that one of her foster mothers had taught her to cook, they would start asking a lot of questions she wasn't ready to answer. "A family friend taught me. She was a caterer. Mrs. Hayes reminded me of her," she said with an affectionate smile.

"Well, we thank her," Libby said. "I think I put on ten pounds tonight." She patted her flat belly. "Five from that chocolate cake alone."

"I'm eating for two. So bring it on." Michelle rubbed her protruding stomach. "We have to get together more often without the men. Plan some play dates for the kids and some for us to take off in the company jets for a day. Have you been to the country club yet?" she asked as they walked toward the front door.

"No. I've been too busy with the kids."

"There's a masseuse there who gives the best massages in the world. I'll call you tomorrow and try to set up an appointment. You could probably use one after today."

"I like that idea." Kaya hugged and kissed her friends goodbye.

After their limos whisked them away, she realized that she was more scared now than she was before they came. She had no idea how to begin planning a seduction, but if what Michelle and Libby said were true, she would have to make the next move. She wanted her marriage to work, but what if she messed it up even more?

Disappointing Bryce in the bedroom posed a far greater threat to their marriage than not making love with him at all.

Maybe she should just let sleeping dogs lie.

Some time during the night, Kaya awakened to the sound of a deep-throated moan. Thinking it was Alyssa having a bad dream again, she turned to wake her up, but her hand landed on a ball of warm fur, instead.

Webster. Like Alyssa, he had the habit of crawling into her bed at nights. Everybody but Bryce seemed to want to share her bed. Well, to be fair, she'd told him he wasn't welcome in it.

It took a few moments to gather her thoughts. The children were at the LaCrosse's. She was alone in the house. Or was she? she wondered as she heard the moan again. She wasn't alarmed since *L'etoile du Nord* was equipped with a state-of-the-art security system that fed into one of Fontaine Enterprises security companies. Innumerable cameras and motion detectors lined the perimeter of the estate. An intruder would have better luck breaking into the White House than this house, Kaya thought, springing off the bed and across the floor to the open door.

If a man was groaning in her house tonight, she knew it had to be her husband. A tender smile spread her lips at the thought that Bryce cared enough about her not to leave her alone in this big house—drunk as he was.

"No…" The cry came from the third-floor master suite.

Half in anticipation, half in dread, Kaya raced down the corridor, bypassed the glass elevator, dashed through the family room, and flew up the flight of stairs to the third floor. She stood in the unfurnished living area of the master suite, and cocked her ears.

She heard it again—louder and more intense. It broke her heart. Kaya dashed off into the direction of the bedroom, and opened the door. There was no need to turn on the light. The glow from the fireplace illuminated the massive form of a man thrashing about wildly on an air mattress on the floor.

Kaya rushed to his side. "Bryce." His flannel shirt was soaked through with sweat and his body was trembling violently. "Bryce," she called again. She leaned over to tap him on his shoulder when he turned and knocked her off balance.

She landed on a massive wall of hard muscles. Steel arms wrapped about her, pressing her cheeks into the damp mat of hair exposed by the unfastened buttons of his shirt. Too stunned to move, Kaya willed her thumping heart to settle down, even as his drummed loudly beneath her ears.

He stopped thrashing, and the groans turned into an inaudible mutter. Realizing he was still somewhere on the threshold of sleep and wake, Kaya tried to ease out of his grasp. But he shifted on his side, bringing her with him.

She wriggled her nose and frowned. He didn't smell like a man who'd spent the night drinking with his friends. He smelled fresh and clean, and his breath held a hint of mint. Kaya smiled. He must have borrowed her toothpaste. The children's was strawberry flavored, and she knew Bryce would not have gone into Haley's room.

She was his wife and even though they had not consummated

their marriage, he still had certain spousal privileges. Having the right to enter her bedroom while she was asleep was one of them. She wondered if he'd stood by her bed and watched her sleep.

Kaya held her breath as Bryce exhaled deeply and burrowed into the duvet, his arms possessively locked around her upper body and one leg around her lower half as if it was the most natural way for them to fall asleep together. The feel of his steel arms and leg holding her prisoner sent Kaya's pulses pounding and her heart jolting. Her nightgown had ridden up just past her thighs and Kaya tried not to think about the weight of his semi-erection under his silk boxers lurking near the junction of her thighs. All she had to do was thrust her hips forward a few inches and their sexes would be connected. Her insides quivered at the thought.

You have to make the next move. Libby's warning rang in Kaya's ears. She swallowed as her fears began to mount. What if Bryce rejected her this time? And just in case he didn't, what if she couldn't please him?

The only two things Kaya knew how to do well were cook and decorate a home. She'd been complimented over and over again for demonstrating those skills. She'd excelled in those areas because someone had taken the time to teach them to her. She'd had no one to teach her about sex—most significantly how to please a man.

Your husband can teach you, an encouraging voice inside her head said. Michelle claimed she didn't have a lot of experience when she met Erik. Now it seemed they couldn't get enough of each other.

What if Bryce didn't have as much patience as Erik? Bryce was a busy man who ran a billion-dollar enterprise. He carried a huge weight on his shoulders, and he held the lives of millions of people in his hands. Every decision he made could either make or break his companies.

On several occasions, Kaya had listened to her former female clients talk about keeping their busy husbands and lovers interested in them. It seemed that sex was an outlet for those kinds of men. They expected their women to satisfy their needs, not the other way around.

What if she couldn't perform to Bryce's satisfaction and he grew bored with her inexperience? She couldn't risk that. She wanted Bryce to desire her.

Kaya sighed as she felt her skin begin to tingle and the ache between her legs increase. She wanted to be with Bryce so badly, to be crushed beneath him as he thrust deeply inside her. She wanted her husband incapable of keeping his hands off her. She wanted to fall asleep every night, and wake up in his arms every morning, just as she was now. Kaya wanted Bryce to remember every single moment of their first time together. The only way to ensure a memorable first time experience was to plan it. She was calling Michelle about those videos and books tomorrow.

In the meantime, there was nothing to do but wait for Bryce's grasp to relax after he drifted back to sleep. Then maybe she could sneak back to her room without him even knowing she was in his bed, in his arms. If he remembered anything at all, he'd think she was a dream.

There was no such luck, Kaya realized in a panic when his eyelids fluttered, then opened completely, giving her full view into his dark, stormy eyes. He stared at her in dazed confusion. Unspoken pain, mixed with some other indefinable emotion was alive and glowing in his questioning stare.

CHAPTER TWELVE

He was fully awake. She could feel the change in the tensing of his body. Uncertain of what to do, Kaya held her breath and merely stared back at him as the air around them became so charged, it crackled. She had trespassed into his private world. A world he allowed no one into. There would be consequences.

His gaze slid lazily to her mouth. He raised one hand and brushed his knuckles across her cheek, so lightly it sent shivers down her spine. The gold wedding band on his finger flashed in the firelight, reminding Kaya that she had the right to trespass. He rubbed the pad of his thumb across her lips as if testing their subtlety. The act was erotically simple.

Kaya swallowed, making a loud gulping sound. "You—you were hav— having a nightmare and—"

"Shh."

One hand at her neck and shoulders eased her closer. He took her face in the other and held it gently. While his fingers tangled in her messy curls, his thumb caressed her cheeks, her chin, the perimeter of her mouth. His eyes held hers captive as he hesitated, waiting for a sign of resistance.

He always gave her time to back out, except on their wedding night. She'd rejected him then. Was he waiting to spare himself another rejection? She wouldn't put him through that again, not after what Michelle and Libby had told her. She had to start taking care of her man like he was taking care of her.

Kaya touched his cheek, liking the feel of his early morning stubble and remembering how the tingling sensation had brought her to an orgasm before. She remembered thinking how awesomely tantalizing morning sex with him would be. She just didn't know that it would be their first time together.

Yes, Kaya realized with infinite clarity, she would make love with her husband. The time was right. No man had ever treated her as kindly and respectfully as Bryce. She trusted him, and she hoped that by giving herself completely to him, she would free his soul from the nightmares that plagued it.

Michelle had said that her love had healed Erik. Kaya hoped she could do the same for Bryce. For the first time since she'd learned of the second will that gave Bryce custody of the children, Kaya felt a measure of peace at the way Michael and Lauren had handled the situation.

Their tragedy had brought her into Bryce's life, and his nightmare had transported her to his bed. His generosity and patience proved that he was committed to this marriage and to her. He needed her to save him, just as much as she needed him to save her. Kaya didn't need videos and books to teach her how to love her husband. All she had to do was follow her heart.

With tears burning her eyes, Kaya held his gaze. "I'm ready, Bryce," she said, the very words creating a pressing need in the deepest recess of her womb. "I'm not reluctant anymore. I'm sorry for making you wait. I'm yours if you want—"

Her apology was absolved in the tender warmth of his kiss. A kiss filled with heartaches, regrets, and unfulfilled promises that were made long, long ago, and a definite yearning to be rescued from the pain.

He wrapped his arms about her lithe body and cradled her to his chest as if she were a delicate porcelain rose, and he were afraid she would slip from his grasp and be lost forever. His lips moved slowly over hers, testing her softness. His tongue gently probed hers, tasting her sweetness. He made no effort for deep penetration, but instead seemed to be absolutely content with exploring the outer regions and fleshy entrance of her mouth.

When Bryce had kissed her like this with Haley lurking nearby, she'd had to curtail her response to him. They were alone in the house tonight. No Haley. No kids. She could scream as loudly as she wanted, and no one would hear her.

The unhurried exploratory rumba of his mouth and tongue sent shockwave after shockwave rumbling through Kaya. As his mouth lavished hers, his hands began a steady path down the unexplored slopes of her body. He caressed her shoulders, the gentle curve of her back, the swell of her hips, the flat surface of her belly, and finally came to rest on the firm rise of her buttocks where he shaped and molded her like a potter shapes clay. The area between her thighs pulsed with a life of its own, and her swollen breasts and pebbled nipples, crushed against his chest, cried out for release.

She wanted something, but had no idea what it was. This man she'd married was taking his time to explore all her pleasure points with his hands and mouth, bringing her into full awareness and acceptance of her own sexuality.

She thrust her hips forward, connecting their groins together. He kept her there with a sure hand plastered on her buttocks. She began to move against him, the sound of their erratic breathing and symphony of erotic moans, heavy in the air.

The thrill of his erection grazing the sensitive button at the head of her womanhood and the exquisite sensation of Bryce's tongue gliding across the inner region of her upper lips sent Kaya into a dizzying tailspin. She had no idea that area was so sensitive, so erogenous.

The familiar shivers of surrender began in the lower region of her belly and spread outward, growing hotter and wilder with their simulated mating act.

Kaya dug her nails into Bryce's chest and screamed his name down his throat when the powerful wave of surrender crashed over her.

He groaned deep in his throat and lifted her, turned on his back, and settled her on top of him. "Sweet baby," he whispered, and held her until she stopped shivering.

His chest rose and fell beneath her cheeks as they both struggled for air.

He hadn't even come. That was just foreplay.

Fire crackled in the air, illuminating the giant rock and wedding band on her finger.

Kaya's old fears, along with some new ones, raised their ugly heads again. She had to tell Bryce. She lifted her head from his chest and stared down into his face. The only emotion she saw in his eyes was passion. Gone were the fear and the pain she'd stumbled upon when she'd awaken him from his nightmare. She was happy she could do that for him. "Bryce. I have to tell you some—"

"I know, Kaya. I don't care. I don't want to talk about it. I don't want to talk about anything. I just want to make love to my wife."

Before Kaya could analyze exactly what he meant by "I don't care", he sat up with her straddled across his waist and pulled off his shirt, tossing it across the empty room. Kaya whimpered when his fingers grazed her thighs before curling around the hem of her nightgown. Without being told, she raised her hands. He pulled it over her head and tossed it next to his shirt.

He expelled a loud breath when his eyes landed on her breasts, standing proud and high as if waiting for inspection. The glow from the fire danced over their naked torsos, and Kaya knew she made an erotic picture for him. It made her toes curl.

"Beautiful," he said, reaching for her.

Kaya sighed and arched her back when his hands closed over her breasts, and he began to massage and mold them—again in the most tender manner as if they would crumble if he pressed too hard. His gentleness, and the thought that he was taking his time to show her how much he cherished her, melted Kaya's heart. She need not fear his size and his strength. He would never hurt her.

Kaya clutched his shoulders as he bent his head to her chest. His lips feather-touched her with tantalizing persuasion as he lavished attention on one nipple—kissing, licking, kissing, licking—for a few heart-stopping moments before opening his wide mouth and taking all he could of her swollen breast into it.

Kaya threw her head back and moaned as her body responded to the demands of his rapacious mouth. Her breasts had never been treated this way, and they were just as captivatingly shocked as she was.

Seated on Bryce's groin, Kaya was acutely aware of the ridge of his sex tucked tightly between the cheeks of her buttocks and the cleft of her love nest. His heat burned through their underwear, soaked with the juices that had poured from her body.

Delirious with desire Kaya dug her fingers into Bryce's shoulders and began riding his erection. She fantasized even a deeper ecstasy as pleasure ripped through her body. When she thought she would explode, he stopped his suckling and kissed his way across the valley of her mounts to the other breast. He gave her time to come down with him, but before she hit bottom, he repeated the erotic cycle by treating this breast with the same devotion he'd treated the other, and when he'd licked and kissed her nipple into confusion, he sucked her into his mouth again.

Kaya found herself walking the same tightrope of desire as a few moments before. This time the intensity increased as Bryce continued to suckle at her tender breast. An intangible cord of electricity ran from her breasts to the vibrating spot between her thighs.

She bucked harder, as Bryce sucked harder. She felt his hand in the hollow of her back as he began to thrust up against her, causing the pleasure to mount inside her. His hands spanned her waist and he moved her up and down, around and around the ridge of his sex as his mouth swooped from one breast to the next like a butterfly that couldn't decide which petal housed the sweetest nectar.

"Come for me, my little sexy wife. Come," he whispered around her nipple.

Kaya raked her nails across his back and shoulders and as she felt herself crashing on ecstasy's shore. Damp and weak, she collapsed against Bryce.

With a triumphant shout, he fell back onto the duvet, pulling her along with him. He wrapped his arms about her and kissed the top of her head. Kaya fought to regain her breath and stop the quakes that continued to rumble through her. This orgasm was a lot stronger than the first one. And they hadn't made love. Her husband was a dangerously skillful man.

No wonder women let him have them with no promise of forever.

"You're beautiful when you come. I should capture you on video so I can watch you over and over again," he said, lifting her head and pushing her damp curls away from her face.

"Don't you dare." She slapped his arm.

"I dare. I double dare," he said with a chuckle. "Did you enjoy that? Those?"

Kaya nodded.

"Want some more?"

She nodded again, this time smiling with anticipation. "I want to pleasure you." She trailed her finger along the contours of his lips then leaned in and kissed him softly as a whisper.

"Hmm." He shook his head. "This is all about you, darling. Tonight's yours. I get pleasure just giving you pleasure. Take off your panties," he ordered, gazing into her eyes.

That one little command sent Kaya's heart racing to the ceiling. With their eyes locked, she reached down and hooked her thumbs into the waist of her panties. She squirmed around on Bryce's huge frame as she wrestled them off and kicked them aside.

His erection throbbed against her wet nakedness with excitement.

"Now my boxers."

Kaya's breasts swelled with desire and her nipples tingled against the hairs on Bryce's chest as she once again reached down to rid him of the last strip of barrier between them. Again, she marveled that she felt no fear of him. She wriggled off his underwear, loving the hard feel of his thighs against her fingers. When she got them around his knees, he waggled around and kicked them off.

Kaya swallowed and shivered as she felt the smooth hot length of him graze her thighs. He was huge, a lot bigger than she'd imagined any man could be. Fear gripped her again. "Bryce—"

"Don't be afraid," he said. "I wouldn't hurt you. I don't want you to do anything but relax and enjoy. Concentrate on your pleasure. Like I said, this is all about you, Kaya."

Somehow his words soothed her. He said he knew. She didn't know how, but she would trust him not to hurt her.

He smiled, lifted her off of him, and placed her on her back.

He immediately bent over her, blocking her view of his lower half. He planted his elbows and knees on each side of her and thus supported his weight.

"You're beautiful," he said, then raised her hands above her head and placed them on the duvet. "Keep them there or I'll tie them together. Now, close your eyes. No peeking. Good. Breathe, slowly and deeply."

Like a child eager to please her superior, Kaya obeyed his temperate commands.

Kaya took a quick intake of air into her lungs as Bryce began dropping a series of butterfly kisses on her forehead, her cheeks, her nose, her chin, and lips. He lingered at her mouth, nibbling, tasting, probing. His hands caressed her face, her shoulders, her breasts as his mouth made a slow trail south along her collarbone, her neck, her throat and down the length of her body. He kissed his way up the mound of one breast, played with the nipple with his tongue and teeth, until she writhed and moaned, then he kissed his way down to the valley and up the other mound, licking, nibbling, kissing.

His hands, sure and steady followed in the wake of his lips. He used his fingertips, his knuckles, his palms to soothe and caress the tingling places where his stubble had grazed. Kaya never dreamed his hands would feel so warm so gentle on her skin. His lips fluttered across the sides of her torso, her stomach, and his tongue dipped into the hollow of her belly button, sending ripples of delight through her. Hypnotized by his touch, her body began to vibrate with liquid fire.

She whispered his name, over and over again as she writhed beneath him.

He groaned in response but was not deterred from searing his blazing trail of desire upon her defenseless flesh. He kissed his way down her thighs to the soles of her feet where he clapped them together and gave her toes a sensuous tongue-lashing. She curled them inside his mouth as her body shattered on yet another orgasm. She never knew the underside of her toes was such a powerful erogenous zone.

As he worked his way back up her legs to her thighs, Kaya reveled in the purely sensual experience of the time her husband took to enjoy every inch of her body. She never dreamed making love with him would be like this. If she'd known, she would never have banned him from her bed.

Kaya's back arched when the stubbles on his chin grazed the tender waxed area of her groin, causing a new and unexpected kind of sensation to throb through her. Her eyes flew opened to encounter his dark passionate gaze.

"I said no peeking," he warned, pressing his chin into her groin and tightening his hands around her breasts. "Close them. Keep them closed this time or I will stop pleasuring you. Do you want me to stop pleasuring you, Kaya?"

She shook her head. "No. No. I like it." She whimpered and closed her eyes.

"Good girl." Bryce waited a few moments before he resumed the sweet torturing of his wife.

Kaya gasped when the tip of Bryce's tongue made contact with the slick folds of her womanhood. He teased her as lightly and steadily as he'd teased her mouth. Her husband was a master at using his tongue to rouse the hottest desires from her. Kaya tried to close her thighs against the deepening pleasure, but he spread them apart, bent her knees, and placed her feet on the mattress. He looped his arms under her thighs and settled himself comfortably between them as if he were about to enjoy a luscious feast.

He played with her swollen folds, pressing them together between his fingers and molding them into a pout. Kaya clasped her hand over her mouth to muffle the feral scream as Bryce dropped hot feather kisses on her wet flesh. With the flat of his tongue, he massaged her with long, sure strokes from one end of her pleasure cave to the other. She felt her inner muscles contracting and convulsing as another orgasm threatened to claim her.

He groaned and let her gently down. She felt his fingers parting her this time. His sharp intake of breath resonated around the empty room as she assumed he was now inspecting the inner regions of her most secret place.

"Lovely," he whispered and lowered his head again.

He thumbed her clitoris as his tongue probed around the entrance to her body. Fire leaped through Kaya's veins and passion radiated from the soft core of her body as Bryce teased her mercilessly, pushing his tongue deeper and deeper inside of her. She wanted to reach down and grab his head, keep his mouth locked to her forever, but he'd ordered her not to move, or he would stop. She didn't want him to stop.

Her senses spun in a surge of scorching bliss. Her fists curved around the duvet and she pulled hard in an effort to stay grounded. Her body arched off the bed as an electrified coil of ecstasy wrapped around her. She felt Bryce's hand on her belly, holding her down as the passion exploded inside her. She screamed his name—long and hard.

He answered with a chuckle and lapped up her hot juices. He kissed the insides of her thighs until she lay sated against the mattress.

Moments later, she felt the hard length of him press into her softness where she burned from his assault. He bent over her, his face close to hers. He smelled of her—musky and stimulating. His lips closed around hers, and his tongue sought entrance into her mouth. For endless moments, their tongues twirled around each other in a dreamy, intimate kiss.

When her heartbeat settled down to its normal pace, he

withdrew. "You can open your eyes now," he whispered in her ear.

Kaya's lashes fluttered open.

"Can you take another one?" he asked, a sexy smile spread across his lips.

"I don't know," she answered truthfully.

"Come on. I haven't put the cream on the pudding yet." He moved his hips so the ridge of his sex skimmed across her slick lips. "Don't you want me inside you?"

She nodded on a frantic swallow.

"I want to hear you say it. Say 'Bryce, my darling husband, I want to feel you moving deep inside me.'"

Kaya quivered as he grazed her again. "Bryce, my darling husband, I want to feel you moving deep inside me."

"Oh, how can I ever refuse such a tantalizing request? Wrap your arms and legs around me, darling. I'm taking your for a ride," he said, reaching down between them.

Kaya stiffened when the broad head probed her, parting her slightly, and hovered at the entrance of her body. Their eyes caught and held. He smiled as he used his hand to slide the tip around her opening then upwards towards her swollen little knob and back down again. He repeated the act over and over again, toying with her, raising her awareness of him, her desire for him.

Something unlocked inside Kaya's heart when she read the heat and the passion buried in the stormy depth of her husband's eyes. She was acutely aware of a burning, swelling, intensely thrilling sensation she'd never experienced before. She wanted to cry and laugh and jump for joy, but her breath solidifying in her throat kept her paralyzed.

She loved her husband.

She loved him.

She was genuinely, giddily in love with him.

Perhaps she'd known for weeks, but she'd been reluctant to

admit the truth to herself. And why wouldn't she fall in love with him? He'd been there for her and the children from the very first day. He'd provided her with everything she needed—a new SUV for the family and a sports car for her personal travel pleasure, an elaborate wardrobe, and license to do whatever she wanted to the house. He'd paid off the lease on her apartment in Palm Beach and had her personal items and her collection of houseplants shipped to Granite Falls.

The day before they were married, he'd added her name to his personal bank account and given her a debit card. Kaya had millions of dollars at her disposal even before she became Mrs. Bryce Fontaine.

He took Jason to school most mornings, and when he couldn't, he sent a car around so she didn't have to face the cold. He'd canceled important meetings to attend Alyssa's dance recital, Jason's karate competition, and accompany Kaya to the hospital when Anastasia was running a fever.

He made sure the pantry and refrigerator were always stocked, and he made it his business to be home for dinner with her and the kids almost every night, during which times they would talk about everything—from Anastasia's first smile to business operations at Fontaine Enterprises. But after the kids were in bed, no matter the time, he would always leave. His nightmares must have driven him away.

Bryce never wavered in his commitment to his family. He was always there, except for church. He left that up to Kaya, and she'd been faithful in keeping that part of the children's lives intact. Perhaps if she demonstrated her love for Bryce, showed him that he was worthy of love, he'd begin attending church again.

Bryce had demonstrated that he trusted her. It was time she trusted him.

Tears welled in Kaya's eyes and a fervent need to love him,

satisfy him, filled her to overflowing. She had waited twenty-three years for tonight, for this carnal act of possession by the man she loved and married. Anxious to welcome him into her body, Kaya raised her hips as the tip of his sex brushed her entrance.

"Easy," he said, dropping a kiss on her forehead. "I'm very large and you're very tiny."

His ardor was surprisingly, touchingly restrained, and she loved him the more for it.

"I want you."

He groaned and thrust gently, testing her tightness. Kaya's eyes widened in fear as the broad tip stretched her opening, gaining more ground at each attempt to enter her. Her muscles screamed from the invasive pain. He pulled back, pushing a bit farther this time, but still with a measure of gentleness. Kaya tightened her limbs about him, digging her heels into his buttocks and raising her hips to meet his next temperate lunge.

The head gained entrance. She moaned and closed her eyes to absorb the pain.

His arms wrapped around her, his large hands spread across her back, cradling her curves into his own contours. "So tiny. So tight. Wet. Hot. Exquisite," he whispered before covering her mouth with his. His hips recoiled and he thrust with renewed force, pushing deeper into her.

Kaya stiffened in shock as she felt Bryce pierced the thin barrier of her hymen. Hot pangs of pain singed through her. Tears stung her eyes. Her mouth opened in a scream. He swallowed it up in his.

"Damn it!" His body froze above her. He kept his hips stilled, locking them groin to groin. He raised himself up on his elbows, gasping for control.

She opened her eyes to encounter the frown on his face.

"You little fool. You're a virgin."

"Not anymore." Despite the pain zapping through her lower

body, Kaya managed a trembling smile. He was hard and hot and heavy inside her, burning, stretching, filling.

"I could have hurt you." He bend down and kissed the tears from her eyes.

"You did hurt me, Bryce. You would have hurt me even if I wasn't a virgin. Anyway, you said you knew."

"I knew what?" His frown deepened.

"I tried to tell you twice tonight, but you said you knew. What did you think I was going to tell you?"

"Not that. Definitely not that. It doesn't matter anymore." His body shook on a laugh, and it caused him to burrow deeper into her, sending a needy tremor to the deepest part of her being. Miraculously, the pain began to subside as her muscles convulsed around him and her body opened and conformed to his enormous size.

Like an awakened, lust-filled nymph, Kaya spread her thighs wider and higher, twisting her hips to snuggle closer to him, wanting to feel him move deeper into her where he belonged. She was so happy she'd waited for Bryce. She'd given him something she could never give another man.

"Don't move, Kaya," he warned in a gruff voice.

But it was too late. Kaya squeezed her muscles around him and felt him pulse in response. She smiled when his eyes turned in their sockets, elated that she had the power to make him lose control.

A passionate madness seemed to overtake him. He groaned, shifting to rest his chest against her breasts and bear his weight on his knees. He began a steady dance of his hips, moving inside her with gentleness that made her heart fill with love and anguish. He reached down and cupped her buttock, coaxing her into the rhythm of his thrusts until together they found the tempo that bound their bodies together.

Waves of ecstasy throbbed through Kaya as Bryce's thrusts

grew stronger and deeper. Yet she knew he was holding back for fear of hurting her. She wanted him to relinquish his control. For weeks he'd been sharing his mind, professional life with her. Tonight he was sharing his body. And she wanted all of him—his arrogance, his dominance, his ego, his uninhibited passion…

"Bryce, please, harder. Deeper," she moaned, unable to control the fire and the love edging though her veins.

How could love be this violently tumultuous, yet purely tender emotion all at the same time? She wanted to dangle on the precipice of pleasure as she'd done three times tonight. She wanted Bryce there with her when the fury of his passion hurled her into the sweet melting haven of delight.

She clung to his shoulders and raised her head, pressing her lips to his damp chest, bucking wildly under him, meeting him thrust for feverish thrust. It was flesh against flesh, man against woman, rushing into an explosive fume of lust as time hung suspended around them. Kaya teetered on the edge as the room began to spin around her. She was losing control. "Bryce." Tears stung her eyes and drizzled from the corners.

"Oh, my sweet wife," Bryce groaned. He caught her arms and crisscrossed them above her head. Their wedding bands joined with a soft click as he laced his fingers with hers and pinned their clasped hands to the mattress.

Moonlight and firelight bathed the tortured contours of his passion-filled face.

He slowly withdrew to her opening then slammed into her, harder and deeper than he'd done before. He rotated his hips in a circular motion against hers, magnifying the wet friction of their mating dance. A pearl of sweat dripped from his chin unto her chest. The room began to spin around her. Kaya's eyes closed and her mouth opened in a silent scream as he withdrew slowly again, then plunged into her, so deeply he moved the air mattress a couple of feet along the cherry floor.

Her back arched. A new flood of tears stung her eyes. Her heart rumbled in her ears.

On the third thrust, he let out a furious roar and collapsed on top of her, his body convulsing violently, his hips pumping wildly in the throes of his orgasm.

Those final thrusts sent spasms of ecstasy humming from Kaya's heart to her toes. Her thighs and legs shook violently around his waist; her toes curled and her fingers tightened around his to the point of pain. Her body constricted as taut as a bowstring as her wet flesh parted on his final thrust, then closed around him, sucking him into her, gripping him, holding him cozily and deeply inside until her heart and body exploded into a kaleidoscope of blinding heat just as he flooded her womb with the hot liquid of his release.

Harsh sounds erupted from them as they lay in a tangled, convulsing web of wet exhaustion, panting for air.

A long while later, Kaya kissed the side of Bryce's head resting on the mattress close to her cheek. So this was what it was all about. No books or videos could have prepared her for this exquisite liberation of her body, mind, and spirit. She was completely satiated, yet oddly hungry for more of him.

The cream was on the pudding. More precisely, inside it.

Kaya tightened her arms about Bryce's drenched body and ran her fingers down the slick muscles of his back. He was a heavy man, but she loved the feel of his weight on her, the rapid, yet soothing thud of his heart against hers. It was the only way she could ever carry him.

He made a sound deep in his throat when her muscles contracted around him. Even though he'd decreased in size, it still stretched and filled her to completion.

Kaya gazed out the wall of windows. A full moon was peeking its way through the line of pine trees that bordered the lake. In a few hours she would have to leave this bed and return to life as it was before. But for now, she would enjoy this new experience of the aftermath of lovemaking.

She started when Bryce rolled over on his back and pulled her on top of him without breaking the union of their sexes. He sat up briefly, searched around for the tangled duvet, and yanked it up and over them.

He kissed her forehead and settled back down. "You okay?" he asked, stroking his hands down the length of her body.

"Perfect."

"I didn't hurt you too much?"

"You were as gentle and patient as a man could possibly be in this situation. I thoroughly enjoyed every second of it. What about you?" she dared to ask. "Did you enjoy every second of it?"

"Oh, God, yes. You're a very sensual woman, Kaya Fontaine, highly charged. I just have to touch you and you begin to tremble, kiss you and you come all over yourself and me," he said with a soft chuckle.

Kaya shivered at the tender feel of his hands on her body. Her skin loved his hands. "I guess that's a good thing?"

"The best. It's been a very long time since I made love like this, Kaya. Years, actually," he added with a hint of desolation in his voice. "I know you worry about the women I've been with over the past few years. Don't, my darling. With them, it was just sex, and it was always extremely basic. I never pleasured any of them the way I pleasured you tonight."

"Well, you do have some special skills."

He chuckled. "I only use them on special women. You satisfy me, you complete me in a way I never expected to be satisfied and completed again."

He didn't have to say it, but Kaya knew he was referring to his time with Pilar. She wasn't jealous of the woman, just sad that Bryce had to go through the horrible experience of her death. She was grateful he felt comfortable enough to be honest with her. "I didn't expect this tonight," she said on a lighter note. "You were supposed to be drunk and stupid and back at your penthouse. But here you are sober, satiated, and in my arms."

"Maybe I was a little stupid for calling you out in front of our friends. I'm sorry for that." He squeezed her. "I was just wound very tightly with my need for you, for this."

"It's okay," Kaya said. If he hadn't called her out, Michelle and Libby wouldn't have given her advice about making the next move, and she wouldn't be in his arms right now. "I have no regrets. But you seemed quite drunk when you left the table, yet you definitely have your wits about you."

He chuckled again. "I was just putting on a show for the others. I'd decided to stay here before the evening began."

"Why?"

"I didn't want to leave you here alone, and since this is Alyssa's first night away from home, I wanted to be here in case she woke up crying for you during the night. I told Michelle to call my cell if she did. I would have gone to bring her home." He stroked his hand down her hair, playing with the tendrils, spreading them over his chest.

Tears escaped from the corners of Kaya's eyes and melted into the hairs on his chest. No wonder she loved this man. He was thoughtful to his core. He risked her hearing his nightmare to make sure she was safe and that Alyssa was taken care of.

In Kaya's eyes, Bryce Fontaine was a true hero. But sometimes heroes were just as lonely, vulnerable, and scared as the people they protected. Sometimes, heroes needed someone to rescue them. She wanted so much to ask him about the scene she'd walked in on, but knew this wasn't the time.

They'd just shared something wonderfully new and present; she didn't want to bring his shattering old past into it. "I'm glad you stayed, Bryce." She pressed her lips into his chest.

"Me too." He cradled her face in his hands and raised her

head. He rubbed his thumbs across her cheeks, wiping at a lingering tear. "Thank you for this unexpected, beautiful gift," he said, his eyes intent as they bore into her very soul. "I could never have hoped for anything so precious. I cherish you and our vows even more now. I hope you believe that."

Before Kaya could respond, he kissed her lips softly then placed her head tenderly back on his chest. "Sleep now," he murmured, wrapping his arms possessively and protectively about her. "You must be exhausted."

Moments later, his breathing grew calmer and, finally asleep, he slipped softly from inside her. Her body missed him terribly, but her senses were filled with the smell of sex and love. He would have no other nightmares tonight.

A smile spread across Kaya's face as she surrendered to the thick blanket of fatigue hovering over her. She didn't know making love was such hard work. But it was a leisure in which she looked forward to indulging herself over and over again.

"I love you, Bryce," she whispered into the night, as her eyelids fluttered shut.

CHAPTER THIRTEEN

Bryce awoke to the soft, warm body of his wife tucked securely against him, the tempting swell of her buttocks pressed into his stomach, his morning erection trapped between their tangled thighs, and the aromatic aftermath of a long night of passion wafting up his nostrils.

He remained quiet and motionless, savoring the simple delight of awakening with a woman—*his woman*, in his arms.

He hadn't had that for some time. Not since Pilar.

He'd had sex with many women over the past few years, but he'd never *slept* with one. He'd always been anxious to leave their beds when his lust was slaked.

Things changed for him last night. When he'd made the decision to sleep at *L'etoile du Nord*, he'd had no idea he'd be making love with Kaya, but once she was in his bed, there was no turning back. Once it was over, he'd honestly intended to steal away from the bed and the house after she fell asleep. But some unknown force had kept him grounded.

His wings had been clipped, and he didn't mind one damn bit. He'd finally found a cozy nest that made him feel at home, that offered him warmth from the cold, shelter from the storms of his life.

Only now he realized how much he missed this intimacy of lazing around in bed the morning after a night of passion, of making love in front of the fireplace while snow or rainstorms raged outside. He missed the simple pleasure of going into the office with a smile on his face, knowing his woman was waiting at home for him at the end of the day.

Bryce sighed deeply and tightened his arms about Kaya, grateful that their time of separation had come to an amazing end. He'd so wanted to spare her from the speculations surrounding their marriage he knew were fueled by his continued residency at Hotel Andreas. He'd wanted to move into *L'etoile du Nord* after they were married, but he couldn't when his nightmares had been resurrected and were still so fresh. He wasn't ready to discuss Pilar with his new wife. He couldn't bear Kaya's pity or her sympathy.

But as fate would have it, she offered him neither of those emotions. Instead, she gave him love in the purest, most innocent and passionate form.

She must have been curious about his nightmares and his screams ringing through the night, yet she'd asked no questions. He was certain she knew he'd been dreaming about Pilar, the wife he still loved, yet she hadn't turned away from him. She'd loved him instead.

I love you, Bryce.

Bryce closed his eyes and opened his heart as the whisper of those four little words caressed his tormented soul.

Kaya loved him.

Her declaration had reverberated through him again and again long after she was asleep.

Her love had kept his nightmares away at least for the rest of the night. He'd never been able to fall back to sleep after being jarred awake. But he had last night. Kaya had calmed him.

Bryce's mind reeled from the pleasure of his serendipitous discovery. Of all the things he could have imagined Kaya to be, a virgin was not one of them. He'd tried to go slowly then, but once he'd been sheathed inside her tight heat and felt her velvet muscles contracting around him, he'd lost all control.

Bryce gritted his teeth. That jerk of her ex-boyfriend had lied to him. If he ever laid eyes on that worm again, Bryce swore he'd choke the life out of him. He was so happy Kaya had had enough sense not to let that weasel touch her. She would never know what he'd witnessed in her apartment the night he'd flown down to Florida to confront Jack. The thought of it still made his blood curdle.

Even before he'd returned home or knew that there was a second will that gave him custody of the children, Bryce had decided to marry Kaya in order to keep her in Granite Falls, far away from Jack. He was determined to bring her under the protection of his house and his name. After what happened to Pilar, no one would dare question his motives when it came to protecting his wife.

Bryce held his breath as Kaya turned completely around in his arms.

He gazed down at her delicate face bathed in the early morning sunlight streaming through the glass wall. She was so beautiful, and she was his. He kissed her forehead and stoked his hand down her back.

"Hmm," she murmured, and snuggled closer to him.

He bent his head and kissed her lips.

Her eyelids fluttered open, and her chocolate eyes peeked up at him.

"Hey, you," he said, smiling at her.

"Hey." She seemed confused for a moment then color rose to

her cheeks when his erection brushed the insides of her thighs. Her lashes crash-landed and her chin dropped to her chest.

"Oh, no," Bryce said, hooking a finger under her chin and raising her face. "You don't get to play coy, Mrs. Fontaine. Not after the night we just shared. You practically seduced me."

"I seduced you?" She was immediately on the defense. "The way I remember is you had a nightmare. I came to wake you up. You knocked me over. Held me prisoner in your arms. Made me take my panties and your boxers off, and had your way with me. I didn't seduce you, Mr. Fontaine. You seduced me."

"Oh yeah, you're right. I did do that, didn't I? I'm sorry. Wouldn't happen again."

"I'm sure you are. And it better happen again." She socked him playfully.

"Ouch," he uttered on a laugh. He captured her hand and flattened her palm against his chest. Compared to him, she was so small. His protective instincts mounted inside him. He caught her other hand and laced his fingers with hers, their wedding bands fusing together like their bodies had fused last night. He wondered if she remembered saying she loved him, or if she knew he'd heard her.

Bryce had declared his love for only one woman in his lifetime, and he'd been unequivocally certain when he'd spoken the words. He cared about Kaya; he enjoyed being around her, and now with her, but he didn't know if he loved her. He'd closed his heart to love and bared it to lust for so long that he'd forgotten what love felt like.

"I was dreaming about Pilar when you woke me last night," he said, feeling it was time his current wife knew about his late wife. Maybe opening up to Kaya would help clear the cobwebs from his mind. "I was dreaming about the night she died."

"I know." She squeezed his hand. "Do you have the nightmares often?"

Bryce gave the room a swift sweep of his eyes. It was the one floor of the house he never had the heart to finish after Pilar died. This is the place where they would have fallen asleep each night and awakened each morning locked in each other's arms, just the way he was locked with Kaya right now.

He took a moment to let that awareness sink into his brain. It wasn't as troubling as he'd expected, but surprisingly comforting instead.

"You don't have to talk about it," Kaya said.

"I want to," he responded, realizing she'd taken his silence as hesitation to talk about Pilar. "One of the reasons I don't live in this house is because it reminds me of Pilar."

"You used to live here together?"

"No." He took a sharp intake of air into his lungs. "We spent countless hours, days, weeks, planning this house, our dream home where we would raise our children. Pilar died shortly after we broke ground. It was just too painful being here on the site so I just walked away with no intention of ever finishing it. But then I realized that it wasn't just the site of our home that brought about the raw aching pain in my gut, the crushing heaviness in my chest. I hurt when I did the things we did together, visited places we'd gone as a couple."

"Like church?"

"Especially church. Music was Pilar's passion. She played the piano, the harp, and the violin, and she composed songs. We used to sing together, you know."

Her eyes caressed him, undressed his soul. "Libby told me. We sing her songs in worship service. Such beautiful lyrics and music. Did she write the lullaby you sang to Anastasia that day we met?"

He nodded. "It was the last song she wrote." He'd found the sheet of music on the dining table. Pilar must have been working on it when Victoria arrived at their mountain villa.

"What happened, Bryce?" Kaya's voice was a choked whisper, barely audible above the hammering of his heart in his ears.

"Pilar thought I'd been unfaithful to her."

"You, unfaithful? Why would she think something so absurd?"

Bryce frowned as he studied Kaya's face.

Well, were you? was the question everyone had asked, including his parents and his minister. He even had to defend himself to Pilar as she lay dying in his arms.

The trust he read in Kaya's eyes told him that she didn't doubt him for one fleeting moment. No one had ever had such unquestionable faith in him. Except his grandmother. She wouldn't have doubted him, either.

Bryce took another deep breath. "There was this woman, Victoria. She was my personal assistant. She was a hard worker, extremely intelligent. Never too tired or too busy to do anything I asked. We spent a lot of late nights working, sometimes over dinner. We were getting along well—professionally, I thought."

"But she wanted more," an insightful Kaya murmured.

"I didn't know that until I brought Pilar to Granite Falls."

"She wasn't from here?"

"No. I met her in a hotel elevator in Chicago while I was there on a business trip." He smiled with the memory. "She was crying because she'd just been turned down for an audition she'd had all her hopes set on." He held Kaya's gaze. "Well, you know the rest."

"It was love at first sight." She dropped her gaze so he couldn't read the expression in her eyes.

Bryce had felt an intense connection with Kaya when he'd met her in Steven's office two months ago. It *was* possible for one to fall madly and deeply in love more than once in a lifetime. But there were too many other issues going on at the time for him to analyze those feelings. There was still a lot to be sorted out between them. He was old enough and wise enough to know that sex wasn't some magical pill that fixed troubled relationships. He and Kaya were troubled. Their marriage was not built on trust and love.

"Anyway, Victoria's attitude to me changed after Pilar and I were married," he continued. "She was very professional when we were in public, but cold and calculating when we were alone. She called my home at odd hours of the night to ask silly questions. I had our number changed. But when she left a naked photo of herself on my desk, I fired her."

"And that made her mad."

Bryce nodded, wishing for the millionth time that he'd seen how deranged that woman was. "She threatened to sue me for sexual harassment if I didn't pay her a substantial amount of money. I told her to go right ahead. You see, my logic was that paying her off would make me appear guilty of her accusations. I wasn't about to let her defame my name and malign my reputation. What I didn't know at the time was that she'd befriended Pilar behind my back. They'd been having lunch together, gone shopping together, and whatever else women do together. Pilar was lonely; she had no friends here, so it was easy for Victoria to ingratiate herself into her life, become her best friend, her confidant."

Bryce thought he'd been enough for Pilar, but he'd been so wrong. Women need women, just as men need men as friends. Victoria was the catalyst for the creation of the Billionaires' Brides Club. He and his friends realized the importance for their future wives to be as close as they were. He was glad Kaya was getting along with Michelle and Libby, two women he knew would never hurt her.

"Go on," Kaya whispered, bringing him back to the present.

He breathed deeply. "A few days after I fired Victoria, Pilar called me at the office and asked me to hurry home because she had wonderful news for me." The blood began to pound in his veins. His hands tightened around Kaya's. "When I walked into our home, Victoria was holding a gun to my wife's head."

"Oh, Bryce." Kaya pulled her hands from his grasp and wrapped her arms about him, holding him close to her heart.

"I tried to reason with her at first, then I began taunting her to make her angry at me. It worked. She let Pilar go and aimed the gun at me. I implored Pilar with my eyes to get out of there. I would have taken a thousand bullets for her." Tears streamed down his face, and melted into Kaya's hair.

"As Pilar inched toward the door, Victoria started talking about she and I making love together. I heard Pilar gasp just before she knocked over a table laden with crystal ornaments. The shattering glass startled Victoria. She fired toward the noise. I watched in horror as Pilar fell to the floor, her blood pouring from her body in a thick, crimson stream. That's when I begin to scream in my sleep, like I did that night."

"Oh, Bryce." Kaya's voice broke as she began to shiver in his arms.

Bryce wrapped his hands around her, his sobs echoing hers. His friends and family had cried over Pilar's death; they'd cried for his loss, but no one had cried for his pain, for the years of torment he'd endured, until this very moment.

Kaya was the soothing salve in the aching wound of his heart.

Last night he'd been reminded of what it felt like to make love to a woman he cared deeply about. This morning he was reminded of what it felt like to have a woman care about him. Amazing, what the comforting touch of a woman could do for a man.

"I hope Victoria rots in prison for what she did," Kaya said when their sobs stopped.

"She's in hell where she belongs!"

Kaya drew back and stared up at him, her liquid eyes opened in awe. "Did you kill her?"

"No, she saved me the trouble. When she realized what she'd done, she put the gun to her head and pulled the trigger."

"You wouldn't have killed her, though."

"Oh yes, I would have, Kaya. That woman killed my wife and my unborn child."

"Pilar was pregnant?"

He swallowed on a shockwave. "She was five weeks along. Erik confirmed it. She was going to tell me over a candlelight dinner that night."

"She must have been so happy."

"She was. We both wanted children so badly. It was one of the reasons we got married so quickly. We planned to have at least five. With her dying breath, she tried to tell me about the baby. We didn't even have a minute to share the blessed news of creating a child out of our love. Victoria robbed us of even that precious moment."

"No wonder you're so attached to these kids, especially Alyssa. You try to hide it, but I know she's your favorite. I see the way you look at her with love and regret in your eyes."

He brushed his fingers through her hair and traced his knuckles along her forehead and cheek. "My child would have been Alyssa's age if he or she had lived. It was only after Alyssa was born that I started building *L'etoile du Nord*. I had to make at least one of our dreams come true."

"Why did you name it *Star of the North*?"

"My grandmother used to call me her little Northern Star. She used to take me to church every Sunday. She had a lot of faith in me." He chortled. "She packed me off up here to boarding school when I started hanging out with the wrong crowd in Queens. If it weren't for her, I wouldn't be where I am today." He paused. "She always used to tell me to surround myself with successful people, to listen to them, learn from them. When she died, she left me a small fortune. She was a millionaire, and nobody knew—not even my dad, her son."

"Whoa. Where'd she get that kind of money?"

"As a young girl, she worked as a waitress and bartender in an upscale Manhattan restaurant. Apparently she used to listen when her wealthy customers discussed their portfolios. She invested her tips in gold, oil, technology, or whatever was on the stock menu. She continued to invest her entire life and never touched the money again. My grandfather didn't even know she had those stocks. My dad was so mad. He'd worked hard as an insurance salesman, while my mother worked as a hairdresser. But the thing that really pissed him off was that Grannie made him get a second job to pay for my tuition at Granite Falls Prep School, especially because it wasn't his idea to send me there."

"She sounds like quite a character. It's nice you two were so close," Kaya murmured on a smile.

"We were very close. She lived with us and took care of me while my parents worked, so I was closer to her than I was to them. She died shortly after I graduated from Harvard. She went to sleep one night and just never woke up. It was as if she thought her job of nurturing me into manhood was done. I still miss her. Some star," he said on a sigh. "I don't even go to church anymore. If she could see me now—"

"She would say what a wonderful man you've become, personally and professionally. She would be proud of you, Bryce. Like I am." She stroked her hands up and down his arms and around his back.

Kaya's vote of confidence sent a warm flush through Bryce. She was so openly sweet and trusting as he used to be before Victoria scarred him. Now, he trusted no one. He didn't even trust himself. "My experience with Victoria taught me to be cautious. That's why I had to deal with Jack before he became another nightmare," he said, deciding she should know about him, just in case he ever tried to contact her.

Ignorance really wasn't bliss.

She stared at him in gaping confusion. "What do you mean you dealt with Jack?"

"I flew down to Florida the night of the funeral and paid him off to sever all ties with you. I ordered him to buy a one-way ticket to any place out of the country. I wasn't about to take any chances."

"Did you beat him up, Bryce?" she asked. "Is that why you had those bruises on your knuckles the next day?"

"Yes."

"Why?"

"He deserved the beating I gave him after the way he treated you. He was lucky to escape with his life. I told him if he ever set foot in New Hampshire, I'd break every bone in his gangly body."

"You didn't have to beat him up, though."

Yes I did. Jack had said some horrible things about Kaya. Lies he'd believed until last night. What was he to do? He knew Kaya had spent time in juvenile detention, and because the records were sealed, he couldn't confirm nor repudiate Jack's lies.

She's a whore, man. She sold it on the streets. She was locked up for prostitution.

Jack's lies weren't the worst of it. When Bryce had knocked on the door of Kaya's apartment, he was greeted by a half-naked Jack, and a woman wearing a robe he was sure belonged to Kaya. The jerk was screwing another woman in Kaya's apartment, in her bed, while she was out of town. That bit of information he would never tell Kaya. It would devastate her.

If the limo driver hadn't pulled him off of Jack, Bryce knew he would have killed him.

"Why'd you beat him up, Bryce?"

"He said some things about you."

"What kind of things?"

"He said you'd been a teenage prostitute."

She went stiff, and sudden anger lit her eyes. "What the... Why would he say something like that?"

Bryce cleared his throat. "Why do you think, Kaya? He was angry, jealous. He couldn't have you, so he tried to make me not want you."

"Oh, my God," she blurted. "You married me in spite of his lies that you didn't know were lies until last night."

"Yes."

She chewed her bottom lip pensively. "Is that why you demanded the blood tests before we were married?"

"Yes, but that was for your safety, too. I've always used protection with other women, but I needed to know that I was okay." Kaya could have simply told him that she'd never been with a man. She was probably trying to save him face. He'd also thought that it was shame or fear that had caused her to reject him on their wedding night. It was the reason he never made any more sexual advances. He didn't want to scare her, but give her time to heal and trust him.

"That's what you thought I was going to tell you just before we made love?"

"Yes again."

"And you didn't care."

"Nope. I didn't care. God knows I'm no saint when it comes to women. I was in no position to judge you."

She looked at him with dreamy eyes. "You're a good man, Bryce Fontaine. Genuine. A lot of other men would have run the other way."

"I'm glad I'm not a lot of other men. You're a rare breed,

Kaya, and I'm happy you agreed to marry me." He drew her closer and planted a soft peck on her lips.

"Why did you go to Florida in the first place?" she asked.

"To warn Jack to stay away from you and the children. I wasn't going to sit around and wait for another Victoria to happen. I wouldn't have been able to live with myself, deal with the guilt if anything ever happened to you or the kids."

"Bryce, what happened to Pilar and your baby wasn't your fault. That woman blind-sided you. You couldn't have foreseen what she was capable of."

His mouth twisted wryly. "I could have put a restraining order on her. I could have paid her off. I could have charged her while she was pointing the gun at me. I could have picked something up and thrown it at her. Every time I think of that night, all these scenarios go through my mind. Bottom line is, I failed to protect my wife and baby. If it weren't for my arrogance, my neglect, Pilar and my child would be alive today."

"You can spend the rest of your life 'could having' yourself to death and it wouldn't change anything." She cradled his face between her palms. "A wise little boy told me that his daddy used to say that it's a waste of time to regret things we should have done. We must learn to pick up the pieces and move on."

He wondered if Kaya had moved on from her past. He was still in the dark about her relationship with Lauren and their father, and the "it" they never spoke about. He still didn't know why Kaya had spent time in juvenile detention or why she'd been in foster care. Where was her mother? Had he done the right thing in burning the report the detective had sent him, or should he have dug deeper into his wife's past to really get to know her? Seemed he was doomed to repeat his impulsive behavior. Were they mistakes or blessings?

"Pilar believed Victoria's lies," he said, surprised that he'd even spoken the words. "She told me she forgave me. It hurts that she questioned my fidelity, my commitment to her and our vows. Perhaps if we'd taken the time to know each other before jumping into a marriage less than a month after we met, she would have had more faith in me, in us."

Her lids slid down over her eyes.

"Oh, that was insensitive of me seeing you and I were also married weeks after we met."

She glanced up at him and spoke with a quiet, but desperate firmness in her voice. "I know why we got married, Bryce. It was different for you and Pilar. You were in love. Don't be sorry about it." She paused. "Sometimes even people we've known for a long time surprise us. I've known Jack since we were kids, and yet when he dumped me so unceremoniously, and now after the lies he told you about me, I realize that I really didn't know him at all." She linked her fingers with his again. "But you, I've known you for less than two months, yet I feel… I feel—"

"What do you feel, Kaya, dear?" Would she tell him that she loved him in the light of day when he was fully awake and gazing deeply into her chocolate-brown eyes? Bryce had no idea how he would respond if she did.

He held his breath waiting, but then the moment was lost when his cell vibrated on the floor beside the mattress. With a groan halfway between relief and regret, he reached out and snatched it up. "Hello."

"Hi, Bryce. I trust you're sober."

"Hi, Michelle," he said on a chuckle. "I'm sober. Very sober." He winked at Kaya. "I guess you're ready to get rid of our kids?"

"I'd love to keep them for the rest of the day, but I have to leave for Manchester soon. I have a book signing in a couple hours at the Youth Center."

"Oh yes, I totally forgot. Congratulations on the release of your second book. Make sure you bring me back a signed copy."

"I will, Bryce." She cleared her throat. "Um, I'm taking

Precious with me, and Jason wants to go along. We're flying down, so we wouldn't be gone all day, just a few hours. Jason will be back home in time for dinner. Is it okay?"

"Hold on. I'll put you on speaker phone." He pressed the speaker button, and frowned at Kaya's attempt to stop him by flailing her hands in the air and mouthing the word "No".

"You guys are up and about already?"

"We're up, but not about. We're still in bed."

He chuckled when Kaya covered her face with her hands and groaned.

There was a long pause, then, "Oh," from Michelle.

He could hear the shock and surprise in her voice. Had Kaya told her and Libby last night that they hadn't consummated their marriage? Well, that was the purpose of the brides club—for the wives to confide in each other. He wondered if they'd given his virgin bride any ideas. "We're newlyweds, Michelle. These things happen," he said in a velvety tone.

"You're preaching to the choir, Bryce," she responded with a chuckle.

"Is it okay if Jason goes to Manchester with Michelle and Precious?" Bryce asked Kaya. "Michelle has a book signing. They're flying down, so he'll be back in time for dinner."

Kaya dropped her hands and glared at him. "It's okay, Michelle. Just remind him that since he's taking today off, he has to work on his science project all day tomorrow."

"I'll tell him."

"I'll have Bryce bring over a fresh change of clothes for him when he picks up the girls."

"Great. You two go back to doing whatever it was you were doing. Kaya, we will talk later," she added rather dramatically, and then hung up.

Bryce set his cell phone on the floor and leaned over Kaya.

"You heard the woman. We should get back to whatever it is we were doing."

"We were talking," she said pointedly.

"Not anymore." He pulled her gently to him.

"You have to pick up the girls and take Jason a change of clothes," she said, pushing against his arms.

"Methinks the lady doth protest too much." He captured her mouth with his and tried to nudge her legs apart with one of his knees.

"I'm sore, Bryce," she whispered against his lips.

His heart jolted. He raised his head and stared down at her. "Oh, sweetheart, I forgot last night was your first time." He squinted his eyes. "You know if you'd told me you were a virgin, I would have been a lot more gentle and patient. Because I didn't know, I may have torn you."

"You probably did, and I did try to tell you." She graced him with an accusatory slant of the eye.

"With something that colossal, you should have tried harder."

"Well, maybe if I'd known *you* were so *colossal*, I would have shouted it at the top of my lungs."

"My sexy wife has a sense of humor," he declared as hearty chuckles erupted from his throat. He kissed her on the forehead and rolled off of her. "You need a day or two to heal before we make love again, and I know just what will help the process along. Stay right there."

Kaya's eyes were glued to Bryce's gorgeous body as he eased his way over to the edge of the mattress. They'd made love last night bathed in the light of the moon and the flames from the fireplace, but the only part of his anatomy she'd had glimpses of were his wide chest and powerful shoulders, and strong upper arms as he'd been bent over her, plunging into her over and over again.

Kaya felt a surging ache between her legs at the memory. If

she weren't so sore, she knew he'd be inside her at the moment, taking her to love's passionate pinnacle and then pushing her over the edge where she'd crash and burn in the melting flames.

She smiled at the thought that she was a woman now—Bryce Fontaine's woman, his wife in every sense of the word.

She—little insignificant Kaya Brehna from Palm Beach, Florida—was married to one of the wealthiest, most powerful men in the world. And that amazing man had not only shared his body with her, but a part of his heart and soul as well. He'd opened up to her and told her about his deepest darkest hurts and fears. He'd cried out his pain in her arms.

She'd given him something of herself she could never give to any other man, and he'd shared something of himself she was sure he'd chosen not to share with any other woman since Pilar.

That knowledge filled Kaya with insurmountable affection for her husband.

Somewhere, she'd heard that women have sex because they were in love and that men have sex because they were looking for love. Kaya wasn't sure about the latter part of that statement, and whether or not Bryce was looking for love, but she knew she'd given herself to him because she was in love with him.

As Bryce pushed off the mattress and stood to his feet, Kaya's eyes were drawn to the corded muscles of his shoulders and back. She gasped at the long angry welts along his smooth brown skin. In her passion, she'd marked him, but he seemed to wear his passion wounds with pride. She bit her lips as her gaze continued down his narrow waist that tapered off into the tight sinews of his dimpled buttocks, and the sturdy pillars of his thighs and long hairy legs supporting his humongous frame. Her heart fluttered as she recalled her heels digging into him, spurring him toward the flaming precipice of passion, roaring all the way like a champion thoroughbred stallion. She'd satisfied him. Her smile deepened at the simple awareness.

For a few moments, he stood with his back to her, giving her time to admire him before he walked slowly from the room, down the corridor toward the *His* and *Hers* bathroom and dressing suites.

When she heard water running into what she was certain was the smaller, woman's size Jacuzzi, Kaya covered her face with her hands and groaned. Was he disappointed that she couldn't make love to him again for a few days? *She was.* She didn't want to wait that long to be with him again, but the ache in her body warned her that it was best. She wondered if this was what it was like for all virgins, or was it because her husband was so huge?

She'd never really given sex that much thought. She'd never had a serious boyfriend until Jack, and even though he'd tried to make love with her, she'd never even been slightly tempted. And thank God, after the jerk he'd turned out to be. How could he tell Bryce such nauseating lies about her? What the heck was wrong with him?

Kaya dropped her hands to her chest and raised her eyelids when a shadow fell across her. Her gaze collided with Bryce's. All thoughts of Jack vanished from her mind, and her heart began to hammer in her chest at the sparks of eroticism she read in the dark recesses of Bryce's eyes.

He stood at the foot of the mattress, straight as a sturdy oak tree. As Kaya took in the background of the Corinthian-columned balcony, the blue skies, and the evergreen pine tree line, one thing became clear to her: Bryce Fontaine didn't blend in. He stood out. He had presence like no other man she'd ever known.

Kaya licked her lips as her gaze slid down the wide chest to his stomach. She'd heard of six-pack abs. Bryce had eight. Divinely ripped and corded. She lowered her gaze to his hips and the turbulent root of his sex in its half-awakened state, surrounded by a thatch of curly dark hair—hair that had tickled the waxed area of her groin as they made love. She shuddered and swallowed when his sex jerked against his thigh in anticipation and excitement. How in heaven's name had she taken him into her little virgin body last night, and enjoyed it so thoroughly at that? It must have been a miracle.

Kaya had never seen a real live naked man before. But she was wise enough to know that they could not all possess the same generous virility as Bryce Fontaine. There was an awful lot of him. He'd definitely broken the mold. No wonder she was sore. And no wonder he hadn't allowed her to see him or touch him last night, because honestly, she would have run from his bed screaming. But now…

"Your bath is ready," he said looking her over seductively. He knelt on the mattress and scooped her up in his arms.

Both of their eyes became riveted to the dark stain on the duvet. His body tensed, and feeling a sense of embarrassment, Kaya nuzzled her face into the warm comfort of Bryce's neck and looped her arms about his shoulders. "I'm sorry."

"Don't be," he said, carrying her from the room. "It's normal." He knelt beside the Jacuzzi—strategically positioned under a low window overlooking the lake—and lowered her gently into the warm water. "I sprinkled some baking soda into your bath. It will help soothe your aches away. Got the idea from Grannie," he added with a grin.

"Oh, this feels good," Kaya murmured, as the jet streams immediately began massaging her body. She hadn't realized she was so achy, like a big truck had run over her. Well, one had actually, she thought, taking in the look of contentment on Bryce's face. He'd run over her and right through her, forging paths on the uncharted terrain of her body.

"I'll leave you now," he said.

"You don't have to go." She enjoyed looking at him. She liked having him close. They'd been apart for so long on so many different levels that she was afraid that if he left, he wouldn't come back.

"Oh, yes, I do." He traced a finger across her eyebrows. "If I don't leave, I will scoop you out of this tub and take you back to bed. But we do need to wait. I want your next experience to be even more fulfilling than last night."

Kaya didn't think that was possible, but only time would tell. "How long do we have to wait?" Her own eagerness surprised her. She'd never craved anything this much.

"A couple days at the most." He paused. "I have to pick up Alyssa and Anastasia. And I'm giving Haley the day off. You, the girls, and I will spend the day together. Would you like that?"

She nodded on a smile.

"Close your eyes, relax, and enjoy your soak. I'll see you downstairs when you're ready."

"Thanks, Bryce."

"No, thank *you*." He leaned in and kissed her lips, then pushed to his feet and left her.

Kaya nestled into a more comfortable position, rested her head against the spa pillow, and closed her eyes. A smile graced her lips when she heard the shower in the *His* bathroom.

A day with Bryce and the kids sounded splendid. It would be the first time that they would spend time together like a true family.

Dear Lord, she'd told him that she loved him.

Had he heard her?

CHAPTER FOURTEEN

Kaya's heart swelled with a sense of fulfillment as she watched Jason, Alyssa, and their friends trek through knee-deep snow to toss snowballs at each other. It was hard to believe it was only two months ago that tragedy had crushed their spirits and taken away their will to live.

With lots of therapy from Samantha, love and patience from her and Bryce, and constant interaction with friends, they were back on course, behaving like normal children again. Even Anastasia was thriving, she thought, glancing down at the baby nestled in the crook of her arm, gnawing away on a frozen teething ring and drooling from both corners of her mouth.

Thank God she was finally sleeping through the night. Even though she had a live-in nanny, Kaya's maternal instinct propelled her out of bed each time Anastasia awoke in the night.

Kaya placed her feet on the ottoman in front of her and glanced around the four-season porch off the kitchen. Large potted plants from her Palm Beach apartment were scattered about, giving her a sense of connection to the place where she'd grown up, the place she no longer called home. This place where children frolicked in the backyard snow was now her home. For the first time since she arrived in Granite Falls, Kaya felt a sense of belonging with the town, with *L'etoile du Nord*. She could safely credit her growing assimilation to what she and Bryce had shared last night and the amazing day they'd spent together.

After her soothing soak in the Jacuzzi, she'd dressed and come downstairs to find a lovely bouquet of white and yellow orchids—that Bryce knew were her favorite flowers—waiting for her, and a card that read: *Thank you for last night, and for listening. Yours Always, Bryce.*

Kaya tingled from the memory of the "thank you" kiss she'd given him in return. If her body could have handled him, she would have definitely taken Bryce upstairs to her room where they would have spent the rest of the day. But he said they needed to wait a few days before indulging themselves in each other.

After a cereal breakfast at home, she and Bryce had taken the girls to Pine Forest Petting Zoo in the neighboring town of Evergreen, where they'd run into Libby who was babysitting her niece, Courtney. Since it was a sunny, pleasant day, they'd all taken a horse and buggy ride around the farm until Alyssa and Courtney cried "hungry". Realizing that Alyssa was having such a good time, Kaya had asked Libby if Courtney could spend the day with them. Her sister was happy to oblige, and so was Libby who wanted to spend time with Steven.

Upon leaving the zoo, they'd driven into town and enjoyed a leisure lunch at Marble Pond Terrace, then walked through the mall window-shopping. Of course Alyssa had batted her eyelashes at Bryce and dropped 'a one hundreds of kisses' on his face until he caved and bought her a new doll. Now that she understood why he was such a pussycat when it came to that child, Kaya forgave him and allowed him to buy her a diamond bracelet from Forsythe Jewelers on Main Street.

Kaya extended her arm and stared at the pink diamonds

sparking against her tan wrist. She smiled as she recalled the stares and attention they'd received from the other customers and passersby, who'd done double takes when they recognized Bryce.

She and Bryce had spent time in public with the kids before, but today had been exceptional. Today, she didn't have to pretend that she was happy. Her smiles were real. Unpretentious. And for the first time since she became Mrs. Bryce Fontaine, Kaya didn't give a damn what people thought of her marriage. She'd flashed her wedding band with pride instead of trying to hide it, as she'd done in the past. She'd melted into Bryce when he put his arms about her and kissed her openly as they strolled along the Esplanade that ran along a portion of the Aiken River. He'd lingered for the benefit of Lester Cobbs, a relentless local reporter who'd been following them around town. Kaya had no doubt she and Bryce would be the talk of the late-night gossip.

On their way back home, Jason had called to ask if Precious and Ethan could come over for the afternoon. How could she say no when Alyssa had Courtney?

As she watched the children, Kaya couldn't help but fantasize about the little ones she and Bryce might have one day. They hadn't used protection last night. They hadn't spoken about children or any of the important issues normal couples discussed, but she was sure that if he were opposed to the idea, he would have taken precaution. Neither one of them had expected to end up in bed together last night, but there were other methods of birth control that he could have practiced.

A smile ran away with Kaya's face. Two months ago, when she was thinking of marrying Jack, she'd had no desire to have children. Fate had given her three, and here she was, dreaming of another—maybe two or three more with Bryce.

"A penny for your thoughts."

She glanced toward the kitchen slider, where Bryce leaned against the frame with Webster in his arms. He'd left her alone on the porch to make some business calls. It was Saturday, and although he didn't have to go into the office, it didn't mean he was free from his responsibilities as CEO of Fontaine Enterprises. Kaya was grateful he'd turned off his cell during the day to give her and the children his undivided attention.

"That's all you're willing to pay?" she threw back at him. "Word on the streets is that you can afford a lot more. My thoughts aren't cheap, Mr. Fontaine."

"Don't believe everything you hear," he said, pushing off the door and coming to sit in the chair next to her. He settled Webster on his lap and continued to pet the cat. "Were you thinking about me?"

"You're so full of yourself." She transferred Anastasia to her other arm, so the baby was facing him.

Anastasia immediately lit up and started kicking her arms and legs in excitement when she saw Bryce. He had that effect on women, Kaya thought as his nearness began to have a drugging effect on her.

"I'd rather be full of you, or more precisely, have you full of me." He curled his fingers around a lock of her hair and played with it.

"Excuse me. Child present. Don't listen to your Uncle Bryce," she said, placing her hands over Anastasia's ears. "He has no morals."

"It's nothing she hasn't heard or seen before. Her parents were extremely amorous in front of them. They let their love show, so to speak." He leaned in and brought his face close to hers. "Like this." He moved his lips on hers in a warm kiss, filled with passionate promises that transported her back to the mattress on the floor of the master suite.

Her whole body trembled with memories and anticipation.

Finally, reluctantly, he released her. His eyes were warm as he gazed into hers. "I had an excellent time today. It was nice being out with you, holding your hands, watching the smiles on your face," he said in a voice husky with emotion. "I enjoyed all my women, even this cranky little one." He bent his head and kissed Anastasia on both cheeks and nuzzled his nose in her neck before capturing Kaya's gaze again. "For the first time since we've been married, it feels like a real family."

"For me, too." Kaya's heart fluttered.

He sighed, sat back in the cushioned chair, and stretched his feet out on the other ottoman. He stared at the kids as they competed with each other to make the most perfect snow angel. "They seem like normal kids again," he said, his eyes sparkling with contentment.

Kaya's heart ached for him. He looked like a man who was appreciating the moment, but who nonetheless teetered on the threshold of his past and his future, uncertain about which to embrace.

They hadn't talked about his living arrangements, whether or not he would remain at Hotel Andreas or move into *L'etoile du Nord*. They hadn't talked about the four words she'd whispered just before she fell asleep last night.

Why the heck had she told him she loved him? *Because you do,* the voice in her head replied. It was foolish of her to bare her heart like that.

Kaya still wasn't certain Bryce had heard her. She was too afraid to ask. If he hadn't heard her, asking would open up Pandora's Box. Embarrassment kept her from bringing it up. What if he'd heard her and simply decided to ignore her? He might lie so she wouldn't feel rejected, but then the matter would be out there and they'd have to deal with it. *Awkward.*

Yeah, he'd talked to her about Pilar, but that didn't mean he'd automatically stopped loving his late wife and started loving his present one. It just meant he trusted her, felt comfortable with her. It didn't mean he loved her. It was best she pretended she'd never spoken the words.

Kaya turned her head as the patio door burst open. A blast of cold air and five very loud, very wet children came rushing through it. Webster leaped off Bryce's lap and bolted into the house.

"Oh, no you don't!" Bryce sprang to his feet as the children started to go after Webster. "You're all stripping down to your clothes before any of you take one step inside."

Kaya smiled with amused wonder as the children began making a hasty pile of boots, mittens, hats, scarves, and gloves on the granite floor, all the while keeping one eye on the stern-faced giant towering above them. She'd be scared, too.

"I need help." Alyssa tugged at the laces of her boots.

"Me, too." Courtney fidgeted with the strings on her hat.

Bryce slid to his knees to help Courtney and Alyssa while the three older children who were done divesting looked on impatiently.

"We want some hot chocolate," Courtney said.

"And a cookie," Alyssa added, stepping out of her snowsuit.

"And what's the proper way to ask?" Bryce enquired, with a playful twist of his lips.

"Pleeeeaaaassseee," they yelled in unison, jumping up and down.

"I'll go make the hot chocolate," Kaya said, transferring Anastasia to her shoulder.

"I can do it, Aunt Kaya." Jason smiled at her. "You just stay out here with Uncle Bryce and enjoy the view." He extended his hand toward the thawing lake and the clear blue sky. "I'll make it just like you taught me."

Kaya frowned. What was he up to? *Enjoy the view?*

"I can help," Precious said. "My mommy taught me how to make hot chocolate, too." She walked over to Kaya and gazed at

Anastasia. "You're so pretty. You're so pretty," she chanted as she started tickling Anastasia's tummy.

Anastasia squealed with delight and tried to grab handfuls of her hair. Kaya had learned to keep her hair out of Anastasia's reach. The kid had a killer grip.

"She's *my* sister." Jealous Alyssa rushed over to stake her claim. She threw her arms around Anastasia and started showering kisses on her face.

"My mommy is gonna have another baby. I hope I have a sister. Boys are yucky," Precious said, stepping back.

"Don't you love your little brother?" Bryce asked her, rising to his feet.

She sat on the edge of the ottoman, her brown eyes shining with affection. "I do, but he's annoying, and he bites. See." She pulled up the sleeve of her sweater and pointed to a red bruise on her upper arm. "He bit me because I wouldn't let him have Bradie."

Kaya had met Bradie, Precious' rag doll that was as dear to her heart as Snoopy was to Alyssa's.

"He's just trying out his new teeth," Bryce consoled her. "And he bites you because you're sweet."

She rolled her eyes. "That's what my daddy says. But he's still yucky."

"I'm a boy. I'm not yucky," Ethan declared, stepping into her face. "You're yucky."

"Hey, don't talk to her like that." Jason placed himself between Precious and Ethan. "She's a girl. You're supposed to be nice to her. You never yell at girls."

Ethan glared at Jason. "We never hung out with girls 'til she moved back up here. Now all you do is talk about Precious all the time. It's no fun playing with you anymore."

"He talks about me? What does he say?" Precious placed her hand on her heart and flashed her eyes at Jason.

"He says—"

"Hey!" Jason cut Ethan off, his grey eyes flashing angrily at his friend.

"Okay guys, you all need to calm down," Bryce said, walking up to the trio.

Wow, Kaya thought, Jason really had it bad for Precious. And why not? She was an adorable little girl. So this was what her future would be like if she and Bryce had kids? She loved the sibling and friendly rivalry going on around her. She never had that growing up. She never had friends—only Jack, and he was as protective of her as Jason was with Precious.

Too bad Jack didn't stay that way.

"Are you and Auntie Kaya in love?" Alyssa wrapped her arms about Bryce's legs and peered up at him.

Kaya held her breath. "Why do you ask, Alyssa?"

"Jason says you are. 'Cause Uncle Bryce gave you flowers and he was playing with your hair."

"Yeah, we all *sawed* it." Courtney nodded perfunctorily, as she wiped a red, wet nose.

"Oh, you all *sawed* it, huh?" Bryce pinched her nose.

"They're gonna have a baby," Precious announced out of the blue.

"What?" Kaya blinked several times. "What are you talking about?"

"You were kissing. And that's where babies come from," Precious stated in a voice of authority.

"Babies don't come from kissing," Jason corrected her.

"Yes, they do." Precious dug her heels in. "That's how my brother Erik was born. Michelle and my dad were kissing, and Erik started growing in her tummy. And then my daddy and Michelle got married and she became my new mommy." She threw her hands in the air. "They're always kissing and now she's gonna have another baby."

Kaya thought Ethan looked dazed and confused before he said, "You know, she might be right. Ever since my dad came from England to live with us, he and my mom are always kissing. And now I have two brothers."

"See, I told you." Precious swung her head, causing her long thick curls to bounce off her shoulders and down her back. "That's why I don't let boys kiss me. I don't want a baby. My mom says they're a lot of work."

Kaya stifled a laugh as Jason rolled his eyes in boredom and impatience.

"Can we just go make hot chocolate, please?" he shouted.

He was such a serious little boy, a trait she'd come to recognize over the weeks. He didn't talk much, but he observed everything and everyone around him. Bryce had told her that he took after Michael in that aspect.

Kaya had been as naïve as Precious and Ethan at this age, but something told her Jason knew exactly where babies came from. She applauded him for demonstrating restraint and not educating his friends about a subject matter that was best left to their parents to explain. He was a wise little boy, and Kaya loved him with all her heart.

They'd been getting along very well over the past weeks. She'd taught him how to play chess and a couple of card games, and the other night after dinner while Bryce played with the girls on the floor in the playroom, Jason had finally won his first game of Chess. Kaya smiled, remembering the look of triumph in his eyes. Even though she frequently expressed her love to him, he'd never reciprocated. She understood that he wasn't ready. "Go make the hot chocolate, Jason," she said, nudging him on the shoulder.

He made a dash into the kitchen with Precious and Ethan in his wake.

"I'd better make sure they don't burn down the house," Bryce said. "Come on, little ones." He extended his hands to Alyssa and Courtney.

"We wanna play horsey," Alyssa said, tugging Bryce to his knees.

"Girls, as much as I would love to play horsey with you, Uncle Bryce is really tired. He had a very long and enchanting night." His gaze held a sensuous flame as he smiled at Kaya. "I think I've given all I can for one day."

"I'll give you 'a one hundreds of kisses'," Alyssa told him.

"Me, too." Courtney smiled, sweetly. "You're nice, Mr. Bryce. I like you."

"I love you, Uncle Bryce." Alyssa didn't let anybody trump her.

"Well then 'a one hundreds of kisses' is what he gets," Kaya said with a grin. He was irresistible to women, no matter the age. "Go on girls, show him how much you love him." Kaya giggled as the girls jumped at Bryce, knocking him into the pile of wet snow gear. "And make him count every last one of those kisses."

Anastasia squealed with excitement and reached out her chubby arms to the frolicking trio, wanting to join in the fun.

"No, baby. You'll get hurt. How about you and Auntie Kaya go play with your toys?"

"Count, Uncle Bryce!"

"Kaya!" Bryce bellowed as she hopped into the kitchen. "Get them off me."

"Count."

"One, two…"

Grinning from one ear to the other, Kaya closed the slider on his cries and left him to the mercy of the girls.

Her heart fluttered with the knowledge that Bryce would make an excellent father one day. He would adore his children and protect them with his life. They would have him wrapped around their little fingers, especially his daughters, she thought recalling several memories of Bryce dancing to the tune of "You Are My Sunshine" with Alyssa on his feet, her little arms wrapped around his legs, and Anastasia clasped to his chest—the way Michael used to dance with his daughters to their favorite song.

Her children would have the father she'd longed for all her life, Kaya thought, her love for Bryce deepening and spreading inside her. He would never abandon them, not for any reason.

As Kaya removed handful of clothes from Michael and Lauren's closets, she felt an overwhelming presence of their spirits in the bedroom they once shared.

Yesterday was Youth Day at church and all children, five and over, joined the adults instead of going off to Youth Church. Chris Kipfer the youth pastor had delivered a message entitled, "Let it Go."

She remembered how attentive Jason had been as he sat beside her, and at one point she'd seen a tear roll from the corner of his eye. He'd quickly wiped it away, at which point Kaya had turned her head and acted as if she hadn't seen it.

Many times he'd shut himself in this very bedroom for hours, and when he emerged, she could tell he'd been crying, even though she never heard a sound coming from within.

This morning, while Bryce waited for him downstairs, he'd called Kaya up to the second floor. "Pastor Chris said we have to let go of the old so God can bring new things into our lives," he'd said while they stood outside his parents' bedroom. "You told me I'll always carry Mommy and Daddy in my heart. I want to remember them in my heart, not in there," he'd added, pointing toward the bedroom. "Can you pack up their clothes for me? I already took the stuff that I want to keep."

"Are you sure, Jason?" she'd asked. "You don't have to rush this. It's not like we need the bedroom for anything else."

"I'm sure," he'd responded with a nod.

"Okay. I'll pack up their stuff and put them in storage. When you and your sisters are older, you can decide together what to do with them."

"Thanks, Aunt Kaya." He'd paused then said, "I'm glad Mommy and Daddy asked you to come take care of us, and I'm sorry I was mean to you at first. Can you forgive me?"

"You were hurting. Never apologize for hurting. And I forgave you even while you were hitting me. But if you ever feel the urge to hit me again, be prepared for a fight. We'll be wearing gloves and dancing around in a boxing ring."

He'd looked at her for long moments, grinned, then suddenly put his arms about her waist. "You're a cool aunt. I love you."

Kaya's heart had trembled inside her and tears had flowed freely from her eyes as she'd held that little boy close to her. He'd come full circle and had accepted her. They were good now. Solid. A real family. She was so happy she could do this small favor for him.

Kaya opened a shoebox she'd pulled from the back of Lauren's closet and stared at a red sweater decorated with white snowflakes folded inside. It was old and faded, and the threads around the collar were coming apart.

It was identical to one her father had sent her for Christmas when she was twelve years old. It was the last Christmas gift she'd gotten from him. She'd kept hers too, right next to the one picture she had of her father.

Kaya picked up the sweater and noticed the other items in the box: an old leather wallet, two worn ties, a money clip, a tarnished silver watch—all of which she was certain belonged to her father—and some pictures of him, Lauren, and Lauren's mother. There was nothing of monetary value, but she would have gladly traded them for the jewel tucked away in that safety deposit box in Palm Beach.

Here were the personal items that her father used, wore, day after day. She touched each item, using her fingers to bridge the years that separated them. *How she still missed him.*

Her fingers brushed against a purple envelope lying at the bottom of the box. Kaya picked it up. It was addressed to her, in Lauren's handwriting. With her heart pounding with curiosity, Kaya plopped down on the edge of the bed and ripped it open.

CHAPTER FIFTEEN

My Dear Sister, Kaya,

If you're reading this letter, it means that I'm smiling down from heaven and that you've agreed to care for my precious little babies. Thank you so very much, Kaya. We didn't get the opportunity to meet on earth again, but I have faith that we'll meet in heaven one day.

A tear slipped from Kaya's eye onto the page. She wiped it away quickly, fearing it would smudge the ink.

I guess you know by now that we've been living in Bryce's house because ours burnt down to the ground. That day, I came face to face with my own mortality, and shortly afterward, I started writing this letter to you—just in case life throws us another curve ball and this is the only way I can explain everything to you.

We tend to go along from day to day, thinking that this is all there is to life, but God has His way of reminding us that we're just pilgrims, passing through a foreign land on our way to eternity with Him. We should never get too comfortable here.

Speaking of comfortable—or not—everyone must be wondering why Michael and I didn't leave the children with Bryce. We know he loves them and would treat them as he would treat his own. He's a good man—loving, gentle, and big-hearted. We even thought about making both of you legal guardians.

But we know Bryce, and didn't want our children to become pawns in some custody battle. Bryce is very possessive of those he loves, and could be difficult and domineering in his desires to protect them at times. You'll understand as you get to know him better. You can't help but love him for his devotion, though.

Kaya couldn't stop the smile that burst through her tears.

Kaya, I chose you, simply because you're my sister. I wanted my children to know you, the only living relative they have. I didn't want to do to them what our parents did to us by keeping them away from their family.

I wish we'd grown up together, loving each other as sisters, sharing secrets and talking about boys and clothes and makeup. Every time I look at Alyssa, I imagine what you must have looked like as a little girl. She has Daddy's big, brown beautiful eyes, just like you.

Kaya paused to take deep gulps of air into her lungs.

Our father loved you, Kaya. Many times I would catch him looking off into space and when I asked him what he was thinking about, he'd say, "A beautiful little princess I used to know." And then his eyes would get all damp with tears.

When I met you at his funeral, I knew that princess was you.

Kaya bit her lip to stop from crying out.

I may have had our father to tuck me in at nights and walk me to the bus stop in the mornings. I may have had his hugs and kisses every day. But you, my little sister, always had his heart. If you remember nothing else about him, Kaya, remember this: our father loved you. He longed for you up until the day he died.

"Oh, Daddy," Kaya moaned, curling her fist around the locket.

I don't know if you're aware of the reason he stopped seeing you. I didn't know until after he died and my mother explained you to me. Just in case your mother never told you, here's the story mine told me:

Our father is from Africa, the country of Ghana. He came to the United States as a foreign student and this is where he met my mother, who was also African. They fell in love, married, and had me. Years later, he met your mother and fell in love with her. It is customary for the men of his tribe to have multiple wives, so he saw nothing wrong in marrying her. Soon after, you were born. Daddy was afraid to tell your mom about us, not knowing how she would react, and since his work took him away from home a lot, it was easy for him to live a double life. Anyway, your mother became suspicious that he was having an affair, and it caused problems between them. That's when Daddy moved out of your apartment permanently. You were about five at the time.

Your mother had him followed and when she found out about my mother and me, she threatened to have him deported or locked up if he ever came near you or her again. I'm sorry you had to grow up without him, Kaya, but if he'd followed his heart and fought for you, he would have lost us both. To him, giving up one daughter was better than losing two.

Kaya's tremors were so violent, the king-size bed shook, but she forced herself to keep reading.

I would have loved to share all this with you in person, perhaps sitting on the back porch watching the children play in the yard. But God would have it differently. He knows best.

Kaya, please believe that I loved you. And that I know in my heart you will love my children and raise them with the same love and care I would have. I hope having them in your life will bring you some peace and somehow make up for all the years you were separated from Daddy, and for those you and I were apart.

God bless you, Kaya, my beautiful little sister. My children are in perfect hands.

Love,

Lauren.

Kaya folded the letter in her fist, curled up like a baby on the bed, and wept for all the years she'd spent being resentful and jealous of Lauren. *For what?* She'd wasted countless opportunities to know her sister. She'd give anything for one smile, one hug from Lauren now.

But it was too late. *Way too late.*

Kaya had no idea how long she'd wept, but she pulled herself together, sat up on the mattress, and unfolded the letter. Lauren had started a second one at the end of the first.

Well, Kaya. There's a slight change in plans since I wrote this letter to you.

You see, Michael is a bit wary about giving the children to you since he has never met you. You're my sister, and I feel comfortable with it. However, he has known Bryce for a very long time. He loves him like a brother and he trusts him with our children, and that's where the second will comes in.

We decided not to void the will we had Steven draw up because I wanted you to meet the children. I knew you'd fall in love with them and would want to be in their lives, simply because they're family. We hoped that by the time the more recent will was read, no matter the outcome, you wouldn't be able to walk away from them, and that you and Bryce would work something out, thus the stipulation prohibiting you from taking them out of Granite Falls if I survived Michael.

Kaya's jaw dropped. She had no idea there were conditions in the second will if she'd gained custody. Did Bryce know? Why would he keep it from her?

Kaya, please don't be angry with me. Michael and I did what we thought was best for everybody. We hope we didn't cause too much upheaval to your and Bryce's lives.

A chuckle escaped Kaya's throat. "It was one of the best decisions you ever made, my dear sister. You brought Bryce and me together, and I thank you for that."

Kaya gazed out at the sun rising over the lake. A warm shiver rushed up her spine as she recalled her short-lived romantic tryst with Bryce in the kitchen earlier today.

He'd snuck up behind her and backed her into the refrigerator.

His kisses had been voracious, demanding, almost punishing as his hands had roamed over her body with a desperate intensity in his touch. She'd gasped in sweet agony when he'd pulled her robe open and slid one large hand inside the neckline of her nightgown to cup the breast closest to his palm, while his other hand slid down her thigh to the hem of her nightgown. He'd pulled it up slowly until his knuckles brushed the insides of her thighs.

"Spread your legs," he'd ordered as his thumb caught the crotch of her panties and pulled it away from her body. "God, you're so hot and wet already."

"Bryce," Kaya had whispered, grabbing a handful of his shirt for support as her knees had buckled from beneath her. "What are you doing?"

"Testing," he'd said, gazing into her eyes.

"Test— Ahhh…" A shock of desire had shaken Kaya to the core as Bryce glided a finger inside her.

"How's that?" he asked, pulling it out and driving it slowly back in, going way past knuckle deep.

"Goo…goo… good."

"What about this?" he'd rasped, sliding another finger inside as his thumb caressed the little bud that governed the level of her arousal.

"Oh, God." Kaya had closed her eyes as passion zinged through her and her muscles clamped hungrily around his digits.

"Any pain?"

"No… No," she'd managed as her legs trembled and her hips began moving in a rhythm that matched the tempo of his fingers. "It feels good… so good…"

"Auntie Kaya, where are you?"

"Damn. We're finishing this tonight," he'd uttered on a groan as he pulled his fingers from inside her, and hastily helped her fix her clothes.

Kaya shivered from the memory of the passionate promises

in his eyes as he'd brought his fingers to his mouth and sucked her juices off of them.

"Sweet," he'd muttered before stepping out onto the patio mere seconds before Alyssa sauntered into the kitchen.

She was so ready for him, Kaya thought. She knew that if Alyssa hadn't called out for her at that moment, she would have slithered to the floor and let Bryce take her right there in the kitchen, or on the marble countertop, or the kitchen table—wherever he wanted her. She would never say no to him again.

"I love him, Lauren," she said, a smile spreading across her face in anticipation of being with Bryce tonight.

Would he leave after dinner as usual, and then sneak back into the house and her bed in the middle of the night when Haley and the kids were asleep? Even though they'd consummated their marriage, their relationship still wasn't normal. There were issues that needed to be worked out—his living arrangements, for one. She wanted him to move into *L'etoile du Nord*. She wanted to fall asleep in his arms every night and wake up next to him every morning. She wanted her husband. *Period.*

Kaya had no idea if it was better to bring up the subject before or after they made love again. With a sigh of uncertainty, she glanced down at the letter and read the last paragraph.

If I could offer you one bit of advice, Kaya, it would be that you must live. Life is too short. Do all the things you want to do before it's too late. And whatever you do, don't run from love; don't hide from it. Embrace it with wide-open arms, for after all is said and done, Love is all we have.

I love you.

Your sister,

Lauren.

"I love you, too, Lauren, and I pray that Bryce would grow to love me as much as Michael loved you."

Bryce stared absentmindedly at the team of engineers, machinists, geoscientists, electricians, and environmentalists seated around the conference table at Fontaine Enterprises. The monotonous hum of their voices bounced off the walls and echoed in his ears, but their words were lost on him.

He'd psychologically detached himself from the discussion a while ago when thoughts of his wife had surged to the forefront of his mind.

It had been three days since they'd made love, and during those three days, he'd been reliving the sounds of the sexy little sighs and moans coming out of Kaya as he'd kissed his way up and down her body. He couldn't shake the sensations elicited from the smooth touch of her small hands gliding along his back and arms, and the velvety softness of her moist heat clamped around him.

And God, her aroma, her musky, arousing aroma was forever etched into his brain.

Every taste in his mouth, every scent in his nostrils, every touch to his skin sang "Kaya". He'd been infected with her, living and breathing her. His desire to have her writhing beneath him again was driving him out of his mind. He'd reached his limit this morning when he went to pick up Jason for school and found Kaya walking around the kitchen in a white satin robe that clung provocatively to the sweet curves of her hips and buttocks, reminding him of the pleasure her delectable little body had brought him.

It had taken all his strength to tear himself away from *L'etoile du Nord* with nothing but a quick squeeze of her breasts, a hungry smooch of her mouth, and the velvety feel of her wet, tight flesh gripping his fingers as he'd cornered her against the refrigerator. All he'd wanted to do was pick Kaya up, toss her over his shoulder, march up the stairs to her bedroom, and spread her out on her bed where he would have spent the rest of the day performing licentious acts on her body.

But the house was too crowded and he'd had to get Jason to school. By the time he reached Granite Falls Elementary, Bryce had known he'd have to break a rule or he'd pop a vein in his brain if he denied himself of Kaya any longer.

He'd love to whisk her away on his jet to a honeymoon destination of her choice, but he couldn't do that until he knew the kids, especially Alyssa, could cope without them for more than one night. Since they couldn't go away on a honeymoon, he would bring the honeymoon to them. He planned to make tonight exceptionally special for both of them.

It was time she got to know him. Really know him. She'd begged for deeper penetration that night, but Bryce was wise enough to know it would have been a mistake to grant her request. He remembered too vividly the look of fear and surprise in her eyes the morning after when she'd gazed at his naked body for the first time. The fact that he was the first man she'd seen naked had deepened his affection for her. He'd given her something he'd never given another woman.

Bryce knew he was more heavily endowed than most men. When he'd first began experimenting with sex, he'd been ever so eager to show off for the girls, but when some of them—especially the petite ones—backed out of their promises, he'd learned to be discreet, ease them into the experience of taking him. Many were surprised that their bodies could stretch that much to accommodate him, and even more surprised at the depth of pleasure he brought them.

Even Pilar had been a little bit scared of him.

His size was the reason he'd kept Kaya literally in the dark as he'd made love to her. He hadn't wanted her to touch him or see him, even though at the time he was unaware that she was still a virgin—the first one he'd ever had, Bryce thought with a deep sense of admiration for her. Now that she knew that she could handle him, he would have no trouble enticing her back to his bed. If her eager response to him this morning was any indication, he knew she was ready to proceed with the sexual phase of their marriage.

Their first time had been under cover of night. Their next time would be in the light of day, Bryce suddenly decided. He couldn't wait for tonight. He wanted Kaya to enjoy the pleasure of seeing exactly what he was doing to her.

A groan echoed in the room.

"What was that, Mr. Fontaine?"

Bryce shook his head as he became aware of the constriction in his groin. *Damn! Damn! Damn!* He was hard as a rock. It was a desperately horny man who developed a hard-on while sitting in the middle of a conference room surrounded by his colleagues and subordinates.

The men stared at him, waiting for him to offer some brilliant complement to their discussion. He had nothing. They had assembled to discuss wind turbine models and power, wind maps, access roads, environmental aesthetics and nuisances, and everything else associated with Fonandt Wind Energy, an emerging wind farm corporation owned by Fontaine Enterprises and Andretti Industries.

Fonandt Wind Energy would be one of the few wind farms in New Hampshire, and its expected net production would tremendously exceed all the others put together. The other wind energy companies that were providing power as far south as Boston and north to Vermont were already petitioning the state to restrict the size of Fonandt's farms. They knew, as Bryce did, that it was only a matter of time before he gobbled them up. It was the nature of the beast.

As important as this meeting was to the success of Fonandt

Energy, Bryce knew it would be wise to reschedule. He couldn't concentrate, nor could he contribute anything meaningful to the meeting. He cleared his throat. "Gentlemen, I must confess that I'm a bit preoccupied. It would be in our best interest to cut this meeting short and reschedule."

"But, Mr. Fontaine, this *is* a reschedule. You postponed our first meeting a few weeks ago when one of your godchildren was ill."

Bryce turned his attention to Marcus Spencer, the chief engineer at Fontaine Construction. "Yes, I did do that, Marcus, and I apologize for all inconveniences this will cause each of you, but—" he added, pushing back his chair and rising to his feet now that he'd regained his composure, "since you all work for me, it's my prerogative to cut short or reschedule a meeting as often as I please. If any of you think I'm wasting your time, please feel free to express yourself."

He looked from one man to the other, and when he was satisfied that none of them would dare challenge him, he closed the folder in front of him. "Mrs. Grant will be in to reschedule at each of your earliest convenience," he stated on his way to the door. "Good day, gentlemen." He opened the door then closed it upon his exit.

"Elaine, is everything all set?" he said, coming to stand in front of the desk of his personal assistant, a stout, kind-faced woman in her forties.

Elaine smiled from her chair behind her desk. "Yes Mr. Fontaine. Everything is in place as you ordered."

"Thank you."

"There's a change again," he said. "Could you please schedule another meeting with the gentlemen?"

"Yes, sir."

"And I don't have any other appointments for the day, correct?"

"No, sir. I cleared your calendar up until Wednesday and rescheduled all your appointments. I already uploaded the revised agenda to your phone."

"I appreciate that."

"It's what you pay me to do, Mr. Fontaine."

Bryce chuckled. "I will be leaving shortly."

"I understand, sir."

He was sure she did, Bryce thought as he smiled down at her. Elaine had been his personal assistant for the past four years, but he'd known her for much longer. She was still a faithful member of the church where he used to attend with Pilar, and Michael and Lauren—the church Kaya now attended regularly with the kids.

Elaine had seen him through the beginning and end of each relationship in between. She'd sent flowers, picked out jewelry— most of which he'd seen for the first time on the necks or wrists or dangling from the earlobes of his then current interest. She'd signed birthday, Christmas, and Valentine cards—none of which he'd ever seen. She'd made dinner reservations, and covered for him when he was in no mood to deal with the unpleasantness of unpredictable female mood swings. He'd had no patience for them, and it was usually his cue to end the relationship.

He'd noted the look of relief on Elaine's face when he'd brought Kaya to Fontaine Enterprises and introduced her as his wife. Elaine didn't know Kaya, yet the warmth in her green eyes had assured Bryce that she thought he'd chosen wisely in marrying Kaya.

Elaine was among the very few people in this world whom he trusted.

"When you're finished with them," he said, jutting his chin toward the conference room, "take the rest of the day off. Take your husband out to dinner at *Andreas*. As you know, I have an open reservation there. Tell them I sent you. Order anything you want, on me."

Elaine's eyes lit up as if she'd just won the lottery. "Thank you, Mr. Fontaine. The only time Bill and I dine at *Andreas* is when you take pity on me."

"When are you going to start calling me Bryce?" he asked, beaming at the joy on her face at such a simple favor.

"On the day your first child is born."

Bryce closed his eyes briefly as a dull pain reverberated in his gut.

"Oh, I'm sorry, Mr. Fontaine. I should not have said that. Me and my loose tongue."

Bryce reached across the desk and touched her on the shoulder. "It's okay, Elaine. It doesn't hurt as much anymore. And I do hope that Kaya and I have children. I need an heir to leave all this to."

"I'm glad to hear that. She's a lovely girl. And I'm sure you'll have your full share of beautiful children."

Bryce's lips split on a wide grin. "I'll hold you to that promise. You will call me Bryce the day my firstborn enters the world," he stated, walking across Elaine's office towards his.

Once in his office, Bryce closed the door and headed for the wall of glass that overlooked the immediate vicinity of downtown Granite Falls and the towering mountain range in the distance. It had begun to rain. He loved making love when it rained. A little lightning and thunder wouldn't be unwelcome either.

He pushed his hand into the pocket of his suit pants and pulled out a black strip of lace—his wife's panties from three nights ago. He brought it to his nose and inhaled deeply. Kaya's scent, her taste—like a fine wine with an earthy erotic undertone and a soft delectable finish—were natural aphrodisiacs. Bryce groaned as he felt his temperature rise and his sex engorge with blood and need.

With his free hand, he pulled his cell from its clip at his waist and speed dialed.

"Hi," he said upon her "Hello".

"Oh, hi, Bryce."

The sound of her voice, the echo of his name on her lips made his heart tremble in his chest. "Where are you?" he asked, knowing exactly where she was. He didn't want her to know he kept tabs on her. He knew where she was every moment of the day. Paranoia had taken up residence inside him since the first time he kissed her. His protective instincts had soared to new heights that night in the library when he'd realized the kind of man her ex-fiancé was.

"I'm at the country club with Michelle. We came in for an impromptu spa day."

Bryce smiled. There was nothing impromptu about her visit to the country club. He'd commissioned Michelle to take her in for a manicure, a pedicure, a full-body massage—the works, from head to toe. He wanted her completely relaxed and feeling lovely, desirable, and special tonight—well, today now. "What time will you be done?"

"We're actually finished. We were just enjoying a cup of herbal tea before we leave. I have to pick up Alyssa from ballet. Haley dropped her off but Anastasia is asleep and she can't leave home. And Jason has karate after school."

"It's all been taken care of," Bryce said.

"It is? How?"

"Libby is on her way to pick up Alyssa. I've arranged for a car for Jason. It will take him to karate then home. Libby will stay at the house with Haley and the kids until you get back."

"Back from where? Bryce, what's going on?" Panic edged her voice.

"Nothing to worry about, darling. I just need to see you

alone. We need to talk without the distraction of the kids or anyone else."

"Yeah, I guess we do have some issues to discuss, but I thought we would talk after dinner tonight, if we're not busy doing other things."

Bryce smiled at the hope in her voice. He did promise her that tonight they would finish what he'd started in the kitchen this morning. "It can't wait that long. Our issues need to be addressed as soon as possible. I found myself free this afternoon."

"Oh, okay. You want to meet somewhere? I drove over with Michelle, but she can drop me off wherever you want. I can come to your office."

"There's a car outside waiting to take you to my penthouse. I want you to go up and wait for me. Can you do that?"

"Your penthouse?"

The skepticism in her voice was apropos since she'd never been to his penthouse. Until three days ago, he wasn't ready to share that part of himself with her. His penthouse was where he communed with the ghost of his late wife. He'd never taken a woman there before.

But Kaya was not just any woman. She was his wife. And if he wanted their marriage to work, he had to share all of himself with her, even Pilar's ghost. "Yes, my penthouse."

"Okay."

Bryce took one last sniff of the panties and stifled the groan that lodged in his throat. *Has she missed them at all?* he wondered. He had to make sure to snatch a fresh pair. "I'll see you soon, Kaya," he said, returning the lacy underwear to his pocket.

"Okay. We'll talk soon."

Bryce chuckled after he hung up. Yep, they'll be doing a lot of talking, but not with words. Bryce walked to the huge mahogany desk in the middle of his spacious office and placed his phone on it. He shrugged out of his suit jacket and threw it over the back of his chair. On his way to the bathroom adjoining his office, he began loosening his tie and belt.

He didn't want to waste time showering once he got to the penthouse.

§

Forty-five minutes later, Bryce opened the door of his dimly lit penthouse to the sensual sounds of soft music floating from the surround sound stereo, and the earthy aroma from pillars of burning candles spicing the air.

He stepped inside and his breath caught in his throat at the sight of his wife leaning against the back of the sofa—one black stiletto-clad foot, slightly bent, one hand resting seductively on her thigh, and the other holding a juicy red strawberry, dipped in whipped cream close to her half-opened mouth. Her curly brown hair fell like a mystical curtain down the sides of her lovely face, grazing her shoulders, and hugging the curve of her back. Her eyes were wide and luminous, and full of enchantment and expectation.

"Don't move," he ordered when she made an attempt to straighten up. "And don't talk," he added when she opened her mouth to speak.

She settled down obediently, but not before she brought the strawberry to her mouth and closed her succulent lips around half of it, a wicked smile flashing in her eyes as she brought her hand seductively to rest against her voluptuous cleavage, spilling over the pink lacy bodice of her outfit. She was glowing.

Bryce swore he would have come in his pants if he hadn't recently taken a cold shower. He'd been anticipating this moment; he'd left orders for her to follow, and she'd obeyed. *Good girl.* But God, he didn't expect her to look this freaking tempting and irresistible like a centerfold lingerie model straight out of the latest issue of Victoria's Secret. Bryce didn't know Kaya was the first thing he would see when he came home, much less find her standing in such a provocative pose. She must have asked the front desk to let her know when he arrived. His little recently deflowered bride was staging for him.

He loved it!

She made an erotic picture as she stood there, clad in the sexy lingerie he'd left on the bed for her to wear—innocent and sinful all at the same time, he thought, admiring the soft curves of her brown body through the silky black mesh that made up the lower half of the garment. The shapely beauty of her near-nakedness taunted him. He knew well the full weight of her firm young breasts in the palms of his hands, the smooth texture of her broad areolas and the hard knob of her brown crusted nipples against his tongue, and the sleek sensation of her moist heat opening for him like a morning flower opens its petals to the magic of the sun for the first time.

He quivered at the thought of running his hands up her smooth legs to the sensitive area between her thighs, hooking his fingers in the thin strip of lace running along her delicate hips and pulling her panties down her thighs to her dainty little ankles.

Knowing his wife's copious reservoir of love juices, Bryce could bet that the crotch of that thong was already soaked. Oh yeah, he was keeping those.

He dropped his keys on the table next to the door and shoved out of his jacket, letting it drop behind him. Without taking his eyes off of Kaya, he hastily stripped off his clothes and tossed them in a pile on the floor near the door. When he pulled down his briefs, his sex sprung out with an excited slap against his stomach. He heard Kaya's intake of air into her lungs. Bryce couldn't remember ever being this hard. It was pleasurably painful, and there was only one thing that would stop that ache.

He advanced slowly into the room, his eyes taking in the numerous bouquets of flowers placed strategically about, the red and beige velvet drapes hanging from the windows, blocking out the rain and the world, and the oversized decorated pillows strewn along the floor. A trail of red rose petals began at the foot of the short flight of stairs and extended up to the second floor.

The hotel crew had done an exceptional job preparing the place, and he was sure the bedroom was as romantically decorated as humanly possible. Bryce's eyes caught the red stage and ramp on the floor in front of the burning fireplace—all set and ready for action. Because of his and Kaya's huge differences in stature, he'd requested that two sets of sexual position aids be delivered—one for the downstairs and one for the bedroom. He doubted they would make it that far.

Finally, he stopped in front of his wife, her entrancing eyes twinkling with mischief as she gazed up at him with half of the whipped cream-covered strawberry sticking out of her mouth. "You look ravishing."

She made a guttural sound in her throat, halfway between a moan and a chuckle.

He picked her up, and hoisting up her gown to her waist, he sat her on the back of the sofa. He settled his body between her parted thighs, his hands pressed into the small of her back. He opened his mouth over hers and bit into the portion of red strawberry extending from her lips. Their lips stayed glued together and their tongues worked in unison as they consumed the piece of fruit, chewing, offering, receiving, and swallowing in an oral mating dance until there was nothing but warm breath left between them.

"That was delicious," Bryce said against her lips, savoring the tastes of strawberry, whipped cream and woman on his tongue— tangy, sweet, smooth, wet, and hot. While exploring the soft lines of her back, her waist, and hips, Bryce closed his eyes and nuzzled his nose in the hollow of her neck, breathing in the intoxicating smell of her skin and reveling in the enhanced ultra-silkiness caused by the lingering traces of massage oil. She felt like warm honey under his palm, and for the first time in years, Bryce felt truly blessed.

"And this?" she asked, wrapping her legs around his waist and turning her head slightly to reclaim his mouth as if it belonged to her and she had every right in the world to it. She kissed him deeply and possessively, spurting a hunger in his belly that awakened every single nerve cell in his body. He felt like a helpless log tossed carelessly into a fiery furnace.

Bryce groaned as Kaya hooked her arms under his and began to massage his neck and shoulders with enthusiastic strokes of her hands. As her mouth moved under his, she worked her way down his sides and back, using her palms and her fingertips to blaze a trail of desire down his body. It was the first time she'd fondled him, and he loved the sensations she created in him.

He shivered in her embrace when her hands came to rest on the hill of his buttocks. He groaned as she molded his cheeks in her hands then raked her fingernails over him. Who had taught his inexperienced bride such wantonness? Bryce wondered as his erection, trapped between their stomachs, throbbed with anticipation and need.

A moan of ecstasy slipped through her lips, and he eased his body a hair's breadth away from hers, raised his head, and stared into her eyes. Her pupils were dilated, the amber specks around her irises sparkling, her lips quivering in barely contained desire, her face frozen in a hypnotic state.

"You look exquisite in this, but it's gotta go." He bunched the mesh of her gown in his fist and she extended her hands above her head for him to pull it off. He tossed it on the sofa and his eyes feasted on her alluring figure clad in nothing but stilettos and a black thong. His hands returned to the small of her back. "Touch me," he rasped as his cock pulsed restlessly against his stomach.

She licked her lips as her hands trailed lightly around the sides of his body toward his belly. Bryce felt lust ripple through his chest as her fingers brushed against the hard length of him. He sucked in his breath when she touched the sensitive tip with the pad of her thumb.

"You like that?" she asked, staring up at him with the most incredibly sexy bedroom eyes he'd ever seen.

He swallowed in an attempt to control his breathing as she used her fingertips to lubricate the broad head with the pearly liquid that oozed out of him.

"It's so hard and hot," she whispered, rubbing her palm up and down the length of him like an unsure child—gently, lightly, tentatively, yet so amazingly rousing. "So huge and strong and beautiful."

No woman had ever called him beautiful.

He held his breath and dropped his gaze as her hand attempted to close around him. Wasn't even close. She moaned and dropped her gaze as her other hand joined the first. She still was unable to cover the girth and length of him with her hands stacked up on each other.

Bryce watched in fascination as his massive sex throbbed in her small hands, the veins running the length and width of him so engorged with blood, they appeared as big as her slender fingers trying to span him. Her jungle-red fingernails only served to escalate his desire. An elemental need to conquer her, control her, and pillage her raced through him.

She gazed upward, imploring him with her exotic eyes as she slid her hands up and down him, around and around, squeezing and testing the weight and strength of him.

"Kaya." Fire shot through his system and, as his ache for her deepened, Bryce thrust against her hands, encouraging her, teaching her how to stroke him, and soon she found his cadence, using her hands interchangeably to play him like a flute—lightly, softly, urgently—short-circuiting his senses.

An incessant must-have-it-right-now hunger rolled through Bryce.

CHAPTER SIXTEEN

With his breath racing out of control, Bryce placed his hand on Kaya's, staying her, and stepped back, pulling himself from her grasp. "I'm not wasting it in your hands, baby," he said when her eyes clouded with confusion.

He gazed at her sexy mouth, opened in awe and passion like a freshly cut peach. He longed for the thrill of that mouth sucking him, the nip of her dainty white teeth grazing him, and the tickle of her little pink tongue licking him, but that kind of pleasure would have to come after he soaked himself in the heat of Kaya's essence, feel her soft female flesh stretching to take all of him. *Deep.*

"It's time, love. I must have you now or die."

Her eyes glazed with desire and lust. "I want you inside me. I want to love you, and I want you to love me, right here." She hooked a finger into the crotch of her thong and pulled it back with one hand, exposing herself to his view. "I'm not afraid of you, Bryce," she said, pushing a finger of the other hand inside herself and moving it back and forth. *Slowly.*

"Whoa." It was the most erotic sight Bryce Fontaine had ever seen. His knees buckled. With one arm along her back for support, he reached down with the other and pulled the leg of her thong wider. He dropped to his knees and buried his face between her thighs. "No, put it back in," he rasped as she pulled her finger out.

With a moan, she kicked off her stilettos. They fell with soft thuds on the carpet behind him. She raised one leg and planted her heel on the back of the sofa, draped the other over his shoulder and reinserted her finger. *Wait.* The knuckles of two fingers disappeared inside her heat. She clasped her free hand to the back of his head and began to stroke herself like a nymph who'd pleasured herself a million times before.

The clicking sounds of her fingers entering and retreating from her body was enough to drive Bryce mad. He dropped quivering little kisses on the insides of her thighs, holding her in place with his strong hands as she began to tremble from the effect of her fingers and his lips. When the rhythm of her strokes increased and her breathing grew more erratic, Bryce angled his head around her working hand. He closed his mouth on her scented heat, specifically on her little swollen bud, and proceeded to enjoy his wife, alternating his devotion between licking, blowing, and kissing her until she threw her head back and screamed.

As her body jerked and quivered, he lapped at the juices that ran down the back of her hand. Thank goodness she was so small or he wouldn't have been able to hold her up, so strong was her orgasm.

"My turn to be inside you," he groaned past the constriction in his lungs as her fingers slipped from inside her and her grip on the back of his head relaxed.

With Kaya trapped in the throes of her climax, Bryce pushed to his feet. He lifted her off the sofa, pulled off her wet thongs, and tossed them on her gown as he took the few stumbling steps toward the stage and ramp.

"I want you like this." He laid her face down on the ramp, her upper body sloping downward away from him, and her lower half on the incline, her palatable derrière nice and high and in perfect alignment with his groin.

Dear Lord. Bryce groaned as his gaze skidded across Kaya's body laid out vulnerably before him. She was a work of divine art. Unable to help himself, he knelt behind her, splayed his hands across her cheeks and bending over, he literally kissed her sweet ass.

"Ooh," she murmured, turning her head to gaze back at him, her hair cascading down the side of the ramp like a silky cloud. She looked like a woman who was made simply for lovemaking, for the pleasure of one man, and that man was he. Bryce saw no fear in her, only love, surrender, trust, and passion. Steamy passion, burning brightly in her eyes. It made him long for things, wish for things that he'd been denied for too long.

"Take me," she whispered, licking her rosy lips and wiggling her buttocks at him.

His cock slapped against his stomach like an impatient, agitated snake, anxious to strike.

Straightening up, he edged closer to her and nudged her thighs apart with his knee. He shuddered as his thighs brushed the silky upper curve of hers. He reached forward, and with one hand on the small of her back pressing her into the cushiony ramp, he guided himself with the other. He felt her tremble as his head knocked against her opening, as if asking for permission to enter, but not waiting for a response.

Moans rumbled from both their throats as he slid into her tight heat as far as he dared go. He felt her slick flesh part for him, then contract around him, holding him snugly in its velvet prison. He held her hips in place as he pulled back and pushed forward, easing in a couple more inches.

"I want all of you. Don't hold back." She slid carefully and slowly back and forth on him like a lust-injected wench.

Bryce glanced down to the electrifying sight of his cock buried halfway inside her. It was pure bliss, enthralling esthetic bliss to see the darker length of his masculine sex protruding from the softer, lighter swell of her womanhood. A series of fiery tingles raced up and down his spine as her heat wrapped around him, burning up his flesh. "As you wish, love."

Tightening his hold on her hips, Bryce withdrew completely and rubbed his tip in circular motions around her opening, along her spread lips and up toward her little swollen knob, tickling it with his tip. He repeated the action several times and when she began to moan and push back for more, letting him know she was ready, he pressed against her entrance, swung forward on her backward thrust, and plunged deep.

She let out a spiral scream, then another. Her legs jerked up in reflex, her heels slapping into his buttocks, her hands reaching back to press against his stomach as if to push him away.

Her reaction drew her slippery passage tighter, increasing the friction between their flesh and his excruciating pleasure. A team of wild horses couldn't drag Bryce away. The animal in him had been released and he held her down, flexed his buttocks and kept forging forward until he felt his tip of his shaft hit bottom and the wet opening of her flesh kiss the hairs on his groin. She had it all.

He uttered a low groan and closed his eyes against the force of the passion that rolled over him. He was deep inside her. He felt every quiver of her trembling body burning up each and every inch of his cock packed inside her. Bryce didn't think he'd ever been this deep inside a woman before, and the thrilling sensations sent hot tides of passion swirling around him, hypnotizing him to the point of dizziness.

He forced himself to breathe calmly enough to savor the feel of her silken heat, spreading, squeezing him so exquisitely tight.

Kaya's bravery in opening herself to him, giving him complete control of her body, had awakened a sense of power in Bryce that he never knew existed. Kaya had crowned him King of Passion.

But he had hurt her, he thought as she quivered under him. As her whimpers rose above the music, Bryce leaned over her and rested his chest on her back, his arms over hers, making his upper body one with hers, relishing the head-to-toe, skin-to-skin connection they shared.

"I'm sorry, darling," he said, his heart breaking at the tears streaming from her eyes.

She moaned on a quiver, her eyes glued shut, her mouth slightly parted as she panted from a mixture of pleasure and pain.

Intimate addict that he was, Bryce gathered Kaya in his arms and drew her further into his body, loving the feel of her damp skin melting into his. He kissed the side of her face and the corner of her mouth as he began to rock tenderly against her, kneading his groin into her buttocks, around and around in an undulating wave-like action. He stayed with her, locked in a timeless haven of delight until he felt her muscles relax around him and her breath—warm and moist against his cheek— deepen, as her pain melted into desire.

Finally, she began to dance with him in a sea of ultra-sensual ecstasy, her mouth opening as deep sexual sounds radiated from inside her and resonated through him like a mating call of the wild.

"Yes, that's it, baby. That's it," he whispered as her body welcomed him and merged with his in the most intimate, sensual dance of his life. She rolled with him in a beautiful cadence, heightening his passion as the deepest part of her body gently and lovingly caressed all of him.

"Oh, Kaya, you're so beautiful, so lovely, so exquisite. Yes, yes…"

Her pleasure moans rumbled through Bryce like a runaway freight train, building his need, driving his lust. He eased up and dropped kisses on her neck, her shoulders, her back, as his hand cupped her firm breasts. He rubbed his palms over her mounds until her tender nipples hardened against his palm. He turned her sideways and licked her nipples, loving the feel of the pebbled flesh on his tongue.

She started to shake and quiver and moan and writhe. Recognizing the signs, Bryce sucked her breasts harder and was erotically rewarded with the tightening of her muscles around him. Her body stiffened for a few seconds then a warm gush of moisture bathed his shaft.

It wasn't a strong climax, just a sweet, enchanting release of emotion, as if her body was showing its appreciation for the delight he was bringing it. Her juices trickled along his length and seeped out against his groin, spreading warmth down the insides of his thighs, like a river of love.

As her breath came out in a long moan of surrender, Bryce switched his movements to an in-and-out motion, slowly at first, withdrawing partially and driving in again over and over, feeling her soft wet flesh part and spread for him. He fought to control his thrusts, waiting for her to catch up. The agonizing slow pace of his movements added to his pleasure, and he felt his cock growing thicker and harder as she opened for him, taking him in with her whole body, then gripping him on his endless journey to Nirvana.

They breathed together in timeless euphoria. Holding and releasing, giving and receiving, as their bodies became one, as their souls connected and rejoiced, and their hearts beat as one unit.

"Harder. Deeper," Kaya finally whispered, shoving backwards into his groin.

Her invitation was a passionate challenge, hard to resist.

Bryce completed his downward thrust, moving deep inside her and staying there for a few gut-wrenching moments, pumping and grinding into her. Content that her moan was one of pleasure and not pain, he raised his upper body away from hers and trailed his hands down the wet slope of her back and curled them around her waist.

"Hold on to the ramp," he instructed, as he began to thrust back and forth. The time to be delicate was over. The beast was ready to devour its prey. He held her hips and pumped into her with hard, long strokes, pulling out all the way and slamming her back into the ramp. A tsunami of pleasure overtook him, and he worked his way in and out of her body with brute force.

Kaya's moans, her groans, her screams, a distant rumble in his ears. Her buttocks crashed into his groin as she matched him hard thrust for hard thrust. Bryce closed his eyes and slid deeper and deeper into her softness, their flesh making hard slapping sounds as they sped towards a sweltering pit of desire. He lost all sense of time as Kaya reared back like a wild tigress and took him—all of him—energetically and physically, until he felt as if his skin, his flesh, would melt away from his bones, taking everything, but the parts where their bodies were fused so intimately, so erotically, so wildly.

Dear God, she felt like heaven itself.

Bryce gritted his teeth as bolts of fire rushed up and down his spine. His skin tingled, his stomach cramped with the force of his oncoming climax. He heard himself screaming Kaya's name over and over as deep, earth-shaking tremors crashed over him. He felt himself spinning, falling, crashing as liquid heat bubbled at his groin, then rushed along his sex.

Kaya grunted with each thrust and her tiny body tightened around him.

When she moaned and pushed back against him one last time, Bryce plunged forward with one final deep brutal thrust and collapsed on Kaya's back. He felt her muscles convulse around every inch packed deep inside her, pumping him, sucking him, demanding that he release his love inside her. His body shook violently as he erupted, spurting his seed triumphantly within the deepest parts of her being. His climax felt endless and wonderful as his sex continued to jerk on its own inside her. He closed his eyes and lost consciousness, surrendering to the pleasure currents that pulled him under.

They lay in a wet panting heap, trembling and gasping, their breaths echoing around the room as their lungs fought for oxygen. Neither of them could stop the spasmodic twitching of their bodies as a series of mini pleasure aftershocks reverberated through them.

Much later, when his consciousness returned, realizing he must be crushing Kaya, Bryce rolled onto the floor, bringing her with him. He groaned as his sex slipped from inside her. He spread her out on his chest, belly to belly, the way he loved to hold her, and combed his fingers through her damp strands of hair.

Their breathing was calmed now, their bodies languid and sated. Bryce didn't care if he died right now. He'd touched heaven. Or maybe he *had* died and entered heaven for one splendid moment when all his vigor left him. He felt as weak as Sampson must have felt after Delilah cut his hair.

Women were dangerous. Bewitching.

Reclining atop Bryce's chest, Kaya smiled and inhaled deeply, loving the masculine, musky smell of him and the tickly sensations his chest hair aroused in her nipples nestled inside the curly strands. She loved that he enjoyed holding her this way, on top of him, where he knew she would be safe from the weight of his body. She lifted her head and grinned down at him. "I've never heard a man make those kinds of noises before. I don't think I've ever heard anything make those kinds of noises."

He grunted and raised his hands to hold her damp hair at the back of her head, away from her face. "Honestly, me neither. I didn't know I could make those kinds of noises. I've never come that hard. I swear you're going to be the death of me, woman." He pulled her down and kissed her full on the lips. "I enjoy you so much. You make me crazy."

"And you me," Kaya responded, amazed that she wanted more after that wild ride he'd just taken her on. When Bryce had first lost control, she'd been a little afraid that he'd rip her apart, damage her permanently, but when the feel of his strong hands gripping her hips sliding her back and forth onto him, his powerful pelvis pounding against her buttocks, and his enormous cock sliding and grinding so majestically inside her, some devilishly wicked spirit had overtaken Kaya—mind, body, and soul. Pleasure had pumped through her veins and spurted out of her and around her like molten lava running down the crest of an erupting volcano.

As her body had burned like a Salem witch's, she'd lost her mind, caring about nothing, wanting nothing but for Bryce to engulf her, devour her, brand her with his love. She never knew her heart could race so swiftly, pound so heavily. She never knew her body could open so completely, uninhibitedly, and fearlessly for a man. She never knew she could endure such a pounding and live to smile about it.

"I didn't hurt you, did I?" Bryce asked, brushing his knuckles along her cheeks. "I mean, after that initial rude invasion."

"That was painful. But then you loved me so gently and

carefully that soon my desire began to grow even stronger than before. I loved everything. I loved your fury, your passion. I love the way you master me, control me. I love giving myself entirely over to you. I trust you, Bryce."

"I know you do." His eyes darkened with emotion as they gazed into hers.

What Kaya really wanted to say was that she loved him. But once again, fear and embarrassment lodged the words in her throat. Overcome with shyness, she turned her head away from him and looked around the room he'd prepared for their reunion. He'd turned his penthouse into a romantic lover's den, and Kaya wondered how many other women he'd brought here. How many satisfied lovers had lain in this very spot with him after a long session of lovemaking.

"Hey, what's this?" he asked, placing his hand under her chin and turning her face back towards him as if he sensed she'd left him. His eyes bore into hers, searching out the deepest secrets of her soul.

Kaya wanted to cry. "I'm thirsty," she said. At least it was the truth. "And a little hungry."

His eyes narrowed as if he didn't believe her and then he said, "Me, too."

"Is it normal to be this hungry and thirsty after sex?"

"Only after good sex."

"Good? Is that all it was?"

He groaned when she socked him in the side. "Okay. Okay. Exceptional, mind-blowing, knock-the-ball-way-out-of-the-park, blockbuster sex."

She giggled and snuggled into him. The lighter side of him was a safe place for her to hang out. She couldn't afford to get mushy around him. She didn't want to pressure him, force him to tell her things he didn't really feel. His desire for her was the one thing she knew he couldn't lie about. "Do you think it will always be like this between us?"

His arms tightened around her. "I don't think either of our bodies is equipped to handle this kind of lovemaking every single day. Three times a week at the most, but I promise we will make love frequently and that you'll always enjoy it."

"I'll hold you to that."

"You better." He smiled. "Hold on." Kaya clutched his shoulders as he pushed up to a sitting position, causing her to straddling him. "This is the next position we'll try," he said, his warm gaze making her skin tingle. "But we've gotta eat first. I have no strength left in me. You squeezed me dry."

With a smile in her heart, Kaya rose to unsteady feet. As she stood over Bryce with her private parts inches away from his face, she jutted her hips at him and she said in wicked jest, "You can eat this."

He leaned in and gave her a quick smooch right on her landing strip. "That's dessert. But before we can get to that course, I need to order dinner. Anything special you want?"

She stepped aside to let him up. "Surprise me."

He pushed to his feet and stood towering above her. "I'll join you in the shower after I order dinner," he said, smacking her playfully on her butt.

"Ohh, that feels good." Kaya giggled.

"Yeah. Don't give me any ideas," he warned, stepping over to a table and picking up the house phone.

With warmth spreading across her heart, Kaya headed for the stairs, surprised she could even walk straight.

Hours later, after they'd shared a delicious dinner of raw chilled oysters, an assortment of grilled vegetables, and Lobster

Newberg as the main course, Bryce and Kaya sat huddled together on the sofa in his bedroom and watched the rainstorm through the windows that overlooked the White Mountain Range.

Kaya's lips spread on a smile as she recalled the steamy shower she and Bryce had shared before dinner. She'd enjoyed the tender way he'd soaped her up and given her a thorough washing. She'd reciprocated, loving the feel of his smooth tight body under her palm as she lathered every inch of him.

He'd tried to ignore his mounting arousal, but when it became evident that it wouldn't simple go away, he'd lifted her up in his arms and lowered her unto his hard heat. Kaya's toes curled as she relived the memory of being shattered into a million glowing stars as Bryce's raw sensuousness brought her to a satisfying climax.

He hadn't sought release. His only desire, he'd said, was to please her. Kaya was quickly realizing that she had an incessant ache, a deep, constant craving for this man. It was shameful enough to bring a blush to her face. She wondered if it would always be like this, or if the novelty of making love with her husband would wear off.

Kaya couldn't remember ever being this happy. Not since she was a little girl and her father used to sit with his arms around her, much like the way Bryce was holding her now. He reminded her so much of her daddy, who was just as huge in stature, but who had the biggest, gentlest heart she'd ever known.

Before Bryce, her father and Mrs. Jackson were the only two people in this world who'd been truly good to her. They were the only two people who'd told her they loved her and meant it, and now they were both gone. Kaya shuddered at the knowledge and a tear slipped past her lashes and landed on Bryce's arm.

"Kaya," he said, easing her away from his body to look into her eyes. "Baby what is it?"

"I was just thinking about my dad, and Mrs. Jackson, the only two people who ever cared about me."

"I care about you." His hands were steady and sure as they caressed her upper arms through her satin robe.

She had no doubt that he loved her body, but did he love her heart? "I mean when I was little."

"Who's Mrs. Jackson? A favorite teacher?"

"No. She was one of my foster mothers."

Kaya watched Bryce's chest rise and fall on a deep sigh. The fact that her heart wasn't palpitating in her chest proved that the moment had arrived when she could trust him with her past. How could she not after what they shared today?

He settled back against the sofa and pulled her back into his arms. "You want to talk about it?"

"I think I'm ready."

"Take your time. We have all night." He tucked her snugly to his side and draped his arms about, offering her comfort and protection.

Kaya took a deep breath and rested her hands on Bryce's thighs, feeling his strength and heat through his silk robe. "Jack was right about me spending time in juvenile detention, but it wasn't for prostitution."

Kaya waited for a gasp, a twitch of shock at her confession, but got nothing. She turned her head and gazed up at him. "Did you know?"

He nodded, his eyes sweeping her face apologetically. "After that fight in Steven's office the day we met, I hired a detective. I was determined to use every means necessary to get custody of the kids, even if it meant bringing you down. Your record was sealed and I was ready to find a way to unseal it. But," he continued, his voice holding a hint of shame, "after we kissed that night in the library, I burned it. I didn't care anymore, because I think somewhere in the cold region of my heart, I knew we would end up where we are right now. Besides, hurting you would have hurt the kids. I'm sorry."

"No need to apologize. You were fighting for children you love. I wish I had somebody to fight for me when I was a little girl." She settled back against him, reveling in the comfort and strength he offered her.

"Tell me about that little girl, Kaya. I want to know her."

Kaya faltered on a smile. "She's scared."

"I'm holding her hand. Why did little Kaya spend time in juvenile detention?"

"She was arrested for shoplifting." What a relief to get it off her chest. She hadn't spoken about that dark period of her life since she walked out of that place, eleven years ago. The events had been sealed in her heart, just as surely as the records of her crime had been sealed by the court.

"What did she shoplift?"

"Food."

"Why?"

"She was hungry."

He sat up again and held her hands while he gazed into her eyes. "Why was she hungry? Where was her mother?"

"She'd abandoned her."

His eyes flashed anger. She lowered her gaze to his hand that covered hers on her lap. His touch was warm and comforting at first. Then, as the silence and his anger grew, his fingers tightened.

Kaya soaked up his compassion like an old, dried-out sponge that had been pulled from the broom closet and dunked into a tub of hot water. Nobody had ever stood up for her. Nobody had been surprised that her mother had simply walked off and left her. She was just another unwanted child in Florida's child welfare system.

"Where was your father?" His grip loosened.

"He left when I was five years old." It was so much easier to talk about him after reading Lauren's letter. He'd done what he had to do. If her mother had turned him in, he would have gone to prison, and or perhaps deported since he wasn't a citizen, and neither she nor Lauren would have known him. They may not have known each other, and she would have never met Bryce, the one man in this world she knew she was born to love. "This morning Jason asked me to pack up his parents' things and put them into storage."

"He told me. It's a good sign. He's accepted you. He trusts you."

She nodded. "I found a letter in Lauren's closet that was addressed to me. You'll understand our relationship and the secret about our father better if you read it." She went to the table in a corner of the bedroom and withdrew the letter from her purse. "It was in a shoebox that contained some personal items of my father. It cleared up a lot of doubts and confusions I used to have about him. I don't understand how the box survived the fire that destroyed their home," she said, walking back to the sofa.

"When Lauren came to Granite Falls, she left some boxes in a storeroom at Fontaine Enterprises. She never got them until after they moved into *L'etoile du Nord*."

"It's a good thing then. Lauren would have been heartbroken if she'd lost the only tangible memories she had of Daddy," she said, handing Bryce the letter.

Kaya sat sideways on the sofa, close to Bryce and watched the play of emotions on his face as he read Lauren's letter. When he folded it and handed it back to her, there were tears in his eyes. There were so many issues in that letter that they needed to discuss, but she felt she should address the most pressing one.

"They didn't mean to hurt you by giving the children to me at first Bryce." Kaya laid the letter on the coffee table. "Lauren wanted them to know the only family they had. She was giving me a second chance."

"I think they were giving both of us second chances by not destroying the first will." Bryce chuckled. "She tried to get me to meet you, you know?"

"Really?"

"Mm-hmm. She asked if it was okay if she sent you a picture of me. I said absolutely not."

"Why? You didn't think you would like me?"

"Kaya, as you know, I had the worst reputation with women. Up until eight weeks ago, I was a player, and I didn't want to toy with Lauren's little sister's emotions. Our friendship would have been ruined when I ended it like I ended all my prior relationships."

"You think you would have been able to walk away from me?"

His eyes caught and held hers. "I don't know. It would have been very difficult, more difficult than any of the others. But I was in a different state of mind, a different level of maturity in my life. I think you and I came together at the right time. Any sooner, and it could have been disastrous."

"Maybe you're right. It wasn't until after I met the kids that I realized I could love someone without fear of them leaving me." She sighed. "Did you know about the condition in the second will prohibiting me from taking the kids out of Granite Falls?"

"I didn't. I'm as surprised as you are."

She believed him. "I guess their lawyer was only to reveal the condition if I got custody. What if I had?"

He stroked a finger down her cheek. "I still think we would have ended up exactly where we are."

She smiled knowing that was a fact as well. "You remind me of my dad."

He cocked his head. "Really? In what way?"

"The way you are with the kids. So patient, gentle, and devoted."

"That's a sweet compliment. Were you close to him before your patents split up?"

"Even after they split up. I used to see him every Sunday. We would go to the playground, the zoo, and the museum. Daddy loved to browse through museums. We used to have so much fun together." She smiled easily at the few precious memories of spending time with her father. But just as quickly, it disappeared with thoughts of Nadine's daily abuse. "My mother, on the other hand, was plain old mean. They fought constantly. It was usually about money. She always wanted more."

A tear slipped from her eye as she recalled the day her father walked out of her life. "Daddy was the only happiness I had as a child. Nadine knew that. She couldn't bear the thought of me being happy. She told me that he left because he didn't love me, and I believed her, until this morning when I read Lauren's letter. I spent so many years hating him for leaving me with her."

"Your feelings were apropos. I can't believe you and Lauren had no knowledge of each other's existence. How did you finally find out about each other?"

"At Daddy's funeral. I was twelve. Lauren was practically an adult."

"You must have been shocked out of your minds."

"We were. We didn't quite know what to make of one another. I was jealous of her, because she'd been raised by the father who'd abandoned me and a mother who obviously loved her and was there for her. We exchanged telephone numbers, but then my mother left right after our father died. One night she went out with boyfriend-of-the-month and just never came back. When I woke up the next day, her clothes were gone. The child support check didn't come that month, you see."

"What did you do after she left?"

"I stayed in the apartment," she said, burying her face in her hands for a moment. "Even though she'd been a despicable mother, I wanted to stay where she could find me, just in case she decided to come back. She was my mother, the only family I had."

She shuddered as the sting of Nadine's neglect ripped through her like an old wound that ached on a rainy day. "I was so stupid to think that her feelings for me would change." She pushed to her feet and walked to the windows. The rain was coming down in torrents and Kaya felt that in some divine way, it was washing her hurts, her fears, and her anger away. She felt as if she were being reborn.

"You were just a little girl. You were scared," Bryce said, following her, putting his arms about her. "It's natural to want your mother at any age."

Kaya folded her arms across her middle as her stomach quaked with the memories. "The food in the apartment ran out, then the phone and electricity were cut off. I managed without the phone and the lights, but food I couldn't live without, naturally. It wasn't so bad during the week. I had one of those free lunch cards.

"The weekends were horrible, though. When I couldn't stand the hunger, I would go to the local supermarket and eat my belly full of fruit, bread, cheese, whatever was easily accessible. One day, the owner caught me sneaking out with a bottle of milk and a box of cereal. He called the cops and I was sent to a juvenile detention when they realized I had no one to take care of me. I had to stay there until my trial."

"He pressed charges against you? A child?" Disbelief rang in his voice.

"He was tired of the local kids stealing from him. He was making an example out of me," she said. "Luckily for me, my case worker knew the owner of the store and she persuaded him to drop the charges. Since my mother was nowhere to be found, I was placed in foster care."

"Tell me about your life in foster care."

"Some were good. Others not so good. I moved around a lot. During that time, my mother came back into the picture and wanted me, but my caseworker found out that the man she was living with was a registered sex offender. He'd done time for molesting a couple underage girls, so the courts denied her petition, and the two of them took off."

"Dear God. To think of what could have happened to you if she'd won custody."

Kaya shuddered in his arms. "I try not to think about it. I try no to think that my mother could have been that heartless and sick to barter me off to that man. Anyway, when I was sixteen, I was placed with Mrs. Jackson. She ran a catering business. She was nice to me and she taught me how to cook. I stayed with her even after I turned eighteen and was no longer a ward of the state. She helped me get my degree in interior decorating. She showed me that a woman doesn't have to give birth to be a mother, and just because you gave birth, doesn't make you one. She died a couple years ago."

"I'm so sorry." His voice was barely a whisper. "Did you ever try to find your mother?"

Kaya traced a finger down the cool surface of the glass. "I hired a P.I. once. I just wanted to know why she couldn't love me, why she hated me so much. He found her in New Orleans dancing in a nightclub. She always wanted to be a dancer. She's very beautiful. People used to say I look like her. Anyway, she told the P.I. that she didn't have any children."

"Oh, Kaya." Bryce held her tightly to his chest, his body shaking on a sob. "I'm so, so sorry you had such a horrible childhood. I will make up for it. I promise, darling." He turned her around and pressed her head into his chest, his tears falling on her face, melting into hers.

Kaya held on to him like her life depended on it. She had been abandoned and rejected so many times, by so many people —her father, her mother, her foster parents, and Jack. She couldn't lose Bryce, too. She was so deeply and helplessly in love with him. He said he cared about her, but he couldn't say he loved her, because deep down she knew he was still in love with Pilar.

While they were having tea at the country club, Michelle had told her about the difficult path she and Erik had taken to get to where they were today. Michelle said she'd been patient with Erik because she knew he'd been in love with, and then hurt by his first wife, and that that kind of love and betrayal was not easily forgotten. Kaya would try to be as patient with Bryce as Michelle had been with Erik.

"At least I know my father loved me, even though he wasn't around to protect me," she said.

"His love was protecting you." He raised her face and leaned down to kiss her lips ever so softly, not seeking passion, but offering comfort and support.

"Yeah, I think so. You know that locket I wear sometimes?"

"The one shaped like a fist?"

"Yes. Daddy gave it to me the last time I saw him. He told me that there was a code inside it that would open a safety deposit box at a bank in Palm Beach. He told me not to go to the bank until I was eighteen."

"What's in it?"

"A huge diamond, a document of authenticity, and a letter from my father explaining how he came into possession of the diamond. It belonged to my great-great-grandfather. Some Englishman gave it to him for helping him escape from Kimberley, South Africa, during the 1899 Anglo-Boer War."

"I'm aware of that siege. It lasted about four months. That mine yielded one of the biggest diamonds in the world—the Star of Africa. It weighed in at eighty-three and a half carats, I think. It was given to King Edward the Seventh of England, and is now part of the Crown Jewels collection in the Tower of London. I've seen it. Do you have any idea what such a diamond is worth?"

"Quite a bit. I was tempted to sell it when I found out the kids had no money, but then the situation changed, and here we are. I would have hated to part with it. It is all I have of my family's legacy to pass down to future generations."

"Some things are worth a lot more than money. I still have my grandmother's old coffee maker. Every time it breaks down, I get it fixed."

Kaya chuckled. "I was wondering what that old contraption in your kitchen was."

"Now you know." He kissed the top of her head.

"Since I'm married to one of the richest men in the world, I'll put the diamond in trust for Jason, Alyssa, and Anastasia, and the children you and I will have."

His eyed darkened. "Are you trying to tell me something, wife? We made love three nights ago, and I think there's some kind of test out there that can give results as early as the next day."

"You're not opposed to us having children?"

"Not at all. I want children. Lots of them, and I can't think of them having any other mother but you. I watch you with the kids and I know you'll be the best mother in the world. You're patient and affectionate, and you can cook," he added on a chuckle. "That's all children need. If you can love the children of a sister whom you once resented, I know you will love our children."

"And you'll be the best father," Kaya told him, gazing up at him with love and wonder in her eyes.

"Let's go to bed," he said, taking her by the hand and leading her across the room towards the huge bed. "I want to hold you, let you know I'm here, show you how much I care."

Like an obedient child, Kaya followed Bryce, and when he pulled down the covers, slipped off her robe, then his own, and lifted her gently unto the bed, Kaya knew that she was exactly where she belonged. *Home.*

But was Bryce? The fact that he was still living in this penthouse told her that he was still holding on to Pilar. He was still out in the cold, maybe closer to home, but not completely. Their roles had switched. She was no longer the reluctant bride who was not only afraid to make love with her husband, but who was also afraid to love him. Bryce was now the reluctant groom.

Yet, when Bryce joined her on the bed, Kaya opened her arms to him. Maybe, just maybe, he would come home tomorrow, she thought as he laid her out on his stomach, wrapped his arms about her and captured her lips with his.

"I want you like this. Woman on top, all night long," he said, capturing her mouth with his.

Their lovemaking was slow and tender. Passions peaked. Emotions swelled, and tears fell, as they loved each other into the wee hours of the morning.

CHAPTER SEVENTEEN

Kaya awoke to the faint hum of distant voices. She opened her eyes and tried to focus in the semi-darkened bedroom. She reached out her hand and groped around the bed. Bryce was gone. The place where he had lain and cradled her while he transported her from one thrilling orgasm to the next last night, was now empty and cold.

Kaya turned on her back and strained her ears to the sounds. She could distinctly make out the low, baritone pitch of Bryce's, and another equally low male voice that she didn't recognize. She couldn't fully make out the conversation, but she could tell that it wasn't pleasant.

When she heard the higher-pitched tone of a woman's voice, Kaya jumped off the bed and reached for her robe. Shrugging into it, she tiptoed toward the foot of the stairs. The voices were louder, but she still couldn't make out the conversation.

With her heart pounding in her chest, Kaya eased quietly down the stairs until the hum became distinct words. She plopped down on a step just before the stairway curved. Out of sight, but within hearing distance, she wrapped her hands around her legs and rested her chin on her knees. The position in which she was sitting took Kaya back to the day when her parents had made her sit on the steps outside their apartment while they argued inside—the day she'd seen her father for the last time. Her heart thundered with anxiety.

"Why do you keep shutting us out of your life, Bryce? Just like your first marriage, we had to read about this one from the latest issue of Granite Falls People Magazine. We almost didn't make it for your and Pilar's wedding. And we weren't even aware of this one. My own son has been married for over a month and I just heard about it yesterday." The woman sounded close to tears.

His parents, Kaya realized with a mixture of curiosity and confusion swirling inside her. Why hadn't Bryce told his parents about her? She hadn't given any thought to his relationship with them. He'd spoken of them briefly and affectionately the two times he'd mentioned them, but because her own experience with the parent/child relationship was so warped, Kaya never thought of asking Bryce about his. She'd thought it normal. Whatever normal was.

She would never have guessed there was any discord between them. Bryce was a master at masking his emotions, except those that were related to sex.

"A month," his father reiterated. "We've spoken on the phone several times, and not once did you mention that you'd remarried and raising your godchildren. I have three grandchildren and I didn't even know it."

"You weren't here," Bryce stated in a tone Kaya thought quite despondent.

"Yes, we were in Asia, but you could have mentioned it in a phone call. We would have flown back for the ceremony and then gone back to finish our work there."

"That's it, Mom. You are never here. You're always there, and everywhere, but here," Bryce declared as if holding a raw emotion in check.

"So we're back to that," his father stated in an irritating voice. "We're back to your childhood. We had to work, Bryce. You know that. We had to work to provide a decent life for you."

"Because we love you. We wanted the best for you," his mother said on a sniffle.

"I know you love me. I don't doubt that. But you weren't there when I was sick, or scared, or even when I was happy about some simple accomplishment. You let Grannie raise me. The best you can give your child is yourself, Mom. That's what Grannie gave me. Herself."

"Well, if she hadn't made me work two jobs, sometimes three to pay for your boarding school, especially when she could have afforded to pay for it herself, I may have been free to spend more time with you," his father retorted defensively. "I still can't believe she was sitting on all that money when I was breaking my back."

"You wouldn't have spent more time with me." Bryce chuckled sarcastically. "She made you pay for my education because she wanted you to have a part in my success, Dad. Haven't you figured that out, yet? She didn't do it out of spite or meanness. Because you were working so hard, it made me work harder to make you proud. I received full scholarships from every Ivy League college I applied to."

There was a long, brittle silence then Bryce spoke again. "After Pilar and I were married, I asked you to move to Granite Falls so you could get to know her, and be near me and the grandchildren we planned to give you. But your friends and your life in New York were more important than me."

Kaya's heart felt as if it would burst. She covered her mouth with her hands to keep from crying out. *It's natural to want your mother at any age,* Bryce had said yesterday when she'd told him about her mother's abandonment. Apparently, there was more than one way to abandon a child.

"I didn't tell you about Kaya and the kids because I don't want them to get close to you and then be disappointed when you don't show up as you promised. I don't want them to ever feel that anything or anyone is more important than them."

Tears slid from Kaya's eyes.

Bryce loved her.

He either just didn't know it, or couldn't say it yet. The knowledge warmed her heart.

"I'm sorry if that's the way we've made you feel all these years, son," his mother said, breaking the silence that was growing tight with tension. "We didn't know. You're so big, and strong, successful, and important. We didn't think you needed us."

"I'll always need you, Mom, Dad. Always." His voice trembled with emotion. "I don't resent you. I just learned to live without you. The question is, do you need me?"

"Oh, Bryce. My baby. I need you. I need you."

Kaya heard feet shuffling across the hardwood floor, then thuds as if arms were being slapped about each other.

Kaya didn't even know her sobs had reached the trio in the kitchen until a shadow appeared on the stairs below her. She held her breath as she peered through her tears at Bryce, clad in jeans and a sweater, standing with one hand on the railing, staring up at her.

His eyes were red, his face puffy. She knew that he knew she'd been eavesdropping, but there were no traces of judgment or concern in his countenance.

He reached out his hand to her. "Come, meet my parents."

"I'm not dressed," she said, staring down at her bare feet

with red toenails sticking out from beneath her robe. She ran her hands over her rumpled curls, trying to brush errant strands from her face.

"It's okay. They're family."

There was nothing for Kaya to do but walk down the stairs toward him. He put his arms about her shoulders and led her silently into the kitchen where his parents were standing around the island, expectant looks on their faces as if they were waiting for Michelle Obama to appear.

Bryce stood behind her, his hands still resting on her shoulders, his thumbs massaging the nervous muscles in her upper neck. "Mom, Dad, this is Kaya, my wife. Kaya, these are my parents, Henry and Lillian Fontaine."

"Oh my God, Bryce." Lillian clasped her hands to her mouth, a wide smile on her face as she stared at Kaya. "She's gorgeous. Absolutely gorgeous."

"Kaya. What a lovely name for a lovely girl," Henry said.

"It's nice meeting you," Kaya said, looking from one to the other, not quite knowing what to make of them. They must have been aware that she'd been eavesdropping on their emotional and extremely private conversation with their son.

Henry Fontaine was tall and broad with a full head of salt and pepper hair. Bryce was a chip off the old block with the same wide forehead, thick brows, prominent nose and lips, and a strong jawline and chin. His eyes, though, Kaya noted with interest were his mother's—dark and intense, with tenderness lurking in the background. Lillian was a few inches shorter than her husband, and sported a curvaceous body that looked as if it spent a lot of time at the gym. Her long black hair was done up in a sophisticated style away from her long attractive face. Kaya remembered that Bryce had said she used to be a hairdresser. With all the little girls in the family, Kaya thought her skills would come in handy.

"Can I hug you?" Lillian asked, opening her arms wide.

Bryce pushed her forward, and Kaya fell into the soft, welcoming bosom of her mother-in-law.

"Welcome to the family, dear," Lillian said, as she clasped Kaya in a tight, genuine hug.

Kaya glanced up as Henry came up behind his wife and, reaching around her with long arms, he hugged Kaya's shoulders. "Yes, daughter, welcome."

Kaya smiled at him, knowing that if she were fully dressed, he would have hugged her to his chest. But he was a gentleman, just like his son.

She stood back when they released her. "Thank you, um—" She had no idea what to call them. Lillian and Henry? Mr. and Mrs. Fontaine? Or…

"Mom and Dad is good," Lillian said, astutely picking up on her uncertainty.

"Okay. Mom and Dad, thank you."

"Maybe you should get dressed now," Bryce said, placing his hands on her shoulders again. "I'll order up some breakfast."

"Okay," Kaya turned to walk out. She needed to breathe and compute.

Bryce pulled her back, and leaning down, he planted a quick kiss on her lips. Even with his parents standing a few feet away from them, Kaya felt the effects of his magical touch.

"Everything will be okay," he whispered against her mouth, then gave her a tender push toward the living area.

"Don't be too long," Lillian called after her. "We have a lot of catching up to do, plans to make, missions to accomplish."

Lillian's first mission was to convince Bryce—no, Kaya thought, her first mission was to *demand* that Bryce move out of his penthouse and into *L'etoile du Nord*. For a husband and wife to sleep under two separate roofs, she'd said, was no way to start a marriage, much less maintain one.

Bryce being Bryce had kicked up a storm of protest, but Lillian Fontaine, Kaya had quickly learned was not a woman who took "no" for an answer. *Like mother, like son*. Two days after they'd arrived in town, Lillian had gone to Bryce's penthouse, packed up all his clothes and had them delivered to the house while he was at work. She hadn't even left him a pair of boxers.

As Kaya sped along Route 80 in her brand new white *Maybach Landaulet*—a wedding present from Bryce—she smiled as she remembered the fury in Bryce's eyes as he'd stormed up the stairs and into the second-floor balcony family room at *L'etoile du Nord*, and ordered his mother to stay out of his life.

"You asked to have me in your life, remember?" Lillian had sweetly responded, never missing a beat as she rocked Anastasia in her arms. "I'm only doing what I know is best for you, your wife, and these children."

He'd glared at his father, who was hunched over a chessboard, deeply concentrating on his game with Jason. "Were you part of this?"

"She's your mother, son. And what your mother wants, your mother gets. You know that. Besides, think of the perks," he'd added, winking at Kaya, who'd been trying to fashion Alyssa's hair into two French braids, the way Lillian had taught her.

"What are perks?" Alyssa had enquired, petting Webster who was sprawled out next to her on the sofa.

"Perks are good stuff," Jason had answered. "Checkmate!"

"Argh!" Henry had groaned. "Who taught this boy to play Chess?"

"The coolest aunt in the world." Jason had beamed at Kaya.

Anastasia had let out a tremendous burp and everyone doubled over with laughter.

"Goodness," Lillian had said, wiping Anastasia's mouth with the edge of a baby blanket. "I'll have to have a serious talk with this child, teach her how to burp like a lady."

"You do that, Mom, and since it's Haley's night off," Bryce had growled, picking up Alyssa from Kaya's lap and walking over to deposit her on Henry's, "you two old busybodies can take care of the kids while I go enjoy my perks."

He'd scooped up a giggling Kaya, tossed her over his shoulder and climbed the stairs to the third-floor master suite like a formidable caveman on a ravishing mission. In the bedroom, he'd dumped her unceremoniously on the air mattress where they'd first made love, and came down on top of her. They didn't leave that room until noon the next day.

That was weeks ago.

Winter had finally melted into spring, and April showers were working hard to prepare the ground for blooming May flowers. Henry and Lillian had since moved to Granite Falls, and were staying at *L'etoile du Nord* until Bryce found them a suitable home close by. He said he'd build one if he had to.

The kids loved having "wicked cool" grandparents and had began calling them "Grandpa Henry" and "Grandma Lillian". Alyssa was finally sleeping through the night in her own bed, and Jason was lavishing Kaya with hugs and kisses in front of his friends, like he used to do with his mother.

Lillian's second mission was helping Kaya furnish the third-floor master suite. It was elegantly and romantically decorated with three base colors of red, gold, and beige, and an enormous rotating bed that was situated in the middle of the bedroom. It was raised on a round platform with three wide steps that ran the perimeter, leading up to it.

Most nights, moonlight lulled her and Bryce to sleep in each other's arms and most mornings, the sun kissed them awake, still locked together in satiated bliss. Kaya loved waking him up in her own special way. Morning sex had become a natural part of their daily routine, and it was the hardest part of the day—no pun intended—for Bryce because he was never happy to leave her bed.

He'd kept the penthouse, and sometimes Kaya would meet him there for a quick lunch and a "marital romp", as he put it. And the times when he couldn't get away, he'd summon her to his office for a quickie on his desk, or his couch where he conducted his professional business. Sometimes, she just showed up and surprised him. Talk about mixing business and pleasure.

But best of all, Bryce's nightmares had all but ceased, and last Sunday, his parents had enticed him to attend church with them.

They had all morphed into a wonderful, loving, happy family.

Yet, something was amiss.

Bryce had still not told Kaya that he loved her, even though he frequently showed her in countless ways, like jetting her off to Paris or Milan for a day or two and showering her with priceless jewelry. The one thing that touched her most, though, was his daily delivery of white and yellow orchids to the house. She knew he signed each card on a daily basis, because he would always refer to some event that happened the night before.

Why couldn't he tell her that he loved her? Kaya wondered as she made a turn onto Evergreen Drive in downtown Granite Falls and spotted the steel and glass tower of Fontaine Enterprises looming ahead of her. Before Kaya could analyze her actions, she'd passed the street to the post office—the reason she'd come into town to sign for her father's jewelry that she'd had sent from the bank in Palm Beach—and was heading toward Fontaine Enterprises.

Bryce had not come home last night, but had stayed at the penthouse. He'd reassured Kaya that all was well, and that he just had to concentrate on a huge international business deal that was to take place the next day. However, right on time, her orchids, with a card stating that he missed her, was delivered that morning.

As Kaya pulled into her personal parking space in the underground garage, next to Bryce's silver-grey Lamborghini, her heart began to beat faster. As she walked toward the elevator, she felt like she was spying on her husband, but that thought was foolish since she'd surprised him many times in the past by showing up announced. He'd always welcomed her. This time would be no different.

Kaya stepped off the elevator onto the tenth-floor that housed the private quarters of the CEO of Fontaine Enterprises. In addition to several conference rooms, there were only three offices on this floor: Bryce's, Elaine's, and Libby's.

Kaya strolled tentatively down a short hallway to discover that Elaine wasn't at her desk. She checked her diamond watch. Well, it was noon. Both Elaine and Libby were probably at lunch. She glanced at Bryce's half-opened door as knots formed in her stomach. Should she call and let him know she was here, or should she just barge right in? She stepped closer and male voices drifted from inside.

"I definitely think it's the way to go, Bryce. I mean the Chinese are…"

Kaya smiled as she recognized Massimo Andretti's voice. She'd met him at the last Club gathering that had taken place at the LaCrosse's home. She'd instantly liked Massimo, or Mass as his friends called him. He was tall, wide-shouldered, and handsome like the rest of the gang, but his reputation with women far exceeded Bryce's. Kaya had taken comfort in the knowledge that there was a bachelor who trumped her husband in infamy. She wondered about the woman who would dare to tame the Italian playboy's heart. She almost felt sorry for her.

Feeling a sense of rightness, Kaya walked bravely through the door. Massimo stopped in mid-sentence and glanced up at her, his bright blue eyes and his smile warming her. He immediately got up from the table where he and Bryce were hunched over some piles of papers.

But when her husband turned around and let his dark gaze slide lazily over her, Kaya's heart began to pound and her knees felt weak. She still couldn't understand how he had the power to make her tremble every time she was near him.

He pushed to his feet and came toward her. "Darling, what a wonderful surprise."

She melted into his arms, loving the smell and feel of him. "I hope my interruption doesn't cause a problem. I know you're very busy men running huge corporations."

Bryce released her and stood back. "I think we covered all the bases for now," he told Massimo. "We're scheduled for another meeting with the Fonandt crew in a couple weeks. We'll have more details then."

Massimo walked toward them. "You look more beautiful each time I see you, Kaya." He brought her hands to his lips and kissed the outsides of her wrists. "I haven't seen my brother this happy in years. He's a lot more pleasant to be around, and sports a stupid grin on his face all the time. You've worked wonderful magic on him."

Kaya smiled shyly up at him and laced an arm around Bryce's waist. She knew that grin very well. It was the grin of absolute happiness and complete carnal satisfaction. She wore it, too. "It's what a good wife does for her husband. You should get one, Mass."

The grins on the men's faces vanished as they exchanged wary glances.

"That's my cue to leave. Catch you later, buddy," Massimo

told Bryce. He bowed courteously to Kaya before practically running out of the office.

"Did I say something wrong?" Kaya asked as Bryce closed the door and locked it as he always did when she visited him.

"It's a long story. And I'm forbidden to talk about it." He took her hand and led her across the spacious room toward the couch.

"Even to your wife?" As they passed his desk, Kaya tossed her purse on it. Hopefully, she'd be hunched over it later with Bryce pumping inside her from behind.

"I'm sorry, darling, but I can't discuss it with you. It's Massimo's business, nothing to do with us," he said, pulling her down on the couch beside him and wrapping one arm about her while holding her hands with his left. "Now, to what do I owe the honor of this wonderful surprise visit?" He leaned over and kissed her on the lips, his face breaking into the stupid grin Massimo had just mentioned.

Kaya knew that in a minute or two, they'd be naked on the couch. They were incapable of keeping their hands off of each other when they were alone. Her body quivered with anticipation, and moisture gathered between her legs. "I missed you last night, and since I came into town to pick up that package from the post office, I thought I'd— Oh my God," Kaya whispered as she glanced down at Bryce's hand on her lap. The ring on his finger wasn't the one she'd put there. Without being told, she knew that it was the one Pilar had given him over five years ago. No wonder he couldn't tell her that he loved her. He was still in love with Pilar.

The mountain of desire that had been building inside Kaya crumbled into dust.

How could she have been so stupid to think that she could make him forget his first love? Tears welled up in her eyes. She fought out of Bryce's embrace and struggled to her feet, stepping back to put distance between them. She couldn't bear to be near him right now. Her stomach crunched up in painful little knots, and blood rushed to her heart and lungs, making breathing painful and difficult. She felt as if she was about to explode, or faint, or vomit, or all three together.

Bryce pushed to his feet. "Kaya, what is it? What's wrong?" He reached out to her.

She jumped back, bumping into his desk. "Don't touch me!"

"Kaya. What is the matter with you?"

"You're still in love with her," she said, glaring at him through her tears as she pushed the words past the scorching pain in her throat. "You're still in love with Pilar. You're wearing her ring, Bryce. You took mine off, and you're wearing hers." She dropped weakly against the edge of his desk and covered her face with her hands.

Bryce stared down at his finger as the sounds of his wife's sobs tore into his chest and his gut, and ripped his heart wide open. *Damn!* How could he have been so careless as to wear Pilar's ring to work? How could he be so stupid and insensitive to be wearing it at all?

Over the past weeks, Kaya's love for him had taken him to heights of ecstasy that he never dreamed he'd experience again. In fact, they had taken him beyond any he'd ever experienced before. At first, he'd thought that it was just the amazing sex, the undying fire and unquenchable lust between them, but as the days turned into weeks, and months, Bryce had come to realize that in addition to Kaya's exquisite little body, her tantalizing touches, and her mesmerizing smile, it was her warm heart, her pure mind, her vivacious spirit, and her virtuous soul that had captured him.

He was hopelessly and undeniably in love with her.

Bryce ripped the ring from his finger and tossed it on the table where it rolled before nestling between the piles of paper. *Damn it!* He hadn't worn it for weeks, but yesterday had marked the six-year anniversary of Pilar's death.

He'd wanted to mourn her alone, the way he'd done for the past five years. That's why he hadn't slept at *L'etoile du Nord* last night. How could he lie in Kaya's arms at approximately the same hour, six years ago, when Pilar had lain dying in his arms?

It didn't seem right, fair. He'd just wanted to let Pilar know that he hadn't forgotten her like everyone else had, that even though he'd moved on, she would forever be in his heart. He'd always been so careful to return the ring to its secret place in the drawer of his nightstand. Perhaps he was wrong to omit Kaya from that part of his life, keep secrets from her.

Bryce's hands clenched into tight fists at his sides, as he watched his wife slumped against the desk. Her sobs had ceased and her face was still buried in her hands, and an occasional shudder rocked her lithe body. He wanted to reach out and pull her into his arms, tell her how much he loved her, but he was afraid, afraid she'd reject him, and they'd be right back to where they'd started months ago. He never wanted to hear her say, "Don't touch me," ever again.

"Kaya," he said softly. "I'm sorry. You don't deserve this. It's just that—"

He stopped when she raised her face and stared at him. Icy fear twisted around Bryce's heart when he saw the pain and dread in her eyes. The only other time he'd seen that look in her was the moment she'd found out that he had custody of the children. That moment, Bryce had sworn that he'd never cause her that kind of pain and distress again.

But he had, and it horrified him. It made him feel as small as a bug to have hurt her.

"It's what, Bryce?" she asked in a choked whisper. "It's just that you still love Pilar, and it's the reason you've never told me that you love me?"

"Kaya, I…" He let his voice trail off. She was right. He'd never told her that he loved her because he was afraid to. He'd told Pilar every single day that he loved her. It was the last thing he said at nights, and the first thing in the mornings. After she died, Bryce had wondered if he'd loved her too much. Was fate jealous and had decided to punish him for loving another so deeply?

He'd known for certain that he loved Kaya when he'd walked into the nursery the day they met and found her holding a screaming Anastasia. She looked awkward and scared and had no idea what she was doing, but yet Bryce had looked far into the future and seen a more experienced, confident Kaya, comforting their own baby in that very room. When she'd squirmed uncomfortably while he explained the varying textures and sizes of nipples, he was ready to plant his seed inside her and watch her belly grow with it.

And now here he was, about to blow that dream to hell.

He took a step forward, his fingers itching to soothe her damp curls away from her face, the way he always did after they made love. "Kaya, you know how I feel about you."

"Then why can't you tell me, Bryce? Why can't you tell me you love me?" She glanced at his hand.

He held it up and pointed to his ring finger. "I took it off."

She uncurled from the desk, unmoved, and tucked her hair behind her ears. She straightened her shoulders, an air of sophistication and confidence in her countenance. Her brown eyes were full of life, pain, and unquenchable warmth as she held his captive. "Bryce, I know a part of your heart will always belong to Pilar, and I don't begrudge her that. But I will not have you longing for her, wishing she were still alive, and lamenting over what could have been. I will not share you with her, not in that way." She swallowed. "I told you that I loved you the first time we made love. I don't know if you heard me or not."

Bryce decided that now would not be a good time to admit or deny that he'd heard her.

She sighed deeply, and even in her state of displeasure with him, a gentle softness deepened her voice. "I love you, Bryce Fontaine. I love you with every beat of my heart, every inch of my skin, every thought of my mind, and every light of my soul. I love you."

Bryce closed his eyes as her words washed over him, bathing him in divine wonder, bliss, happiness. "Kaya—" His voice and body trembled.

"But as I said, I will not share you in that way with Pilar. You have to choose, Bryce. You have to choose whose wedding ring you want to wear. You can't switch back and forth between us."

"Kaya, I don't—"

She put her hands up to stop him. "Anything you say right now will seem contrived. I don't know why you took off my ring and put on Pilar's. Only you know the reason. So whatever it is, you need to fix it, deal with it. Get over it. Do whatever you need to do, but don't come home until it's done, until you're ready to tell me that you love me, give yourself to me completely. You promised to love me, forsaking all others—that includes Pilar. You have to prove that you meant it." She picked up her purse from his desk and stumbled toward the door, her stifled sob twirling about the air in her wake.

Bryce watched helplessly as his wife walked out of his office. He stumbled backwards onto the sofa, holding his chest as a tightening gripped his heart. At least she didn't tell him not to come home, just not to come home until he could be completely and openly honest with her.

He couldn't lose her. She was his world. All she had to do was smile at him, slip her small hands into his, and the universe melted away. Love wasn't an invitation to heartbreak. It was the doorway to happiness.

Bryce pushed to his feet and walked over to the table where he'd tossed Pilar's ring. He picked it up and, folding his fist around it, he walked out of his office.

CHAPTER EIGHTEEN

The morning sun was bright and the breeze coming off Lake Michigan was pleasantly cool for a Chicago spring. Adjusting his sunglasses, Bryce climbed out of his rental car and skimmed the perimeter of the cemetery, happy there was no one in sight. People didn't usually visit cemeteries in the middle of the week and this early in the morning, especially after an unexpected early-spring snowstorm like the one they had last night.

He went to the passenger side, picked up a bouquet of roses and a screwdriver from the front seat, then taking a deep breath, he began walking down Celestial Path, paying little attention to the snow-dusted monuments and statues along the way. He would have buried her in Granite Falls, but her parents wanted her in Chicago. He'd obliged, since in all fairness, he hadn't known her that long.

His heart beat faster and his pace grew slower at each step he took toward her grave. Part of him wanted to turn back, to keep holding on, never let go of what they had, of what they could have been. Another part propelled him forward, the part that wanted to live, to move on, to be happy once again.

Finally, he reached the grave under a poplar tree where Celestial Path and Happy Avenue intersected. *What genius named these roads?* Bryce wondered, pushing the screwdriver into the side pocket of his wool coat. And what had enticed him to bury Pilar here, in this very spot?

He'd spent the past three days in his hotel room, mustering up the courage to visit the resting place of his wife and child. He'd been here several times over the past six years to reassure them that he still loved them, that he carried them in his heart every day. Today, he'd come to say goodbye.

He bent down and brushed a fresh layer of snow off the tombstone, then placed the roses below the inscription on the headstone: *Pilar Sanchez-Fontaine and Unborn Child. Beloved Wife. Beautiful Daughter and Sister.*

Bryce swallowed a moan as tears burned his eyes. She would have been a great mother if she'd only been given the chance. She'd been so excited when she'd called him that night.

"Hurry home, darling. I have something to tell you. Something that would make you very happy."

"Did you finally decide on the right color tile for our bathroom?" he teased. *She'd been so indecisive about what to do with the master suite.*

"This is even better."

"So tell me."

"It's a surprise and I'd rather tell you in person."

"Pilar, you know I hate surprises."

"You'll love this one. I promise."

Bryce shook his head, and pulled off his sunglasses, shaking his tears off the frame. He'd been living in the past for too long. He had to move forward. Standing upright, he pushed his hand in the pocket of his slacks and pulled out the wedding band. He held it in the palm of his hand, and the white gold coruscated against the sunlight, almost blinding him.

He closed his fist around it.

"I told you that I would love you forever. And I will. Just not in the same way I did when you were here with me. You see, darling, there's someone else. I— I— um, I married someone not too long ago. She's sweet— like you were. She loves me, and she makes me happy. I love her, too. Problem is, I can't tell her how I feel until I let you go."

He chuckled on a sniffle. "You know me. I'm a one-woman man. When I'm with a woman, I'm with her, and no one else. I kept my promise for as long as I could, Pilar. I don't want to lose Kaya. Yes, that's her name. Kaya. Kaya Brehna-Fontaine. She's Lauren's sister. Half-sister. You would have liked her."

What was he saying? His late wife would have liked his current wife, the woman he loves?

He pulled the screwdriver from his pocket and began to dig a hole where the tombstone and the hard ground met. When he was satisfied that it was deep enough to protect against vandalism, he dropped in the wedding band and covered it up. He would be back when the snow melted and the ground softened to give it a permanent burial.

He needed to do this for now. Kaya had meant it when she'd told him he couldn't come home until his heart was completely free to love her. She hadn't even let him into the house to pack his clothes. She'd sent his father to his penthouse with a suitcase already packed.

He wanted to go home.

"We did have some happy times," he said, rising to stand at the foot of the grave. "I'm sorry it was so short, and that I didn't protect you. Please, forgive me for that. I will always remember you and the baby our love created. I often wonder which one of us he or she would have most resembled. Either way, our baby would have been beautiful because our love was beautiful."

Bryce cast his eyes heavenward to a deep-blue, cloudless sky then back to the grave one last time. One day, her soul, up there, would return to her body, down here, and they would be reunited. But for now...

"Goodbye, Pilar, my love. Goodbye, my sweet babychild."

Blinded by his tears, Bryce turned his back on his past, and walked up Celestial Path, toward the future that awaited him in Granite Falls.

Naked, his body warm from his shower, Bryce stood at the top step and gazed down at his sleeping wife. She looked so small, so childlike lying in the humongous bed. He eased down on the edge of the mattress, trying not to disturb her—or perhaps he should disturb her, he thought, reaching out to brush her soft curls away from her face bathed in moonlight.

He could live a thousand years, Bryce realized, and he would never tire of gazing at Kaya. She had the longest, curliest lashes, the daintiest nose, the sexiest lips, and the hottest mouth. He'd taught her how to pleasure him with her mouth, and a fiery ache settled in Bryce's loins as he recalled the abundance of indescribable pleasure the strong suction of those lips and mouth brought him.

It had been four days since he'd last seen her, yet it felt like a year to Bryce. He never wanted to go a day without seeing her again, even if it was only by satellite. He wanted to gaze into her fiery brown eyes every single day for the rest of his life, and tell her that he loved her. How could he not love her when she epitomized the various cultural meanings of her name: forgiving, restful place, home, wise child. But most significant of them all: pure and beautiful body?

Bryce drew back the covers and scooted down next to Kaya. Wearing clothes to bed was something they'd both realized was a waste of time. They made love almost every night, sometimes three and four times, into the morning hours, and sometimes beyond. After missing a couple of early morning meetings when he couldn't drag himself away from Kaya's tantalizing body, or when he awoke to the suction of her hot mouth on his swollen sex—her favorite way of waking him up—he'd had to rearrange his regular schedule at the office. The times when he absolutely had to go in early, he groaned all the way in, but then he'd groan in a different way later on in the day when his insatiable wife showed up in his office, wearing nothing but a warm winter coat.

With misty eyes, Bryce gazed at Kaya's slender, naked body, mesmerized at her beauty, grateful that she'd waited for him, chosen him to love her, enjoy her for the rest of their lives. She belonged to him. Only him. Until he met Kaya, until he'd made love to her, Bryce never knew that he could long for, ache for another human being this much. She'd turned him into a Kaya addict. It was a high he never wanted to come down from.

Reaching out, Bryce eased his left arm under Kaya, his right arm across her, and pulled her close, the warmth exuding from her soft skin seeping into his pores, making his heart tremble, his limbs weak.

He tightened his hold and burying his face in her hair, he breathed in her sweetness.

"Bryce?" she whispered, stirring against him, her warm breath tickling the hairs on his arms.

"Yes, baby, it's me. I'm back. I'm home." *He was home. Kaya meant home to him.*

She turned completely around and nestled her face in the hollow of his neck. "I'm glad."

No explanations were necessary. His being home was enough for her.

"Kaya." Bryce turned on his back, bringing her on top of him then reached up to turn on the bedside lamp. He wanted to look deep into her eyes. "Wake up, baby. Look at me."

She raised her head from his chest and her eyelids fluttered a few times as she tried to adjust her pupils to the soft light. "Hi." She gave him a sleepy smile that made his toes curl.

He cupped her face in his hands. "I love you, Kaya Brehna-Fontaine," he said, his voice trembling with the emotions that swelled inside him. "I love you with every cell in my being, with every breath in my lungs. I love you, and I will tell you that every day, several times a day until you beg me to stop."

"I never will," she said with a tremor in her voice. Tears pooled in her eyes as they darkened with love and passion. "Say it again."

"I love you, Kaya. I love you. I love you. I love you…"

"I'm pregnant." Her eyes were wide as she stared at him, waiting for a reaction.

Bryce went stiff as his heart stopped beating for a few seconds. He closed his eyes to let the information sink in. He swallowed the lump that lodged in his throat before he asked in a trembling voice, "Are you sure?" He didn't want to get his hopes up, seem too happy, tempt fate again.

"Yes. I'm sure. I've been having morning sickness for three days now, so I bought a test. It was positive. I went to see Erik this afternoon. I'm four and a half weeks along. You're going to be a daddy, Bryce. You're going to have your own baby."

Tears spilled down Bryce's face as Kaya's sweet words wrapped him in a silken cocoon of euphoria and sent a warm glow flowing through him. Kaya was going to have his baby. "I love you. I adore you. I worship you." The pads of his thumbs brushed her cheeks, her lips, her forehead.

"I know. I've known for a long time. I just needed to hear you say it. *You* needed to hear *you* say it."

"I was afraid I'd lost your trust, not your love, that you wouldn't forgive my infidelity, because that's what it was. I was cheating on you with Pilar."

"I thought about making you grovel, but then I spoke with Michelle today and she told me how people thought she forgave Erik too quickly for hurting her. Even when they were apart, she still loved Erik and she knew he loved her, and she wasn't going to waste time making him beg, just to make a point, especially in the condition she was in at the time. She said it's punishment enough when people realize they mess up, and may lose everything they love because of their stupidity. She said love isn't about groveling or revenge, or hurting you because you hurt me, but that love is just what it is: *love*. It's pure and kind and forgiving. She said life is too short to hold grudges and toy with the emotions of those we love, and that I should just open my arms to you when you came home."

"Michelle is a very smart woman, and I'm so happy you two are getting along. You need friends like her and Libby." *True friends Pilar didn't have*. But his life wasn't about mourning Pilar anymore. It was about loving Kaya and celebrating the creation of his baby growing inside her. "I missed you, love."

"I missed you too, so much. I love you so much, Bryce, my heart hurts from it."

Bryce reached a hand down between them, and spreading his palm across her belly, he caressed her gently. It was so tiny and flat. He wondered if his child had room to grow in there. He eased her onto her back and kissed his way slowly down her body to her stomach. He planted a series of kisses on the soft skin there before laying his cheek against her.

He felt Kaya's hands on his head, her fingers burrowing into his hair, caressing him as he savored the newness of being told he was going to be a father. It was a gloriously rapturous feeling, so strong, so intense that Bryce couldn't help but weep softly.

He felt like the Biblical Job who'd lost everything he loved, but whom God later blessed, twofold. Finally, he lifted his head and gazed up at Kaya, noting the lingering tears in her eyes.

"You make me so very happy. Happier than I ever imagined I could be."

"You deserve to be happy, Bryce," she replied with love in her eyes and voice.

His body shuddered on a strong emotion. "Now that my parents are here to take care of the kids, I want to take you away on a honeymoon. I want to be alone with you for a few weeks, block out the rest of the world. Anywhere special you want to go? Just say it and we're there."

Her smile was radiant. "Disney World."

Bryce cocked his head, his brow wrinkling. "Disney World?"

"Oh please, Bryce. It was the one place I wanted my daddy to take me when I was a little girl, but we didn't have the money to go."

Bryce's heart ached with the pain and neglect she'd endured as a child. He moved back up in the bed and rolling onto his back, he brought her to lie supine on top of him again. "Okay, sweetheart, I'll take little Kaya Brehna to Disney World."

"Can big Kaya Fontaine come, too?" she asked with a mysterious twinkle in her eyes. "She'll give you a one hundreds of kisses."

His body shook with laughter. "She'd better."

"And she promises to dress up in the outfit of your favorite princess, and you can have her any way you want, Prince Bryce, my Royal Highness."

Bryce's heart jolted in his chest. "I love the way you think, baby, but we're only spending a week in Disney World—too crowded. After that, I'm jetting you off to a private island somewhere where you can be the Naked Queen for three weeks, and I'll be your Hard Dark Knight and bow to your every demand."

"See, we make a great team. And I do have demands," she

said, lowering her head to lick and kiss the sensitive hollow of his neck, an extremely erogenous zone of his that she'd discovered.

Oh yes, she did have demands, Bryce thought, as his heart began to pound in his chest.

The thought of Kaya in a princess outfit straddled across him, riding him with her head thrown back and her long, curly hair swinging across her back, or her bent over a table with pink lace, chiffon, and mesh hiked up over her head while he took her from behind, or with her lying on her back with her legs draped over his shoulders and the dress bunched at her waist while he thrust madly into her, brought heat and vigor to Bryce's sex, filling him with an overwhelming need to be with the now Naked Queen Kaya, in her, show her how much he desired her, wanted her, loved her. Four days was way too long for him not to have made love to his wife.

"Are you up to making love, My Queen, see how hard you can make this dark knight?" he asked reaching out to turn off the light.

"What kind of stupid question is that? I should have your head just for asking."

Bryce chuckled. "Oh, you shall have my head, My Lady, anywhere you want it."

He pulled her head gently upward and met her halfway, swallowing her giggles into his mouth. Her lips were warm and gentle as they joined his in a deep, soul-wrenching, tantalizing kiss. Her hands came up to caress his face, her fingers burrowed into his hair.

Bryce's hands trailed eagerly down her soft body, caressing every sacred inch of her. He sighed in pleasure as his hands moved to cup her delectable buttocks. She rubbed against him and curved her body, allowing him to easily dip his finger between the apex of her thighs, to thrust one deep inside to find her hot and wet, ready for him.

With a bit of maneuvering of their bodies, Bryce spread her thighs over his and eased his turgid aching erection inside her warm slippery channel. She trembled on a long deep sigh of desire as her muscles closed and tightened around him. Each tremor resonated deep inside Bryce, past his flesh to his heart and soul.

He angled his head and captured one swollen breast in his mouth and suckled her. The thought of his baby's little mouth nursing at her breasts in fewer than nine months deepened his hunger. He moved to the other one and loved it just as voraciously, then with his hands on the lovely arc of her buttocks, guiding her, he began to thrust up inside her, slow, deep, and steady. Her sighs and moans and the undulating movements of her body on his sent deep, earth-shaking tremors surging through him.

Flames of passion churned deep within both of them, pushing them higher and higher to that pinnacle of delight where the only way out of the sizzling vortex that whipped them about was to crash and burn. They cried out each other's names as the hot tide of passion pulled them under, then eject them up and out into the universe, where they exploded, shattering into a million glowing stars. Yet one body, one mind, one soul.

They clung to each other, soaked and trembling, fighting for air.

Reclining on his stomach with his still hungry cock buried inside her, Kaya spoke. "Bryce?"

"What, sweetheart?"

"My panties have been disappearing."

Bryce held his breath, his stroke down the hollow of her back temporarily halted. "I wonder where they could be."

"I found a few in the pockets of your trousers. And I know why you take them."

Bryce chuckled. "You got me."

He groaned as her muscles contracted around him as if to punish him.

"You're a dirty, dirty man."

His laughter floated up from his throat, and he felt the vigor return to his cock, full force. It was going to be another long night of passion. Supporting Kaya's back with his arm, Bryce rolled over and pinned her to the mattress. "Can't help it. I love the way you smell, love. And you're right; I'm dirty. Just let me show you how dirty I am."

He reached down to where their sexes were joined and lathered his fingers with her hot juices now mixed with his. He smeared it all over her face, her neck, her chest, loving her girlish chuckles as she wriggled around in an attempt to elude him. He was never letting her go.

He kissed her deeply, and as her laughter turned to desire and she began to move provocatively under him, Bryce buried his face in the hollow of her neck. "What's the count?" he asked against her skin. They'd been practicing Taoist Secrets of Love.

"Nine," she whispered on a shudder.

Bryce recaptured her mouth as he began to thrust with measured strokes. Nine shallow quick thrusts, one deep and long, nine shallow, one deep, nine shallow…

Bryce repeated the mesmerizing cadence until Kaya's erotic groans and unintelligible words floating from her lips, the unrelenting convulsions of her thrashing body, the thumping of her heart under his, and the sheen of moisture covering her body told him that she was trapped in the relentless cyclone of a series of tumultuous orgasmic waves. She was drowning, raking her sharp nails into his back and shoulders, pounding her heels into his buttocks and thighs, bawling out his name, and the only way he knew to save her was to jump into the water with her.

All the blood in Bryce's body rushed to gather in a sizzling whirlpool between his legs. He thrust with abandoned speed and intensity—just in and out, back and forth at his body's will, for his mind had gone numb.

When the dam broke and the torrential waterfall of his seed flooded her womb, Bryce bellowed Kaya's name, then dropped his head in the hollow of her neck and filled his lungs with her intoxicating aroma.

As he succumbed to the passionate undertow of love, lust, and desire, Bryce thought that if anyone ever asked him what love smelled like, his reply would be, "*Kaya.*"

THE END

NOTE FROM THE AUTHOR

Dear Reader,

I hope you enjoyed following Bryce and Kaya on their journey to love and *Happily Ever After* in The Mogul's Reluctant Bride. May you find your own true love, and if you have already, cherish them with all your heart.

Blessings,
Ana

ABOUT THE AUTHOR

Inspired by the strong heroines and flawed alpha heroes in the stories she read as a young girl, *New York Times* and *USA Today* Bestselling Author, Ana E Ross writes steamy and sophisticated, multicultural contemporary romance novels. Her drama-filled stories feature charming, powerful, larger-than-life billionaires and strong, independent women who fight and love with equal passion.

Born and raised in Nevis, Ana now lives in the Northeast, U.S., and loves traveling, tennis, yoga, meditation, everything Italian, and spending time with her daughter.

www.anaeross.com
ana@anaeross.com